# THE DRAGON OF RUSSIA

ALSO BY JESSICA PIRO

**THE PHOENIX TRILOGY:**

Ascension of the Phoenix

The Dragon of Russia

Dueling with Snakes

**COMPANION SHORT STORIES:**

The Panther's Pride

The Crane's Dance

The Tiger's Patience

**SHORT STORY:**

It's the Small Things That Matter

# THE DRAGON OF RUSSIA

Book Two in The Phoenix Trilogy

JESSICA PIRO

THE DRAGON OF RUSSIA



www.jessicapiro.com

Cover Designer: Faera Lane

ISBN: 979-8500564320

*For everyone who has struggled with demons.*
*Let Leila's experiences prove that you aren't alone,*
*and that you can find balance.*

To change a person must face the dragon of his appetites with another dragon, the life-energy of the soul.
-Rumi quotes-

# I.

*I could live here.*

Few sights could compare to the warm, welcoming palette of Michigan in summer. No clouds had marred the sun shining on the trees during her two-day stay, and now it sparkled on the clear waters of the lake outside her window; everything advertised warmth, comfort, tranquility, and a sense of settling down.

*No, not until Foster is dead,* the Phoenix declared. *New York City draws him, not a boring place like this. We will wait there for his return.*

The Phoenix was right. Leila couldn't get distracted. But… her eyes returned to the lake. What if she left uninteresting and routine New York City for a place like this? She could forget revenge, forget Foster and David, and hide in this wilderness. Didn't she deserve happiness too?

*We won't find happiness until he's dead. You know this.*

A light groan followed by the sliding of a shoe on the wood floor sounded behind her. She didn't turn, not wanting to lose sight of the scenery despite the Phoenix's attempts to dilute its beauty. If she opened the screen door, she'd be free.

*Why can't I run? Wouldn't it be easier?*

*After what we've been through and devoted, you want to give it up? No, your regret and guilt would kill us.*

*But I'd be safe. No one would ever get hurt again trying to protect me.* Leila placed her hand on the rough wood framing the screen window, preparing to push.

*Don't be naïve! Foster wouldn't stop because you did. He would hurt everyone you left behind because we weren't there to protect them. Because you only thought of yourself. Because you were cowardly.*

"Wha—" someone said behind her.

She pulled her hand off the door. *Fine, I get it. I can't run. I can't stop.* For the first time, clouds passed over the sun, and Michigan darkened. It wasn't as inviting or promising of a carefree future.

"Detective Wells?"

She still didn't bother to turn, but the Phoenix became her voice as it did so often now. "I honestly thought you were smarter than to run from me."

He grunted, and the chair creaked as he struggled against his handcuffs. "I thought you couldn't come here."

"I can't unless I'm invited." She propped against the cabin wall, still refusing to look at him. "I was going to let you go—let the ones that call themselves 'detectives' claim you, but they were having trouble. In two days, I tracked you here to your cabin."

"Then you're done. You got me."

"Technically, yes. I'm taking you back to New York for the trial of murdering Howard Stanen, and that would be it—I did my job."

She let the apprehension grow by trailing off. "But…?"

"Howard Stanen tried to redeem himself by turning you in—he had good intentions. Since you know who I am, you know I go beyond what I am called to do and make it a personal priority to see things through.

"I know your supply comes from here and that you are one of the leaders. You are going to tell me where to find the drug labs, I will relay the locations over to the detectives, they and the rest of the nation will be rid of one less drug cartel, and we will return to New York where I will go on about my business and you will go to prison."

Astonished that she had everything planned like a vacation agenda kept him speechless until the ridiculousness of it all brought out his laughter. "Turn on my guys? Are you serious? You've grown too used to getting your way. The famed Phoenix can't scare me!"

She let him enjoy his laughter for a while. "What about death?"

It disappeared. "What?"

"Aren't you afraid of dying? Most people are."

"Are you threatening me?"

Leila finally turned to face Emilio Delgado-Valdez, originally from Puerto Rico and now a U.S. citizen, cuffed to the wooden chair she had found in his abandoned-cabin-getaway. The Phoenix gloated at his blanching. "I'm promising you."

"You-you can't do that… You're a cop!"

"You think that will stop me?"

"It should!"

"I'm not the Detective Leila Wells from before, am I?"

Valdez tried to stare her down, but the Phoenix overwhelmed him into backing off. After weighing his options, his shoulders slumped in defeat—there wasn't a doubt in his mind now. "It doesn't matter. I'm dead either way."

"It matters because I'm sure they won't be so merciful in their killing tactics." His face turned white, confirming what Leila figured the drug lords would do to him when caught. "Or, you could live in cushy witness protection, and they'll be here in prison. It's just, you will always be watching your back.

"I prefer an eye-for-an-eye, but you can convince me otherwise." Leila folded her arms and leaned against the wall. "So, what will it be?"

"I'll never snitch."

"You sure? There's nothing I can do to change your mind?"

"We all die in the end."

"Brave words." She pushed off the wall and walked toward him. "But hollow."

His eyes widened at the sight of her gloved hands. "Why are you wearing gloves?"

She kneeled beside him. "To keep my fingerprints off the syringe you shot up with to overdose on heroin. Why else?" She tied his arm off and grabbed the waiting syringe on the floor.

"I wouldn't overdose!"

"Tell me a junkie, like yourself, wouldn't. Picture it: the walls closing in about you as you trapped yourself, me breathing down your neck, and the reminder of the drug cartel coming for your head if one of them gets caught. You have a way out; why not escape it all with one last high? That is what I will tell them. Now, convince me it won't work."

His bottom lip quivered as she pulled up the syringe, removed the cap, and tapped it to test the needle. "No one will believe you."

"And who would believe a drug dealing-murdering-junkie over a renowned detective with no incriminating evidence?"

Valdez couldn't argue. She patted his arm to ready the vein, then looked at him. "Last chance."

His mouth flopped like a fish, speechless. His eyes remained glued to the syringe holding his death.

She gave him longer to recover but then lowered the needle when he still didn't speak.

The needle just touched him, not enough to even puncture. "Wait, wait!"

She pulled it back and looked at him.

Trembling, his eyes nearly shook out of his head as he spilled his guts on where to find the drug cartel, who would be there, and even others in different states. His tongue was still running when the time ran out and dirt crunched under the tires of the police cars.

Leila took off the tie and threw it across the room where she found it. "Thank you, Emilio." She emptied the syringe on the floor, then tossed it away too.

"For what? Who was that? What are you doing?" he asked, all running together.

"For telling me what I needed to know, the cavalry I called for while you were out, and emptying the syringe of water."

The Michigan detectives broke through the door with their guns out. Once seeing Valdez apprehended and Leila at ease, they put up the guns and relaxed. She told the squad where to find the hideout of the drug cartel.

"You played me!" Emilio yelled at her as the detectives relayed the information into their radios.

"It's called a police tactic." She freed him from the chair and—

The mention of her name snapped her out of her memory of the mission she just returned from. After dragging herself to her bedroom, Leila had collapsed onto her bed and kicked her boots off—too tired to sit up and take them off.

She had turned the television on behind her for background noise to eliminate the normal sounds of the city. But her name on the news made her turn up the volume.

"...didn't just go to Panordom to help Jamaal Gordon like she said. She went to escape the guilt of David Neal, Jr.'s death, to heat up her anger, and to use it as an excuse to search for Bryan Foster. I mean, why do you think she goes away on so many missions? She's using the police force for her own gain! Watch this—you can see how defensive she becomes when Detective Neal and Bryan Foster are brought up."

One of the last interviews she had given, without Jamaal, replaced the talk show host. She hadn't changed since the tournament: same long, jet-black hair pulled back in a ponytail, slim face with high cheekbones, and hazel eyes, only they held a constant edge and rarely crinkled in laughter now.

The interviewer insinuated the motive for Leila going to the tournament, and she shut him out to keep a hold on the Phoenix. Her body tensed, her voice grew hard—not like she was open and friendly with him in the first place—and her eyes steeled and became empty voids: signs of her restraining the Phoenix.

The clip returned to the talk show host. "With any mention of that tragic night or why she went to Panordom, Leila lets the Phoenix take her place. She is fragile, and she hides that part away so no one will doubt her strength. I believe Leila Wells is a time bomb; her control—if I can even call it that—on the Phoenix will vanish when someone, or another incident, tests her restraint, and she will blow up. Leila Wells is dangerous, and we can't rely on her to keep anyone safe—especially from herself."

She mashed the power off and tossed the remote away. Hitting the floor, the batteries exploded from the bottom.

Face obscured by the pillow, she just lay there. Murderers waited for her return from Panordom to become active. As nonstop as it had been, keeping busy gave her plenty of excuses to escape the media. Even though her interviews had stopped, she still made it into the gossip magazines or talk shows—they had plenty to say about her.

*Of course you can't rely on me. I'm not the same.*

*Let them say what they want. They don't matter. Only we matter, and Foster,* the Phoenix said.

She folded her pillow over her head. Was letting David go so early a necessity? Why did she allow the Phoenix free reign?

*Because you need me, not him.*

*Only to avenge him. David was guiding me toward my role.*

*What is your purpose?* She couldn't find an answer. *You're the only one who can stand up to Foster. You survived to stop him from hurting others. They don't understand your pain and the need for revenge because they've never been through it. Don't listen to anyone that doesn't know.*

The vibrating of her phone pulled her focus off responding. She discarded the idea of ignoring it as someone might need help. Leila reached back a hand and fumbled around on her nightstand until her hands clasped around it.

The number wasn't the captain's, Heath's, DeMarcus', or the station's, so it wasn't an emergency. Neither was it David's parents, Hyun, Nuan, or Jamaal. Leila opened the multimedia message, anyway.

**Sry 4 l8 delivery! Trouble w/ file transfer. Hope every1's good! Maso**

Leila's mind snapped out of sleep as the picture loaded: the picture Maso Bonucci had taken of their group on the return trip from the tournament. Luke Zheng's smiling face making his eyes nearly unseen; Jamaal hesitant like he stood on eggshells; her strained smile because of the Phoenix; Rinieri Anton's arm around her; and Miguel bearing over her. Shamus Shauns grinning beside Maso, then the Spaniards, Miguel Del Toro and Alvaro Munoz, in the back row.

Miguel Del Toro. His name brought warmth. She remembered their intimate dance, the prickling of stubble as he spoke in her ear, and her lips tingled with the memory of his kiss, hard and needy.

The Phoenix shoved him out of her mind, angry that she had thought of him so fondly after four months.

"Relax, will you? I know he's not meant for me, so I won't be obsessing over him. I cared for him, I can't deny that."

*Thinking of him will take away your focus. For what? For nothing.*

"It wasn't for nothing. He's proof that I can move on and love another."

*Only to get hurt again?*

"I…" She paused. What if it happened again like with David? Terror seized her; no, she couldn't suffer another love dying. She'd ensure her life didn't go on anymore.

*That couldn't happen with me. I wouldn't hurt you; another can. Trust in me. I will protect you from ever being hurt again if you rely fully on me.*

Leila put her phone back on the nightstand. Building another relationship only to have it torn down wasn't worth the heartache. "Please, don't. I can't… Not again." She pulled the sheets over her shoulders, shaking uncontrollably, scared of that possibility, and tears blurred her vision.

Warmth blanketed over her, knocking away the cold fear—and it wasn't the bed sheet.

*I won't. I will protect you as long as you don't step out from under my wings.*

Comforted that the Phoenix sat perched and watching over her, Leila calmed down, and exhaustion finally took hold.

# II.

The elevator bell dinged, and Leila entered the refurbished 5th Precinct headquarters. No more clamor of ringing phones, taps of computers, dial tones of fax machines constantly spitting out 'Wanted' flyers, and officers chatting or arguing. All that usual noise, now held back by a glass wall, had been reduced to a constant buzz. The four desks of the detectives sat segregated by the glass wall, though the door endlessly swung open and invited the noise in. Still a busy beehive, just a quieter one.

Captain Sullivan had figured out her anonymous donation. He confronted her about the money and threatened to lay her off for a while if she didn't take it back. After the Phoenix made it clear that there was no discussing a return, the captain renovated the station and put the rest in a savings account—but with a tight lip at being bashed by one of his detectives.

The renovation didn't solely focus on the squad room: the interrogation rooms were installed with better lighting, chairs that did not wobble, and smudge-free one-way glass; a sturdy stairwell led up to the filing room now secluded behind windows; and plush cots replaced the old lumpy ones, providing better sleep in the bunks. Modern whites, silvers, blacks, and grays replaced the outdated color schemes throughout the station. In the conference room, new software allowed face-to-face meetings—how the Michigan police reached them.

"Welcome back to the Hive!" DeMarcus Dixon greeted from his usual position, legs propped on his desk and hands behind his head. Being the third of their squad—since David, the second, died—didn't affect the black man's cockiness. He still boasted about running down and tackling criminals.

"You're looking productive." She sat at her desk, previously David's—she couldn't bear the sight of his empty desk.

"You know we can't get anything done without you, Queen Bee."

The Phoenix eyed him; Heath stepped in to hold her back. "So, how was Michigan?"

As the second of their squad, and also a good friend, Heath Fonda did that a lot now—intervened before the Phoenix could go on the warpath. The blond man might be strong enough to hold her back now; he had won a bench-pressing contest a few weeks ago—D went to support him; Leila didn't. Socializing wasn't appealing anymore.

She stared at where DeMarcus' head was before Heath blocked her line of sight. "Uninteresting," she stated flatly and turned back to her desk.

"Really? I heard differently," the captain said. She looked up at the police chief; even though he stood planted, dissatisfaction plain on his face and in his voice, he looked old and tired. Ever since David's death, stress lines were more prominent, and he constantly appeared worn down and defeated. He had aged twenty years from that experience. The Phoenix making its presence known didn't help either.

"What did you hear?"

"I would be more concerned with another criminal complaint against me."

"That's nothing new, Captain—they always complain."

"But they don't usually sing the same song."

"Did I go beyond what I'm allowed to do?"

"According to him, that tactic sounded questionable."

The Phoenix faced him directly. "Am I being investigated?"

"No, but it's high time I do something—I've let this drag on too long. You're on desk duty until I say otherwise. You can help with the cases, but you can't leave."

Her mouth opened—her dark side about to lash out—but Leila recognized irritation in the captain's eyes and seized control before the Phoenix could go too far. Her punishment would become worse if she acted like before. Then, her outburst had been a surprise; now, he had had enough.

She gave a small nod. "If you say so."

The captain breathed in deeply, glanced at the other detectives watching, then turned for his office.

His door shut, and still, no one made a sound. She turned to her partners who were staying silent, knowing better than to get involved. "So, what's this case?"

DeMarcus snapped to attention; he headed to the touch screens and pulled up the crime scene photos as he spoke. "We have five possible suspects but have nothing to nail one." Three women, all killed with their jugular severed, popped up on three screens, then the five driver's licenses of the suspects appeared on another.

"All from Hell's Kitchen, and all women killed with their own steak knife found at the scene, but no fingerprints or fibers pinpointing the murderer," Heath added as he joined him.

Leila moved to the screens. "That would make it too easy."

"We know the killer is left-handed." Heath gestured at their necks. "The cut grows shallower as it exits at the left. Someone right-handed wouldn't swing like that."

She tuned them out, droning on about how three of the five suspects had been singled out from dating each of the women, their routine visits to explain the connection of one suspect, and their opinions on the case as she searched for the smoking gun. It didn't take her long to find it studying the crime scene of victim #3.

"The one with burn marks is the winner."

The men silenced. "What?"

"Why?"

"Valerie was cooking." With her thumb and index finger, she maximized the picture of the kitchen by sliding her fingers apart, zooming in on the wall with scorch marks. "She defended herself by throwing grease on him… At least she fought."

Heath tried to give them some credit, "Maybe the others didn't get a chance to."

"No, they invited him in. He wanted them to know he was there for revenge. The others didn't even try. Weak."

The men stared, stunned; Leila bet they considered responding. They wisely chose to remain silent—pretending like nothing happened—and headed back to their desks.

"What were you whining about with Brooke this time?" DeMarcus asked his partner.

"I was not whining. She blows everything out of proportion."

"About what?"

"A waitress giving me a longer smile than usual for a tip. I'll admit, the girl was flirting with me big time, and she wasn't bad to look at, but Brooke was there; she saw me brushing her off. I didn't flirt back."

Their continuing conversation became unintelligible as Leila focused on the murdered women. How pathetic it was for them to lie down and die. They invited their killer in, encouraging him to take his chance. Victim #2 kept drawing her gaze; when she looked, the girl's face transformed into Leila's—eyes open in shock and betrayal, so weak and spineless to try to defy her fate, naïve to think she was untouchable to provoke Foster, submitting without any resistance to her own death, and not thinking she could go on without David…

Leila tore her eyes from the screen. Her anger toward the victims was her way of reflecting it off her. She had nearly become one herself until the Phoenix gave her the strength to stand on her own. As the only one who fought back, Leila wanted to relate to Valerie, but she found herself more like victim #2.

"You two don't get along!" DeMarcus' voice brought her out of her depressing thoughts. "You come here always complaining about her. She's toxic for you. Get rid of her!"

"D, I'm serious about this girl!"

"Are you sure you're not just crazy about the benefits she gives you?"

Heath was ready to punch him as redness crawled up his neck.

Leila stepped in. "That's enough, D. You have a job to do."

The two partners straightened up at hearing her temper prickling—it could be unleashed on them again.

They would have to wait for Randall Thimes to return from his flight tomorrow; Heath and DeMarcus made a hasty getaway, still bickering with heads bent toward each other.

Leila went back to her desk, irritated that she was left doing paperwork while they did real police work. Before getting started on reports, she looked over to the wall of fallen comrades. David's crooked smile, brown hair, or chocolate eyes did nothing to her—no rush of memories, and no increase in her heart. Not a single element that she missed him. The Phoenix ensured nothing could slip in and break her stature. He was never anything to her.

*It's better that way,* she reminded herself as she turned back to her computer screen.

"NO DELAYS; HE'LL BE HERE in thirty minutes," DeMarcus said as he looked up Thimes' flight schedule from Chicago.

Leila continued to type. "Go have fun." Without another word, the two detectives left.

As soon as the elevator doors closed, her mind flew to Foster, as it always did when she was left alone. She minimized the report she was working on and searched the archives for any suspicious behavior or crimes sounding close to Foster's MO. Nothing raised a red flag—in state or out.

*There must be something, somewhere. He couldn't stand falling off the face of the earth.*

*Unless he's doing it on purpose,* the Phoenix suggested.

Realization struck her. *He knows me just like I know him. Foster has studied me…*

*So?*

*That doesn't bother you? I can't do anything he wouldn't expect. Why, though?*

The Phoenix had nothing to say.

Instead of punching something in frustration, with one angry breath and a hard click of the mouse, she closed the archives and hung her head in her hands. The more she looked, the worse she wanted a scrap of Foster's existence, so she could find him and kill him.

Footsteps headed toward the captain's office, halted, then began again but toward her. She recognized the pattern of the footfalls and how heavy they fell on the floor. The shoes would be the black dress shoes of the captain's. She prepared for the confrontation.

"Captain," Leila greeted when the man stopped at her desk without opening her eyes to see.

"Lei." His weight eased down on the corner of her desk—she couldn't escape him now. "We have to talk."

"If it's about Michigan, you know the story."

"It involves it."

"Then if it's also about David, you know that story too."

"Lei, please… I don't want to start another argument."

She looked up at him. "Say what's on your mind, and I'll try not to respond."

"There have been fourteen complaints against you, Lei. I'm putting my foot down."

"Do what you think you must."

His arms crossed over his chest, displeased at her careless attitude. "Nothing gets to you anymore."

"Do you want me to be emotional?"

"No, but I wish you would show some kind of reaction."

She had to look down. "It's not going to happen."

"Lei, I'm worried about you. Becoming numb to the world can't be healthy."

"It keeps me safe; I can't get hurt again if I don't get attached."

"But then you also can't feel happiness."

Her hand popped the table as she looked back up. "What else am I supposed to do? Just let Foster go? Pretend like nothing happened? He is always in my head, enticing me after his ghost. He is mocking me! I have to find him; I have to end him, and then I will find some peace."

Captain Sullivan took her outburst like she was telling him how her day went. "You've gotten too close, and now he's in your head. You know better than that, Lei. Take a step back."

"You don't understand. I can't; I just… can't. I need to get away, but there's nowhere far enough. He's always going to find me. And the Phoenix won't let me go."

Quite a few officers passed through before he spoke, all with questioning glances but not daring to approach. The captain ran a hand down his face, then let out a heavy sigh, considering something.

"What if… it's a place you weren't prepared for?"

"Like what?"

He had an idea from his hesitancy to answer. "I'm not saying, but it's not like Michigan—far from it. A friend has contacted me, scared about his safety, and from what he told me, I am too."

"What's the job?"

"I don't have all the details, so I'm not sure."

"If this job happens, it sounds like it'll be off the record."

He shifted in unease. "Yes, it would be."

"Is that the reason you're worried?"

"In a way, yes. You'd be alone with no backup, but I'm mainly concerned that if I do send you, will it help you by getting some space or make it worse?"

Leila looked at him. "If I don't know 'til the last minute, I highly doubt Foster would be there."

His blue eyes locked with hers. "My case and point."

She understood. Being away from the force's reputation, she would look for Foster unceasingly through—more than likely—unorthodox methods, and if she failed, she'd be more driven to find him, incoherent to anything else.

"Once I get the whole story, I'll decide whether to get involved or not. It also depends on how things go with—" He cut himself off.

Her body jerked to attention, especially at the regret in his eyes. "With what, Captain?"

He didn't get to answer due to the arrival of DeMarcus and Heath dragging in an unhappy Randall Thimes in handcuffs. The fresh burn marks on the right side of his face looked nasty, painful, and incriminating.

With a smile toward them, DeMarcus led the murderer to the interrogation rooms. Heath lingered, eyes shooting between Leila and the captain, unsure if he was interrupting something.

Captain Sullivan broke the ice. "Everything went smoothly, I hope."

"Yeah. It was in his eyes that he wanted to run at the sight of us, but he didn't." Heath turned to her. "He probably knew that the Phoenix would be after him if he had gotten away." He left to join the interrogation.

She froze at him unintentionally reminding her of linking Foster's ploys.

*That's why Foster is lying low: he* knows *I'll come after him. But there has to be more to it…*

*Who cares? the* Phoenix said. *He's going to die by our hands. Don't get caught up in his mind games.*

This was all a part of the games he liked to play, but Leila cared. No matter how twisted or cunning, all veteran felons accepted either incarceration or death was in their future, but no criminal had goals to die.

Foster had reasons for everything he did and was doing, and Leila needed to find out what before killing him.

# III.

Leila practiced her Five-Animals Kung Fu at Hyun's dojo every Saturday morning and Sunday evening. The ritualistic workout allowed her to get away—escape the Phoenix's anger and fury at Foster, guilt because he still lived, grief over the loss of David, and frustration over knowing Foster had plans… and not knowing what they were. Focusing on her moves and landing just right to transition into another stance kept her from dwelling on her memories, thoughts, and emotions.

Since Leila won the Ruler of the Realms Fighting Tag Tournament and placed the championship belt on display there, **Hyun's Gym** became popular. Because people mostly came to watch her practicing, not even using their gym memberships, Hyun set certain times aside so she could workout in private. Doing so took the pressure off them both—Leila wouldn't lose control over the Phoenix at scrutinizing fans and harm Hyun's customers.

For now, she trained in the middle of the wrestling mat, ignoring the training dummies—she only used those to release suppressed energy. Performing her moves by herself kept the Phoenix's fire at bay by allowing a little out, but she knew it could explode at any moment. Enough force would blow the fragile cap off.

Slipping smoothly from one stance to another helped clear Leila's mind: she danced around the floor in Crane, then dropped down into Panther and crept like she stalked prey. Finished familiarizing herself with the different stances, she turned to battle mode by imagining she was back in the tournament.

Leila leaped to avoid an attack when the fighter charged, dropped into a roll, and attacked. Another fighter appeared behind her after she finished the first; she blocked their hit and spun her leg out in Tiger's Tail. They jumped over it; staying in Tiger, she flipped back, then launched up to kick her opponent.

Another attacker replaced the fallen, and she quickly moved into Snake. Remaining low, she lashed out with her hands as she slithered toward her opponent. They moved out of the way and pulled back their arm to strike; she ducked under the punch, changed to the Dragon mentality, and threw a strong palm at their chest.

She ducked into a roll as another approached. Rising out of the roll, Leila changed into Phoenix, then froze. The form became a grinning Bryan Foster. Rage consumed her, and she lunged for his throat. He deflected her hit, and his uppercut connected with her chin.

Pain didn't throb since Foster was imaginary, but Leila stumbled back anyway, playing out this pretend fight. She had never heard his true voice, but Foster chuckled. Deep in his throat and mocking.

The Phoenix released a frustrated yell through Leila as she re-engaged the mental ghost of Foster.

They continuously exchanged hits and never separated. When the fight was real, it would resemble this: up-close and personal. At one blow, he faltered; Leila took advantage by slapping him across the face, then flipped backward and her foot met his chin. She landed into the Phoenix as he collapsed, but another Foster-mirage appeared, and the routine continued.

Leila lay spread-eagled in the middle of the mat, eyes closed, focused on her breathing when footsteps approached.

"Working out is good and everything, but I'm afraid you'll push yourself too far soon," Hyun began.

"Are you talking about exercise or my reliance on the Phoenix?" she asked.

"What do you think?"

Leila opened her eyes and looked at Hyun-Ki Myung. "The Phoenix."

"You wouldn't be wrong." He reached down a hand to help her up. "Come on; Nuan has some tea brewing."

SEATED IN THE BACK LOUNGING room, Leila had her hands wrapped around a steaming cup of Oriental tea that Nuan Hataye had made. Both were slightly different to 'typical' East Asians: Nuan's pale skin always had a beautiful soft pink undertone, large, rounded eyes, and her nose was thinner than most Chinese women, and Hyun wore his black hair long in a ponytail when most Koreans had short hair, and then there was his above average height at 6'2". Hyun's fiancée perched on the couch's arm he sat on with her hands full too. The painted flowers on their cups reminded Leila of their wedding in spring.

While taking a drink, Leila couldn't figure out what Hyun meant before. She lowered her cup to ask. "Did you mean my dependence on the Phoenix could be bad?"

Hyun sighed. "One day, the Phoenix will become uncontrollable. You keep it at bay by wearing yourself out fighting—but not it. You've told us it has gotten harder to resist your dark side from emerging, and we've seen the strain. All your efforts seem to have empowered it while draining you. When the Phoenix pushes you aside and takes your place, what will you do?"

She had realized that, too, but she couldn't handle the consequences of doing nothing. Refuse to unleash the Phoenix safely here and hope to keep it from detonating in a critical moment? Hurting or possibly killing someone? Impossible.

"I don't know. I can't think of anything else I can do." She cut her eyes at him—the Phoenix was rising, insulted. "Can you?"

"I'm not… accusing you of not doing enough. Fighting before the week starts is your truce with the Phoenix: your anger will stay back unless you call for it as long as you let it loose every weekend."

"You have to fight fire with fire, don't you?" Leila threw in.

"Usually, you end up with ashes."

The room fell silent until Hyun released another breath. "You can't tame the anger you're relying on. It will eventually break your hold and do what it wants. When it does, it will be disastrous."

Nuan placed a hand on his shoulder. "Leila, this change that has come over you frightens me. I know it must scare you a little… or, at least, it will."

She hesitantly looked down at her tea. "I understand your desire for revenge, but vengeance is never the answer. You become so focused on retaliation that it controls your life. If you achieve it, you're no better than the person you exacted it on. You can't return to a normal mindset once everything's over. But, do you know what truly scares me?"

Leila shook her head.

"I'm scared that you will lose who you are, Leila—you will lose your heart and the personality we all love and admire. You've regained an essence of that Leila if just more light in your eyes, but I'm terrified of you falling back into that abyss you were in when David died… only worse. No life in your eyes; no hint of a soul; no sign of you trying to return. Just the hard, emotionless Phoenix." She shuddered, picturing it.

"I'm not going to let that happen, Nuan," she stated with certainty, reassuring the Asian couple she wouldn't.

"You won't, but the Phoenix won't care if that happens," Hyun said. "Your anger will twist you to get what it wants: revenge against Foster. I'm telling you, if the Phoenix goes free, its anger will consume you."

Leila had to plead her case. "But if I fight against it, I could douse its fuel, and the Phoenix will die out. Then what will I be? The emotional, fragile woman everyone believes I am. I have to prove them wrong!"

Nuan placed a hand on Hyun's shoulder to stop him from speaking. "Are you trying to convince everyone that you are strong, or are you trying to convince yourself?"

Leila didn't want to answer. She was exactly what she had said inside—she had piled hardened layers over her shell to appear strong. "Both, I guess."

She looked at them. "That's why I rely on the Phoenix. My anger makes me feel strong and not weak. It gives me the drive to keep on living. The Morning Glory reminds me of my promise to David of finding the one I'm meant for, but the Phoenix is real; I can feel it. That's what I need right now: something physical."

# IV.

"Details?" Leila asked when she, Heath, and DeMarcus ducked under the crime scene tape. Forensics walked around the small apartment, taking pictures and documenting notes about the two victims covered with white sheets.

A coroner answered her without looking up from the bodies. "Two males, both Caucasian and in their thirties, killed with a single gunshot to the head—probably with a silencer—and" —he pulled out the thermometer to measure their body temperature— "time of death between ten and midnight last night."

"Any gang tattoos or marks?"

"None."

After putting on gloves, she squatted and pulled the sheet back to look herself. The one closest to her was abnormally skinny, pale, and nerdy with broken glasses. By appearances, probably a computer whiz. The one lying beside him epitomized a John Doe with unremarkable features and an average build. Nothing immediately stood out on them.

The sickening sweet smell of their brain matter invoked memories of Detective Jamie Washington's suicide, caused by Bryan Foster killing his partner. Leila folded the sheet back over them quickly. This was a different case—no point in reviving her anger.

"They looked like some good boys. What did they get caught up in?" Heath asked over her shoulder.

She stood. "We won't find out by searching their bodies."

The detectives dispersed to separate sections of the apartment the deceased men shared: DeMarcus searched a computer desk with opened and unopened envelopes as a computer tech ran through the laptops for anything suspicious, Heath dug through the beds, nightstands, closets, and drawers, and Leila took the kitchen and living room.

She checked the entertainment center, opened movie cases, ran a gloved-hand through the couch's cushions, peered into coffee tins, moved boxes of nearly empty cereal—even looked inside them—for anything the deceased wanted hidden. Nothing. A few minutes passed as they searched.

"Tech hasn't found anything on the hard drives," DeMarcus called from the other room.

She walked into the bedroom Heath was checking. "There's got to be something here," he said. "They were executed to keep silent."

"Or were loose ends," she said.

Through with searching in and under the bed, Heath moved to a closet as she flipped through pictures on the top of a drawer. Few pictures of the nerdy boy adorned shelves throughout their home, but there were many of the other, arms draped around girls with a drink in hand.

"Lei."

The quiet but urgent call of her name made her discard the photos and head over to Heath in the closet. He remained rooted to where he stood, eyes glued to whatever he found, not turning at her approach. Once she joined him, she froze too.

A hidden door in the closet led to a room equipped with tables, lights, magnifying glasses, wire clippers, T-9 explosives, and wires… Wires everywhere—bombs. Posted on the walls were extremist posters, pictures, and campaign posters with Mayor Priest's face and other political faces scratched out or stained with red paint saying 'corrupt'.

Leila took control. "Evacuate the building, calmly, and call the Bomb Squad."

They slowly backed out, telling everyone to drop everything and get out. There weren't enough officers to spread out on all floors, so the forensics team helped get occupants out of their rooms and outside at a safe distance. During the evacuation, Heath radioed for the Bomb Squad as he provided an arm for an elderly lady.

After ensuring a safe perimeter was set up before the apartment doors, Leila radioed the captain. "This isn't a cut-and-dried case; a Ten-thirty-three against the mayor and other party members."

"Bomb Squad?"

"En route."

He took a breath to maintain his stability, but his voice still faltered some at the bomb threat. "Be careful."

"Ten-four."

As she hung up, the Bomb Squad's mobile unit pulled up. The bystanders parted, and some even backed off farther in precaution as men jumped out and headed through the barricade. A well-built man with a buzz-cut, clearly militarized and in command, approached with his unit following.

"Shiers. What do we have?"

"Detective Wells. A room heavily supplied with explosives. First floor, room 132, and try not to blow up my bodies—I still have a case with evidence in there."

"That's why we're here." He treated her with a smile, carrying more than politeness and shooting the Phoenix's defenses up. "Excuse us." Shiers went back to the mobile unit to don his safety gear.

She watched him, intrigued that even under the circumstances, and the Phoenix's proudness notorious for shutting down interest, he would attempt to flirt.

*He's a fool thinking he could openly approach us. If the bomb doesn't burn him, I will,* the Phoenix said.

Shiers ascending the apartment's stoop followed by two other dark green, bulky, slow-moving aliens caught her attention. They disappeared inside, and Heath and DeMarcus moved over to her.

"Now we wait," Heath said.

"Anxiously," DeMarcus added in.

Heath looked at his black partner sharply.

"What?"

"You have a lot of faith."

"I'm just stating it like it is. We can't see what's happening; we don't have any warning when to take cover."

Once again, they started trading barbs, so she tuned them out by scanning the pedestrians. Faces of worry, puzzlement, and obliviousness all blended together. Arms crossed to maintain comfort, eyes searching for an explanation, and heads turning to respond to their neighbors were expected. Her eye caught one not performing the telltale signs of nervousness.

He stood among the civilians, not too close nor too far, and not uneasy like the others—he appeared calm and assured but interested in the progression of the situation. Instead of leaning toward the opinions surrounding him, he lent an ear to the police officers' discussion.

Leila moved away from her partners, zoning in on him. She didn't turn or reply to Heath's questioning call.

Her approach caught the man's eye. He casually turned and moved through the throng of people.

She quickened her pace. "Stop! Police!"

He didn't hesitate; he grabbed each person to the side of him, threw them sprawling and colliding into others behind him, and took off running. Leila fell right into step; she leaped over the fallen entanglement of people and gave chase.

The suspect flew down the sidewalk, ramming into people and throwing them behind him as obstacles. Nothing threw off her run. Desperation shined in his eyes as he stopped and whipped around with a gun.

"Everyone, run!" Leila yelled as she jumped behind a parked car for cover. At the pop of the gun, people began screaming and running.

She unholstered her Glock and leaned around the car's bumper to see the suspect… and found him running again.

Cursing, Leila took up the chase again. She couldn't risk shooting him for she could miss, and the bullet might hit a bystander. Energized by the chase and from being shot at, the Phoenix gave her extra energy to push herself harder.

Nearing a busy intersection, he looked behind to see her steadily gaining.

He took a hard right and slipped between two parked cars. Right as he did, Leila copied but jumped onto the hood of the car behind his and leaped off.

She dove into him, and the momentum sent them sprawling to the middle of the road. His gun went skittering across the pavement, and she held onto him so he couldn't escape. A car horn snapped her head up to see a van skidding as the driver slammed on the brakes at them flying into the street.

Leila yanked them both free from death's grasp as the van screeched past. Unfortunately, the van's sudden brake check threw the following vehicles into hysteria: horns blew, tires squealed as they swerved and braked, and metal crunched as the cars slammed into each other.

The accused thanked her by driving his elbow into her nose. She stumbled back into a parked car, but the Phoenix took over by bouncing off, striking him into a daze, then catapulting him backward over her knee—all without being able to see through watering eyes.

He hit the ground, hard. She frantically wiped her eyes to see if he attempted to flee, but he was face-first on the concrete, unconscious.

People gathering closer to the spectacle and the car horns angry at the instigator of the accidents made her flash her badge, warning them to back off. They did.

"Lei, are you okay?" Heath asked as he finally caught up.

Remembering her sore nose, she tried to stop the bleeding with a finger. She remained bent from slamming into the car. "I'm fine. There's at least one of the terrorists."

"I hope this was a small cult." He handed her a napkin from his pocket, then set to throwing handcuffs on the unconscious man.

"Did you do that?" DeMarcus asked when he arrived, nodding toward the traffic jam.

"He should've looked before running into the street."

"A 'safety first' lesson?"

She looked at him. "I saved his life; I should be thanked, not scolded."

"I don't think he sees it that way." Heath had roused the apprehended man and hauled him to his feet, scowling nonstop at Leila.

"Doesn't matter what he thinks."

After DeMarcus retrieved the suspect's gun from under a car, they followed Heath as he led the criminal back down the two-and-a-half blocks to where they started to find Shiers waiting, helmet off but still in his bulky armor. He considered the suspect as Heath took him to an officer's cruiser, then turned to Leila.

"Grow bored?"

"Something else promised more excitement."

"The bombs were all disabled; we're taking them with us for precaution, but we'll log everything for evidence. But there is something: bombs were set out for an attack against the mayor today."

Leila looked to DeMarcus; he already pulled out his radio. "On it."

He moved off, talking with the captain about the next threat.

"Oh." Shiers turned back to her. "We didn't disturb your dead."

She pulled the napkin away after the bleeding stopped. "Thanks."

"Are you sure you're okay?"

"I've taken harder hits than an elbow to the nose."

He nodded in agreement. "You have."

The Phoenix glared at him. *What does he know?*

*He probably watched the tournament.*

*That's not the hits I'm talking about.*

"Detective Wells?"

He pulled her out of her internal dialogue before she could react to what the Phoenix was talking about. She donned her mask—hiding her emotions—and offered the unbloodied hand. "Thanks for the assist, Shiers."

He took her hand, but confusion flickered in his green eyes at her shutting him out then returning. "No problem. Until next time."

"Not under the same situation though," Leila added.

"Bomb threats are the only time I see New York's Finest—or the Phoenix."

The Phoenix bristled again. *Get your eyes off us.*

"Seems that way."

"I can think of another way of meeting you, and it doesn't involve explosives."

She stiffened from the hot anger and defensiveness of the Phoenix at the nerve of the man asking her out. *Who does he think he is? This hothead better go before I show him a real explosion.*

Leila fought against her dark side to remain in control. She needed to refuse him without causing a scene. “Sorry, but I don’t see that happening.”

His hopeful eyes dimmed in disappointment. “Maybe I’ll see you next time, then.” With a forced smile in farewell, Shiers headed toward the Bomb Squad’s mobile unit. As soon as he entered, the van pulled out and left.

With his departure, Leila now realized that Heath had re-joined them… and witnessed the conversation. Through his silence, he was just as disappointed as Shiers at her not taking the offer of a date.

She looked at DeMarcus coming back to avoid snapping at her blond partner. “The captain?”

“He sent word to the mayor, but nothing has crossed him yet.”

“Maybe we foiled the plan,” Heath suggested.

“I guess we’ll have to see, but we have bodies getting cold.” Leila turned away from them and headed back up into the apartment complex, wondering if the bomb threat was a ruse set by Foster to get her moving.

“AT APPROXIMATELY 10:30 A.M., POLICE responded to the scene of two deceased men and discovered a plan for an act of terrorism against Mayor Priest. The Bomb Squad arrived—led by Kirby Shiers—and successfully disarmed the explosives. As the bombs were being handled, Detective Leila Wells—also known as ‘The Phoenix’—took up pursuit of a suspect. The chase spanned several blocks and instigated a traffic jam, but the suspect was apprehended, seen here in this video a civilian submitted."

The reporter was replaced by a phone recording of Leila diving into the suspect, her pulling him out of the van's path, him ramming an elbow into her nose, and her ending it by striking him repeatedly, then flipping him over onto his chest. The video stopped and the anchorwoman replaced it.

"As you saw, Detective Wells single-handedly confronted the suspected terrorist and saved the mayor and the city of New York from a possible devastating attack. The NYPD assures that they will solve this double homicide and have the murderer arrested, if not already. But if you have any information concerning this case, please call the number at the bottom of your screen.

"Even from the extensive pursuit and bomb threat, no other casualties or severe injuries were inflicted thanks to Detective Wells, New York's Finest, and Kirby Shiers and his Bomb Squad. Whether you believe Leila Wells is a danger or not, once again, the Phoenix's actions have saved many lives." The reporter shuffled the papers on her desk, getting ready to announce the next story.

Leila kept her eyes down at the case file of the two men throughout the news report, but she raised her eyes at the mention of the video. She watched long enough to realize her takedown of the suspect would be considered police brutality through others' eyes. The talk shows would likely thrash her later, and she'd see cries of outrage on magazine stands tomorrow.

Her focus was back on the file, but she felt eyes turn on her at the end of the news. Most believed their stares of annoyance at always hearing her name were safe behind the glass wall, but the pinpointing glare from the Phoenix jolted them back to work.

After surveying the room—the Phoenix's glare encouraging more dropped gazes and shuffling of feet to get away—Leila closed the file and went to check on the interrogation. She joined the captain in the last interrogation room, watching Heath and DeMarcus grill the suspect through the one-way glass.

He didn't acknowledge her presence with a smile like he normally did. The man being interrogated clearly nagged the captain—his crossed arms didn't unfold, the twisted lips and scowl looked permanent, and he glared through the one-way glass. The suspect should've been squirming under the captain's scrutiny.

"Am I needed?" she asked after watching their lack of progress.

"No. They may be slow, but they're working on him."

"Not from my perspective. I could get him to talk quicker."

"I think you've done enough. By the way, congrats on getting him."

"Heath's the one who collared him; I just tackled him."

"Never wanting to take the praise, just like…" Captain Sullivan trailed off. He glanced at her, unsure if he had gone too far.

"David," she finished. She twitched her lips for a forced smile to show that any mention of him wasn't touchy ground. Leila kept her gaze ahead, pretending to observe her partners but stared into the void to prevent the captain from seeing the hardening of her eyes from the Phoenix ensuring that she wouldn't react.

The captain's concerned gaze bore into her. "I know," she finally replied to ease the thinking that he had brought sorrowful memories back to the surface—memories she had buried six feet under in a hidden resting place so nothing could dig them up.

Heath's bad-cop persona came through as he threatened the suspect for harming Leila. The suspect balked, declared that he had nothing to do with the murders—he was there to retrieve the bombs—and it ended with him asking for a lawyer. At the magic word, Heath and DeMarcus left, and the captain turned off the speaker.

"He's telling the truth; he didn't kill those men," Heath said, sighing.

"But he's involved with those who did," DeMarcus said.

The captain nodded. "I'll talk with the D.A. and get her to give him an offer that if he names who did, he'll get a lesser charge. But for now, try to find them before she arrives so we don't have to offer him a deal."

# V.

Joel Brannen didn't give up any names, but he did relinquish the address of the organization's base of operations—an old paint factory near the Brooklyn Heights Promenade. Still new, this group didn't even have a name yet. It sounded like a group of young adults trying to instigate unrest against the government, but regardless, they killed two people and intended to murder others.

As Leila approached the tall, concrete building with Heath and DeMarcus, she glanced over at the tourist attraction. Like nearly every day, people visited the Esplanade. Joggers, bird-watchers, and couples flocked to it because the long walkway under shady trees ran alongside the scenic view of the Manhattan skyline across the Hudson River.

David had liked to visit it, too. Other than Central Park, they came there a lot to get away from the chaotic city. He said the open water in the New York Harbor drew him.

The corner of her lips pulled up at a memory. Some joggers had passed, inspiring David to run, but—trying to impress Leila—he had jogged backward. Not seeing where he headed, he banged into a trashcan, tripped over it, and fell in with the garbage.

"Lei?" DeMarcus said, pulling her back to focus.

"We're just here to find names of this organization's members," she said. "Search for any evidence, but if you see one wire, get out and call the Bomb Squa—"

A staccato of automatic fire cut her off and sent the detectives ducking for cover. Leila and Heath dropped behind a parked car; D hid behind another. Bullets dented the cars and shattered glass, coming from the second-story windows of the paint factory.

"Ten-thirteen. Shots fired. Requesting backup," Heath said into his radio.

She and D returned fire, and once done, Heath's Glock popped beside her. Only three of the fifteen windows were open and had M4 rifle barrels sticking out. With their poor aim, the shooters were inexperienced, probably scared, and trying to ward off the cops.

*They shouldn't have started firing, then,* the Phoenix said. *More are coming now.*

*Like I said: scared.*

As the expert shooters in their classes, Leila and Heath took out a hostile each; the third must've given up seeing their comrades fall as that particular gun barrel withdrew from the window.

Now clear, the three detectives rushed toward the paint factory. Before they crossed the ten feet to the wide-open bay, a man burst out of a side door running.

DeMarcus took off after him. Even after continuous orders from the black cop to stop, the fleeing man didn't. Just as Leila and Heath reached the loading bay, DeMarcus had caught up with the suspect and tackled him.

"I'll take the first floor," Leila said, and Heath nodded.

They entered the painting factory with guns up, seeking further hostiles. A quick scan revealed none, so Heath hurried over to the iron stairs leading up to a catwalk. Once he vanished, she heard him ordering someone to get on the ground.

Still alert, Leila crept through the huge loading bay. Tables, ancient conveyor belts, and strewn garbage filled the room tall and wide enough to stack two eighteen-wheelers on top of each other.

"Lei, the kid says—" Heath began.

A hand suddenly shot out from behind a table, knocking the gun out of Leila's grip. She turned to meet her assailant, rising to a height way above her and twice as wide. And as she struck at him, he blocked her hits and fought back in Taekwondo. A rudimentary form—not polished; probably picked it up on the streets—but martial arts, nonetheless.

The Phoenix grew excited.

He didn't pose much of a challenge, though. The Phoenix toyed with him, using basic fighting techniques, but then it became bored. She dropped low in Panther to dodge a punch, then grabbed a hold of his leg and used it as balance as she cartwheeled, her boots striking him across the face. He flew to the side, banging into a conveyor belt track—probably already unconscious before he hit the metal.

"That there's another?" Leila finished for Heath. "I know. He's down."

DeMarcus came in hauling his suspect in handcuffs, and backup arrived soon after. Heath had already called for ambulances for the shot victims, and a paramedic checked out Leila's suspect. He would just suffer a severe headache when he eventually came around.

THE SUSPECTS QUICKLY THREW THE one Leila fought under the bus for killing the two men in the apartment and confessed to plotting the attack on the mayor. Even if they hadn't admitted their crimes, the apartment and the painting factory held plenty of evidence to convict them.

So, another case solved.

It used to be that after a successful case, she and David shared a congratulatory cup of coffee. Leila held onto the tradition, even though she drank alone. The Phoenix hated it, but she couldn't let it go yet.

Since Heath and DeMarcus were somewhere else, Leila practically had the squad room to herself. Propped against the table holding the coffee pot, she drank her cup while staring at David's picture on the wall.

Not even a full year had passed since he died. Reflecting on her changes, she huffed. She hid emotion by never looking anyone fully in the eyes so none could see her deadness. People expected her to be strong; she feared someone seeing past her façade of strength to the cowering woman within her. To be exposed.

Disgusted, she averted her eyes and knocked her drink back—still warm, but not scalding hot. Her acts of heroism fooled everyone, but she couldn't trick herself. She knew David's death made her fragile. If life struck her another devastating blow, she wasn't confident that she would remain standing.

*That's why I'm here,* the Phoenix assured.

The Phoenix kept her together—nothing could break her now. Memories could, though.

A hand strayed up to knead her coldest wound. David had kept his word on backing off at her insistence. He hadn't spoken to her, visited her dreams, or warmed her wound with his presence in four months. Doing so had her relying solely on the Phoenix, but now he only existed in her memories.

*He's not needed now; you want what you will never get back.*

Movement in the entryway brought her eyes up to see two people coming in.

David Neal, Sr.'s mustache was now completely gray, but his hair, along with Julianne's, remained mostly brown. Neither of them had aged or looked defeated with a gloomy atmosphere at losing their only child. They had taken David's death better than anyone, especially far better than her.

Since they had taken a vacation to the Canadian Rockies, she hadn't seen them for the whole summer. It was hard, but she forced herself not to rush toward them.

Leila smiled warmly for the first time since returning from Panordom. She would always have their love and support if no one else gave it. If it wasn't for them, she honestly didn't think she could continue with life.

"You both look well."

"Mountainous air does that," David Sr. said.

"It was so lovely, Leila. You should've come," Julianne said.

She meant it, just like when she whole-heartedly invited her at the beginning of June. Leila had declined, needing more time to adjust to the Phoenix. She had planned on having control over her dark side by now.

"I still wouldn't have been good company."

Concern washed over their features—Julianne tried to mask it. "Oh nonsense, you're always good company. It would've been better with you there."

"I have to disagree with you, Mrs. Julianne."

Leila's blunt denial stunned her.

"You'll be on your feet again once you find some steady ground," David Sr. encouraged.

The Phoenix's stare shocked them. "I must wait for someone to provide for me? This is where I'm to be."

They stared at her like an alien had taken her place. Julianne's green eyes twinkled with threatening tears, stung.

She had never snapped at them, never allowed them to see the Phoenix. For the first time, the Phoenix retreated in shame, and Leila ducked her head under the guilt. "I'm sorry, I shouldn't have… I don't have control over what the Phoenix says, but now you see why I couldn't go. I didn't want to hurt you like now… I can't say anything right anymore."

"Hey, Mr. David and Mrs. Julianne!" Heath greeted as he and D walked in. "What are you doing here?"

David's parents explained that they just felt like popping by since they hadn't seen everybody in a while.

Standing there, Leila realized that she didn't belong with them anymore—by holding onto David when they had moved on and putting up a front that she was okay, she made things worse. On the outside now, she saw how her struggle with the Phoenix was such a nuisance to their lives.

Suddenly, Leila's coldest wound thawed and warmed. David's presence broke through the Phoenix's shield, and Leila felt the warmth of reuniting friends.

She glanced at David's smiling detective picture. *Fidelis ad Mortem,* Leila repeated the police motto.

*"Faithful unto Death. And even afterward,"* David replied.

# VI.

After putting her Nissan in park, Leila kept her grip on the steering wheel. Her nerves shouldn't be shot after finally hearing and feeling David again. She hadn't revisited him since returning from Panordom. So, guilt? Shame for ignoring him?

*This was my choice, and he agreed. I had to.*

Anger swelled within her—like she had been offended. He was an intrusion in her yield to the Phoenix, a numb contentment.

No, that was the Phoenix talking. She had longed for his presence and now had him… Could she go back to the Phoenix? He wouldn't be constantly talking to her—she had asked him to back off.

She looked over at the freshly bought bouquet of flowers. *I have no choice; I gave him a promise to move on without him.*

Releasing a breath for courage, Leila grabbed the flowers and stepped out. The whole time she sat in her car deciding whether or not to visit David, she hadn't looked at his grave. Seeing his lonely headstone under the willow tree without a single change—other than the complete recess of the bump—opened the carefully sealed floodgates of her memories.

She shut her eyes in an attempt to stop them and felt the Phoenix rushing to her defense. *No. Not yet. I want to feel again, even if it's pain.*

The Phoenix backed off, displeased, but not absent—its presence lingered like a shadow.

Leila refocused on David's grave and made her way up to it, wincing in pain at the memories of her wounds like they had just been inflicted. She stopped at his feet, and after a while of staring at the words chiseled into his headstone—not finding a single word to say—she sat.

Still, long moments passed as she couldn't find the words to express her feelings. David didn't start the conversation either, allowing her to begin when comfortable. She fingered a soft petal in the bouquet of flowers. Why did she become so distant from everyone? She didn't feel at ease talking with anyone anymore.

"Once again, you are lost in thought, not hearing my approach." She turned to the elderly grave keeper, standing at a distance to maintain her private bubble. "I know I am not that silent."

"My thoughts are too loud now."

"You must find somewhere to quiet them."

"Where?"

"Not here." He considered his cemetery for a while. "Somewhere larger… quieter… empty."

"That doesn't sound like New York."

"Certainly not. But until that time comes, would you like to talk?"

Leila didn't. Just like with the psychiatrist, she didn't think it would help; it was her situation, and she would have to figure it out.

"Or may I just ramble to you? Hearing the troubles of an old man may help."

After further deliberation, Leila nodded beside her. Perhaps he would become background noise so she could focus on speaking to David.

The grave keeper thanked her as he shuffled closer, then gingerly eased down. Bones popped against each other with age. He released a big sigh when he finally got settled.

"Before you know it, time takes everything from you: your beauty, your health, your life, and even your joys."

He was quiet for a moment, giving her time to respond if she wished to. "Elaine was the joy of my life. I couldn't talk so openly with another or laugh as deeply. I thought I knew love, but not the merging of souls that we had. If she wasn't in the room, I couldn't breathe right. Yes, we fought, but there was never discomfort; we knew each other in and out, so that's why we quarreled—to test our love.

"When she passed, I knew nothing—like a child longing for direction. I was lost and without hope of living without her; she was my reason for living. I built a wall around me, nursing wounds I had inflicted upon myself—wondering why I still lived, and so discouraged that she had left me.

"But then one day, I sobered up, and I realized I was feeling sorry for myself. I had my soulmate for thirty-seven wonderful, beautiful years. And, my soul hadn't been broken. I realized she was still with me, for when souls touch, they can never be parted."

He paused for a breather and realization settled over him. "And now you've answered the question haunting me these nine years without her: I was kept alive to tell you that you're not alone. I am proof that it will improve, through time and effort. And I'm sure I'm not the only one."

Leila stared at him. Once again, she was told that David wasn't her soulmate; not only from David telling her, so moving on would be easier, or because the Phoenix needed fewer distractions to focus on Foster but from one who *had* his soulmate. And none of that corresponded to her and David.

Their souls didn't fuse together. They fought—a lot—and she had always felt superior. When she first lost David, she could do nothing, but now, and she hated to admit it, she didn't need him. That was why he urged her to participate in the tournament.

The grave keeper didn't say any more. He wasn't waiting for her to reply either; he just sat beside her, looking beyond David's headstone, at peace with the quiet. It still took her a while to regain her voice.

"I guess I needed to hear that I'm not alone. No one really understands. Thank you."

"Anytime, dear. But, I think, I don't fully understand either but better than most."

She looked at him to explain.

"Losing Elaine did not bring out a darker side in me. That, I do not understand, and I do not think anyone will unless they have one themselves."

*Him.*

He shifted so he could get up. "I've talked enough for one day. You came here to spend time with him, not me."

She helped him up. "I think I come now expecting you."

"Why?"

"I can't talk to him like before. It's not the same now. But if I stop coming, I might lose this last connection, even though it's strained."

He looked at her for a long time, his tired eyes seeing the fragile spirit she tried to hide.

"Not even a year has gone by, and you have grown ten years older. He is dead, and you are not; you realize that you can't keep going on like before. You must find who you can talk to."

"That's the problem. I want to, then I don't."

"Which is greater?"

She debated for a while. "I'm not sure."

"Sounds like you're at the fork in your road. You may pull yourself down the wrong road on your own, or someone will help you decide. You just have to wait."

She gave a dry chuckle. "I'm so tired of being patient."

"Jumping the gun is never a good thing. We often find our soulmates when we are not searching, but rather when we open ourselves to the realization that we deserve it." He waved farewell and left the way he came.

Leila turned back to David's grave, now finding the words she wanted to say. It came out harsher than she intended though, "Before, why give me a spark? Why now?"

*"The Phoenix has kept you cold too long. I thought it time you felt warmth."*

His voice soothed her like drinking a warm cup of soup—her body relaxed, feeling lighter as if all her burdens vanished. But she could feel them lingering behind her where the Phoenix waited, held back for the time being by David. It didn't matter now that he wasn't her soulmate; he had held her heart.

"Thank you; it was nice."

*"You think I shouldn't have…"*

"No, it's not that. It's like going into a warm building after being outside in the cold. I must go back out, but it will be colder than before."

David hesitated. *"I hate to say it, but it's going to get colder than you can expect."*

"What can I do?"

*"Trudge through to your next warm building."*

She understood his metaphor—until she found him.

"So, this means he's close."

*"Closer than before but still far away."*

"Death really has changed you, David. You're not snarky." Leila tried to force humor, but it fell flat.

*"You need me to be serious now; not sarcastic."*

She laid the bouquet at his headstone. "How much longer must I suffer this torment?"

*"Too long. Much too long. I wish this had never happened to you."*

"You're not the only one."

*"No. Everyone that meets you can see you're hurting, and those who know you can see the mask you wear."*

Her dark side glared at the headstone through her eyes, and she couldn't keep the Phoenix out of her voice, "I don't need pity."

*"I know you don't, but you're going to get it no matter what unless the person understands your pain from experiencing it themselves."*

Leila thought back to Shiers' reaction to her shutting him off to argue with the Phoenix. Confusion had swept over his face, but interest also sparked in his eyes—he wanted to know why.

"Shiers wouldn't have understood, would he? He likely only asked me out because I'm pretty and as an experiment—to see how far he could go…" Her hands clenched. "Adrenaline junkie."

David hesitated. *"You're not entirely wrong…"*

"So, it's good I turned him down."

*"You know I can't tell you what happens… but yes. He would've taken part in this weather you're to storm."*

"Would he have been trapped by this storm or was he a cause of it?"

The leaves of the willow swayed under his sigh. *"Most of the time, we bring our storms with us."*

# VII.

Everything appeared the same as she ascended to the second floor: the goldfish still held occupancy in the garden's fountain except their number had grown, and new faces stared at the white visitor.

She stopped at the fifth door, trying to hold onto her courage as the Phoenix kept trying to pull it from her so that she would run.

*This is pointless. What good will come of talking to him? He never mattered.*

*He was my friend.* The laughter of the girls strengthened her nerve as a hand raised to knock. *And they were my family.*

A weight approached the door. She could feel his eyes on her through the peephole. Still, the door didn't open. With his long hesitation, he wasn't going to let her in. He hadn't forgiven her yet. She deserved his rejection; she started to head back down to her car when locks clicked, and the door opened.

Leila turned back around to Jamaal Gordon standing in his doorway. Other than his neck being thinner from lack of fighting, he looked the same. Dreadlocks held back by a rubber band. Wide, open brown eyes, but his beaming smile didn't greet her—caution kept his features taut. He waited for her to make the first move. But she could also feel an eager air around him that he wanted to burst her touchy defenses and hug her.

A long, awkward silence passed between them. She would take the first step to breach it. "Hi, Jamaal."

It still looked like hearing her voice was a surprise. "Hi, Lei."

"How have things been?"

"Good; fame from winning the tournament isn't so new anymore, so I get some privacy now."

"That's good. Wish I could say the same."

Awkwardness came up again until Jamaal uprooted himself and walked to her. He grabbed her shoulder, and relief washed over him to where he smiled and pulled her in for a hug. "I thought I was imagining things, but you're actually here."

She returned his hug just as tight and long—she had missed him far more than she would admit. But it strongly resembled their last long hug after the Changeling fight—him needing her, and her as hard as stone. He made the comparison too.

Jamaal stepped back, his face falling some with disappointment. "But you're not here, are you?"

"I am more than I have been."

"At least you're trying."

The Phoenix started to snap at him—that there was nothing she needed to change—when her name was squealed, and two dark forms barreled into her.

"Miss Lei! We've missed you!"

"Where have you been?"

"Why haven't you come back?"

Their greetings and questions all ran over each other in a hurry. Leila knelt so Zaira and Eve could wrap their arms around her neck.

She forced enthusiasm. "I've missed you too, but I've been too busy to come back."

"You need to be less busy!" Eve fussed.

"I need it."

Eve's forehead scrunched. "Why do you need it?"

"Yeah, why do you need it?" Jamaal chimed in.

Leila looked at him, and the Phoenix came out. "Because it's a part of me—without it, I'm nothing."

The former partnership stared at each other, but luckily the girls remained oblivious to the tension in the air. "Mommy and Daddy gripe about being busy," Zaira said as she grabbed Leila's hand and dragged her into the apartment.

Jade Gordon lingered in the kitchen that doubled as a dining room. She knew that Jamaal had told her about the Phoenix from the way she was anxiously wringing her hands, looking on the verge of running to the door, yanking her family back inside, and kicking her out.

But she put up a strong front for her girls by giving Leila a nervous smile. "It's good to see you again, Leila."

"Same here."

Eve kept the silence away. "Are you going to eat with us, Miss Lei? We're having lasagna and garlic bread! Please?"

She looked to Jade for approval. "I'm not sure if I should. I just came by to say hello."

The girls turned to their mother. "Please?" they begged.

She relented to their pouts. "You can eat with us, Leila; we have plenty." The girls cheered. "Perhaps it will be like old times."

Zaira hurried off to help her mother with finishing the salad and cutting the lasagna, Eve pulled Leila with her to fold napkins and disperse the silverware, and Jamaal passed without a word to fill the glasses. She hadn't felt this uneasy and out of place even when they were strangers.

The food was blessed, and they began to eat. At first, the girls didn't want to eat, instead informing Leila of everything she had missed and the outcome of their summer break. After some stern warnings from their parents to eat, they did but still giving Leila snippets of the happenings when they swallowed.

"Are you coming with us to Jamaica, Miss Lei? It's going to be a great vacation. Mommy and Daddy grew up there," Eve said.

Leila tried not to let the parents' sudden jolt and eyes shooting to her sting. But they did. "No, I don't think I will. It's a family vacation."

"But you are family."

*At least the girls don't have a cold shoulder,* the Phoenix mumbled.

*You did this, so don't you place blame.*

"I haven't always been. This is a special trip just for you, Zaira, your mom and dad, and your grandparents."

"Oh."

"Will you come see us fly off in a plane?" Zaira asked.

Leila looked for Jamaal and Jade's disapproval but didn't find an outright objection. "I think I'll be able to do that."

Eve began to babble on about her first plane ride with her sister chiming in until Jamaal reminded them of the hour. The girls bid her goodnight, then were ushered to their bedrooms by their father.

Silence fell on the women like a rock. Jade quickly grabbed some dishes and retreated to the sink. The Phoenix wasn't going to let her apologize for the severing of any connection—especially since it didn't feel it deserved the blame. Leila grabbed the remaining dishes and carried them to her. Jade acknowledged her help with a nod.

"When are you leaving?" she asked after sitting back down.

"August 8th; nine in the morning," Jade said, then shut off.

"I'll be sure to mark the date—unless I'm not truly wanted."

Jade stopped cleaning the dishes. "The girls want you there." She hesitated before turning. "I do too, and so does Jamaal." Taking a seat, she hurried to explain. "Jamaal has been torn up about how you two stopped talking. It doesn't look like it, but we are happy to see you again; we've missed you. We just… don't know how to show it since the Phoenix sees something negative in everything, even when there's nothing there. We're fragile; we can't take its constant demeaning. I hate doing it, but it's easier to remain cold."

"I second that."

"About remaining cold or that you hate doing it?" Jamaal asked when he came back in and seated beside his wife.

"Both. I feel guilty seeing how I'm received, but I feel safer. Disappointment doesn't hurt."

"This is only temporary though, right? Until you get…" He trailed off.

She kept his gaze until he had to look away from her severity as a yes. His heavy sigh spoke of his disagreement with her decision, but he changed the topic to avoid an argument. "So, any news on London?"

Leila shook her head, withdrawing more heavy sighs from the couple. After returning from the tournament, Jade expressed concern about London's disappearance—he had yet to show up or contact her. For Jamaal and Jade's peace of mind, Leila filed a missing person's report.

"Maybe he went back to England," she suggested.

Jamaal shook his head. "He wouldn't have without telling us. He's shady, but he wouldn't stoop that low."

A thought began to rise from the Phoenix; she fought back against it—Foster couldn't have been involved; she would find London alive. But it lingered like heartburn. No amount of medicine could rid her of it until it was proven right.

# VIII.

The files held Leila's attention until the phone began ringing incessantly on her desk. Without removing her gaze from the missing person's file, a hand answered the phone and balanced it under her ear and neck. "Wells."

"Detective? This is Coroner John Hall."

His name brought back her first memory of his voice when he had called to say her parents were dead. She brushed off the apprehension of Deja-vu the memory caused. "Hey, John."

"How are you doing, Leila?"

"I've been better."

"I probably won't improve things. I have something that may interest you. Are you able to come?"

Leila shifted her gaze from the file to the clock on her desk. "Sure, I have time. See you soon."

She hung up the phone, closed the file, and stood to leave. "Headed to the morgue; be back in a bit," she announced to Heath and DeMarcus as she walked out.

AFTER A SHORT DRIVE TO reach Metropolitan Hospital, and making her way through the chaotic Emergency Room, Leila caught a free elevator and headed down to the morgue.

Luckily, she found John Hall to be the only coroner present in the chilly and confining morgue, observing a body lying on the examining table. The other coroners gave her the creeps with their searching eyes. John had an odd sense of humor, and his lanky body, overlarge hands and feet, and shallow face made him a strange-looking man, but at least he had a heart.

"Hey, John. What do you have for me?" she announced as she pushed open the swinging door.

"A body!" he said cheerfully as he pulled up the white sheet to cover the deceased's face, then removed his safety glasses.

"That *is* what one tends to find in a morgue. Anything to them?"

John grinned as he motioned for her to follow him to the vaults. "He belongs to a missing report you filed."

She refrained from a frustrated sigh. "Be more specific than that, John. I've filed quite a few missing persons."

"Well, he'll be specific for you," he said as he opened one of the doors and pulled out the table with a covered body occupying it.

"Some officers fished him out of the Hudson this morning. He's almost impossible to recognize from being in the water for a few days, but his tattoos are what tipped me off." He pulled the sheet back to the middle of his chest.

He was quite pale and had short red hair. His face was definitely unrecognizable from the swelling and absorption of the water. Leila could barely make out the swirling letters of a tattoo wrapping around his neck.

"London Calling?" she asked to make sure she had read it right and received a nod from John. Dread overcame her that she had found London, Jamaal's ex-fighting partner who hadn't been seen since last October.

"I recognized the tattoos from a picture of one of your missing persons, but I wasn't sure until his fingerprints came back and proved it to be him: James Leroy Hareing III, also known as London," he read off the file he had grabbed, then handed it to her.

"How did he die?" she asked as she scanned the report.

"A combination of things: the breaking of his trachea, and the massive amounts of water in his lungs."

"Drowning?"

John nodded. "In a way, but this was no accident. The breaking of his trachea didn't kill him, so into the Hudson he went to ensure that he would die."

"Any clues on who murdered him?"

"No. No prints on his entire body. I know someone murdered him, but I can't prove who."

Leila just stared at the lifeless man's swollen face as Bryan Foster's face appeared in her mind. But why would he kill London? What would he gain?

*Ensuring Jamaal and we would be put together…* The Phoenix's thought froze her blood. The possibility scared her. The only reason she and Jamaal fought together was that London had disappeared, then he never showed again…

"Detective? Did you know him?" John's question brought her out of her horrifying thoughts.

"No, I didn't. A friend knows him— Well, knew him." Now whether to tell Jamaal that London was dead or not…

He remained quiet as he observed Leila thinking over a decision. "Well, do you know any family or relatives to contact?"

"I don't. I'll contact the CA, and they'll see about next of kin."

John's mouth twisted into a frown. "Well, hopefully, they'll find someone, and they can afford to have his body shipped overseas. I hate it when the deceased can't get a proper funeral." He recovered the dead man's face, then pushed him back inside the vault and closed it.

The closing of the door snapped Leila out of her thoughts. "Thanks for letting me know he was found and notify me if anything else comes up about his death."

"Sure thing."

After handing him back the file, Leila left the morgue afraid that the reason for his death involved Foster. She had assumed right last night.

LEILA SEARCHED CONTINUOUSLY THROUGH COLD case files for murders similar to London's death—anything to prove her feelings wrong. Foster *couldn't* be the culprit—breaking necks wasn't his MO. But the more she looked for evidence and continuous failures, the stronger the Phoenix's declaration became.

*Why do you fear? We've been waiting for some kind of trail, and here it is. This means he's closer to being killed.*

She set aside another report. "I'm not afraid of getting him; I just want to make sure."

*When have I been wrong?*

"I must have some basis for condemning him of London's death."

*He's a murderer, and he's set on you. What more do you need? You're just stalling.*

In frustration at the Phoenix nailing her and her failed searches, she knocked papers and files off the desk. She hung her head in her hands and closed her eyes instead of screaming.

"I don't want to believe that Foster knew exactly how to get to me. I don't want to be the reason for both David and London's deaths. If so, Foster has some plan, and it revolves around me. That is what I'm afraid of."

*Not just Foster.*

"I know; Xander too." She massaged her temple. "Why target me? What's so special about me?"

The Phoenix struggled for an answer, and its unease transferred into her. It had a hunch and wasn't sure if it should share.

Before her dark side could decide, the captain called for her through the intercom system.

"Lei, you're needed down here."

She had ducked her duties for too long searching for scraps that probably couldn't be found. Leila picked up the papers and files she had knocked off, continuing her debate with the Phoenix as she left.

*What do you know? Tell me.*

*It's just a guess…*

*Liar, you never guess; you're too sure of yourself.*

The sight of four faces turned to her caught her attention. *If I'm right, this will—* The unfamiliar fourth face slowed her descent, but the recognition of concern, worry, and plain-out seeking forgiveness on the three faces she knew stopped her foot from reaching the next step. The foreigner was a Caucasian likely in his mid-twenties. He had blond hair and a youthful, innocent-looking face—a newbie straight out of the academy. She knew exactly what had transpired.

He had accepted the only job open at the station: David's position. He was her new partner.

Leila focused on at least getting down the stairs before she fell. She didn't hesitate a second to go up to the men with her head level with theirs. The Phoenix was surely present in her eyes from the men jerking into caution, but the complete emptiness she felt inside was an immense comfort.

"Lei," the captain began, breathing in deep to settle himself. "This is Spencer Ghent, our fourth man. He'll be your new partner."

She finally looked at the young man's welcoming face, then down to his outstretched hand. She hoped she hid her features well enough from her struggle with the Phoenix not to show her anger or to completely deny the youngster before he had a chance to prove himself.

*Look at him! He will be nothing close to what David was.*

She forced a small, small smile and accepted his hand. "I'm Leila Wells."

"I know who you are. Perhaps you could show me a few moves, Phoenix."

*I could show you some now.* She wrestled irritation out of her voice. "Perhaps."

The captain cleared his voice, recognizing the tension in his best detective and knowing she would break if he didn't give her space. "It's time you see real work, Ghent. Heath, D, catch him up on your case. Lei, I need to talk with you."

He turned toward his office, Ghent moved off under D's guidance to the screens, and Heath caught her eye as she put the files on her desk. His sympathetic gaze offended the Phoenix.

"Lei—"

"I don't need comfort." She turned from him and disappeared into the captain's office.

He shut the door behind her. She went straight to his desk but didn't sit down—instead placing her hands on his desk, she focused on maintaining even breathing, preventing the Phoenix from getting out. Leila knew this day would come, but she could never be ready. Never could she accept someone replacing David.

*In his position or in my heart?* she asked.

*Both.*

The captain sighed. "Lei, I'm sorry."

"Don't apologize. You needed to fill that place; we haven't been as productive since David died. You're just doing your job."

"Just like it's your job to act hurt and deny him so soon?"

Leila turned on him. "I am not hurt."

"Then what is this?"

She couldn't hold his gaze for long. What was she doing? She struggled against the Phoenix every day, so she couldn't blame it. She did feel hurt—hurt that the captain had moved on, leaving her behind to continue moping.

"I'm trying to accept the fact that I'm the only one who hasn't moved on yet. I can't let David go, and that gives the Phoenix power over me." It started to deny her, but Leila silenced it. It was the truth. She looked over at Ghent with Heath and D discussing the newest homicide.

The captain caught her attention by moving in for a hug. "I hoped this move would make you realize that. I don't have the strength to confront you."

"It's going to be hard seeing someone in his place."

"Yes, it is—for all of us. But if it was easy, it wouldn't help."

Unfortunately, the Phoenix found a button to push; she looked him straight in the eye. "But I will tell you this, Captain: if he mentions that he's trying to be better than David or to replace him… I won't rein myself in—and you, Heath, or D won't be able to stop me."

He stiffened because of the fire in her eyes. "I know you will. I hope he doesn't get close enough to feel the heat."

She looked back at the men, then to David's picture on the wall. "He won't have a warning. One slip up and he will burn, along with anyone in my way, I swear."

Leila left his office and stopped before joining the men, eyeing the innocent Ghent. She definitely had a thing or two to show him, and it wasn't just martial arts. He was in for a hard awakening. It would be his last mistake to take her on. She decided it better—and safer—to go cool off before joining them. No one would be able to emerge from her fire.

# IX.

She practiced at Hyun's Gym to quell the Phoenix's anger. The exercise junkies gawking at her explosive moves didn't bother Leila; she barely noticed their presence. Ignoring them was for their safety—she probably would've turned on them if they started pestering her for autographs or pictures.

The main cause of her anger today: Ghent.

They had gone to an abandoned warehouse to take a gang by surprise. Of course, the leaders bolted, so she and Ghent headed to the roof for one. Ghent messed up, affecting her, and the criminal escaped. Replaying what happened following that hardened her moves.

"Everything okay? You're here early," Hyun commented from the entrance to the exercise area.

"Will be," she answered without taking her focus off the intricate moves of the Snake. As she danced around her imaginary opponent, she struck him with sharp hands, ducked under a hit of his, and retaliated, then went back to advancing toward him. To finish her opponent, she blocked a hit of his and ducked under the arm to drive a sharp head into their armpit.

Leila remained frozen in her final move—legs twisted beneath her holding her low to the ground, her right arm in front of her after fending off the punch, and her left striking underneath with the hand still sharp like a snake-head.

After releasing a long breath, Leila untwined herself and straightened. She turned to Hyun propped up against the Shoji door but saw phones in everyone's hands, filming her practicing.

The Phoenix flared back to life, angered at everyone enjoying the show—not dissipated like the extraneous activity should have done.

Her movement snapped the mesmerized crowd out of their trance. One ran up to her, making her bristle at the emerging Phoenix. "Detective Wells, can you give me an autograph?"

Noticing the change, Hyun hurried over to intervene before something happened. "Lei, want some tea?"

His voice brought Leila back to the surface. "Sure." She turned back to the woman asking for an autograph. Back in control now, Leila took in the expectant fan and felt many eyes and camera lenses eyeballing her. She nodded and accepted her offered pen, receipt, and checkbook to use as a firm surface—she didn't need to disappoint a fan and have the denial go viral, slandering her name.

Her agreement had others running up for either an autograph or a photo. Hyun stood beside as a bystander, ensuring everything stayed calm.

Finished with signatures and pictures, Leila retreated with Hyun from the gushing crowd. Hyun took her to the back where he heated up tea while Leila collapsed into a couch.

"Alright, so what happened?" Hyun began.

She released a sigh before starting. "Captain hired an idiot to take David's place about two months ago. He hasn't done anything right in my eyes. Yesterday, he caused me to lose a criminal by foolishly tackling me, thinking I was the criminal—I'm sure you read it in the papers."

He nodded.

"I went back to the warehouse today to see if I could find him and bring him in, reclaim my title of only losing one criminal. But I found him dying of an overdose. The paramedics tried to keep him alive. Now I've lost two criminals."

"He's still new to the force, Lei. He's eager to prove himself—especially to you."

"I know, I know. It's just if it wasn't for Ghent, the man wouldn't be dead."

Silence took over the room. "Can I ask you something?" he asked as he poured the Oriental tea into cups.

"Sure."

He turned with steaming cups in hand. "Why do we fall?"

"To get back up." Her answer was monotonous, having heard this lecture many times before.

"And what if we don't get up?"

"We lay in defeat." She accepted the cup Hyun handed her and took a sip.

Hyun took a sip as well. "And what does that represent?"

"That we've given up. But Hyun, I haven't surrendered; I've just… given in."

He contemplated her words for a while, then leaned forward. "Is that better or worse than giving up?"

Leila thought hard but couldn't find an answer. She shrugged. "I guess we'll see."

LEILA AND HEATH BECAME PARTNERS again after she persuaded the captain that Spencer Ghent couldn't be with her until he became more experienced and wouldn't embarrass her again. Ghent's reassignment with DeMarcus allowed Leila to accomplish policework without blemish or criminal fatality, and Ghent was safer under D's capable wing as he learned the ropes.

A month passed with Leila and Heath working together again, deflating the media's excitement at her screw up. A case worked up of a group of single mothers getting revenge on bankers who had scorned their love by robbing their vaults and killing them. Killian Youngend, the CEO of New York Progressive Bank, was the next target.

Scared of the scorned lovers coming for his heart, Killian wanted to run. Leila convinced him to go to work or the women would know something was up—probably knowing his schedule. Being spineless and cowardly, she didn't think he deserved protecting. He was a conniving banker, too, but she had sworn to protect the innocent, so they went to stakeout the bank.

As they infiltrated the building undercover—guns and bulletproof vests hidden underneath shirts, and her wearing a hat to prevent recognition—she fought off Deja-vu. This wasn't the bank where David and eight others died. Different scenario, too, with women being the criminals, not Bryan Foster. She straightened up but couldn't shake off the apprehension thick in the air.

Acting as a couple, Leila and Heath passed a bent over Ghent working on his fake deposit slip. The sight of him brought out the Phoenix. Through his stiffening, he felt her glare.

"I know why you're so hard on him, and I can understand," Heath began as he took a seat to wait for their pretend meeting for a loan.

"Do you?"

He gave her a warning glare. "You're not the only one affected by David's death. He was my partner too. He left a huge hole, and the captain is trying to patch it up with Ghent. We need this as a functioning station—as partners. Yes, he has made mistakes, but D and I acknowledge that he's at least trying; we expect errors because he's new. So, why can't you?"

"He hasn't proven himself yet."

"Because you haven't let him. Every time he tries, you shoot him down. He looks up to you, and you're letting him down by not being open."

She kept scanning the bank, refusing to respond.

Heath chuckled. "You also need to tone down your seriousness: you're scaring us and intimidating him."

"He should learn to work under pressure."

"Maybe you could ease up on him a little."

She eyed him.

He brought up a hand with his fingers almost pinched, showing a small space between his thumb and index finger. "Just a little bit."

"It depends on how he handles today."

"Come on, sit. Speaking of toning down, we're supposed to be blending in, not sticking out. I'm sure others are getting nervous."

After seeing people glancing at her periodically, Leila took a seat.

"What's got you so wired up?"

Images of that night at Citizen's First Bank flashed in her head. Like a transparent film lay over her eyes, the seven dead security guards littered the lobby mixed with the throngs of people. Even though not marble stairs, Leila and David hurried up to the third floor—

She shut her eyes, blocking out the memory. "I haven't been to a bank since."

He understood what she meant. "Is it just memories or do you feel something, like that night?"

She shook her head. "It's not as strong, but something's—"

"Suspects entering bank," a lookout outside of the bank reported into their earpieces.

Leila looked at the entrance; five women entered, all with large purses. Two were blonde, one a red-head, and two brunettes—she bet those were wigs.

"Lei, if—" Heath began; she held up a hand to silence him. As expected, three women headed toward the lines for the bank tellers while the other two were lookouts at the front: one sitting at a bench by the window and the other beside Ghent.

Hands clenching her chair's armrests, she forced herself not to intervene. Seeing where her gaze went, Heath placed a hand on her fist. "Have some faith."

She wasn't able to not stare holes into Ghent, praying he wouldn't mess up again. The three women continued to advance in their lines, and the woman beside Ghent struck up a conversation with him. He forgot his work on the fake slip and talked with her.

Leila watched them, but so did the other lookout by the window. Uncomfortable with what she saw, she pulled out her phone and messaged the rest of her partners. The one laughing with Ghent ignored her buzzing phone, but the other three women retrieved their phones to read the message. Whatever the text, the women glanced around them as they exited the lines.

"We can't let them go," Leila whispered to Heath as she stood to intercept the criminals.

"You've been compromised; apprehend suspects," the lookout confirmed. Before Leila could do so, Ghent heard the order, and in his excitement, he jumped up to arrest the woman, but fumbled at his gun.

"Cop!" she yelled in warning before easily disarming him and aiming the gun between Ghent's eyes.

Ghent raised his hands in surrender. The woman seated at the window apprehended the bank guard, and the other three spun around with their guns out, demanding the identity of other cops as they ordered everyone to get down.

"I don't think so." One of the robbers caught Leila reaching for her gun. "Take it out and put it on the ground. Kick it away, and you, by the sofas, do the same!" Heath's Glock clattered on the tile floor.

"You know the routine: hands on head and get on your knees."

Leila did as she was told. By the benches lining the back wall, DeMarcus looked at her from down on his stomach—his cover wasn't blown yet.

Her captor regained her attention by knocking off her hat, then she retreated smartly to a safe distance. "The famous Phoenix, on her knees and held at gunpoint. You don't seem that great to me."

"Should I remind you?"

"Remind me that you're a woman who lost her man and doesn't know what to do with herself?"

Like a dam bursting open, the Phoenix surged through, enraged at the insult. The Phoenix taking over in Leila's eyes startled the woman; she stepped back, alarmed.

"I used that to win a fighting tournament, and I don't need anyone."

Her hand shot up to knock the gun up, and she spun to trip her. As she fell, the gun went off; the bullet whizzed by Leila's ear and struck something behind her. Whatever it hit dropped heavily to the floor. With a swift punch across her face, Leila knocked the woman unconscious and grabbed her gun.

The other two spun to face her as she charged at them. Not trigger-shy, bullets ripped through the air. People screamed.

Leila shot at one woman's thigh before diving toward the two robbers, landing in between them. As the women turned again, she rammed her palm into one woman's nose to break it. The robber stumbled back, blood squirting from her nose as she dropped her gun.

Leaning into a back handstand, Leila wrapped her legs around the brunette's neck—the one she shot in the leg—and then pulled her legs back so the woman flew into the other. Like she figured, the wig flew off, revealing short black hair. Their collision echoed, and they remained stunned and in a tangled heap on the floor.

Leila rose with guns in both hands, aimed at the women acting as lookouts staring at her, shocked at her quickness.

"Drop it." The guns clattered on the tile floor, and they raised their hands in defeat.

The rest of the undercover officers came alive then: retrieving their fallen weapons and aiming at the defeated robbers, making sure the civilians were safe, or calling headquarters for reports.

Leila breathed out the Phoenix, thanking it for its strength. She looked where the woman fired: the sitting area where she and Heath had sat… with him missing.

"Heath!" she screamed. As she sprinted toward the encircled sofas, she could only see pieces of that night: Bryan Foster's green eye, the table Foster threw her onto after breaking her arm, David jolting still when the last bullet drilled into his head. She hurdled over the chairs. Falling had shifted the order, and he lay with his hand over the right side of his stomach.

She ripped open his shirt, expecting blood. His torso wasn't covered in red—the bulletproof vest did its job.

"I'm good. It just hurts like Hell," Heath complained.

Leila hugged her partner. "Thank God."

His arm slid around her back for the return hug. "Sorry for the heart attack."

She helped him to his feet, holding onto him until he was steady. A pale Killian Youngend spoke with another officer.

Heath chuckled. She followed his gaze to two female robbers limping with slumped postures: one with a bleeding nose and the other with bruises and a bleeding thigh. An officer tried to rouse the unconscious one.

"Dang, I missed seeing you in action. All I've ever seen is you on TV," Heath griped.

"It's not that impressive."

DeMarcus jogged over to them. "It was too impressive! I thought I would get a chance to shine until she creamed them. You good, man?"

"Vest got shot, not me."

DeMarcus continued to gush about seeing Leila fight. She spotted Ghent coming their way, and the Phoenix exploded back to life like a firework.

*"No, not here. Later. The public doesn't need to see,"* David suggested.

Leila turned to a side exit. "I'm headed for the House."

"What's the rush, Lei?" DeMarcus asked.

"Keeping Ghent alive for the time being."

# X.

Leila's hands shook. Blistering fury bubbled under her skin. She hadn't experienced this much hate since she thought she saw Foster back at Panordom. Paperwork at her desk couldn't keep her still; her legs kept her moving. Maybe the repeated patterns she walked would calm her down… Along with walking to dispel energy, she read a file over and over again in hopes that the nonsense words would glaze over the Phoenix's anger. The words blended together, and the brisk pacing kept her limber—nothing would distract the Phoenix.

Her constant pacing made Captain Sullivan come out of his office. "Lei, what—"

"Not now. Please, not now."

He watched her walk the aisle separating the four desks, back and forth. "Heath will have a bruise, nothing more. Was it that he—"

"No," she interrupted him again, this time before he could compare his shooting with David's.

"Then what's the meaning of making a groove in my floor?"

"The cause of him getting shot."

"Which was?"

She considered telling him as she reached the end of the aisle. Turning back around to confess, Heath, D, and a smiling Ghent walked in. Her anger spurred her to lunge at him and beat that smile off his face to where he wouldn't smile again.

"Is something funny!" Seeing the dangerous inferno in her eyes, Heath and D bravely formed a human blockade between her and Ghent.

Ghent dropped the smile and acted puzzled.

"Don't you play dumb!"

The captain inserted himself. "What is going on?"

"Heath wouldn't have been shot if not for this idiot!" He cowered behind his blockade, flinching when her scorching eyes landed on him.

Captain Sullivan looked at her restraining herself to his newest recruitment, hiding from guilt and fear.

"Can someone explain?"

Ghent tried to stand up for himself. "I got too eager to make an arrest, and I messed up; I'm sorry. According to her" — he attempted to glare at her, but her fire devoured his, and he recoiled— "I caused Heath to get shot."

"It was your fault! You made the one at the window suspicious, probably smelling rookie all over you. Then, wanting praise, you fumbled at your gun, obviously revealing this was a trap for them!"

He leaned over his partners' shoulders. "That didn't get Heath shot! I didn't trip the one who fired the bullet."

Heath's arm came up to hold her back. "Don't you dare put this on me! I did what I've been trained to do: take down criminals who become immediate threats to the public. If not for your foolishness, they wouldn't have pulled their guns out—you put everyone in danger!"

"I'm sorry!" His own temper rose. "I messed up! I know this!"

"A police officer doesn't have room to screw up; you are the difference between life and death! Because you messed up, *again,* Heath was shot and could've died! The first time you failed, someone did die! And you shouldn't be apologizing to me; you should be apologizing to Heath. He's the one you could've killed."

Ghent glanced at Heath.

He stopped him. "No need to apologize, man. I know you didn't mean it."

Ghent turned back to Leila. "He understands that I didn't do it on purpose."

"I'm trying to make you understand that you must be more responsible for your actions. You can't think only about yourself now; others are relying on you to keep them safe. Accept that or many others will die. You're in the real world now; this isn't the academy where mistakes are expected."

He rubbed his forehead in frustration. "Fine; I forgot. She was flirting with me, and I got carried away. My fumbling got Heath shot. Happy?"

DeMarcus added his hand to restrain her as she surged forward. "Watch your tone with me, boy. I am the best cop in all of New York. I didn't get this way making mistakes; I earned this title, and you better respect me. I can have you out of this job and stripped of ever becoming a cop in the entire United States in the blink of an eye. Don't push me."

*"Calm down, Lei. He's just a boy and isn't as experienced as you,"* David said to soothe her.

It did.

"Calm down, Lei," the captain also added.

She sighed; David's voice smoothed over the Phoenix's anger. Feeling the tension in her body relax, the men holding her back released their grip.

"Ghent, I know you have promise, even though I wanted to deny it. You are filling a role I wanted to believe no one could fill—I wanted to find you lacking. As much as I hate it, I have to step back and let you work without my pressure. But you can't make mistakes anymore if you want to keep this job."

Then he said it.

"Well, if you hadn't made the mistake of going into that bank without backup, David Neal, Jr., would still be alive, wouldn't he?"

The Phoenix detonated. She knocked Heath and D out of the way to tackle Ghent. He didn't get to squirm beneath her before a fist slammed into his jaw—cracking under her fist—and another punch dented his skull. Fists rained down, and yells echoed around her, but the Phoenix had full control. It would see Ghent dead.

Heath's arms trapped hers and yanked her off the immobile, bloody pulp. He had trouble maintaining his hold because of the blood making her slippery and her thrashing. DeMarcus appeared beside the unconscious Ghent, checked him quickly, and called for an ambulance.

The Phoenix roared, needing to finish what it started. She continued to fight against the arms holding her; they loosened from the strain.

"Let me go!"

"Leila, that's enough!" the captain yelled. His hands grabbed her face, but he flinched from her murderous eyes.

"I will kill him!"

"I will not have his blood all over my station!"

"Get out of my way or yours will join his!"

Her head snapped to the side from his slap. Him raising a hand against her stunned her for a moment. The Phoenix glared back, taunting him even further to give it a reason to kill him too.

The captain faced her eye to eye, finger in her face. "That's enough, demon. I will not tolerate fighting here. I will arrest you and fire you myself. Now, where is Lei?"

His threat shocked the Phoenix for a second, giving Leila the chance to blink to the surface. She had gone too far, allowing the Phoenix to take advantage. It raged against her that she took back control. Even though she kept it restrained, it still slipped in through her voice.

"I can't let him get away."

"He's not; he'll only be going to the hospital. But you are suspended until I say otherwise."

After waiting to see how she would react, Heath let her down. As soon as her feet touched the ground, the Phoenix re-woke, seeking to finish Ghent off.

*"No, Lei. Leave before you do go too far."*

David returned the reins to her. She pulled herself away from searching for Ghent, and without a word, the gathered officers quickly gave her a wide berth as she headed for the stairs. It was a struggle not to turn around. David's spirit couldn't reach her from the Phoenix wrapping its wings around her to prevent its anger from leaking out.

*LET ME OUT,* THE PHOENIX had continuously hounded—she headed to the only place she could. She walked in, told Nuan to make sure no one bothered her, and went straight through the pale Shoji doors. Leila ignored Hyun teaching his Taekwondo class, hoping she could slip in, release the Phoenix enough to where she had control, and escape without dealing with his philosophical questionings.

She didn't bother to stretch and warm-up or even wrap protective tape around her hands; she just released all control and let the Phoenix have at it. Immediately, the punching bag transformed into Ghent. Forgetting all her techniques, Leila let out the hot anger as she struck it in sloppy haymakers and kicks. Being precise and calming herself through the stances didn't matter, getting back control did, and exhausting herself was the only way to do so—and the safest.

"You know better than fighting outside of your forms." She tensed at Hyun's voice, even though dripping in concern. He had shown up too soon; the Phoenix was still very much present. "They reflect composure and help you maintain it."

She didn't respond. Leila couldn't afford to pull the Phoenix's focus off the attacks.

"What happened?"

"Nothing," she answered.

"Doesn't look like nothing."

"Later. Please, it's not safe for you right now."

"I can handle the Phoen— Is that blood?" True horror shook his voice. "Is that yours? Are you hurt?"

"Ghent's."

"How did—" She could feel him approaching… dangerously close.

"I tried to kill him."

"Alright, talk to me; what happened? What did he do?"

"Not yet."

He released a frustrated breath. "Let me help."

"I don't need any help."

"Lei—"

The Phoenix turned on him. "Leave me alone!" The fist aimed for the punching bag smashed into his jaw instead. Not prepared for an attack, the hit felled him. Nuan yelled his name as she ran into the practice arena; she dropped down and helped him sit up, checking out the hit.

Realization hit her: she had struck Hyun. The Phoenix dropped back in shame, leaving Leila exposed and speechless at what she had done.

"Hyun—"

"Get out." His words came through clenched teeth as he nursed his injured jaw. "The Phoenix isn't welcome here anymore."

Nuan looked up from her fiancé with tears of disbelief in her eyes. Hyun refused to look at her.

She didn't know what to do. If Leila apologized, he wouldn't take her words as truthful, and she wanted to touch him, to comfort him in some way, but he'd probably flinch at her touch. Nor did she want to just obey his order—it would look like she was running away in shame.

"I said, get out." He didn't raise his voice—kept it even—but a firm edge showcased his anger.

He needed space, and so did she. She couldn't even voice an apology as she stepped around them and left.

THE DOOR SLAMMED BEHIND HER, probably shaking some pictures on the walls of her neighbors' apartments.

"What is your problem! Why did you do that! I don't care about Ghent, he needed a beating, but Hyun…"

*They were thinking you're weak. I showed them that you aren't. No one will doubt you now.*

"That wasn't the way to do that."

*No? Remaining silent and doing nothing was?*

"I was piecing myself back together; everyone could see I was trying on my own. Now you've ruined that! I have to start all over again, building back everyone's faith in me—"

*You were playing the role of a damsel in distress, waiting for her hero. There is no hero. I'm the only one who can save you.*

She shook her head in defiance.

*I speak the truth; you know it in your heart. I'm only trying to protect you.*

She scoffed. "Protect me? From making a fool of myself? You did that."

*From being hurt again. Having your hopes built, only to be torn down.*

Her reflection in a hallway mirror stopped her rampage toward her bedroom. Not a single hint of gentleness, understanding, or compassion. The old Leila was gone—only the harsh Phoenix could be seen. Was that all others saw in her now?

*You're still holding back. You've yet to give in fully to me. Once you do, you won't be hurt again. You won't feel guilty; you won't feel again. Isn't that what you want?*

"Can't you see what you're doing? You're hurting everyone around me; you're the problem."

*I brought you back to life. I give you the drive to keep living. This charade of going back to routine is driving a wedge between us, and you're losing focus on Foster. If you'll just—*

She cut it off. "Shut up! Just, shut up! I'm tired of hearing about Foster! My life does not revolve around him!"

*Once you realize that it does—*

Leila shut up her reflection by driving a fist into the mirror. Pain shot through her hand as glass exploded, shattering into even more pieces as they struck the ground along with drops of blood.

*"Lei, calm—"* David began.

She pressed her hands against her ears. "NO! Leave me alone!"

*"Please listen to me."*

"No more. It wasn't that you couldn't let me go—you kept that connection so I would grow tired of hearing you, but not being able to touch you! You're part of my torment!"

*"Lei, that's not—"*

"No, that's enough, David! I can't take this anymore! Go! I don't need you!"

With hands cradling her head, not caring about the blood soaking into her hair, Leila slid to the floor and sobbed. Too much had happened, and even more went on in her head, making things worse. Neighbors knocked on her door, calling out to see if she was alright, but she ignored them, too busy hating her-self for destroying her last normal tie with Hyun.

# XI.

She sat against David's headstone. Leila didn't come to talk with the grave keeper—she hoped he wouldn't appear as usual like a sudden apparition—or with David, she came for the quiet. Woodlawn Cemetery was the only place where the Phoenix remained mostly silent.

The painful throbbing brought her gaze down to her bandaged hands—beating Ghent broke some skin but hitting the punching bag at Hyun's without protective tape split the cracks wider. Shattering the mirror had sliced glass shards through her hand. But hitting Hyun trumped all her pains; it felt like she had assaulted a brother—her heart held more bruises than he did. Her hands would heal easier than him forgiving her… if the Phoenix ever allowed her to apologize.

His kicking her out voiced his frustration—tired of giving all he could and making no progress. She was tired too. Striking out at him could've been intuition kicking in; she had pushed the Phoenix into a corner, and it lashed out to save itself. Perhaps she couldn't push anymore.

She banged her head against the headstone. No, she couldn't give in. Leila needed balance, and that wouldn't happen by driving each side to the edge. The constant tug of war was wearing her out, and if not careful, she would surrender to the wrong side.

Preventing that required her to admit that she couldn't save herself. She couldn't do it alone. Someone had to save her. She had to show weakness.

Leila shook under the sudden chill—not only did the Phoenix dislike the idea, but she herself feared to do such a thing. She had to be the strong one that others relied on. She always had been.

She glanced at David's grave, expecting a remark at least by now, but she had told him to go, and it seemed he had done so. Maybe he understood that she needed more space, or he hid in shame from her telling the truth…

She shook her head at the Phoenix's thought. It wouldn't make her turn against David; his voice provided the only security she could latch onto. She had lost herself in her anger, and it had lashed out at him from things getting too pressured. There were too many voices, and she needed her own for once.

"A lot of good it did me," she said to the cemetery.

*"This… episode will prove useful,"* David said. *"You know what to listen to now, but it will still be a challenge to pick it out of the cacophony of voices telling you what they think you should do."*

"I thought I had scared you off."

*"Never. I know when to back off. And I will never be gone. Not until you are ready."*

She thought about his words. "You're saying that I *needed* to hit Hyun?"

*"For you. You needed to be shown what could happen if you lost control."*

"Ghent wasn't enough?"

*"No; you have no attachment to him. Attacking him gave the Phoenix more fuel; attacking Hyun doused that fuel before it could get too dangerous."*

She watched a funeral procession of cars meander through the cemetery to the gravesite deeper within. With all the cars, the deceased was much loved. Leila wondered if the surviving loved ones knew what grief and torture awaited them. Could she be the only one to experience something like this? Was she that alone, even in her heartache?

*"No, you are not alone."*

"He has gone through the same?"

*"Your emotions and your actions, yes—through an experience similar to yours but not the same."*

She watched the final car disappear beyond her view. "Will he be open to me?"

*"As much as you will be to him."*

Leila smiled at his answer, taking that as a no. "How common we will be."

*"More than you can imagine. He is just as hard-headed, but he will succumb to his heart sooner."*

"I will hold out longer than him? Sounds like he isn't much of a fighter."

David chuckled. *"Wrong. Fighting isn't his second nature; it's his first. He would rather hit you than spend time talking. He just knows what voice to listen for."*

"We are alike."

*"Far more than we were."*

Another reminder that they weren't soulmates; they weren't meant to be together. But they were for a while. What if…

*"Stop. That kind of thinking only causes more heartache. We weren't meant to be together; that's how it is."*

"You're right; I don't need anything else. I have to face the facts: you are gone, you aren't coming back, and I am someone else." She looked down at her hands again. "I just can't believe this is who I am. This rage can't be me. I'm becoming my own destruction. Can't I be in some denial?"

*"He will expose who you are by showing himself and letting you in. Something—he will admit—he doesn't do either. He is the salvation you're looking for."*

"But he's out there, and I don't think I can leave again; I'm too comfortable."

*"You know you have to leave, for yourself and others. Your future isn't here, that isn't going to change. New York holds your past. You've let my memory chain you down. But your life here is dead. Out there is where you can live again. How can you keep your promise to me if you force yourself to stay?"*

Leila let out a shaking breath. She loathed facing the truth after trying to deny it. "I can't."

*"Then go live."*

"But how can I when—"

David interrupted. *"Your future doesn't change. The journey may, but not the outcome. If you're meant for something, it will happen."*

LEILA LAY BESIDE DAVID'S GRAVE, close to drifting off, but not because of the stillness or the warmth of the August day, more that it was reminiscent of Central Park—lying underneath their tree with David stretched out beside her, hearing his slowing breathing as he drifted to sleep and watching the explosion of colors in the sky.

Her life had exploded but not as beautifully. Her sky bled with too much red, and there was not enough blending to make it a masterpiece. She couldn't take out one color to put more of another in—it wouldn't be her painting. Using those same colors, and a blank canvas, she would repaint.

She shifted—what was she saying? She couldn't start completely new; she couldn't throw the ugly one away and begin anew. The paint had dried and couldn't be peeled off. Using the old strokes and brushes, she would paint over what was already there.

Too poetic. And she wasn't an artist.

Maybe he was.

He would know how to fix her painting from repainting his. She had the colors, and he could show her how to change the brush strokes…

A presence interrupted her musings. She ignored it, figuring another mourner had come to visit a grave and looked at the woman asleep at a grave, or if the grave keeper, he would leave her alone.

But it lingered. The grave keeper didn't hold that aura, and a mourner wouldn't be so rude with a strong spirit demanding her attention. The longer it stayed, the more she felt its warmth, comfort, and how her heart pounded with life. Longing to know why this presence felt so different, she opened her eyes in expectation.

Nothing. She sat up, expecting to find someone watching her from afar. Nobody was around her. Leila was alone.

She knew what she had felt, and she could still feel it—her heart wanting to burst out of her chest, her spine tingling in anticipation, and goosebumps shivering with nerves. But none of it from dread. These emotions belonged to meeting someone for the first time and clicking… Finding your soulmate.

Nerves and fear shot her to her feet. Now was not the time to meet him; she wasn't ready. Where was her car? She parked it right at the curb, in sight of the grave, but her black Nissan wasn't there. Leila patted her pant legs for keys but didn't feel them. Something wasn't right. Body trembling, she began to leave David's grave to search for her car or run home if she had to.

A space to her left shimmered in gold and white flakes. She stopped, recognizing the light from that enveloping David in The Between. It wasn't the same, though—not as blinding or as other-worldly. The faint shimmering solidified into a portal of gold, tall and wide enough for her to step into.

Her heart seemed to stop—everything she felt came out of this portal.

And it called to her.

Like a marionette on strings, Leila moved toward the portal, hypnotized by the gentle and beautiful light. She stopped at arm's length, uncertain on what to do next. Her feet wanted to run, but her heart ached to know more.

Hesitantly, she lifted a hand, and it drifted through. She expected some kind of change, but nothing was there. Nothing solid. It was as if she reached into a bubble of air warmed by the sun.

Disappointed, she pulled her hand back and wondered why it would appear if it didn't have something to show her. Then the light churned like a shifting cloud…or like smoke being disturbed. She stepped back. A creature as dark as the Changeling couldn't emerge out of something so light and airy. Could it?

No form stepped out. The light slowed from its disruption, and where it grew still, eyes appeared—brown eyes of a man. Leila cringed, shielding herself under his powerful scrutiny; she had never felt so exposed. But something resided within, covered up by the immediate intimidation that drew her closer.

As she looked, a cornucopia of emotions took her breath and left her with tears. Soul-wrenching sorrow, pangs of heartache with every beat, a will as firm as stone, unshakable courage and bravery, cunningness, sheltered kindness, and sensitivity. A longing for love. To possess so many emotions at one time, let alone have them hidden away… She hurt for this unknown man.

Her hand lifted to search for the face the eyes belonged to; she understood what he felt. She wasn't alone.

Without warning, the eyes disappeared.

"Wait, don't go!"

They didn't return. The light grew disturbed again, and she waited for the eyes, hopefully giving her another chance to locate the face—to know he was real. But it solidified farther down near Leila's waist. Just as her eyes dropped, a hand reached out.

She jumped back in shock. It didn't grope blindly for her; the hand remained submissive, like offering his hand and waiting for her to accept. Since it stayed still, Leila approached to look.

The large hand was pale but definitely not soft—the man worked for those callouses. Slightly paler than his skin were multiple puckered lines, scars long smoothed over many years. A man with a hard past—probably the origination for those emotions. She wondered if those hands softened when touching her skin…

His hand waited.

Once again like being pulled by a string, Leila's hand reached for his… but David. She yanked it back and looked behind her. His grave remained there: cold, alone, and dark. How could she be so selfish, taking his warmth and light?

She looked from his silent grave to the warm light where the hand waited for her to choose. Leila was torn between the hope of the physical, spiritual, and emotional love she felt in the eyes and the memory of love David provided. He wanted her to move on, but how could she when she still had a tie to him? She looked to the portal. Could this man help loosen it?

Leila released a long breath to steady herself and placed her hand in his—

The buzzing of her phone on her nightstand jolted her awake.

*A dream.*

Leila didn't know whether she was crestfallen or relieved as she stretched, threw off her sheets, and reached for her phone. Remembering her suspension, it wasn't a call from work.

The Phoenix's anger at Ghent and at the captain's punishment rushed into her. It deflated once she reflected it back for hitting Hyun and unleashing on David. The Phoenix withdrew, unhappy that she continued to fight back.

Now fully awake, she grabbed her phone and unlocked it to see an appointment reminder: August 8th, the Gordons leave for Jamaica.

Releasing a heavy sigh, she got out of bed. They invited her only because the girls did. Leila plopped back down. The girls would be disappointed, but their parents would probably be relieved that she wouldn't be there to cause a scene. Or would they be just as disappointed that with her no-show, she wasn't trying as hard to fight against the Phoenix—like she had led them to believe?

She massaged her temple; she had just woken up but needed aspirin. The shower would help first.

She would go if only to send them off before she could get around to hurting them like everyone else.

# XII.

"Miss Lei!" The youngest black girl clambered down from her perch atop her father's shoulders at the sight of her emerging out of the crowds in J.F.K. International Airport. She ran full blast at her.

Leila knelt so she could throw her arms around her neck.

"I'm so glad you came!"

"I told you I would try," she said.

"Work isn't busy?"

"Not right now." *It might not be for a while.*

She stood with Eve in her arms, gushing nonstop about her excitement, and hugged Zaira who appeared silently, unlike her sister.

"You don't seem as excited."

"I am, but I'm not."

"Nerves?"

Zaira nodded but kept her eyes on the ground. More than just nerves were plaguing her.

"It'll be fun; visiting your grandparents; living on a beach…"

"It'll be a really fun vacation!" Eve piped up. "The best ever because I've never been to the beach!"

"Yes, it will," Jamaal encouraged when he approached and hugged his oldest daughter. "There's nothing to worry about. Grandma and Grandpa aren't *that* scary."

He tickled Zaira to pull out some giggles and lift her mood. When he asked the girls if he could speak with Leila alone, she set Eve down, and they hurried back to Jade sitting in the terminal lobby. She waved in greeting, but her eyes betrayed the mother's unsureness about her presence.

"Zaira's realized what it means when we packed up the apartment," Jamaal whispered when they were alone.

"So, you have decided to move back?"

"Yeah. Jade and I want to go home; New York isn't the place for us."

"I hope it works out for you."

Becoming serious, Jamaal dropped his voice even lower. "Any news?"

London's dead body flashed in her mind, bringing along her suspicions on his death. Learning the truth would ruin his excitement about going home. "Sorry, still nothing."

He looked at her as if he suspected she lied. She avoided looking away—proclaiming guilt. Giving up, he took her answer with a nod and opened his mouth to speak when his eyes dropped down. "Lei, what happened?"

Her bruised and bandaged hands. "Hit a few rough spots this week." *Literally.*

"I didn't read anything in the papers…"

She gave a dry laugh. The captain must've prevented the media from getting word of her beating of Ghent. "Well, that's good news for once." The furrowing of his brow wanted more of an explanation. "Fighting the Phoenix has turned physical now."

Concern seeped into his eyes; Leila looked away before it turned into pity—and before the Phoenix accused him of considering her weak.

He rubbed her shoulder in comfort. "Is there anything I can do?"

Telling the truth was necessary now. "You leaving may be the best thing." She looked at him. "Prevents me from hurting anyone else."

Jamaal's hand fell from its comforting gesture in shock and more worry. Her pointed look told him all he needed to know.

Leila turned away again. "I've been woken up; I had to be shown the damage I've caused, and how I'm losing everyone. So, it's safer if everyone stays back until I can find some distance myself. In a way of words, David said that things will work out, but I don't know where I will be going. Maybe it's better that I don't."

Her confession—and what it implied—stunned him. Jamaal still looked in search of words when seating for first-class was announced. Eve bounced to her feet and fussed at her father to hurry or they would lose their seats.

Pain wracked his face. "Lei—"

She hugged him to stop his disagreement. "No, go. This is what you and your family need." Leila pulled back. "And me too, if you'll give me that."

"You know I would give you anything."

"Before, I don't think you would've. Until now, we haven't really spoken."

His face fell in shame.

"It was my fault too." She urged him to go. "Eve's about to panic if you don't claim your seats."

Jamaal opened his mouth, but Leila denied him the chance to speak. "We can't delay it any longer: it's time we go our separate ways."

He let out a heavy breath and nodded. "I know."

She lifted his face. "You know I see things through to the end, so I *will* find myself again."

Jamaal smiled. "Then we'll come back to welcome you home."

"Daddy…" the girls whined.

"Jamaal," Jade joined in with a frustrated undertone.

He hugged her tightly and kissed her on the cheek. Jamaal held her gaze for a long time before turning and joining his family heading for the reception desk to scan their tickets.

Once approved, the Gordons waved to her in farewell before disappearing through the terminal gate. Leila moved to the windows overlooking their plane's dock and the runway to keep some connection to the family a little while longer.

After loading all the passengers, the bridge retracted, and the plane backed out to taxi down the runway strip. Following two other planes, theirs finally appeared already gaining lift-off. She had sight of the Air Jamaica tailfin—painted black, green, and gold for the country's flag—for two seconds before they were gone.

Their leaving hurt just as much as hitting Hyun and having him disown her. Everyone she knew and cared about ended up leaving. All because the Phoenix drove them away.

Leila turned from the windows. She only had herself… for now.

# XIII.

A few days suspension turned into a full week before the captain contacted her, but only to inform her of a required evaluation with Dr. Moretti.

The gentle blue walls in the psychologist's lobby were meant to stimulate calming—instead, they seemed too bright and unsettling. The Phoenix fumed inside her, disgruntled at this mandatory assessment.

*Why are we punished for reminding Ghent of his place? This is unfair.*

*To be fair, the captain should've fired me. So please, hold your tongue, so I can portray stability.*

If the Phoenix would've been a person sitting across from her it would've crossed its arms, grumbling.

*Please, just this one time,* she begged.

The unadorned wooden door opened, and Leila stiffened, preparing for the shrink's penetrating words, and hardening herself against unveiling emotions. The Phoenix approved the defense.

"Leila, good to see you. Come on in." Dr. Moretti waved her in as he held the door for her.

She entered his office—expectantly arranged, simple, and promoting an organized mindset. The Phoenix scoffed at the absurdity of the place. Leila took the seat where Dr. Moretti gestured, not in front of the desk but where two rigid chairs faced each other.

Her shield rose even higher at the open space between the chairs. Nothing separated them, which encouraged the exchange of feelings without a buffer. It gave him the advantage of noting body language and seeing the emotions patients wanted to hide. The setup either coaxed a patient into feeling relaxed enough to speak their mind or inflicted unease at being exposed.

To show indifference, she crossed her arms and legs, one foot dangling in the air.

*He wants an emotion? We won't hide our anger,* the Phoenix said.

*Please be quiet,* Leila said.

Dr. Wes Moretti took his seat across from her and picked up a notepad and pen. He looked the exact way as she first saw him: graying hair, black-rimmed square glasses, button-up shirt, tie, jacket, khakis, and an easy, take-your-time aura.

He began. "You look ready to start."

"So we can get this over with."

"Still not comfortable talking about your feelings?"

"I won't ever be."

"One day, you will; I'm just not the right listener."

A long pause settled between them as he looked her over. "I guess I'll get straight to it then." He tapped a file on the side table beside him. "I know of your attack on Detective Spencer Ghent last week. I warned you that if your stored-up emotions were not properly confronted, they would become a danger to others. That is what happened here."

The Phoenix wasn't going to give him the chance to lecture and belittle her. Leila couldn't stop her tongue. "No, I'll tell you what happened. Ghent stepped out of line, twice. He caused a man to die, and he endangered others while getting a fellow officer shot. I was the only one willing to hurt the rookie's feelings by setting him in his place. My emotions had nothing to do with it—I was angry, and he knew it. People get angry every day, and they're not forced to face themselves."

"But those people don't lose so much of themselves that they nearly kill their partner and threaten to do the same to their captain."

Unconscious of it, the Phoenix smirked. "But he didn't die. I let him live, so he'll always remember it and get his act together."

He shook his head. "You didn't let him live; Detective Heath Fonda had to physically restrain you and pull you off Detective Ghent's unconscious body."

He leaned toward her. "That is not anger; that is rage—long stored up at not being released in your desired direction. I know of your dark side—the Phoenix as it has been named—and of the revenge against Bryan Foster it wants you to exact."

Dr. Moretti tapped the file beside him as the Phoenix flickered in her eyes at being called out. "I have been updated on how you have changed, Leila. And I have given advice on how to prevent an incident like this from happening."

"A lot of help it did."

"I'll be honest, I did not expect the Phoenix to be this extreme—to have this much domination. You went to Panordom believing you could learn to control it, but it controls you."

She huffed. "Why does everyone think I went because of the Phoenix? All my life I've struggled against a dark side because it frightened me." It was her turn to lean up. "I left needing space to determine what to do about David's death. Going there, fighting in the tournament, made me realize my dark side would help me—it wasn't something to repress. You told me to find a drive; something strong and from within to keep me going. The Phoenix is it."

He looked at her in his unnerving way. "Maybe you haven't found the right drive yet. A healthy one would not cause this much turmoil, and you don't see how it has changed you. It has fed you the belief that you need it to retain control. The Phoenix is breaking you down, so you'll give up fighting and give in to what it wants."

She clenched against the Phoenix declaring denial. Hyun and Nuan had voiced the same concern—tried making her face the truth of her downward spiral—and she brushed them off. Leila owed them another apology.

"I have begun to see it," she said quietly.

"Too late though." Dr. Moretti leaned back and laced his fingers together, a small smile pulling at his lips. "But not entirely.

"This is good. I wasn't expecting this improvement. From what I have been told, you weren't showing any signs that you were fighting against the Phoenix." His eyes flickered down to her bandaged hands. "I hate it had to turn physical before you could see it."

Leila forced herself to let out an emotion she had held back for so long. "Thank you for that."

His body reacted to seeing a better emotion. "All you want is an acknowledgment that you are trying. May I ask what has brought on this self-awareness? Besides the obvious reasons."

She debated whether to tell him of her connection with David. Dr. Moretti remained still as she thought, allowing her time, and not pressuring her. The Phoenix couldn't believe she considered telling him—it was too personal to share.

"My promise to David, and David himself."

He nodded in understanding. "In his memory."

"No, not only in his memory but him—his voice."

His eyes skewered her in disbelief. "You're hearing his voice?"

"I'm not imagining him." The Phoenix's anger rose in her voice.

Dr. Moretti raised his hands to slow her anger. "No, it's good that you think you can hear David."

"I think? I *know* I hear David."

"Leila… when some people go through as much grief and blame as you have, their conscience mimics the voice of the one they held dear."

She stared at him. David was the only thing keeping her sane. "I am only hearing my conscience? David's voice is a ghost?" The Phoenix exploded and shot her to her feet. "THAT'S A LIE! HE IS WITH ME, ALWAYS!"

He retracted from her outburst. "I know it's hard to accept, but it's—"

"NO!"

"What are you trying to hide from, Leila? Acknowledging the fact that you've been relying solely on yourself this whole time—not the Phoenix or David—will help you gain control over yourself."

She headed for the door. "I'm done with this."

"Please, Leila, one more thing! What did you hope to accomplish by going to the tournament?"

His question didn't stop her hand on the doorknob—not asking herself that beforehand stopped her. "David told me I needed to break away from him, and leaving would be the start, so I did."

As she thought about it though, she could've gone anywhere; why there?

"For escape, too. I also thought that tournament could be the perfect test for me. My confidence had been shaken—I needed to see if I knew myself inside and out."

Dr. Moretti didn't respond for the longest time, and she didn't turn to see if he would, too stunned at what she had admitted.

"I won't deny or downplay that those events on the island made you realize your strength. Even though the Phoenix can be touchy" —Dr. Moretti paused, probably expecting a lashing from

Leila's dark side— "I think it can be beneficial. You can't have darkness without some light. There's a reason the Phoenix is there, you just haven't found the exact purpose of it yet."

She had begun to think that too. With the level of the past events being at extreme, the Phoenix was using her. Surely her dark side wasn't meant *only* for revenge. What was its full use?

*Tell me,* she begged.

*Until you stop fighting me, you'll never know.*

"I think that's enough for today, Leila. We can only loosen so many emotions in one day. May we meet again? I would like to see your progress."

Leila stood with her hand on the doorknob. She didn't throw open the door, laughing as she left. It surprised her that she stayed, debating—infuriating the Phoenix and probably astonishing Dr. Moretti.

She turned, met his eyes, and without a word, she nodded. True happiness lit the psychiatrist's face.

He hurried over to his desk to mark the next appointment date and time on a card. Retrieving it, she made her way out… looking forward to the next meeting, not that she would admit it.

# XIV.

The next day, the captain called her again, but not just a quick ordering.

"Dr. Moretti told me he's seeing progress in you."

"I don't know whether to call it progress or not," Leila said. "It's more like we're acknowledging each other's claim of me."

"There's no doubt that you're improving."

"How's Ghent?" She squirmed under the Phoenix disliking her for thinking of his well-being.

He sighed. "He was released yesterday with a broken jaw, a few broken teeth, eight stitches above his eyebrow, and a cracked skull. They kept him so long in fear of spinal damage or bleeding on the brain. From how he looks, he'll be out for a while."

Leila cringed—not at the listing of Ghent's injuries, but at the captain's deadpanned displeasure. "Captain… I'm sorry. I know Ghent needs the apology more than you, but that needs to be face-to-face."

"I do appreciate the apology, but it *will* mean more when I see you speak with him again."

"How are Heath and D?"

"As expected, they know it was the Phoenix—not you personally—and are still snapping at each other like puppies."

She chuckled. "Sounds like I didn't disrupt things too badly."

"No, still the same daily grind." He paused for a moment. "Which is why I'm making this call."

She let him take his time, steeling himself for the conversation. "The same old routine isn't enough for you anymore. The consistency is aggravating the Phoenix and making you jumpy, I guess. What you need is something different."

"Sounds like a change of scenery again."

"It would—if you accept the job. Remember me mentioning the friend needing help?"

The one he mentioned before Heath and D came in with Randall Thimes. "I do."

"I've decided he does need help, and I'm the only one to give it. And so, I wish to send you."

The Phoenix appeared. "Trying to get rid of me, I see."

The other end remained silent, taken back from its lashings.

Leila yanked on the leash to pull the Phoenix back. "I'm sorry, Captain. It just… See? I'm still a work in progress."

"I've debated sending you because of that very reason."

She couldn't let the opportunity to leave slip away. "Regardless, I need some distance. David implied things would work out for me to do so, and this is it."

"Are you sure?" He was giving in.

"Absolutely. Where am I going?"

"You won't know until you get the ticket from me at the airport tonight. Just pack warm clothes for a week and leave your badge—it's useless over there."

SHE SKIPPED VISITING DAVID'S GRAVE to meet the captain at J.F.K. International Airport on time. Speaking with him might talk her out of her spontaneous volunteering for a vague job in an unknown destination.

He stood at the curbside with a ticket and passport in hand. As soon as she approached him, they headed to her terminal.

Captain Sullivan turned serious by laying out her job description. "My friend's name is Herman Petrishchev. He may seem rude and paranoid at first meeting, but he has a soft heart—it's his way of guarding himself in his line of work. He is a spy for us, but he also furnishes ships, submarines, and other marine equipment for our War on Terrorism. But now the Chechen—terrorist groups—have caught wind of his involvement and are focused on him."

*With a last name like that, he must be Russian or Ukrainian,* Leila mused. *Maybe I'm going to one of those countries…*

"You'll act as his bodyguard as he goes around cutting all ties leading the Chechen to him. Since this is off record, you won't have any immunity over there. More than likely, you won't be welcomed with open arms for being an American, either so you won't be using your name—in hopes you won't be recognized. He doesn't know the detective I'm sending is Leila Wells. Your alias is Harper Nathaniels."

The Phoenix swelled up with indignation. *How dare he want us to go unnoticed! We deserve better respect!* Leila held back its tongue by eyeing him; he lifted his hands in defense. "It's what I came up with last second. Since you're someone else, there's no mention of the tournament, showing your skills, or external arguments with the Phoenix."

"Captain, I know how to blend in."

He nodded quickly like his nerves were getting to him. "I know you do; this is just different surroundings. This is in a country that doesn't take kindly to foreigners meddling in their affairs."

"You're concerned about me. I—"

He stopped her to interrupt. "You won't have anyone over there to rely on. No one will have your back. You will be alone, Lei."

The realization of what he was conveying hit her—like being thrown into a pit of darkness, she'd have no support on how to get out. Because of her isolation, an idea formed in her head;

she couldn't miss this opportunity. The Phoenix angrily pushed back at her thought, disgusted she would think such a thing.

"Maybe I shouldn't let you go," the captain mumbled, fidgeting with the plane ticket and passport. "What if something happens? What if—"

She grabbed his shoulders to make him look at her. "Captain, I can do this. I *have* to do this. I will be fine."

He considered her words, absorbing her certainty for his own confidence. He released a long breath and nodded. "You will be fine. You're strong."

They began again for their destination. Once they arrived, the captain turned to face her fully.

"I want you to promise me this: If anything goes wrong, get yourself out of there. When it comes down to your safety or his, choose yours. You are more important to me than him."

His statement shocked her. "I still matter to you?"

He kissed her on the cheek. "No matter what you do, you can never fall out of my love."

The receptionist announced first-class as they were speaking, so Leila missed the destination. "Captain, I still don't know where I'm going."

He jolted into action by handing her the fake passport and ticket—St. Petersburg, Russia.

Captain Sullivan cupped her face. "Find you over there and bring her back."

"Are you sure I still can? I haven't gone too far?"

"Not to me, you haven't. There are always second chances. I can't prove it to you—that's someone else's job. Mine is to order you around."

# XV.

Her mood matched how Russia greeted her: gloomy, gray, and threatening to rain. For the entire nine-hour flight, the Phoenix tore down her hopes of this change from her drab routine and chance of escape by slamming the captain's actions.

*He's trying to get rid of us.*

*Of course, he is, so he can get back on his feet from you blowing him over. He's trying to get a breather before the next wave of you hits.*

That angered it. *We are one. He is punishing us for being ourselves. He prefers the softer form of us, the one from before. One he can control. We intimidate him; we are seizing his control, and he doesn't like it.*

*No.* Her denial wasn't as strong as she wanted it—the Phoenix's words had seeped into her.

*He's sick of us.*

*I'm sick of you.*

She let the first-class passengers disembark to breathe out the Phoenix—the best she could—and assume the fake persona of Harper Nathaniels. To help disguise herself, Leila wore her long black hair down. She prayed the captain's precautionary measure would hold as she mingled with the Economy Class and followed them to Baggage Claim.

After grabbing her bags, she walked close to other passengers to not be targeted as alone. To her relief, she recognized some of the Russian words, without referring to the translated English beside them—the two years of taking Russian in college were finally coming in handy.

The Phoenix puffed up. *Why are you doing this? Acting meek and afraid; we are stronger than anyone here, and they should know; give us respect.*

*This is part of remaining undercover; I must act unknown like a nobody.*

*We are somebody.*

Arriving in the geometrically designed and generously spaced lobby swarming with tourists, locals, and embarking and disembarking passengers took her attention away from defending herself to the Phoenix. She focused now on locating Petrishchev and avoiding attention as an American, a lost tourist, or as Leila Wells.

Relying solely on the captain's description of his friend—short and stocky, more on the rounded side, with a pudgy face, small eyes, and a balding head—she scanned the airport pickups and the people seated, waiting on someone to arrive, but she didn't find him. However, one of the airport pickups held a card with her fake name on it.

"Detective Nathaniels?" the man asked when she approached.

*No, it's Leila Wells; yes, that one—the famous one,* the Phoenix boasted.

"Yes," she said instead.

"*Добро пожаловать в Россию.* Welcome to Russia. Mr. Petrishchev is waiting for you."

He retrieved her suitcase and duffel bag, then nodded for her to follow him. He led her to an already running black car, gestured for her to sit in the passenger seat, then proceeded to place her luggage in the trunk.

When she opened the door, the sight of a man in the driver's seat—much pudgier than how the captain described him—stopped her in surprise. He turned to her in boredom. She was relieved to see a stubborn strength underneath his age of wrinkles. Maybe the Herman Petrishchev the captain spoke of still existed.

"If you are so nervous to jump at a sitting man, perhaps I should find another detective," he griped with a level voice.

"Forgive me for having my nerves exposed from a nine-hour flight through seven time zones to enter a country possibly hostile to my nationality, only to be greeted by such polite manners."

Leila couldn't help but slam the door when she got in. There went making it through the week without a Phoenix episode. She probably just blew her cover.

Instead, Petrishchev chuckled. "You have fire in you; that's good. We probably wouldn't survive the week if you didn't. Colin said he was sending his best."

The airport pickup knocked on the top of the car in a sign to go. Petrishchev pulled out from under the awning and followed the traffic winding away.

"With the ruse of the pickup so you wouldn't be seen, you're that worried about your life?" she asked.

He nodded. *"Сейчас обо мне много говорят. Будет безопаснее, если я останусь в тени."*

"Didn't catch that part."

"People talk much about me now. It is safer if I remain in the shadows." He looked at her. "You know Russian, Detective Nathaniels?"

"A little. I can read it better."

"I will try to remember."

They grew silent for a few feet. "I've guessed some of it, but how have the Chechen threatened you?"

"They threaten my life and my wife's, but so far it has only been in letters—nothing physical."

"What crimes are they known for?"

"Any kind of terrorism: shootings, political sabotages, bombs…"

"That narrows it down."

He chuckled. "If I knew what to look for, I wouldn't need protection." He looked at her. "I hope I don't get you hurt putting your neck out for me."

"Don't worry about me; just focus on getting your life back." *Because we take priority like the captain said. You're not someone we would die for.*

She turned away so he wouldn't see her disgust at the Phoenix's comment. *He's an innocent and an ally. I am still a cop here; I am here to serve by protecting the public.*

*This isn't America. Russia is out of your jurisdiction. He is not a member of the American public you swore to protect.*

*He needs help, and that's why I'm here.*

*I'm not the only one to think it; you did too.*

"Detective Nathaniels? Is it something I said?"

To avoid answering, she changed the conversation. "How do you think the Chechen discovered your involvement in our war?"

From his hesitation, Petrishchev wanted to know what had happened. "I don't know; we are very careful in our business not to be caught. Our own government would have us executed, so we know how to deal under the table. We don't make mistakes."

"What about a mole?"

"I have considered it, but no one else has received threats; only me."

At their silent agreement of a hiatus, Leila looked out to see Russia. She had never heard of Russia being a popular destination for its beauty, and her eyes bounced from construction site to construction site—at least a good sign they were trying to improve. Every now and then a cleaner, more modern hotel towered over everything else, or the startling bright blue of an Orthodox church dome rose above the utilitarian apartment buildings, but once they vanished, she was left with dull pastels. Nothing of interest.

Better that way though. This wasn't a site-seeing vacation. She didn't need anything distracting her from keeping Petrishchev safe. Nor did she need something to keep Russia in her memory, keeping her heart and mind intrigued. She had to return to New York unscathed by this foreign country.

After thirty more minutes of forced small talk, they finally pulled into a living subdivision—nicer than what she had previously seen. Instead of old tenement buildings, all were two-story identical houses in a cul-de-sac environment. A great and surprising improvement over the crammed-with-the-whole-family living conditions Leila had dreaded.

Petrishchev smiled over at her. "Home sweet home." He got out to retrieve her luggage.

"Maybe." Houses like these seldom held occupants of such pristine, orderly, and normal lives the outsides portrayed.

"*ЕВГЕНИЯ!* WE'RE HOME!" HE ANNOUNCED as he and Leila came through the front door.

A platinum-blonde woman hurried down the stairs, surprising Leila with her ability to descend the stairs in a short-hemmed dress—restricting movement—or tripping in her stilettos.

"Welcome to our home!" She came forward to hug and kiss her on both cheeks. Gold bangles shook as she released her. "Oh, I am so pleased you are finally here!"

At first, Leila couldn't respond. Petrishchev was a short, middle-aged man—not handsome but neither revolting—and his wife was young, possibly mid-twenties, and overly dressed for a first impression. An ideal trophy wife… or gold digger.

"I am too," Petrishchev added, giving her more time to get it together. "*Детектив* Nathaniels, my wife, Evgeniya."

Something flickered across her face: a slight but unsure recognition. "What do you prefer to be called?"

"Harper." She hoped she put enough declaration in her voice.

A bleached-white smile answered her—revealing that Evgeniya didn't buy it. Recognition still lingered in her eyes. "Come, let me show you to your room."

*I don't like this one,* the Phoenix grumbled. *Something's not right.*

*I know. I don't like her, either.*

Leila would keep an eye on Evgeniya. She followed the woman sashaying up the stairs with Petrishchev behind, hauling her luggage.

From what little of the house she saw, they enjoyed luxury with contemporary design in mind: neutral tones, thick curtains, plush couches, exotic memorabilia, vivid paintings—all on display as a sign of their wealth. Everything looked new and spotless; the house even had the distinctive new smell like they slept here but didn't live here.

Her room was no different. It was likely meant as a guest room but furnished and sized like a master bedroom. Colors of gray with a few strategically placed bright colors defined sophistication and class. The massive bed took up a third of the space, and a reading nook sat in the windowsill. She was positive the bathroom had just as much grandeur. The couple had money, and Evgeniya knew how to flaunt it.

"I hope this will be to your liking for your stay," Evgeniya said as her husband walked in and placed Leila's luggage on one of the lounging couches.

"I'm sure it will be fine."

"Well, get some rest. I'll wake you when supper is ready."

Petrishchev placed a hand on her shoulder. "I'm really glad you're here." The husband and wife left, closing the door behind them.

Alone, the frivolous and sizeable room unsettled Leila. Going into the bathroom to freshen up from her flight, she found it as she expected.

Returning, she unzipped her suitcase for the Morning Glory preserved in a Ziploc bag. Leila rarely took it out anymore since it had withered so much that the blue petals were turning brown. After pulling out her phone, she went to the bed and sat. She sent the captain a text saying she had arrived safely, then put it on the nightstand.

Considering the flower for a bit longer, she took it out of its protective casing, put the bag under her phone, and laid back into the bed.

*At least they know to buy comfortable furniture that's not just for show.*

With the faint floral aroma near her nose, she sunk into the pillows and let jet lag take her.

THE RAPID KNOCKS ON HER door came too quickly.

"Harper, food is ready," Evgeniya said—her fake name sounded forced.

Leila forced her unresponsive body up; jet lag had taken more out of her than she realized. She checked her phone and listened to the responding message from the captain wishing her to stay safe. She slipped it into her pocket again, placed the Morning Glory on top of the Ziploc bag, then went to the bathroom to wipe away any sign of sleep.

As she thought of Evgeniya looking like she was trying to place her, it wouldn't be a surprise if she came snooping into Leila's room for evidence of who she was. She didn't like the idea of Evgeniya poking around in her things.

Done in the bathroom, she wrapped the Morning Glory back into its bag. The Russian would probably check her suitcase first. Spotting the entertainment center, she hid it behind various foreign movies in a compartment under the flat-screen TV. Satisfied with the hiding place, Leila headed for the dining room.

She found Petrishchev seated at the table, with his wife almost finished setting it for dinner. Like the rest of the house, the dining room was furnished extravagantly. A different shade of the neutral colors throughout the rest of the house decorated the room: the long black table housed contemporary cushioned chairs of white, a crystal chandelier hung over the center, and a short bouquet of red flowers became the centerpiece. Petrishchev sat at one end, Evgeniya prepared hers at the opposite end, and set Leila in between.

"Better?" Petrishchev asked.

"A little; I won't snap so easily now."

The housewife had prepared a large meal she called *zakuski.* Plates of cold cuts, cured fish, bowls of salads and various pickled vegetables, open sandwiches, hard cheeses, and caviar filled the table. When Leila took her seat, the platters were passed among them so they could help themselves. Leila hoped the Russian cuisine wasn't too spicy.

Silence overcame the dining room as they ate; Leila was tense, feeling Evgeniya's eyes on her every now and then, and holding the Phoenix back from snapping at her. Petrishchev seemed preoccupied with the uncertainty of the days before him and what he planned to do. When the dessert plate was passed around with some sort of pastry—the small squares smelled fruity—Leila felt it her fault for not being cordial.

"Mind telling me the plan you keep running over in your head, Petrishchev?"

He looked up at her after placing his pastry on the small dessert plate. "Just like Americans, wanting to get the job done fast."

"What's the rush? Ready to get home already?" his wife added as she grabbed the empty plates and disappeared into the kitchen.

*You have no idea.* "I just want to make sure you're safe."

The Russian smiled. "Pleases me you say so. Tomorrow we go to Summer Garden to meet Leonid Demidovich, then we meet Kazimir Fedoseev at *Glyanets.* Wednesday, we meet Igor Gromov at JSC Seaport. Thursday, we go to Ruslan Mihailov at Kochech Incorporation, and then you can go home."

"Sounds easy enough."

"*Да. Да.* As long as no Chechen are around."

"If they're like the terrorists I've dealt with before, I'll spot them in time."

Evgeniya returned from the kitchen. "*Муж,* if everything goes well, maybe you can show her *Зимний дворец.*"

Leila's interest piqued. "The Winter Palace?"

Petrishchev looked off. "Maybe free after meeting Gromov…"

"Then it is decided," his wife began. "You will take Harper after Gromov as our appreciation. Something you can remember *Матушка Россия* with." *Mother Russia.*

*I don't want to remember this place,* the Phoenix grumbled. Leila nodded to keep it from voicing its disagreement.

Petrishchev shrugged. "Why not, but we survive the week first."

"You two will be fine; I have faith in Harper." Evgeniya honeyed her confidence too much. Leila looked at her to find the machine in her head still working to spit out her identity.

And when she did—Leila was positive she would expose her alias—it would mean trouble. Those eyes held some dark knowledge.

# XVI.

Leila peeked through a blind at the Russian morning. When she had first woken, it was too dark, but now after getting ready, the rising sun painted the sky with the warming colors of a new day.

The sky shone with promise and invitation, much better than when she arrived. She hoped the promise of the good day it portrayed would transfer into her job for this week: Petrishchev would be successful in starting a new life, her cover wouldn't be blown, and the Chechen wouldn't kill them both. All revolved around one of those possibilities.

Out of precaution, Leila hid the Morning Glory back in the entertainment center. Assuming the Russian couple had woken up, she headed for the door. Upon opening it, her hand flew to the gun at her waist, hidden underneath the jacket—Evgeniya jolted like she had been caught with her ear against the door.

She gave a quick smile, declaring her innocence. "I didn't mean to startle you; I just..." She cleared her throat. "Would you like breakfast?"

*Sure, you did.* "I would."

Keeping a smile meant to ease her but which instead kept her suspicious, Evgeniya turned and headed down to the kitchen. From all of her interrogations, Leila knew when someone was lying.

The Phoenix pulled her attention to the flower. *If she knows the sounds of her house, she will know what you opened,* it said.

Shutting the door, Leila went to the hidden flower, glanced around for another hiding spot, and decided on sliding it under the bed. Now, she left.

Arriving, Petrishchev was reading a newspaper and sipping coffee, dressed in his pajamas. The Phoenix rose in annoyance, angry that he wasn't ready, and she would have to wait.

*Not everyone rises as early as I do,* Leila began.

*It is a sign of having things together, an eagerness of being punctual, having motivation. Is his life in danger not enough incentive to wake up early?*

"Have a good sleep, Harper?" he asked as she came around to her seat.

She bit back the Phoenix's comment on his laziness as she helped herself to the breakfast in front of her—Petrishchev called the small pancakes, *oladyi,* and the oatmeal, *kasha.* Evgeniya pretended to be reading a novel, but Leila knew she listened and dissected every word. "I did."

"Good; we have a big day ahead of us."

*So you should already be ready.*

"I think it is a good sign that Harper is ready—shows how dedicated she is to her job," Evgeniya added in with too much sweetness again.

Petrishchev chuckled. "Are you hinting, *Евгения*, that I have become slow and fat? Because you wouldn't be wrong." He folded up the newspaper and set it down. "I will be down soon, Harper."

Once he left, Evgeniya stood to take his plate and cup. "*Герман* is a good husband." Knowing she would dig into Leila's life, she braced for the questions. She returned quickly. "Do you have anyone back home, Harper?"

*Keep your answers generic, and she won't get anything,* the Phoenix said. Leila kept her eyes on her plate. "I don't."

"I am sorry. Have you ever? Does your job allow you to?"

"Not for a while now."

"I have friends in the police force who have a hard time finding someone outside of their work. If only there was someone like your partner; they understand what you're going through, and they're always there with you." She paused, probably to look for a reaction. "Don't you agree?"

"It would make relationships easier, but we're not supposed to."

"Why not? They would be perfect. I've heard your partner is supposed to be your second half."

*Careful,* the Phoenix warned.

She took a sip of her coffee to think of an answer. "If cops in the same unit date, they could bring about relationship issues—as with all couples—that could destroy their success as a team."

"The decision to choose between your partner's life or an innocent's is probably included in that," Evgeniya said.

Leila kept her face away to avoid responding.

"Certainly, police captains allow their detectives to date…"

Captain Sullivan did for her and David. Hopefully, Evgeniya would accept her tensing as unwillingness to talk.

The Russian's probing took another route. "The detective's life sounds hard; I wonder why you do it. You must have something else on the side, like a hobby." She meant her statements to be rhetorical, but they were anything but. Leila knew she was still trying to get an affirmative answer that would nail her.

"I suppose many do."

Luckily, Petrishchev came down the stairs, fully awake and groomed, disrupting Evgeniya's interrogation. "Ready, Harper?"

She bounced up. *"Да."*

He kissed his wife farewell before heading for the door. Evgeniya's eyes bored into her back as she followed Petrishchev. Leila knew she revealed nothing personal to the Russian, but hoped she had hidden the Morning Glory well enough so her treasure hunt would come up as a bust.

"REMEMBER, IF I START TO feel uneasy, we leave—hurting feelings or not," Leila reminded as they entered the Summer Garden.

"*Да.*"

She wasn't ogling the gardens, awestruck by the multitude of marble sculptures portraying mythological gods and heroes belonging to ancient tales or the abundance of gushing fountains like the other tourists; she was enjoying the tranquility of the place—how the gurgling water soothed, and the silence of the statues calmed. If she wasn't here to suspect every person in sight as a threat to Petrishchev, she would've enjoyed it even better.

Petrishchev didn't look appreciative of his environment at all. He was pale, his eyes shifted constantly, and his walk was uneven—he would speed up, slow down, and repeat.

"You don't have to do my job for me. Focus on speaking with Demidovich and leave security to me."

He chuckled nervously. "I just don't know what to expect."

"That's why I'm here."

They came onto a circle of flowers seemingly admired by the statues encircling them; a man sat on one of the benches, guarded by four other men nearby. Demidovich knew how to hire men for discretion—they dressed as normal civilians and didn't show their suspicion of everyone. She had no doubt they all carried a piece but knew how to hide it.

Petrishchev breathed out deeply beside her. She shared a pointed look with him for a reminder of their agreement, and then he walked toward the seated man with her drifting close.

Leonid Demidovich looked up at his approach. He matched Petrishchev in that he didn't look to be in the spy business—eyes that could clearly be seen, an open aura, and a fresh, trustworthy face; no shadiness. But physically, they were different: he was slim and young with a crew-cut of blond hair.

Petrishchev mentioned her alias in an explanation of her presence. Demidovich nodded in greeting, which she returned, then he rose, and the two men sauntered off, speaking in their rapid tongue.

Leila shadowed the men, giving them enough space for privacy as they terminated their business. Demidovich's own men did the same, on their boss' side of the path and watching her. They weren't trying to place her—like Evgeniya's leering—but it was their job.

By the time they reached the next flower garden, Petrishchev and Demidovich had finished their business. After finalizing it with a handshake, Demidovich looked to his bodyguards for a sign; once they approached, he nodded to her in farewell, and all continued the way they were headed.

"That didn't take long," Leila commented when she walked up to Petrishchev.

"Fedoseev will take longer. I have been in business with him for many years."

"One down, three to go."

He looked at her. "I hope all my meetings go this smoothly."

"You're not the only one," she replied as they headed back in the opposite direction.

THE SUCCESS OF THE FIRST meeting put Petrishchev in a better mood—he jabbered the whole way to *Glyanets*, which he explained to be a restaurant, and suggested the best food to order. But upon arriving, his mood darkened. When he parked, he turned to Leila.

"Fedoseev is not my favorite negotiator."

"Why?"

He took a moment to think. "Let us say that if there is a mole, he would be it."

"So much for wishful thinking that it would remain smooth."

He sighed. "Sounds so."

She looked to *Glyanets*: a simple restaurant with wired chairs and tables set on the patio for guests to eat outside. Five men were seated, but only one of them bit into a sandwich. Kazimir Fedoseev. The bodyguards looked like they belonged to a mafia—dressed all in black and packing heavy. Their strict guard-dog mode made them easy to identify.

*Great way to remain inconspicuous.*

Now she knew why Petrishchev had sought out the captain for help, and why he sent her—she didn't have the look of a bodyguard. She wouldn't draw attention like the mafia rejects across from her. That meant much more safety for Petrishchev.

Leila didn't have to study Fedoseev long to know she disliked him. Hunching over his food like he expected someone to steal it spoke of his greed and possession and being the only one eating showed narcissism. The obvious bodyguards were him flaunting his power. Small, beady eyes labeled him as untrustworthy. She could see why Petrishchev didn't like him.

"Here we go." Petrishchev let out a steadying breath, and then he opened the car door. She followed simultaneously, and they walked over.

To give his men credit, though, they immediately narrowed in on their approach. Experienced bodyguards but were showy when the job required discretion. She received most of the eyeballing, and dread dropped into Leila's stomach: one of them recognized her, but she couldn't tell which behind those dark sunglasses.

An arm stopped Petrishchev. He looked at her in question, and then with fear rounding his eyes, he understood the gesture. His safety depended on her identity remaining a secret. She urged him back to the car without removing her gaze from the men and not toning down the Phoenix in her eyes.

One of the men shot to his feet, shouting at them to wait in Russian. Leila pushed Petrishchev behind her while pulling out her gun. Aiming it at him raised his hands but brought the others to their feet with their own guns. Fedoseev jumped up as well, but he inched behind his men for safety, while also trying to see who caused the disruption.

"Sorry," he struggled to say. He began speaking in Russian, which she couldn't follow, but he did mention her true name.

"What is he saying?" she asked Petrishchev behind her.

"He didn't mean to alarm you. He can't speak English, but he recognizes you as… Leila Wells… the Phoenix. Winner of the Rulers of the Realms Fighting Tag Tournament."

There went her cover. That same recognition slid into Petrishchev's voice.

With a defeated sigh, she ended the tense standoff by holstering her gun. "*Да*, that is me."

He exclaimed and told his comrades who she was as he grabbed a napkin and rummaged in his pockets as he came toward her. He stopped in front of her holding out the napkin and a pen.

"Before I give you an autograph, I want something from you. From all of you," she added, looking around the first man for the others holding napkins.

Their faces fell in puzzlement, so Petrishchev translated. "No one must know I am here. I can't protect him" —she gestured at the man behind her— "if I am busy signing autographs."

With the translation, they all nodded in agreement.

"They promise, Harp—I mean, Leila."

Hoping they meant it, she took the pen and gestured they move to the tables so she could write. As she signed napkin after napkin, Petrishchev moved over to Fedoseev. She couldn't understand all that Fedoseev said, but including his undertone, he was angry at Petrishchev for the scare.

"This wasn't Petrishchev's fault." She didn't stop the Phoenix from hardening her voice or glaring at him. The coward shrank under her gaze. Petrishchev stepped back too, but he looked at her in a new, impressed light.

Fedoseev motioned for them to sit, but at a distance from her, and where he could keep an eye on her.

Very well since Leila could do the same.

IT DID TAKE MUCH LONGER than the meeting with Demidovich. From their expressions, they fought quite often on what needed to be done, which was probably the case.

Following Petrishchev's advice, she ordered what he had suggested for lunch as she waited: *pirozhki*—fried buns stuffed with meat, mushrooms, rice, and onions. She sat at the next table over from where the bodyguards continued to talk about her fights in the tournament.

Neither Fedoseev nor Petrishchev looked pleased with the final arrangement when they finished. With a quick handshake and a final look at her, Fedoseev practically ran off, making his bodyguards scurry after him, but they gave her smiles, thank-yous, and waves of farewell.

Petrishchev plopped down beside her and waved for the waitress to order a shot of vodka. "I need this after that talk."

"Make that two," she added, thinking about the eventual talk with Evgeniya and wondering how she would react.

SINCE THE LIGHT BULB WENT off in her head as Leila confessed, it meant Evgeniya hadn't found the Morning Glory. Petrishchev asked her to retell her victories in the tournament since they didn't watch it. The couple drank in what she said, but Evgeniya's eyes gradually turned into a dark twinkling—unnerving Leila—which she tried to hide by hitting her husband.

"See? I told you I thought she looked like Leila Wells."

He nodded in apology but turned back to her. "Why did you and Colin hide who you were?"

"What I told the men was true. If I had come by announcing my arrival, you wouldn't be having private meetings. My fame would've drawn too much attention and would've put you in even more danger."

"What about now?"

"Hopefully, the men will keep their word, and I'll maintain my cover. Be careful not to let slip my name, Petrishchev; I must remain Harper Nathaniels."

He nodded. "I will."

"If it gets out that Leila Wells is here, you might as well paint a target on your back, mine, and your wife's." Leila looked over at Evgeniya and found her eyes distant.

"Evgeniya, is everything alright?"

She turned at her name. "Oh, yes. I'm still shocked but excited that you are here. I've never—we've never met a famous person before."

Her attempt at being excited through her chatter held an eagerness. The Phoenix turned her stomach over with unease. It didn't like how Evgeniya looked at her with potential, and neither did she.

"This warning includes you too: no one must know I am here."

"Oh, yes. Yes, I know." She stood. "It'll be hard now to remember calling you Harper. Excuse me while I get dinner ready."

Leila watched her go to the kitchen, fighting against the Phoenix threatening to know what she knew. It expected a different type of challenge on this trip—involving searching for Foster.

*She knows something, something dark for us.*

*I know she does, but I can't show my hand too soon,* Leila pointed out.

*Too soon may be too late; it should be now before her plan hurts us.*

*It will be alright.*

# XVII.

Something was wrong.

Arriving at the fully operational JSC Seaport mollified her at first glance with so many workers—the Chechen wouldn't risk an assassination with too many eyes and mouths. But upon entering one of the numerous shipyard container storage buildings, her unease grew the more she looked.

Metal containers of various sizes stacked high on each other created aisles running throughout the building—wide enough for vehicles to retrieve and store containers. Wooden crates created obstacles for those vehicles. Overhead lights seemed to enlarge the containers looming over her and Petrishchev and revealed gaps in between the bottom containers—wide enough for someone to slip through or hide.

The lights didn't reach everywhere though—those gaps were plunged in shadow. Some of the stacked containers threw others below in darkness. Leila kept glancing at those platforms in the shadows, expecting the glint of an eye.

Voices or loud clangs of machinery should've been echoing from workers. But there was only the sound of their walking until even that silenced when they stopped to wait for Gromov.

Leila couldn't even spot a camera. This was too perfect an opportunity for the Chechen to ignore. Her gaze went to a stack of containers with the highest container leaving the one below it in shadow—she could've sworn she saw darker shadows within.

"Harper?" Petrishchev at least had enough control over his tongue to address her with the fake name.

She continued to watch the darkness, willing the shadows to form into a human being. "Something isn't right."

"Like what?"

"I can't say." Her eyes made their routine search but snapped back to that darkness on the containers. "It's just a feeling."

Petrishchev looked around himself. "I'm almost done with all of my meetings. I would have to reschedule this. Must we go?"

The Phoenix still being occupied with Evgeniya and herself being on edge made it harder to focus and think. "The longer I stay here, the more dangerous it will be for you."

Five Russians appeared at the end of the aisle, all in dark attire—four easily identified as the bodyguards—and Igor Gromov just as how Petrishchev described him: tall, long face framed with a goatee, and firm stance showcasing his seriousness.

He greeted Petrishchev with a question mark, wondering why he hadn't approached. Petrishchev looked at her.

"I'll be close but try to make it quick."

He nodded, and with a breath of courage, he headed toward the man. She trailed after him until he reached Gromov and explained her presence. She slightly picked up Petrishchev asking him whether or not his men felt uneasy.

Worry creased Gromov's face as he looked behind to ask his men. He turned back and answered Petrishchev. Leila knew the answer from his men becoming more paranoid with eyes searching and drifting closer to their obligation.

"They haven't, Harper."

"But now I have more eyes. Still, make it quick."

Leila positioned herself close to the two Russians, but with her back to them, so she could watch behind them as the other men supplied surveillance on the other side.

At least they weren't out in the open without shelter. To the left and right, gaps of darkness broke up the walls of metal containers. Stacked chest-high, the wooden crates dotted the aisle. They could hide if the need arose.

Now closer to the container that had drawn her eye before, it became harder to resist looking up there. Leila felt for the gun at her waist as her mind drifted to dark imaginings of what awaited in the shadows. Whether real or not, she outlined human forms…

A sudden clang echoed from her right, drawing all attention, and aims of guns. She scanned the other side for movement as Petrishchev inched closer to her. The Russian bodyguards discussed what they thought of it.

"Lei—Harper?" he whispered, uneasiness sweating off him.

"I don't see anything." Movement in the corner of her eye drew her attention to the bodyguards.

One gestured at them. "Some will check." He pointed at her. "You stand guard."

Three headed toward the containers across the aisle; specifically, toward the darkness between two containers, what they presumed was the source of the noise. The last bodyguard stepped closer to her, so they formed a wall shielding Gromov and Petrishchev.

She switched from watching their cautious approach to the darkness, on alert for some sign the men might miss so she could warn them. A few feet separated the men from the opening when darker shadows within the darkness moved.

"Wait!"

Out of the darkness, a reflective object soared over the advancing men and toward Leila's group. Gunfire cracked the silence, and all three bodyguards crumbled under the bullets as a metal cylinder landed among them, then exploded into white smoke.

The dense fog enveloped them in seconds. Leila dropped to the ground—the vantage from below provided better vision and precious cover.

"Leila!" a panic-stricken Petrishchev yelled.

"Drop to the ground!" she ordered as she crawled to the left, hoping the eye-stinging smoke would be less dense. "Tell the others!"

He translated it to the others behind her. As she hoped, the smoke let up before her. Looking back to where the three body-guards lay dead, men stepped over them, covered head to foot in black, armed with submachine guns, and wearing masks with bulbous eyes and some canister under the chin.

*That's not just smoke.*

"Petrishchev! Stay on the ground, and crawl to the sides!" Rising to a crouch, she sighted the ambushing men. They were unaware of her escape out of the white cloud.

Leila's Glock rang out; one bullet struck a Chechen in the thigh, where he fell with a cry of pain, and another broke the glass of one man's mask as the bullet drilled into his eye socket. He fell back, dead. At her continuous fire, the men scattered like quail, ducking under her fire and taking cover behind wooden crates.

She did the same: hurrying to the nearest group of crates when they spotted her and returned fire. The bullets either thud-ded against her shelter or ricocheted over her head off the metal containers. At each hiatus of the rain of bullets, Leila shot at an-other from a different angle before they spotted her again.

*You should go. They want to kill him, not you,* the Phoenix said.

She changed to a full clip. *Petrishchev is my priority. Now help me focus!*

A new array of gunfire joined in—on her side of the aisle. The heavy rain of bullets slackened as they turned to address the new adversary, and by the sounds of confirmed hits, they bested

Leila's shoot to kill ratio two-fold. She moved to another crate, and from her new position, she found the gunfire coming from the area of darkness that drew her eye earlier.

"Leila! Where are you!" Petrishchev crawled out of the dispersing white cloud with Gromov and the last bodyguard in tow, bellies on the ground, flinching at every gunshot.

Still crouched, she moved around the crates so the ambushing Chechen wouldn't notice her. "Over here but stay down!"

Seeing their safe haven took every thought from them except for reaching it. All three jumped to their feet and ran.

Since they weren't going to heed her order, she stood to cover their retreat when her head spun, and her legs turned to jelly. Leila fell to the floor. Slamming to the ground caused her to pull the trigger, but, luckily, she didn't hit the men running toward her, oddly in slow motion now.

Petrishchev yelled her name. She tried to warn them to get down, but they couldn't hear her voice.

*Tear gas.*

The Phoenix's heat ignited within her, snapping her back from under the heavy fog the gas was blanketing her in. *You're not gone yet. Fight it.*

Shaking her head, everything resumed its natural speed. Affected by the tear gas like her—only worse since they had inhaled more—they swerved like drunkards, tripping themselves up, harsh coughing ransacking their bodies and further messing up their run.

Unfortunately, her misfire and Petrishchev yelling her name caught the Chechen's attention. They directed their fire on the escapees almost reaching safety.

Leila fired back to distract the ambushing men, but Gromov fell, followed by his bodyguard who turned to help him, then Petrishchev.

The men turned their attention on the last survivor. She had to act fast. Leila dove for the cover of the crates as gunfire shot in her direction.

The heavy fire wore through the wooden crate—one bullet whizzed by her ear and embedded into another. With her defenses falling, Leila shifted one crate to reinforce her barricade. A bullet struck the edge of a crate, causing it to explode into splinters and cutting into her face and arms.

*Time to go,* the Phoenix said.

Leila hesitated—this was her chance to save everyone back home. They would be hurt, but at least *she* couldn't hurt them anymore.

*No!* the Phoenix roared. *I am not letting you give up! You're getting out of here!*

A cylinder landed near her feet, snapping her back to the present. She curled in for protection as it detonated into white smoke. The gas wrapped around her, cutting off any visibility, and stinging her eyes.

*Move; you stay, you die. No one will rescue you.*

The Phoenix's determination to survive forced Leila to her hands and knees, groping forward for a space between the crates. Another bullet thudding nearby forced her closer to the ground. It grew harder to breathe, and the longer she searched for an escape, the more the gas burned her lungs. She began coughing hard like Petrishchev did, making her attempts harder.

After finding space between crates, the fog grew less dense, and she could see the outlines of crates and even containers to her left. Coming out of it, she hid behind one of the last crates for cover as she searched for a safe way back outside.

Her clip was empty. The aisle she and Petrishchev had come down was too long and open—she would be shot down with ease. The gap between containers to her left offered an inviting and promising escape. She darted to her only option.

Even with her run off, she made it, but she found the gap tighter than she thought. She became stuck with half of her body in the gap and the other in the line of fire. Leila wriggled into the safety of the gap and slid through to the other end.

She got stuck again on the exit. Busy getting her left leg out of the gap, a voice yelled. Looking up, one of the men tried to follow after. Leila tugged more feverishly until she came free and jumped to the side for cover.

Moving so quickly again dropped Leila to her knees. The Phoenix prevented the fog from creeping in.

*Go. Go! They're behind you!*

It drove her on, even though she could only crawl. Yells from behind made the Phoenix take control since Leila couldn't. Her dark side forced her legs to tighten as she stood and half-stumbled, half-ran to the exit. She practically ran blind—everything spun; because she couldn't see, someone tackled her from the side.

Her head hit the concrete first, and the man falling on her knocked the air out of her lungs. She lay stunned and tried to regain her breath as the man straddled her and wrapped his hands around her neck. The Phoenix came back with a shock. Leila's hands flailed above her: hitting, scratching, trying everything to pry his hands off her neck, and vainly trying to buck him off.

Her attempts made him angrier. With his hands still choking her, he slammed her head against the concrete floor.

The lights increased to blinding, and her body went limp. A steady pain throbbed at the base of her head. She would soon pass out from an inability to breathe, but the man loosened his grip, allowing air back in, and the Phoenix swooped in.

Her palm rammed up against the man's mask. He reeled back in surprise and pain; Leila arched her back and hurled him off with her legs.

He landed heavily behind her. The Phoenix pulled her to her feet and turned to him. The Phoenix wanted to finish him off, but Leila moved to go past him for the exit.

*We need to go while he's distracted!*

Him springing back to his feet ceased her moment to flee. A hand tried to stop the flow of blood under his broken mask. The Phoenix must've stared him down because of his sudden uncertainty by stepping back. Finding his courage, he grabbed small gray balls from his utility belt and threw them at her feet.

Smoke exploded, cutting off her view of him, but it didn't last long. When it lightened, the Phoenix's reflexes caught his punch. With her unsteadiness, the fight lasted longer than it should've. She gained the upper hand by dropping into Tiger to dodge his punch, then spinning with a leg out to trip him.

As he fell, she pounced on him to swiftly knock him out before he fought back. Snatching the broken mask, Leila fumbled to put it on as she headed back toward the exit.

The hairs on her neck rose, but she reacted a second too late. A large arm wrapped around her neck and dragged her back. Leila dropped the mask, and her fingers scratched into his arm to loosen his vise-like grip. Unable to get her feet under her, she couldn't kick at him. He only grunted and squeezed harder at her failed attempts.

She was passing out—she couldn't breathe, and the white spots in her vision dimmed. She didn't have the energy to spend fighting anymore. Her lack of air severed the Phoenix's encouraging spirit.

Suddenly, the weight on her neck disappeared. She choked on the air she gulped in. The Phoenix returned, urging her to hold on, and her vision cleared only slightly. Now on her side, she faced two fighters.

They were tall, lean, and wearing gas masks, but one moved like an experienced fighter, was lighter on his feet, and possessed more powerful moves. In three strikes of a familiar fighting technique, the other man crumbled to the ground—immobile.

Leila saw the victorious man approach through flashes between blackouts. Her sight disappeared, but she felt him reaching for her. Strictly in survival mode now, the Phoenix lurched up to strike the stranger. He pulled back for a second to avoid her swipes, then caught her wrists. They weren't tight and forceful; he merely held her back.

Her vision began to fade, making it harder to focus. The gas mask covered him from the bridge of his nose down but exposed his eyes. Brown eyes—both dark and intense—stared into her soul, making her shrivel inside. But then they ever so slightly softened.

*"You're safe, Lei,"* David whispered.

His eyes reminded her of something, but it flittered away along with her consciousness before she could grab it.

# XVIII.

The back of her head throbbed; Leila kept her eyes closed to seal it off. Focusing on anything else brought the aching of her dry throat and strained muscles to her attention. A wall met her as she tried to remember what caused these injuries. After a while, brief flashes of the shipyard played—Petrishchev crawling out of smoke only to be killed, she fighting with a man, caught by another from behind, and then brown eyes.

Those eyes… David's?

She discarded that thought immediately. David was dead; he couldn't have been there. As firm as a sheet in the wind, intuition lingered that the eyes resembled something.

Blocking out her pain, Leila opened her eyes to a foreign room, simply furnished with the large bed she lay on, a television set, a hefty but damaged chest beside it, floor-to-ceiling windows draped with thick dark blue curtains, a private bathroom, a closet, and a closed door with a man propped by it, watching her.

Never taking her eyes off him, she gingerly pushed herself up to rest against the headboard, fighting nausea at the movement.

He was a tall man—a little taller than Miguel—broad, fit, and lean with slicked back black hair to the nape of his neck. A dauntingly strong and sharp-boned face stared at her, so blank and simple, fear skittered across her skin. His eyes, though, were captivating: brown—matching the eyes of the victor—but so surreal. Intense, cold, hypnotizing, soul-searching eyes that matched the emotionless face. Leila recognized the endless depths of emotions, mostly masking sorrow—the same reflected in her eyes.

Even though he looked indifferent, he projected a refined, gentlemanly essence, and it added to his attractiveness. His firm stance impressed great strength within him—and classified him as a dangerous man to be enemies with. The sharp clothing snug to his strong frame hinted at an officer or a general.

Drawn back up to his eyes, he continued to observe her; his face revealed no sense of concern or hatred of her presence. Unused to an extreme gaze lingering on her had Leila uncomfortable.

The Phoenix rose in annoyance. *That is my gaze! Who is he to make us uncomfortable?*

"How are you feeling?" The straight line of his mouth moved, revealing a deep, strong Russian voice.

"Sore and stiff," she groaned in answer. A hand massaged her bruised neck.

"Not surprising. You took a beating." No concern laced his tone. He nodded to her left. "There's water to soothe your throat."

A bottle of water sat on the nightstand. It had been placed there moments before for it hadn't begun to sweat. So, he knew when she'd wake.

Leila turned back to him. "So, are you my savior… or captor?"

"Neither." He shrugged. "Both. I kept you from being taken by the Chechen, but I don't save people. You are in my home to heal, but you are not imprisoned here; you may leave whenever you wish."

"And where is here?"

"An hour southeast of St. Petersburg." From his blunt and vague answer, he wasn't going to disclose their location.

Leila looked over at the window shielded by curtains; maybe a landmark would help pinpoint their location… She doubted it though—from his attire, unmovable stance, and disinterested tone of speaking, he was a military man who preferred distance, so his home would reflect that.

"I wouldn't make it far, considering I don't know where I am."

"Not many do. Until you wish to leave, I am Dragunov."

She looked at him. Deception probably had no further purpose—she sensed he already knew who she was. "Leila Wells."

No surprise came over his face, confirming her hunch. Dragunov dipped his head in greeting, then turned to leave. "I'll tell the others not to run you off."

"Others?"

"Five others," he replied languidly as he opened the door, then looked back at her. "We are Spetsnaz." He motioned toward the water. "Drink. It'll help." Dragunov turned and disappeared.

*We go from bad to worse,* the Phoenix grumbled.

*How so?*

*Spetsnaz: military Russians, trained to live and breathe war. As if regular Russians weren't enough.*

*Why do you have a problem? I thought you were meant for fighting; you'll fit right in. Or do you feel threatened?* She reached for the bottle of water.

*Careful; it could be drugged.*

*If he wanted to harm me, he wouldn't have rescued me.*

*I just don't like him. Something's off.*

Dragunov proved right: guzzling the water eased the scratchiness in her throat and refreshed her mind still hazy from the tear gas. Feeling more awake now, she eased her feet to the floor and tested standing. Her legs wobbled, but with each step to the bathroom, they became stronger and less likely to give out.

Tending to her needs first, the mirror at the sink was her next attention. Leila looked as terrible as she felt: pale, dark circles under the eyes, and cuts and dark bruises around her neck added color. What the mirror didn't show was the pain of the throbbing in her head, shoulders, and back or the stiffness throughout her body.

She reached up to feel the tenderness of her head, to see if there was any dried blood, but she found it on her bruised hand—twin to the other's condition. After washing her hands, she rubbed her face with the cold water, cleaning the cuts and reducing her paleness. Looking better, she undid her bushy ponytail and combed through her hair with damp fingers.

Brushing her hair was calming, so the ambush at the Seaport replayed in her mind. The Chechen weren't waiting for Petrishchev. They wanted her. Their unwillingness to shoot her explained their intentions. But why?

*Maybe Foster hired them to,* the Phoenix suggested.

Leila stopped, exasperated. *Why do you always think he's behind everything?*

*Can you give a different explanation?*

She shook her head, refusing to answer—no matter what she came up with, it would be a losing argument.

*Fine then. Continue denying what could be, it doesn't change Petrishchev being dead. It'll only grow more dangerous the longer you stay. We should go,* the Phoenix urged.

*And go where? No. I'll wait a week to recover; by then, this will blow over, and I'll go home.*

*A week is too long.*

But a nagging doubt clung on—she only fooled herself; it wouldn't be that easy. Hope is a foolish and damaging thing when unnecessary.

*Are we safe here?* it asked.

*I don't have another choice, do I? It's all I have right now.*

She tied her hair back into a loose ponytail, trying not to pull the tender spots on her head. With nothing else she could do to be more presentable, Leila headed out to go meet the other members of the Spetsnaz. They had likely seen her passed out so being conscious was probably the best improvement.

Her hand stopped from pulling open the door. *Please, mind your tongue. We need them on my side, so they won't just throw me out,* Leila asked the Phoenix.

*Neither do we need their pity. Like you thought, they probably saw you unconscious—carried away from the fight in defeat. How will they view you other than a damsel needing to be saved?*

*They saw me fight back; I have the bruises to prove it. They will know I am not powerless.* She turned the knob.

*And I can show it.*

The door opened onto a catwalk, her room being at the end of the hallway. Two other doors—both closed—dotted the stretch of wall to her right.

She headed for the stairs—toward the male voices—when one of the doors opened, revealing a spiky-headed blond Russian, much shorter than Dragunov. Leila was even taller. Nor was he similarly built to the big man, being small and slender. Not what she pictured a war-hardened Spetsnaz to look like.

When he shut the door behind him, he must've sensed her presence and looked up; surprise lifted his features, and a warm, friendly smile broke out on his charming face.

"Nice seeing you awake again. I'm Alekseev, but I go by Alek." He offered a hand in greeting.

Leila immediately liked him and took his hand without hesitation. His open and inviting aura drew her in. "Leila Wells, or Lei."

Her name didn't invoke a lightening of realization in his eyes—they were already bright and starry. He knew who she was and struggled to speak, "I can't believe I'm meeting you. Never did I think this would happen. I mean, of course, I dreamed about it, and wondered what I would say, but I didn't see it happening. I'm not that lucky. Anyway, I loved watching the tournament, and I fell in love with you… Well, not you—your fighting. Someone's already got my heart. But you were the reason why I watched."

His gushing and cheery disposition kept the conversation from becoming awkward. Apparently, he wasn't just bubbly from meeting a celebrity; it was his personality, and he was a talker.

It all came out so fast, she struggled to digest what he had said, so she couldn't respond like normal. And he still held her hand.

He chuckled as he let go and stepped back, eyes turned to the floor, but a smile in his voice. "Sorry, I didn't mean to fully let go like that. I was going to ease you down gently. Just made a fool of myself, but I'm used to doing that."

Leila finally caught up. Even the Phoenix was amused instead of annoyed like usual at a fan. "No, you didn't. I think I'm still foggy from the tear gas; it's just… new. But thank you."

"About that." Concern replaced his smile as he looked at her battle scars. "Bruises look nasty. You okay, though?"

His playfulness vanished in an instant; she felt lost and needed it back. The Phoenix grumbled in displeasure.

*I'm not growing attached,* she stated.

*You're acting like a teenager who falls head over heels too quickly.*

*No one shows that spirit to me.* "They're just bruises; I'm fine."

"You held your own really well until the tear gas got you—but that affects everyone. I knew your fighting in the tournament wasn't for show." He waved for her to follow him. "I'll introduce you to the others."

She followed the charismatic Russian down the stairs and got a quick impression of the Spetsnaz with their living arrangements: the two-story house held lofty ceilings, vaulted high with sharp edges, and half of the catwalk and stairs opened onto the enormous living room—furnished ideally for six men with couches arranged to view the entertainment center and widescreen TV dominating the center of the room. Tinted glass enclosed a cold fireplace beneath the television. To the left, a sleek grand piano lounged near the back wall of tall windows; heavy drapes covered most, but the sliding door revealed a porch looking out at the Russian wilderness.

Decorated with bookshelves and other space-fillers too, the house embodied more of a home than the Petrishchev's did. Nothing appeared too pristine that it had a warning label of do-not-touch. The lived-in feeling relaxed Leila even further. With the bouncy Russian in front of her and from her impressions of the home, the Spetsnaz wouldn't be what she expected.

Coming down the stairs, to her right sat an enormous kitchen, simply designed again for efficiency instead of appeal, but with classy elements of stainless steel and a weighty dining table. Except for two, that's where she found the rest of the men. Two similarly sized men—at least brothers with their bulkiness, the color of hair, and way of sitting on the bar stools—played poker at the long island separating the kitchen from the living room. Another cooked in the kitchen—much more slender and taller than Alek beside her but with gray hair.

Alek cleared his throat loudly to gain their attention. None turned. He glanced at her in apology and then tried again. They still didn't stop.

He looked at her. "They're stubborn."

"Not as stubborn as you," one of the men playing poker said.

"We've learned to ignore you," the other finished as he laid down a card. They even spoke the same.

"Says the one who gave in to his 'I Spy' game today at the Seaport."

She caught a glance at one's face as he turned to retaliate. "I didn't give in; I was trying to shut him up, or he would've kept asking."

"Ignoring him is the best way, or just let Dragon order him."

"Like you're doing now when I have someone to introduce?" Alek squeezed in.

That made the men stop playing their game and turn in unison. Square faces, cropped hair, open eyes, and cleft chins—identical twins except one had a lighter shade of brown hair.

"Sorry; we didn't mean to be rude," the one with lighter hair apologized.

"We thought Alek was up to his usual antics."

Alek chuckled, too innocently. "What antics? I'm an angel."

"Those we put up with every day." The man cooking approached behind the twins. He looked to be in his forties, but he appeared to still be nimble in his movements. Craters dented the left side of his face from severe burns. His gray eyes held such gentleness—his kind nature radiated, feeling like a soothing balm. He nodded in greeting to her. "I'm glad to see the head injury doesn't seem to be a factor. Any ailments I missed?"

Not only was he the cook but also the medic. "Just stiff."

"A hot bath and a night's sleep is the only treatment I've found for that."

Alek snatched back the reins, "Don't listen to them. They don't know what they're talking about. I provide the only fun in this place; they would miss me if I was gone. Anyway, I have the *immense* pleasure of introducing the boys." The twins started to gripe but he hurried to interrupt them, "Yurii and Yakov Chubais—Yurii, the slightly blonder one, and Yakov, the other with the ugly snarl on his face. Not much of an improvement, if you ask me."

It grew into a scowl as his twin laughed. "I don't see why Svetlana tortures herself with looking at you when you go home." He turned on his brother. "And why are you laughing? We look the same."

"Because he said it about you, not me."

"Moving on," Alek announced as he moved the subject back to introductions. "Our excellent chef and medic, Silvestrov."

He gestured at Leila. "And this is L—"

"Aren't you missing someone?" Yakov asked.

Alek looked confused for a second, then counted. "Where's Ruben?"

"Where he normally is," Silvestrov answered as he turned back to the stove.

Alek held up a finger for Leila to wait as he spun and headed toward the sliding door. He opened it, spoke in Russian to somebody, then returned trailed by a tall, slender man holding a guitar.

"This is Ruben Severnov."

Ruben looked the poetic type with long black hair, a goatee framing his mouth, and equally dark, mysterious eyes. The guitar added to the poet stereotype. If she had to guess, he also played the piano behind him.

Now having met all the Spetsnaz, Leila realized her assumption of what these men would be like had been off. Way off. They were all handsome men and appeared open and friendly, not withdrawn with cruel auras. Physically, Dragunov and the twins fit the bill of soldiers more than the others, but she knew better than to underestimate any of them.

"And this is Detective Leila Wells—or Lei. Also known as the Phoenix, or one of the Rulers of the Realms," Alek introduced with a beaming smile—as if a proud parent on their child's awards ceremony.

The Phoenix awoke in her eyes at being called out, but its intensity winked out—neither Ruben nor Alek reacted to the change in her. Instead, both men tried to hide recognition.

*They've seen me before.*

*Alek said he watched the tournament.*

*No, I mean they are used to seeing me… or one like me.* The Phoenix drifted off to ponder possibilities.

"We know who she is. We don't need you becoming an announcer," Yakov said.

"Something else to annoy us with," Yurii mumbled.

Yakov grunted in agreement. "Alek begged us to watch, and you were good, Leila. You were the favorite there and here."

"I hope he hasn't talked your ear off yet, Leila," Silvestrov said from the kitchen.

Alek frowned at the man's back. "No, in fact, I haven't. I'm going to try and take it slow. I've already apologized for letting some slip through. I couldn't control myself."

"His gushing gets worse when he's excited."

"Or nervous—like meeting you," the twins said.

"It doesn't get any better though." Ruben's smooth, soft-spoken voice made it hard for Leila to hear. He headed to one of the couches, placed his guitar in the space next to him while sitting, and grabbed a remote.

Alek glared at the back of Ruben's head. "Teaming up on me isn't new, but ignoring Lei by plopping on the couch and turning on the television is. Rude."

Ruben didn't look at him. "It's the news."

The offended air in Alek deflated. "…Oh." He looked at her. "They'll have something on the Seaport by now."

When they seated, a news reporter had appeared, and after a few clicks of the remote, she changed from Russian to English.

"We are on-site of an apparent terrorist attack at JSC Seaport that occurred earlier this morning.

"Just behind me" —she gestured at the building— "is where the situation occurred. There is evidence of a gunfight, and twelve men lost their lives. Not all victims have been identified, but among those were Igor Gromov and Herman Petrishchev."

As she recapped the story, clips of the destruction inside the building played: yellow evidence number tags beside bullet casings and tape circling bullet holes in container walls, and white sheets covered the bodies of the twelve men. The pictures of Petrishchev and Gromov appeared, then it jumped to an interview of Petrishchev's wife dabbing at her eyes with a tissue.

"I can't believe this has happened," she wailed through hiccups. "Herman was such a good man; a good husband. It is that detective's fault! Leila Wells! I knew something was wrong with her—hiding under a false name. He wouldn't be dead if she had not come!"

The interview ended, and the news reporter returned. "The woman Evgeniya Petrishcheva spoke of is Detective Leila Wells from New York City. She came under the alias of Harper Nathaniels. All that Mrs. Petrishcheva knows is that Leila Wells came over for business with her husband.

"Detective Leila Wells was not among the dead, and there is no lead on what has happened to the American. We will have further news on Detective Wells tomorrow and an interview with her captain in New York City. The authorities are asking that if you know the whereabouts of Leila Wells, or see her, to alert them at once. Do not approach her and use caution. Call the number at the bottom of your screen with reports." The news reporter disappeared to show Leila's detective picture along with a number below it.

No one said anything as the news flipped to another story. Leila put her head in her hands to cover up the Phoenix's anger shaking her hands.

*I'm going to kill her!*

*And truly make me into the bad guy she portrayed me as?*

*I don't care! She practically killed her husband, blames us, and is acting as the meek victim? I'll reveal her as the lying murderer she is! Everyone will think twice about trusting the next crying woman.*

Leila shook her head at the Phoenix's desire to slaughter Evgeniya. "She did this."

She felt Alek's eyes turn on her. "Why do you think so?"

"She and Petrishchev did not fit, she grilled me about personal matters trying to find out my identity, and then when I came clean, she responded… strangely, like she thought about an opportunity.

"And now she is lying that she didn't know why I was here, and directing blame on me with those innocent tears? She's behind this."

"Sounds like we're paying her a visit." Leila turned to Dragunov standing in a previously closed doorway. "Silvestrov, Leila… make sure Alek behaves." He shut the door behind him and left the house with Ruben and the twins following.

# XIX.

Evgeniya couldn't have made it easier breaking into her home if she had invited them inside. With the media camping in her yard and her marching back and forth in front of the window shielded by drawn curtains while griping on the phone, her distraction let the four Spetsnaz slip through her back door and head upstairs to collect Leila's luggage.

Dragunov sent Yakov off to comb through the Petrishchevs' records for any red flags, Ruben stood guard, watching the clueless woman, and Yurii collected Leila's things.

By the looks of the place, Yakov would come up empty-handed. The Petrishchevs weren't fond of personal items, so they wouldn't have kept anything that left a trail of existence. He understood.

Leila didn't plan on enjoying her stay. Yurii made quick time gathering her belongings since her luggage was barely unpacked. He expected her luggage to show the usual qualities of a woman by packing something of excess or value. But her suitcase only held the basic travel necessities.

A Ziploc bag on the floor caught his attention. That was different from what he'd seen. It wasn't empty—a plain napkin had been shoved inside, and moisture residue had the bag cloudy. Grabbing the bag and bringing it closer to examine, a floral scent wafted up to him.

Evgeniya wouldn't keep a flower—too personal. Nothing he saw Yurii grab of Leila's resembled a flower. He glanced around the room, hoping to spot it.

"Dragon?" Yurii whispered, barely louder than a puff of air.

"A flower," he answered in the same manner. Yurii considered the room before ducking back into the bathroom to search.

Ruben materialized at the door; without a word, he turned around, and Dragunov followed. He joined him semi-hidden behind the corner of the stairs leading down to Evgeniya still arguing on the phone in Russian. She periodically peered through her curtains at the media outside.

Her voice almost rose to a shriek. "I didn't contact you only to kill Herman, you were to catch Wells! My money is gone with her! I knew better than to trust you for the job. I should've done it myself."

She listened to their response, her back growing rigid. She turned from the window to point at the recipient on the phone as if they stood beside her. The hand she jabbed in the air held a blue flower. "Don't you dare say I couldn't have done it! The Phoenix is all for show! She doesn't scare me!"

Ruben looked pointedly at Dragunov as she continued to speak over her caller. The woman was fortunate she hadn't acted on her poor judgment.

Leila was right in accusing Evgeniya of killing her husband, but the news that she sought a reward for her capture troubled him. Not knowing who would offer the ransom made it even more disturbing.

He'd ask Ruben to fill in the conversation he had missed later, but first, he must get that flower. At the sight of it, the Dragon rose within him—infuriated that she held something which didn't belong to her. He felt a possessive need to reclaim it.

The back door they snuck through opened and shut, whipping Evgeniya around. Bubbling with excitement, she abruptly ended the call and jumped into the intruder's arms. He wrapped around her with just as much vigor. The pair exchanged happiness that they could now be together and mushy declarations of love when they caught pockets of air in their frantic kissing. Their passion overtook them on their way to the couch, ripping clothes off the other.

Evgeniya having a lover outside of her marriage wasn't a surprise. Nor was her disregard for the dead in having her lover over for sex, not six hours after her husband had died.

Dragunov turned to the Chubais twins in attendance—Yurii was holding Leila's suitcase, and he had shared the load with his brother since her duffel bag was slung over Yakov's shoulder, but Yakov was otherwise empty-handed. He nodded for them to head out since Evgeniya and her lover were preoccupied.

They headed down the stairs as quietly as they came up. Ruben checked for a different order, but then he shadowed the twins to slip out the back door.

Dragunov went down the stairs like his men, but his eyes switched from the couple having sex to the wrinkled blue flower on the floor, almost covered with the man's shirt. Crouching so she wouldn't see him over the man's shoulder, he crept to where the flower lay three feet from them.

He rolled the crumpled shirt over on itself to free the flower, grabbed it, and snuck backward. Once behind the dining room wall, Dragunov straightened and headed for the kitchen door, raising the delicate flower to his nose—past the natural floral scent, it smelled of her.

ALEK KEPT THE TABLE CONVERSATION from growing awkward as the remaining three ate. Her lack of enthusiasm didn't keep him down—he spoke with Silvestrov and her equally. It wasn't that being thrown into a house of Spetsnaz was uncomfortable, but her thoughts stayed on Dragunov leaving for Evgeniya's and of what they would do.

She decided to be more cordial when Alek stopped to eat the *golubtsi*—cabbage rolls stuffed with mincemeat mixed with buckwheat and stewed in what looked like thick tomato sauce. "Will they kill her?"

Silvestrov looked at her as if she had spoken the whole time. "Not unless she gives them a reason."

"I know you're not concerned about her safety or anything—especially with your suspicions—but Dragon's not going to kill her. He'll find out what she knows and is involved in. Ruben and the twins went for extra help, if he needs it, and also to get your stuff," Alek said after he swallowed.

"But there's a chance they might," she guessed.

Silvestrov nodded. "There's always a chance. It depends on how much use that person brings by staying alive."

"This all sounds too secretive and independent for regular military Spetsnaz…"

Silvestrov smiled, and Alek beamed. "I knew you would notice. Not that we hoped you wouldn't, but you look like a smart one who catches on quickly. I mean, you're also a detective." He turned to the cook. "I'm not helping much, am I?"

"You never do."

Alek turned back to her. "Anyway, what we are: we're not as involved as normal Spetsnaz with the army. Instead of waiting for orders from them, we listen only to Dragon. We're called when secrecy is required." He paused, deciding how much he should tell. "Well, they wouldn't be that secret if I blabbed about it to everyone. I'm sure you can imagine our missions."

She could. *Assassinations and subterfuge have to be included. This is a dangerous group. Best to remain on their good side.*

*All the more reasons to be careful,* the Phoenix said.

"So, why did Dragunov decide to be at the shipyard today?"

Alek speared a mushroom. "He listens in on the Chechen, and he heard about an arrangement there, but seeing you and

Petrishchev meeting with Gromov threw us off. We first thought his bug had been compromised, and the meeting was a diversion. But we were proven wrong, and I'm glad we hadn't left."

"Did he mention my name or my alias?"

Alek shook his head. "Seeing you there surprised him as much as it did us."

She looked down at her plate. "I knew something was going to happen. I warned Petrishchev, but he wanted to get today over with."

"We thought you could see us since you kept looking up at us." Alek changed subjects to bring her spirits back up.

"I didn't see you; I just felt you watching."

"Then I guess we are good."

"*We* are," Silvestrov corrected. "We know how to keep quiet; you don't."

Alek turned on him. "Did I blow our cover?" With Silvestrov's silence, he kept going. "I know how to be quiet—no one had shown yet, and I decided to liven up the boredom. I went quiet when Lei and Petrishchev showed up. No harm done."

Silvestrov chuckled. "Your definition of quiet is to lower your voice. At the sight of Leila, you bothered Dragon like a gnat, asking for the binoculars to see if it was her!"

Alek glanced at Leila. "Why do you embarrass me?" he asked quietly.

"You embarrass yourself; I continue to point it out."

As the Russians bickered, Leila and the Phoenix considered Dragunov's quick decision to go to Evgeniya.

*If there wasn't something about Evgeniya that bothered him, he wouldn't have volunteered to look into your accusations,* the Phoenix pointed out.

Leila breathed out a sigh. *I know. His actions have shown he's concerned.*

"Why did Dragunov leave? What is he worried about?" she asked.

Her question halted their playful jabbing. They looked at each other for an answer; they tried to hide their hesitancy with Alek cheerfully turning to speak, "He wants to ensure that you're not in danger. No worries, Lei. Dragon won't let anything happen to you.

"Can I ask why you came under an alias? I mean, other than the obvious of drawing too much attention to the famed Leila Wells. Or was that the reason?"

Him abruptly changing the subject meant he knew. Silvestrov joining him by nodding his interest showcased his guilty knowledge too.

She wouldn't be distracted. "What do you know?"

The men kept silent, throwing the table into discomfort with them debating what to say. Finally, Silvestrov sighed in defeat.

"We're not going to lie to you, Leila. Dragon's worried there's more than just Evgeniya blaming you for Petrishchev's death. The ambush at the Seaport was too meticulous. You've probably figured out the Chechen were there for you, not the others—which bothers Dragon even more that he didn't know the plan, just the location. He feels that we were led there."

"How could the Chechen have planned you would save me? I could've escaped."

The cook shrugged. "I don't know, but they did. That's why Dragon thinks Evgeniya isn't the one behind this. She may be in front to receive the fault if something went wrong, but the real mastermind is keeping their face hidden."

The Phoenix turned its attention and anger on the faceless enemy—who it assumed was Foster.

*Told you,* it boasted.

*Yes, you did, but I didn't even know I was headed to Russia, how could Foster have known?* Leila asked.

*Foster could've arranged it from the beginning: threatening Petrishchev, making him reach out to the captain for help, which involved you,* the Phoenix mused.

*Come on! That's quite a stretch and unlike his MO.* She paused. *How's Evgeniya involved?*

*She's the diversion; the face like he said. And he has changed his MO with you before.*

She shut down its thought process before David's death replayed.

"We aren't happy about these suspicions either," Alek said, bringing her back to focus. "We knew something was up when they avoided shooting you. When we debriefed while you slept, we agreed that our returning fire surprised the Chechen. Whoever put this together left out certain plan details."

"Perhaps on purpose," Silvestrov mused.

The table fell silent again, all trying to find the missing puzzle piece. Leila tried not to slot Bryan Foster's face onto the mystery orchestrator's body, even though he fit. The Phoenix grew hot, excited about the realization and eager to hunt him down.

*This is why the captain sent me over here, to prevent me from obsessing over Foster,* she said to the Phoenix in hopes of cooling its growing flames.

*He followed us over here or brought us to him,* the Phoenix stated. *We are meant to go after him!*

*And what about the Spetsnaz? I'm to thank them for saving me by leaving and running straight into a trap and dying?*

*They cannot be involved! This is our fight; our duty! This isn't a tag-team fight! And you doubt our power.*

Leila stopped herself from replying—arguing with the Phoenix usually turned outward and violent. Plus, no amount of persuasion could change its mind.

She decided to bring them out of their heads. "Since someone seems to be after me, I didn't notify the Russian government before coming, and the Russian people are suspicious from Evgeniya idolizing me as a threat, there's no suggestion I hop on a plane and head home anytime soon."

*I knew better than to hope I could go home,* she grumbled.

*See? You should listen to me more,* the Phoenix said.

Alek's peppiness returned like he flipped a switch. "No worries, Lei! You can stay here as long as you want, and Dragon will handle getting your name cleared! He won't let anything happen to you, and neither will we."

He pushed his empty plate to the side to place his elbows on the table and propped his head in his hands. "Now onto a happier note, tell us everything about the tournament! Like what we weren't shown on TV and all the behind-the-scenes action. Also, how did you get invited to participate? Oh, and what did you think…"

Alek spouted off questions in a steady string. She couldn't answer before he thought of another question. Silvestrov chuckled as he stood to take the dishes to the kitchen. "Just start at the beginning so he'll be quiet for a change."

Careful to avoid personal feelings or situations, Leila sated Alek's desire about the tournament. Enraptured, he soaked in every detail like a sponge, almost like he planned on using the information to make a documentary. He just needed a notebook to jot down notes. As she continued, Alek would think of more questions or ask her to elaborate on certain fights, and she realized he would never be satisfied. Eventually, Silvestrov was drawn back to the dining table and supplied his own questions.

It neared midnight when the two Russians' questions tapered off—and, conveniently too, for Leila's already sore throat began to ache worse. She had just drunk some water to soothe her inflamed throat when the four Spetsnaz returned.

Ruben came in first, nodded in greeting, and headed for the kitchen to fix his dinner. Yurii and Yakov came in next carrying her duffel bag and suitcase. Yurii smiled at her as the twins disappeared up the stairs.

Leila rose to ask what they had found when Dragunov brought up the rear and closed the door. He looked at her expectantly.

"So?" she asked.

"Exactly as you thought."

"I've added some suspicions to my thoughts—as have you." She hoped Alek and Silvestrov wouldn't be in trouble for revealing their leader's worry.

He observed her, those dark eyes hiding any hint of a reaction. "It is as I feared: Evgeniya is not behind this."

"Did you find out who is?"

"No." Dragunov headed for the kitchen. She wasn't going to be brushed off. Leila barely registered Ruben sitting at the table she left to follow the Spetsnaz leader into the kitchen.

"So, what *did* you find?"

He remained focused on fixing his plate. "She's angry the Chechen didn't capture you for a hefty-sounding reward."

Leila staggered some, taken back. "Reward? From whom?"

"She was interrupted before she could say his name—if that was who she spoke with."

"What do you mean 'she was interrupted'?"

"She didn't marry Petrishchev out of love," Yurii answered as the twins came down the stairs. "More out of money it appeared."

"She didn't waste any time mourning before inviting her lover over. I bet she won't be proper in waiting before marrying the stud," Yakov finished as they also headed for the kitchen.

"Is there anyone who would put a price on your head?" Dragunov asked, directing her focus back to him. She turned to find him in front of her, giving her no room to look at anything but him.

Foster and Xander's faces flashed across her mind, but she discarded them. More precisely, the Phoenix made her refuse to mention them.

*If he knows, he'll take away your right to justice,* it said.

She shook her head. "No. No one I can think of."

He remained pressing in on her, his soul-searching eyes doing their job. Dragunov stared at her like he knew she lied. Leila resisted squirming and fought against the Phoenix from emerging to shove him back and scolding him for pressuring her to confess.

Thankfully, he shifted his eyes off her. "I'm looking into it regardless." When his eyes locked back with hers, they had changed—soft, pitying, and understanding. "Sorry." Without another word, he headed for the room he had emerged from when Leila accused Evgeniya and disappeared behind the closing door.

His sudden departure left her stunned. She tried to ignore the fact that his closeness contributed to her being breathless and puzzled.

She turned to the men at the table, the incomers beginning to eat, and Silvestrov and Alek watching. "Sorry for what?"

"Sorry for what you've been through," Silvestrov said.

"Sorry for what you're going to go through," Yakov added.

"And sorry he couldn't keep it from happening," Ruben finished.

"Things won't be as bad as you might be thinking, Lei," Alek added with a knowing twinkle in his eyes, and Yurii agreed.

Leila felt raw candor from the Russians but more from Dragunov. Not in the one word he said but in his eyes. True sympathy lay in those dark eyes—a brief emotion hinting at the magnitude of emotions within the hard man.

# XX.

Leila didn't sleep a wink. The ambush at the Seaport and staying up late talking with Alek and Silvestrov—and after they came in, Ruben and the twins—had drained her. Being in a house of six Spetsnaz didn't help, either. *None* of the men—Dragunov included—made her uncomfortable, but they were still strangers. Best to stay on her toes, especially since she was a woman.

But she was trained, too—she could defend herself, and they knew it. They'd be stupid to try anything. Because of the Phoenix, they'd probably be risking their lives.

The main reason for her lack of sleep, though, was the worry and guilt taking center stage in her heart.

Yet again, everyone back home dealt with the unknown—her sudden disappearance and condition. Her possibly being dead would cross their minds.

What made her toss and turn was the doubt of them caring at all. The captain, Heath, DeMarcus, Hyun, Nuan, David's parents: she had hurt every single one of them. She had pushed them away when they only tried to help. She wanted to blame the Phoenix but couldn't. Leila had let the Phoenix control her, so the fault fell on her shoulders too. If they didn't care, she wouldn't hate them. She'd understand.

*We are one,* the Phoenix reminded.

*Yes, I know… unfortunately.*

*Every coin has two sides—I am one side, and you are the other. How can that fact be a misfortune?*

She curled up on her side and wrapped around a pillow. *I'm not thinking about it. Fighting will just depress me more.*

*But I…*

She cut it off. *Please. Not now.*

To her surprise, the Phoenix backed off without pressing the issue further… Probably because it didn't feel defensive where it had to prove her strength.

With it withdrawing, another worry took the stage: someone was after her. The Chechen weren't a concern, the one giving orders was. Xander wouldn't part with his fortune for a philistine capture reward, and Foster's style involved drawing personal blood. But she couldn't discard their names that easily.

Even though the captain had feared her being without allies, she had stumbled into a reclusive Spetsnaz team who appeared like they wanted her safe. She could always be proven wrong though—they could change their mind, agree she had overstayed her welcome, and throw her out. Or her being targeted might endanger them, drawn into a blazing whirlwind she so often ignited. The Phoenix could only bring about destruction.

Leila huffed and threw the pillow behind her, giving up trying to fall asleep. Prepared for exposing her limbs to the cold, she threw off the warm sheets. Now fully awake, she rose and headed to her suitcase. She unzipped the top, folded it back, and froze: the Morning Glory sat atop her folded clothes in its Ziploc bag. She had hidden it from Evgeniya, so how did the men know it belonged to her? Also, where did they find it? Regardless, she was touched and comforted by the sight of it, immediately dispelling her dark mood.

She stood with her chosen clothes, placed the blue flower on her nightstand, and headed for the bathroom, hoping her shower wouldn't disturb the others.

After the shower, she checked her reflection. The water had reduced the redness of the multiple cuts, but the bruises had already begun changing color; before long, the black discolorations would dirty her neck. Lack of sleep made her face pale, and bags pulled down her weary eyes. At least her throat wasn't as sore as yesterday.

Leila rubbed cold water under her eyes to help look refreshed. *David, why do I always end up in situations like this?*

*"It's because you are the best person to handle it,"* he answered.

*Are you sure there's no one else?*

David chuckled. *"I'm sure. You are the only one who can go through this."*

Unsure if she liked his answer, Leila finished drying her hair and put it in a low ponytail—minding her still-tender head. She entered her room and considered the balcony blocked off by curtains. Grabbing the Morning Glory, she headed for it.

She opened the curtains to be greeted by the sun waking behind the thick forest. The serene landscape enticed her further. Careful to not make a sound, she slipped through the glass door and shut it behind her.

The morning air seeped through Leila's shirt, chilling her. She leaned against the railing and enjoyed the quaint landscape. A clearing of about twenty-five feet separated the house from the surrounding densely packed forest. Trees of varying heights went back endlessly. Only knowing the chaotic city-life, being isolated from civilization wasn't so bad. The stillness wasn't discomforting but peaceful. Leila inhaled: the crisp, clean air still moist with dew and scented with pine was calming.

*The men chose a great place to live.*

She could've stayed watching the sun ascend and listening to the wildlife waking to the beckoning of the light, but life stirred within the house. Not wanting to be rude by staying aloof, Leila headed back inside.

"Good morning, Lei!" Alek greeted her when she came down the stairs. She wasn't surprised to find him a cheerful morning person—he seemed like one who never lost energy, day or night. He sat at the island dividing the kitchen from the living room; Silvestrov was busy cooking breakfast. "Sleep well?"

"Some," she lied. "Morning, Silvestrov."

"I hope pain didn't influence your rest," he said, worried. He looked back at her, appraising like a doctor looking for symptoms.

"No, it wasn't that I was hurting. Thinking about those back home, especially since they're interviewing the captain today."

Silvestrov gave her a small smile of understanding. "A different type of hurt then."

"I guess so."

"Don't worry too much, Lei," Alek began. "They know you're strong and smart too, so you can handle yourself over here. They just want you home soon." He gave an encouraging smile at the end.

*I'm not so sure they do,* she thought, but she changed the subject so they wouldn't see the frown growing on her face. "Can I help with anything, Silvestrov?"

Alek moaned before the chef could answer. "You shouldn't have done that."

"Done what?"

"Offer help. You're a guest here; you don't have to earn your stay. He takes advantage of free labor. His daughter could warn you of the dangers."

Silvestrov shot a pointed glare at him from the stove. "Klara has chores—it is not child labor. You sound like I force her. She wants to do things with me."

Their trading barbs reminded her of Heath and D, and to an extent, of Shamus and Luke. Alek gave a playful snort. "Who wants to spend time with an old geezer like you?"

"I am only twenty-three years older than you, Alek; hardly making me that old."

"You're still ancient."

"Anyway, I enjoy her wanting to help—it lets me spend more time with her." He turned back to the stove. "You'll understand once Svetlana has your child. You'll want to spend every moment with them, but you can't, and then you'll want time alone, but you won't get it."

Alek pursed his lips as he thought about Silvestrov's words.

Silvestrov looked at her as he pulled the frying bacon out to cool. "If you didn't catch it, I will put you to work."

"If I'm not willing to help, I wouldn't have offered," she defended.

He chuckled. "I think you'll fit in fine, Leila. You're more help than some around here."

"Hey!" Alek yelled, offended.

Silvestrov smoothly retaliated, "I didn't say any names."

"But I heard the undertone—you directed it at me!"

"Then you *can* hear." He looked at Leila. "Start with the muffins, and once those are cooking, cut the cantaloupe and honeydew."

Leila set to gathering the ingredients, then started mixing a new batch of muffin batter—some already rose in the oven—as the Russians continued to bicker.

"What do you mean 'you *can* hear'?" Alek demanded.

"You have selective hearing… unless it's something about you, of course."

"What's wrong with that? Keeps one from obtaining ammunition for gossip. If something was important, I would be told directly. Nothing matters much unless my name is mentioned."

She scooped the muffin batter into the paper cups, and once full, she checked the currently cooking muffins—nearly ready. As she moved to cut the melons, Silvestrov added fried ham to the plate of cooked bacon. "Your selective hearing goes hand-in-hand with your ability to avoid work."

Alek scoffed. "I do work! Do you want me to help you cook?"

"No, definitely not. I would burn the food making sure you weren't catching yourself on fire."

"I know how to cook!"

"Do you, or do you just know not to play with fire?"

"I cook for Svetlana all the time, and the house hasn't burned down."

"Yet," Silvestrov added.

"She loves the *pelmeni* I make for her."

Silvestrov winked at Leila as she retrieved the first batch of hot muffins and slid in the tray she made. "Oh, so that's what Natalia has seen her throwing out to the dogs."

"She— What?"

"Will you two give it a rest?" Yakov begged as he and his twin came into the kitchen. "You argue like a married couple."

"Or cats and dogs," Yurii added.

"The ugliest cat and dog I've ever seen."

Yurii chuckled in agreement as the twins separated, him grabbing mugs for everyone and Yakov checking the brewing coffee. With them in hand, he headed for his brother when he noticed Leila. "Silvestrov, that's cruel making Lei work."

The chef shook his head in disbelief.

"I offered." She smiled at the Chubais twins moaning at the same time.

Leila balanced the plate of muffins and the two bowls of fruit to take to the table. Before Alek rose to help, Ruben swooped in, and with a quiet, "Morning," and, "Let me help," he grabbed the bowls of fruit. After accepting he wasn't a hallucination, she followed him to put down the plate.

"Alek, what are you and Svetlana expecting?"

"A boy, due in late December or early January." His voice held fatherly pride.

Hearing about his upcoming family brought up the memory of her and David talking about children. Luckily, her back was to him, and Ruben faced away from her, so neither saw her pain.

The Phoenix showed up to block any more painful memories from seeping in. She forced enthusiasm into her voice, "Congratulations, Alek."

"I hope for the baby's sake he doesn't look like you," Yakov picked at the soon-to-be-father as he brought the filled coffee mugs to the table.

"Or has your personality," his twin added as he sat beside his brother.

"If you name him after you, you've doomed him," Ruben said.

"It'll be best if he is a spitting image of Svetlana," Silvestrov ended while he put the bacon, ham, and eggs on the table.

"Thanks so much for the words of encouragement," Alek said.

"I'm sure he'll be handsome," Leila said as she took a seat beside Silvestrov.

"As long as he looks more like Svetlana," Dragunov said as he walked into the room. "He'll be fine." He patted Alek's back as he headed for the coffee.

Over breakfast, the men continued picking on Alek by explaining Svetlana's stability to Leila. She sounded steadier than Alek, but Silvestrov whispered that she could slip up like her husband.

"A perfect pair," he whispered. "One balancing the other with enough similarities and differences to keep it even."

With the men ganging up on Alek, it prodded him to mention their own relationships. The table really got talking then. Leila had trouble keeping track of the conversations among the laughter and corrections.

Alek and Silvestrov were the only ones with wives; Yakov, Yurii, and Ruben were dating—Yurii's relationship sounding the most serious. Dragunov mentioned neither a wife nor a girlfriend. Leila threw in a comment every so often to avoid drawing attention. They had watched the tournament, so they knew about David; fortunately, they didn't pry into her situation now.

A phone began ringing, muffled like being behind a door. Dragunov stood, and with an "Excuse me," he disappeared around the stairs. A door opened, then shut, and the ringing stopped.

The men never slowed their playful verbal battle, the interruption disrupted nothing so the phone calls for Dragunov must be a regular occurrence.

Curiosity burned, but Leila didn't know how to inject her question without being rude. Ruben noticed the question mark over her head. "Business."

"The Dragon is in his Den; do not disturb," Alek said as he stood with some dishes.

Silvestrov twisted in his seat, eyeing his trek back to the kitchen. "And what do you think you're doing?"

"Cleaning the dishes since you think I'm not much help," Alek said, putting the dishes in the sink.

"Alek is doing something for a change?" Yurii asked.

"Without being ordered? Take a picture," Yakov suggested.

Alek faked laughter in return.

"Don't break my dishes!" the chef ordered.

On cue, Alek rattled the dishes. "Oops."

"Alek…"

Leila grabbed hers and went to his aid. "Would you like some help?"

Alek considered the pile of dirty plates, mugs, skillets, and various utensils used to prepare the breakfast. But back on the table, more dishes awaited to be cleaned.

He looked at her. "This is more than I thought," he whispered.

They rinsed while the others brought the rest of the dishes but continuously peered over Alek's shoulder, checking his progress. With two washing and drying, soon, the remnants of eating were gone. Leila turned to the table empty from the men cleaning it. Silvestrov approached for Alek's inspection.

"Spotless, huh?" Alek boasted when the chef rubbed a finger across a plate.

He winked at her. "Only because Leila cleaned this one."

Alek's mouth hung open, flabbergasted. "Look: I cleaned these!" —he motioned to his pile of clean dishes. "Those" —he gestured at Leila's side— "Lei did. That plate came from my side!"

"How do you know?"

Alek crossed his arm, smug. "I knew you would pull something, so I prepared."

"Prepared to take credit for what Leila did?"

After being stunned for a second, Alek fired back defensively. Silvestrov took up the offensive with a grin. As they bickered, a soft touch on her shoulder pulled her around to face Ruben.

"Thought you needed rescuing." He gestured behind him. "The news is on."

Leila followed him to the couch where he already set the language to English. The reporter from yesterday sat at a desk with a picture of the JSC Seaport and 'Terrorist Attack?' stamped across it, behind her.

"Last night, we reported on the scene of a possible terrorist attack at the JSC Seaport where twelve men lost their lives. Those men have now been identified as --" Leila didn't recognize any of the names the anchorwoman listed off.

"Also present at the attack was Detective Leila Wells from New York City, New York, but she is currently missing. Local authorities have no leads on what may have happened to Detective Wells or her whereabouts.

"We gained an interview with Detective Wells' supervisor, Captain Colin Sullivan of New York City, that may help further this investigation."

The anchorwoman disappeared to a video of the captain answering questions in a quick conference-like interview. Guilt twisted Leila's stomach at the sight of his disheveled appearance—strained eyes from lack of sleep, gaze jumping from face to face as he struggled to focus on the question, and worry shaking his usually steady face.

*That's what you get,* the Phoenix said.

She shook the self-righteousness off. *No. He doesn't deserve this pain again… I do.*

The captain answering a question pulled her focus off what the Phoenix replied, "I take full responsibility for Detective Leila Wells' presence in Russia. Herman Petrishchev and I were close friends, and when he came to me for help, I asked Detective Wells for assistance. She went to Russia solely for Petrishchev's protection."

A reporter raised their hand. "Why did Herman Petrischev require protection? Does that mean he was involved in dangerous or illegal activities?"

"I am not at liberty to say. It could very well be more damaging to this situation than helpful. Evgeniya's life could be placed in danger as well as Detective Wells'. That is all I will say on that matter."

His blue eyes hardened with certainty and anger. "But I know for a fact that Detective Wells had absolutely no hand in the terrorist attack at the JSC Seaport. Leila is not a threat to the people of Russia. She is a reliable ally."

"How can you say she isn't a danger with her known skill in martial arts?"

"Detective Wells' prowess in fighting is not a threat to innocent civilians. She will fight to protect them, not harm them."

"But what about the Phoenix? That makes her unstable. Especially with her recent attack on a Detective Ghent proving—"

He cut that reporter off. "The accident has nothing to do with the situation at hand."

A nerve had been struck, forcing the reporters to change tactic. "So, are you calling Evgeniya a liar?"

*Yes. He saw right through those crocodile tears,* the Phoenix said. Leila agreed.

The captain had to play politician though. "No. I do not know why Evgeniya said those things. Perhaps she misunderstood Leila's presence…"

Leila understood his trailing off—he probably thought about a possible explosion involving the Phoenix, causing Evgeniya to distrust her.

A reporter asked something, and he pleaded into the cameras. "I only want to know if Leila is okay. Any word on her condition, any news of her whereabouts… or just to hear her voice…" He closed his eyes to regain composure.

When he opened them, he became professional again. "We offer a reward of two-hundred and fifty thousand dollars for Detective Leila Wells' safe return. We won't pursue whoever brings her back to us or ask any questions. You will be free to leave with your reward, and this will all be forgotten. Please, she is important to us.

"And a message to Leila," he added, eyes softening like he knew she watched. "Don't burden yourself about us back here; we are fine. Focus on keeping yourself safe and bringing yourself back to us soon. Please, we need you more than we've led you to believe." The captain swallowed back the emotions too easily revived. "We love you."

The anchorwoman replaced the video. "Authorities are looking into what Captain Colin Sullivan had to say, and everything is being evaluated." Leila's detective picture appeared with the number to call. "Any reports or sightings of Detective Leila Wells should be called in." The reporter switched to another story, and Ruben turned the volume down.

The house remained quiet behind her as Leila held her head in her hands, sorting through her thoughts.

*How can I not think about them? That reward will bring hundreds of false information.*

*They deserve heartache for what they've done,* the Phoenix restated.

*Stop it! No, they don't! They were acting in the heat of the moment—just like we did. Now, help me think.*

The Phoenix fell quiet like it was thinking. After a while, Leila still not coming up with an answer, it sighed like she had missed the solution right under her nose. *Get sighted in town! A picture would be enough evidence to ease them… if they even care about your safety.*

She ignored its last remark. *No, that won't do. I could be captured or killed, and doing so could bring Dragunov and his men's involvement to light. They might be put in danger.*

*Who cares about them? We are to worry about ourselves, not them.*

*I care. It's only right I return the care they've shown so far for me. So, what else could I do?*

The Phoenix backed off, unhappy at her thought, and letting her come to a solution herself.

*I must contact the captain in some way.*

Leila rose and faced the men gathered to see the news report—Alek and Silvestrov still in the kitchen, the twins in the hallway running past the stairs, and Ruben seated on the couch. All except for their leader. "Where's Dragunov?"

"Uhh, it's best to let him come out on his own," Alek said, but his glance at a closed door answered her question.

She headed toward the shut door—the room he had emerged from yesterday.

"Lei, I wasn't picking about the Dragon being in his Den. He doesn't like to be disturbed," he warned.

The Phoenix perked up—this sounded like a challenge. "I can handle myself."

She opened the door without bothering to knock—he probably wouldn't have answered anyway. Cabinets lined the far wall, numerous thin TVs covered the wall to her left, and a table sat in the middle of the room with organized papers and folders occupying it. To her far right, a couch had been turned into a bed. But at her direct right and closest to the door, a large computer desk held three computers and the Spetsnaz leader.

Before abruptly halting and looking at her in the doorway, Dragunov was typing—his look both held curiosity and irritation. One screen held a map constantly changing locked-on positions, the middle held foreign computer codes running halfway down the black screen, and the last held a news report.

*Let me handle this,* the Phoenix begged.

*No; angry demands won't help.*

"Dragunov, I have to ask you for something."

"I saw the interview. Sending a message is out of the question right now," he answered in a deadpan tone.

"There must be something I can do to let them know I'm okay. They can't go through this again…" She closed off before mentioning the likeness to David's loss.

Dragunov didn't react or suggest he understood her desperation. Last night, a smidgen of emotion slipped into his dark eyes; now they just stared at her dully. The Phoenix grew angry at his apparent disinterest.

*He doesn't care,* the Phoenix growled. *I'll make him care.*

He spoke before she could, "I'm working on an untraceable way for you to contact them without delay."

The Phoenix came through her frustration. "Without delay? You, being this secretive Spetsnaz, should already have these means of untraceable messages! What's so different about now?"

"The difference now is you. A famous American entangled in a plot to be ensnared in a foreign country, necessity requiring a message to be sent anonymously across the Atlantic, and the threat of an unknown enemy to the safety of my men for hiding you, causes me to approach this cautiously. If anything isn't secured, I could alert the government and that nameless enemy where you are, and then I put my men in danger." His voice remained blank, but she grasped the underlining meaning—his men's safety comes first.

"So, I'm to sit back and let men take care of me?"

Dragunov's eyes flashed at her contempt, looking very familiar. "Precisely."

"I am not some defenseless damsel in distress!"

"I know you're not, but your situation requires patience. You must lay low."

The Phoenix broke through, taking a step toward him. "Am I talking to a wall? Show some kind of emotion so I know you're human. Register something!"

Her advancement brought out the slightest reaction: his body tensed, and jaw clenched like in expectation of an assault, and even his hands gripped the chair's armrests to stand. That familiar glazing flashed across his eyes. But surprisingly, he turned back to the computer screens and resumed typing.

"I don't do emotions."

She stared at him. The Phoenix expected him to fight back, but when he pulled himself away, it was left disappointed.

"You're not emotionless. I saw sympathy in your eyes last night. You do have feelings, Dragunov; you hide in here to keep from showing them."

With that, the Phoenix slammed the door without seeing how it would register—if it would at all. She hoped she had scorched him some.

# XXI.

Simmering from her confrontation with Dragunov, the Phoenix returned to the couch, eyes glued to the screen. The anger radiating off her kept the Spetsnaz away. She watched clip after clip of "new advancements" in the case and even possible predictions of what could've happened to her—taken by the Chechen, taken by the unknown group who had intervened, killed and her body dumped someplace, or perhaps she had run for her life.

The last suggestion had her laughing dryly. Like she cared about her life anymore? She would've stayed and fought to the death; it sounded like a promising way to die.

*Please! You didn't want to die! If I die so do you. You only think about yourself.* Leila succeeded in snatching back control when the Phoenix struggled to deny her claim.

She joined the men for lunch with less of an imposing aura, but there was still enough present to discourage them from asking questions. Dragunov never came out of the command room to eat, and none of his men ventured into his Den with a peace-offering of food.

Finished with lunch, Leila returned to the couch for more updates, and everyone else scattered throughout the house.

Anticipation hung in the air—something would happen soon. Because of sixth sense, the Phoenix rose in eagerness. Maybe it was just the Phoenix's lingering anger waiting to engulf anyone who ventured too near…

Dragunov's door whooshed open, and he strolled out, smoothly ordering his men in Russian. It was all too fast for Leila to catch, but the determination set in his eyes, his stride for the exit, and the men quickly falling into step behind him tipped her off—he had discovered something.

She jumped to her feet. "What did you find?"

All continued their march to the door, focused on Dragunov's quiet instructions. In her irritation, the Phoenix yelled her question again, and out of politeness, Alek stopped to face her.

"Dragon found where the order for your capture originated. We're headed there now."

"You're staying here." Dragunov's harsh order cut off her interjection to be included.

The Phoenix bristled as she turned on him. "Excuse me?"

"Must I repeat myself?"

"I will *not* be left here!"

Dragunov stopped and turned on her, eyes steel-hard and flashing dangerously—again, triggering recognition. His voice remained calm and cool but demanding, "You will heed my orders."

"Who are you to say what I must do?"

"The fact that you are under my roof."

"I may be in your house, but you can't order me around like one of your men."

"Thankfully, you are not, for you don't respect authority well." He jumped to finish before her furious objection. "You have no place here, which doesn't grant you a vote."

The Phoenix exploded. "You brought me here! While I am here, I have a voice!"

Her outburst broke his restraint; his eyes became just as dark and hollow as hers when the Phoenix emerged—his dark side. "Not to dictate my orders! I brought you here so you wouldn't be tortured by the Chechen. As nothing more than a guest, you listen to what we say. You won't put my men in danger protecting you!"

"I don't need rescuing! I'm capable of defending myself!"

"As I witnessed in the Seaport," he said condescendingly.

She reverted the fist into her voice. "Did I ask for your help? Maybe I wanted to die!"

Dragunov didn't reply. He kept the stare-down, but his eyes narrowed. The deathly silence spoke volumes—her statement disturbed him.

The Phoenix glared back, challenging him to pick up the tension. It wasn't ready for its anger to be cooled and enjoyed someone being able to stand against her intensity and fire back equally.

Replaying her last words returned Leila to the surface. She didn't truly mean it… at least, she hoped. Just something said in the heat of the moment. Realizing how close she had advanced toward the Russian—almost touching his chest—she stepped away. The men all stopped their exit to watch the clash; contemplating what had been said kept them quiet. They probably wondered what would happen next.

To avoid Dragunov's prying gaze, Leila kept her gaze down. It seemed like years of silence until Alek cleared his throat.

"I think it would be a good idea if Lei came."

Her eyes snapped up to the Russian's hesitant smile. Dragunov breathed out, then looked behind Alek to each of his men, agreeing. Only Ruben didn't nod his approval—his answer lay in his guarded eyes.

"You have no problem killing, do you?" Dragunov turned back to her, anger gone and his cool voice back. There was no hint of his dark side.

Her eyes shot to him venomously. "Of course not."

Reassured by either her answer or the look in her eyes, he turned for the door again. "Know I won't save you again."

"You won't have to," she muttered at his retreating back.

LEILA STIFFLY RODE WITH DRAGUNOV to a warehouse a few miles outside St. Petersburg, near the small town of Yekazen. Alek and Silvestrov in the back didn't attempt conversation, knowing the tense atmosphere only needed a spark to ignite. Once they arrived, they would arm themselves. Leila caught the quick, puzzled look Yurii gave his brother before she entered the SUV—they weren't accustomed to doing so. It wouldn't be logical to have her armed after her yelling match with Dragunov. She agreed.

*At least we know now how they recognized me,* the Phoenix said.

*Please stay back,* Leila begged. *I don't need you setting off another explosion with him.*

Nightfall masked their arrival. Dragunov parked in an empty lot behind the warehouse, and Leila dressed alongside the men. Alek gave her a bulletproof vest, a knife, and an AK-47. Yurii strapped on quite a supply of knives. Ruben wore the least armor and was only armed with a knife and the gigantic sniper rifle on his back.

A single flickering light spotlighted the back door of the warehouse. The one-story blocky concrete building seemed normal—not looking rundown or important—but it was conspicuously isolated from the small town.

Dragunov whispering orders brought Leila back to the fully armed Spetsnaz huddled around their leader—now they were intimidating and dangerous Spetsnaz. She understood enough to know the plan of splitting into two teams: Ruben as the designated sniper, and her paired with Alek and Silvestrov. With a searching look at Leila to follow the orders, Dragunov motioned to move.

The flickering light seemed to wave them onward to the back door—their approach was covered. After flattening against the building, Dragunov worked on picking the lock. When the handle turned and the door cracked open, his search for sensors or alarms came up empty; he continued opening it, slow and quiet. Dragunov slipped in so quickly that the warehouse seemed to suck him in, followed by six more shadows.

The dimly lit warehouse housed shelves of hardware supplies and appliances: washers and dryers, wooden beams, paint cans, taped-up boxes, and more. Ladders led up to the top of the towering shelves; Russian men spoke and laughed somewhere, and one—eclipsed in shadow because of the overhead fluorescent light—patrolled the highest stack of inventory. Dragunov had them crouch under the windowsill of an unused room, hidden in shadow. He motioned upward, and Ruben took off without a word, vanishing into the darkness.

Leila strained to see where the Russian had slipped off to until she realized the Spetsnaz crouched with her looked up at the rafters. Following their gazes, Ruben silently crossed the metal catwalk above them. Stopping at a point suiting him, he slipped the sniper rifle off his shoulder, keeping his eyes down on a position past the shelves. Without looking at them, he signed information to his comrades.

Dragunov turned to the rest of them and signed his orders. Leila looked at Alek when he was done. He whispered that there were fourteen hostiles—four elevated and the other ten grouped together, all heavily armed—and they would wait until Dragunov, Yurii, and Yakov's first assault, then flank them.

The Spetsnaz leader motioned for the teams to move to their positions. Alek followed Silvestrov, sneaking toward a wall of shelves encircling the grouped targets. As the blond Russian passed, she caught Dragunov's gaze on her—something tender lay in his eyes. The Phoenix growled in unease, and his regard for her disturbed Leila. Uncomfortable under his gaze, she turned away and followed Alek.

Kneeling behind Alek and Silvestrov in the shadows of stacked inventory, she looked around them—across the white river of light, another hardware shelf awaited. Looks passed between the two Russians, and with a nod shared, Alek took a deep breath, then scurried across the no man's land to safety in the darkness. Leila surely thought Alek would be seen in his vulnerability, but no alarms came from their targets. Not only the smallest but the quickest of the Spetsnaz, too.

Silvestrov motioned for her to stay with him; when he turned back around, she glanced behind at the windowsill they had hidden under. The three bigger Russians were gone. She looked up, and it took her a moment to find Ruben, now stretched out on the catwalk with the rifle aimed.

She took a steadying breath. The Phoenix trembled in excitement—its rage had been halted with Dragunov, but now it could unleash on the ones that wanted to capture her. This could also implement Foster or Xander as being behind it all.

*Or it couldn't.* Leila tried to keep the Phoenix's eagerness down.

A chill and heaviness filled the air as if to coincide with their imminent ambush—no one seemed to breathe, none of the Russian targets spoke, laughed, or coughed. With the abrupt silence, the hostiles noticed the atmospheric shift.

*"Что-то тут не так,"* one said. A metal chair scraped back as someone stood. The loud echoing crack of Ruben's sniper rifle sent a body crashing into the chair.

Chaos erupted. The quickfire from machine guns filled the air, along with the cries of alarm and pain. Individual gunshots and automatic gunfire joined with the others as the fight broke out. Ruben's rifle felled another as Alek, Silvestrov, and Leila emerged from their hiding spots to surprise those who thought of escaping by the open aisle.

Men dropped underneath their pinpoint bullets as they advanced toward the intense gunfire. Silvestrov kept Leila close to the shelves while approaching the backs of their enemies firing at the other end. Alek shimmied down his side of the aisle—most likely to be spotted. Unaware of the danger at their flanks, he dropped two Chechen in one spray of bullets. The closest hostiles turned at the new gunshots and opened fire.

She didn't see where Alek hid, but—predicting how the situation would develop—Silvestrov flung open a refrigerator door for Leila to get behind. He hunkered down with her until bullets stopped thudding into the metal. Still crouched, the chef/medic leaned around the door and pulled the trigger once. Popping around, she found all hostiles on the floor.

When the gunfire ended, an eerie silence took its place. The Spetsnaz team and Leila set out to check the dead for survivors. Yurii found two struggling to breathe and ended their misery with a swipe of his knives.

Killing the Chechen hadn't quenched the Phoenix's need for release. Silvestrov had allowed her to emerge only to kill three.

*Not like we helped much,* the Phoenix grumbled.

Dragunov hauled a survivor to his feet—one Ruben had shot in the shoulder. From the corpses lying around her with precise headshots, this had been intentional.

He pinned the man against a stack and began his interrogation. The Chechen laughed at the question and remarked back to Dragunov's anger. The criminal's eyes roamed from the demands yelled at him until they landed on Leila. Recognition lit his features, and he grinned through his pain. Seeing where his eyes landed, Dragunov banged him into the wall, questioning him again. His smirking reply angered the Spetsnaz leader; with a quick twist, he snapped the man's neck. Leila swallowed a gasp as the Chechen's body slid to the floor.

The sudden death fazed none of them. Dragunov kept his eyes closed as he controlled himself. With a long exhale, he ordered them to find something.

Leila helped with the search, but Alek found what they searched for. "Lei's name and picture are everywhere in it. He's supposed to be the reward's recipient, not Evgeniya. It talks about making her believe she would get the money." Alek handed the folder to Dragunov, and he flipped through it himself.

*That's too simple,* the Phoenix said, and Leila agreed with it.

"So, we done here?" Yakov asked after a while. "Leila out of danger yet?"

The Spetsnaz leader closed the folder. "For now." He looked at her. "But Russia still believes you are a criminal." Caution had more of a presence over the tenderness in his eyes.

*He doesn't believe I've gotten off this easy either.* She nodded anyway. "I know."

Dragunov considered her a moment before looking behind him and up. "Ruben, let's go."

Ruben made no noise as he stood, slung the rifle over his shoulder, and headed down the winding staircase. Alek gave her a warm smile as he walked beside her, following the others out.

*None of them believe I'm safe but won't say.*

The Phoenix tried to re-stir the cooling embers of her anger. *Still trying to be the man by protecting the helpless woman, I see.*

*No, they don't want to jinx their suspicion by making it true.*

# XXII.

Even with the success of the ambush, the week dragged on for Leila. As the cuts and bruises faded, her strength returned, but restless nights sapped what energy she had regained. Watching the effects of her disappearance on the news increased her guilt. Russians suspected everyone around them with no sightings of her, the government was in a frenzy to find her—whether for her safety or to hold her accountable for JSC Seaport, she wasn't sure—and the whole world focused on Russia because of Leila.

Within hours, the discovery of the carnage at the warehouse sparked a story, implicating Leila. Nothing became of it other than locals expressing gratitude that more Chechen members had been killed.

The worst was watching the captain, Heath, DeMarcus, Hyun, Nuan, and David's parents endure interrogations posing as interviews. It looked like they suffered from the same insomnia she dealt with. This resembled almost losing her before, and the ghosts of those emotions strained their faces. They neared breaking—she didn't know how much more they could undergo.

Leila was helpless though. Although the Chechen threat had been neutralized, everyone wanted to claim the reward the captain offered or turn her over to the Russian government. So, she took Dragunov's advice about lying low, but she yearned to break free of the house's confines, feeling like nothing was being accomplished—unfortunately, re-establishing the Phoenix's irritation.

"Umm, Lei?"

She looked away from the television to a cautious Alek. He gave her a quick smile. "I thought to get your mind off home by showing you something. I hope you like it."

He gestured for her to follow, and she did, intrigued. Alek led her through the hallway under the stairs and opened a door to a workout area. It had more than enough for a proper workout: a spacious practice arena and a variety of punching and body opponent bags. The sight lifted Leila's spirits—now she could focus her temper safely, instead of on the Spetsnaz.

Alek walked in with her. "We're not expert fighters like yourself—perhaps Dragon being the closest—but keeping fit is a must among Spetsnaz."

"Does Dragunov fight?" she asked while heading toward the punching bags.

"No, but he's a master compared to us. Only you could pose a challenge."

She punched a boxing bag, feeling her adrenaline pulse for more as it shuttered violently. "How so?"

"He's the only one in our legion to be awarded the *krapovyi beret*—the maroon beret."

"What honor is that?"

"The greatest an officer can get. It goes to the 'most professional, physically, and morally fit' sergeants and officers. Along with others, he went through physical-fitness and shooting tests, survived a twelve-kilometer cross-country run in full combat gear, a hundred-meter sprint, urban-assault exercises—with those annoying wall climbs—acrobatics, and a twelve-minute free-style sparring match with three opponents."

*He would put up a fight.* "Impressive."

"He's the best; he and every Spetsnaz team know it. No one talks about him because his audience doesn't stay alive."

She looked back at him. "Nostalgic?"

With hands in pockets, he shrugged. "I can't deny it. I have to wait three years to see great fights again…" His eyes became suppliant.

"You don't have to beg, Alek."

"So, would you?"

"I can't fight without an opponent."

Alek beamed. "Then I'll let you get to it." But he didn't leave.

She stared at him, thinking he would come out of his trance without her probing him. He instead looked expectant of her to begin. "Alek, I usually don't mind an audience, but now might not be the best time."

He blinked out of his stupor. "Oh, right… Sorry." He gave her a little wave as he headed out before looking back—hoping she would change her mind—but without her assent that he could stay, he closed himself out.

As soon as the door clicked, the Phoenix whirled around to kick the bag. She released her dark side on the small boxing bag. Killing the Chechen increased the Phoenix's need to be unleashed, and Leila's struggle to keep it under.

After a final kick sent the bag insane, she turned to the opponent dummies. Her power knocked opponent bags down one after another. As she continuously stopped to right them again, her mind drifted toward what was happening around her, which increased the force of her attacks.

Trying to clear her name, Dragunov only emerged from the command room to grab something to eat and shut himself away again. The Dragon was in his Den, and she had escaped unscathed from her confrontation with him both times. She hadn't meant to blow up at him, but her emotions running high enabled the Phoenix to slip through.

Risking another trip into his Den, uninvited, or antagonizing him again would get her scorched.

Having knocked down all the opponent bags for the sixth time, Leila took a deep breath. She needed to get in control—exhausting herself was not working, just as Hyun had said. The Phoenix wanted to keep exhorting herself, but Leila picked up the dummies and set them aside.

She centered herself on the mat, released a long and steadying breath, and flowed through the calming forms of the Crane. It soothed her burning desire to destroy something from being helpless to helping herself.

THREE DAYS HAD PASSED SINCE the explosion between Leila and Dragunov, and Leila's daily tranquil routine of practicing through her stances toned down the Phoenix, but their leader's absence and her disheartened mood dragged the men down. Alek wasn't his peppy, charming, snide-remark-making self; Silvestrov remained in the kitchen and rarely picked at Alek; and the Chubais twins seldom showed themselves. Only Ruben seemed unaffected, playing his guitar on the porch.

One evening, Leila was left alone with Dragunov.

Alek explained. "About the third week of every month, we all return to our families. Every now and then, one of us checks in to make sure we're not needed. We'll be back soon though." He patted her arm before walking out into the night, and Leila felt lonelier than before. Now no one provided presence; even though she didn't socialize much, the men being there gave the house essence.

Like burning heartburn, the Phoenix rose, angry at everyone for abandoning her. Leila went to calm herself in the workout room; once finished, she would lock herself away in her room like Dragunov below.

A DISTANT VOICE CALLED OUT to her, but she discarded it—this was the first night in a while that she fell asleep instead of being restless with worry. It called again, closer this time, but she still ignored it. If David, she would feel him; the voice must be a figment of her imagination.

"Leila, wake up." The deep voice startled her, along with pressure on her bare shoulder.

Leila's eyes snapped open to widen further in finding Dragunov bent over and rousing her. Self-consciously, she pulled up the sheets to cover her scars, then noticed he held a phone.

She began to ask what was wrong when he answered, "I found a loophole."

All weariness disappeared as she shot up. "I can call?"

"Yes, but only one person. And you have nine minutes—which is already counting down."

Leila grabbed the phone and hopped off the bed as she dialed the captain's cell—he needed to hear her voice the most.

The phone rang for a while.

"Come on. Please answer," she begged while pacing the floor.

Her pacing stopped when the other end picked up. "Hello?" Captain Sullivan's weary voice answered.

"Captain!"

"Lei? Leila! Thank God, you're alive! What happened? Are you safe? Where are you? Are you okay?"

"Captain, Captain, please I'm okay, but it's too much to explain. I don't have time to talk. Know I'm fine." She looked at Dragunov for permission to mention them; he nodded. "I'm safe with a Spetsnaz team—they saved me in the Seaport."

"Alright."

"Let the others know that we talked but keep it quiet. I don't need the world knowing I'm with a Spetsnaz team or the Russian government will find us."

Dragunov caught her attention by tapping his watch for a warning. "Captain, I'm out of time, but I wanted to ease you. You looked weighed down on the television, and… I'm sorry about Petrishchev."

"Lei, you're safe. That's all that matters. Now get yourself home soon. Love you, Lei."

"Love you too, Captain. Bye." Leila pressed end quickly. She chose the right one to call—the captain understood her urgency and didn't stop her through curiosity. His genuine concern deflated the Phoenix's claim that he didn't care about her. She released a breath of relief, then turned to Dragunov.

He nodded. "Still had time to spare."

She returned the phone. "Thank you so much for this. I feel better knowing he's not completely in the dark."

"The training seems to be helping, but it would be better if you could call someone."

"So, you're not as emotionless as you say—you thought about me."

The Russian smirked. "Only because you're bringing it out."

She shared the smile. "Then it's a good thing I'm here. Now that a message has been sent, you can rest now."

"Perhaps you can too." He bowed his head in farewell, then began to leave, but her calling his name turned him back.

"I didn't mean what I said before we left for the warehouse. I let my anger control me. I don't think so cowardly to… kill myself." Her confession brought heat up her neck.

The twitch of Dragunov's lips cooled her. "I didn't think so, but I'm glad you admitted it out loud. You're too strong to think that." Tenderness reappeared in his eyes, and it was his turn to look away first. "Goodnight, Leila."

He left, almost reluctantly. Relief had replaced the simmering Phoenix, but his acknowledgment of the strength he somehow saw brought warmth—a smile lingered on her lips.

"Goodnight, Dragunov."

# XXIII.

The rest of the week turned out better because of the effect seen in the captain. He continued to give interviews when reporters kept fishing for news, but his eyes held more light, his back was straighter, and he exuded confidence, knowing of Leila's well-being.

Less stress meant restful nights for Leila, and in turn, it forced the touchy Phoenix to withdraw. So, she increased the intensity of her workouts. She maintained her compromise by giving her dark side reign to attack the dummies but pulled it back to cool down through practicing her stances.

After finishing her workout for the day, Leila rested against the wall, holding onto the serenity she gained from emptying her mind through the Five-Animals Kung Fu. This balancing of her and the Phoenix must've been what Hyun had wanted.

"Leila."

Opening her eyes, she looked over to Dragunov in the open doorway. His black eyebrow was raised, questioning her state.

"I'm fine, just being still for a change. What do you need?"

"Your name has been cleared; the government will no longer be looking for you."

He left it hanging.

"...But I'm not safe to go."

His arms folded. "No; the Chechen don't abide by the rules. You must stay hidden until I discover their motive and who is behind them."

Dragunov's eyes steeled. "So, I ask again: Is there anyone who would be out to get you?"

She took a moment to 'fess up. "Yes, I believe there is." Her eyes pierced him. "You knew I had lied. Why didn't you call me out on it?"

"It was not my place to do so."

Once again, she couldn't take the soft change in his eyes for long. She looked back ahead with a quiet, "Thank you."

"Who is it?"

"Actually two; I think they work together." She had been pondering that for a while; the Phoenix agreed with her conclusion though unhappy she shared it with the Spetsnaz leader. Saying their names required a steadying breath—Leila wasn't sure why. "Bryan Foster and Amadeus Xander."

"The tournament host? Why him?"

"Instinct said something wasn't right with him. My feelings have unfortunately been proven right time and time again."

"And this Bryan Foster?"

The Phoenix rose at the mention of his name. "I've been after him for some time, and in spite, he seems to have a vendetta against me."

Dragunov didn't reply. He seemed to be sizing her up, but she refused to give in to the pressure of his eyes by looking at him. "I will watch for their names."

Leila waited for him to say more until she looked over and found the doorway empty—he left without delving into why she closed off indiscreetly on the topic of Foster.

THE NEXT DAY, THE DRAGON emerged from his Den since the others still visited their loved ones. Leila sat in the living room, watching whatever news she flipped on when she sensed him enter the room.

"May I join you?" Dragunov asked.

"This isn't my house." She looked at him behind the sofa. "You can do whatever you please."

His lips twitched before walking around the couch and sitting at the opposite end. "It is politer to ask."

The news broadcasting a large insurance fraud in St. Petersburg brought her attention back to the television.

"Anything new?" he asked after the story concluded.

She sighed. "No. I don't know whether to be relieved or worried that nothing is happening. Things don't stay this quiet; something will blow up."

"Sometimes it is best to be in the middle—to be neutral. Nothing can unsettle you."

Leila thought about it. "But once you grow accustomed, it's hard to get out, and that brings a new struggle: whether I want to or not."

She felt him looking at her. "Is it better outside where the world hurts you or inside where you hurt yourself?"

Silence overtook them. Leila couldn't say for not having an answer. Giving up, she looked over at him and recognized the conflict in his eyes she often saw in the mirror. For his need and hers, she came up with one. "Neither is better, but I don't know which is worse."

Dragunov kept her gaze until he blinked away, releasing a small breath—one of relief that she thought the same or of disappointment, she couldn't tell.

With him looking away, Leila seized her opportunity to admire him—memorizing the hard and strong angles of his face going down his neck and surely mirrored throughout the rest of his body, matching his firm nature. Close enough now, she distinguished scars, blended in from time, marking past struggles and victories. But when looking at her, his imposing aura softened; his eyes weren't as piercing and stabbing, either.

He suddenly turned back to her, set on ending the silence. "How did you go from a detective to winning a fighting tournament?"

She gave him a small smile to show that she was willing to talk, but she averted her gaze so he couldn't see what started it all: David's death. "I taught myself Five-Animals Kung Fu to keep up with a friend learning Taekwondo. We sparred together to prepare him for competitions, and I used my technique to better combat criminals in my career."

Leila broke off, thinking about David's death and Foster causing it, but she recovered to end her backstory. "Fast-forward to helping Jamaal win a street fight, and the following victories got us an invitation to the tournament."

"Is that not illegal in America?"

She grimaced. "It is, but I made an exception that night."

Once again, he didn't probe into her hesitation. "And it just went from there."

She looked at him. "What about you? Alek told me you are the only true fighter out of them. From what he said, you're capable of winning the tournament."

His lips twitched, but he shook his head. "I have nothing to fight for, so I would not win."

"You must have a reason to win?"

"Practice and strength do not grant you the champion, a great heart does. You fought to find yourself; others fought for glory."

Leila looked away, not wanting to see what he knew about her fights in his eyes. But Dragunov speaking—like he hadn't diverted the conversation—brought her back.

"Being raised in the military, and eventually the Spetsnaz, I grew up trained in the Commando Sambo. It is hard to find an equally matched opponent."

"As I have heard." She curled both legs beneath her as she turned to face him. "How did you become known as 'Dragon'? Is it because of your name?"

Dragunov shifted as well to face her. "I'm sure that is part of it, but the imaginings of that mythological creature also give an immediate impression of what I'm known for."

An arm draped along the back of the couch. "I did not have a name when given to the Spetsnaz, and they named me after my preferred weapon: the Dragunov Sniper Rifle."

"When you mentioned that you and the others were Spetsnaz, I was worried," Leila confessed. "I expected you all to be hard, unapproachable, and solely violence-focused, but I'm relieved to be wrong."

As she spoke, the corners of his mouth lifted. "Shocked?"

She chuckled. "A bit. I didn't expect you to be so—"

"Human?"

Leila ducked her head. "Yes. I shouldn't have assumed that; similar stereotypes are put on cops."

"You are not the only one; most think the same. In most cases, that train of thought is true. But we are" —he smiled— "different circumstances."

"Are you trained to be that way?"

Dragunov nodded. "Staying detached makes our job easier. Being a Spetsnaz, you rely on yourself; I know I won't be able to save myself someday, but pride prevents me from asking for help. I am strong, I can adapt, and I am a leader. My team looks to me, along with those that know of me, so I cannot become arrogant, or we would not be as successful."

Being hard, serious, and—if provoked—dangerous, gave Dragunov an eminence to be feared. Being with him now for three weeks had Leila seeing why Dragon was the exact description: he prefers isolation, is usually silent—the polar opposite of

Alek—invokes curiosity in his mystery and is unnervingly cunning and calculating. He's the Dragon of Russia.

Listing off his attributes brought the image of his dark side to mind. The Dragon represented his dark side just as the Phoenix emerged as hers.

"I see we're finally bonding," a voice said, causing Leila to jump, not hearing or sensing anyone coming in. She casually turned like she hadn't been caught to find Alek in the doorway. When their eyes met, his crinkled in pleasure—he had seen.

"Because you weren't here to annoy us," Dragunov retaliated. Even though he meant it in a playful manner, his voice had a snap to it like Alek's intrusion vexed him.

The blond Russian's eyes narrowed. "I wanted to make sure Lei hadn't killed you for refusing her phone privileges."

Leila's cheeks reddened, but Dragunov laughed. She turned to him in astonishment. He had never so much as chuckled, but his face lighting up with merriment and the sound of his laughter… It wasn't musical but a deep, hearty, genuine laugh—one that vibrates the body. Already an attractive man, the Russian laughing in liveliness hypnotized her.

A smile crept across her face. Internal warmth lasted a second before the Phoenix burst back in, hardening everything in disapproval. Dragunov's sudden shift in composure didn't affect her anymore.

"You don't have to worry about my safety, Alek; I'm capable of taking care of myself," Dragunov answered with bliss in his voice.

Leila looked back at Alek, finding him stunned from Dragunov's laugh. *He must never show emotion.*

Alek chuckled himself as he sat down on a couch. "I'm not so sure. Have you seen this girl fight? I know we tried to get you to watch the tournament, but I don't know if you ever did."

"I saw one fight." He looked at Leila. That playfulness twinkling in his dark eyes vanished at recognizing the emotional change in her. "I think you would be a good challenge."

The Phoenix would stake its claim. "You're confident you can beat me?"

"I've seen your moves; you've never seen mine." Finalization hardened his statement like concrete. She wasn't letting him win.

"You've seen only one fight; that's just one set of moves. I have plenty more, and some no one has seen. And I recall opponents fighting in Sambo, so I have experience with your technique."

"Alek mentioned them to me. 'In comparison, they're amateurs.' His words, not mine."

She looked at Alek to find him nodding in agreement.

"Those Germans weren't much of a problem. If you're as great as you say, then I'll relish in a fight." The Phoenix tried to pin the Spetsnaz leader down with its certainty of Leila's skills—facing down another dark side thrilled it.

Dragunov matched her stare. The longer they stared, the higher the heat of them mentally challenging the other rose. Their standoff enticed the Dragon to come out.

Tension thickened the atmosphere; Alek quickly jumped in before another explosion, "Sounds like we need to have a contest…"

The Dragon toned down in his eyes at Alek's voice. "Maybe so."

Angry its challenge wasn't picked up, the Phoenix turned on Alek. "Suggesting this again?"

"This is the first I have heard of it." Dragunov also turned on him.

Alek gaped from one to the other. "I couldn't arrange it if neither of you wanted to participate. You had to drum up interest, and now that you have, the fight's definitely happening.

"But you can't start without me," Alek demanded. "I've got to be the judge to make sure you play fair."

"Don't trust us?" Leila asked.

Alek stammered, "Well… not you, but… we can't have either of you getting really hurt so I can… you know, tell you to pull back if you get too into the fight or violent."

She understood his discomfort: he was concerned about their dark sides emerging and what kind of annihilation would happen because of it. The realization had Leila seizing control over the Phoenix as if in apology.

Dragunov did too. "That may be best, but you might need help, Alek."

"Oh, everyone will be there to watch! There's no chance anybody would miss an excellent fight between you two."

To keep the Phoenix from emerging and its excitability down about the upcoming fight, Leila averted the conversation. "How's Svetlana fairing?"

She caught him smiling as Alek hung his head in dramatic fashion. "Terrible! I swear she's going to rip off my head! Those hormones are killing me!"

A phone started ringing from the command room, and Dragunov stood. "Wait until she's in labor. Excuse me." His eyes landed on hers for a moment, then he blinked away as he walked past, and the door shut behind her couch.

Alek leaned forward but kept glancing at the shut door. "What are you doing? He's never laughed before, and forget about cracking a smile," he whispered, afraid Dragunov might hear.

Leila thought about it. He had changed toward her in the past few days. Her figuring drifted to the Phoenix slipping out and drawing the Dragon out in him. "I don't think it's anything intentional."

Alek's thoughts joined hers. "I think you surprised him when you braved a visit to his Den—I know you shocked us. We don't dare go in there when he's working. Standing toe to toe with him in a yelling match also has to be a factor. You two were terrifying, by the way."

"I got what I needed."

His eyes widened. "You did? You called your captain?"

"He found a loophole in the tracing lines."

Alek sat back with a knowing smile—seeing something she didn't. "He went into overdrive because he saw how desperate you were. But that could never work for any of us. We're not brave enough to take him on. We've been with the man for so long, but we're still afraid of him. You have more guts than any-one."

Leila thought she heard Dragunov chuckling at Alek's comment.

# XXIV.

After a full week, the rest of the men returned. Leila's dread at being isolated with Dragunov had made a pleasant turn, but now with the guys back, she worried the Dragon would shut himself off again in the command room. Instead, their presence seemed to increase his need to visit with them all. The change intrigued them, but they welcomed the modification.

Even with the house full again, she didn't alter her routine: training in the workout room to appease the Phoenix, then watching the news for updates. Seeing improvement in her loved ones back home increased her good mood. They perked up like flowers given much-needed water—the captain had hinted that he spoke to her.

Leila flipped the news off and headed up to her room to grab a cardigan—September brought winter's chill down from Siberia. The green Russian wilderness gradually turned white with light snow.

A shout sounded from the first floor; she turned at the pounding of feet as someone rushed up the stairs.

"I'm going to kill him!" Yakov yelled as Alek made the landing and turned toward Leila's room. The grin on his lips hinted at his newest mischievous endeavor; Yurii was hot on his heels.

Putting on a burst of speed, he avoided Yurii's grab and ran into her room. "Pardon us, Lei!" Alek raced toward her balcony, followed closely by an enraged Chubais twin. She fell back onto the bed as they breezed past her.

He slid into the glass door and fumbled to throw it open when Yurii slammed into him. Laughing, Alek fought against the bigger Russian and somehow shoved him off.

Yurii stumbling backward gave Alek time to rip open the door. The blond Russian ran onto the balcony and launched over the railing. Leila yelled when Yurii recovered, ran onto the balcony, and jumped off in the same fashion. She rushed out as his head disappeared.

Two-stories down, the Russians wrestled each other in the snowy leaves, a mixture of Alek's laughter and Yurii's curses.

Yakov suddenly appeared beside her on the balcony, growled in frustration, then ran back to the stairs. Leila saw why he wanted to kill Alek and couldn't help but laugh at his running back: a black nose and whiskers had been drawn on his face with a permanent marker. She looked back down. Alek pushed Yurii off him again and sprinted to the woods. Similar markings on Yurii's face—only more jagged from waking during the crime—meant both had fallen to the same prank.

Yurii took up the chase after the laughing Russian; Yakov soon appeared and followed his twin.

"Quite a show Alek puts on, doesn't he?" Silvestrov spoke next to her and leaned against the railing, watching the disappearing pursuit.

"Why didn't Yakov jump? He would've reached them sooner."

"Yakov's scared of heights."

It sounded absurd that a fierce Spetsnaz would fear anything. A victorious roar echoed out of the forest—they laughed at poor Alek's exodus ending.

AS SHE HEADED DOWN THE stairs to grab something to drink and one of the brownies Silvestrov had made, voices reached her coming from the dining room behind the wall. Metal clicked and clacked, the smell of gun oil mixed with the chocolate aroma from the kitchen, and something sharp scraped against a stone—she guessed it was Yurii sharpening his knives. The men talked as they cleaned weapons.

Leila hesitated on the stairs, tempted to stay hidden and eavesdrop. Perhaps they would discuss some secret, maybe mention her, or what they *honestly* thought about her staying with them… But being Spetsnaz, she doubted it because they probably already knew she was nearby.

They weren't startled by her appearance when she came into view; all met her with smiles, except for Ruben who never looked up from cleaning his sniper rifle. Various guns lay on the table—some currently in parts so the Spetsnaz could clean hard-to-reach places; others whole—with charcoal-colored cloths under them to protect the tabletop from gun oil. Like she figured, Yurii ran one of his wicked knives against a whetstone.

"Lei! Take a seat!" Alek said.

She did, looking down to hide the smile tugging at her lips in seeing shadows of the cat whiskers Alek drew on the twins' faces. They had rubbed hard to get rid of the markings—based on the red, raw skin on their cheeks—but time and more washing were required to erase the remains completely.

"What are you smiling about?" Alek asked, humor pulling up his lips and sparkling in his eyes. He knew.

"Nothing," she said.

Yakov grunted, and Yurii scraped his knife extra hard, making a loud sound. Silvestrov's lips twisted as he also fought a grin. Ruben had no reaction—seeming to ignore them, but she knew he listened. Alek must've been poking them even before she arrived.

"You know, Lei, I've been wanting to get some pets here," he began. "Cats are the way to go, with their cute noses and whiskers…"

The twin Russians cleaned their weapons with angrier and angrier attacks. Their strong jaws had become tenser, and their eyes flashed.

Alek turned to her. "Don't you think so?"

Leila shrugged. "Sure, I guess."

A loud clang sounded from Leila's left. She looked to see that Yakov had racked the bolt on his AK-47 hard while glaring at Alek.

"Oh! Twins! That would be perfect!" He looked at the twins. "We could name them after you and give each twin the other's name to take care of. What do you think?"

Quicker than what seemed humanly possible, Yurii flung the knife he was sharpening at Alek—it missed his jaw by a hair's width and stuck in the wall with a hardy, resounding thud.

Alek never blinked, just smiled.

"Svetlana won't like finding a cat scratch on my face."

"She won't complain if there's no head to see it on," Yurii quipped. "Keep on, *ублюдок*."

"I bet she wouldn't hate us for long if we killed you," Yakov said. "Knowing you probably pulled some prank to deserve it."

Silvestrov put a hand on Alek's shoulder. "Let's you and I leave before you die."

The blond Russian frowned at him. "But Lei—"

"—Can survive without you," he finished, then pulled up his comrade. "Come on. Sorry to leave you, Leila."

Alek's protests grew fainter as he and Silvestrov headed up to his room. When they left, Yurii pulled out another knife and set to work on it.

Not seconds after the duo left, Ruben finished cleaning his weapon, gathered his cleaning supplies, and left without a word. Leila never got the impression that he disliked her, only that he didn't like to chitchat.

Silence fell on the three that remained.

"Leila," Yurii began timidly. "Can I… ask you a question?"

His hesitant way of beginning had her nervous and worried.

She swallowed. "Go ahead."

The Chubais twin kept his focus down on the knife in his hand, the blade going back and forth. He flipped it periodically to sharpen both sides. It took a while for him to find his voice. "What *is* the Phoenix? I know the Dragon is Dragon's dark side—it comes out when he's stressed, irritated, or furious… but that's it." His eyes finally lifted to meet hers. "Is it the same for you?"

Her dark side stirred at being called out. Seeing an opportunity to stake her ground, it took over and eyed the Russian with a challenge.

"Why do you want to know? Too afraid of the Dragon to ask him? You think I'm softer? Gentler?" The Phoenix scoffed.

He shook his head. "Not at all. I haven't seen much of you, Phoenix, but from *what* I've seen, you're just as terrifying. I feel that I can approach you better."

Leila blinked. Even with the Phoenix offended and lashing out, Yurii wasn't intimidated. Her dark side wouldn't be able to bully these Spetsnaz like everyone else. The Phoenix receded in disappointment and seemed to pout.

The corner of her lips twitched with a small smile—she enjoyed her dark side being powerless for once.

"But, yes, Yurii," she said. "It's pretty much the same."

"So, both of your dark sides are defense mechanisms?" Yakov asked.

*I'm* more *than just something that protects you,* the Phoenix said. *I give you power, strength, and focus.*

*Yes, but…*

Leila finished out loud. "At first, it was. It appeared when I needed extra power or protection. Now?" She trailed off, looking at her upturned hands.

"It's always present," Yurii added in for her.

She closed her hands into fists. "Until I get my revenge. That's what it's here for."

The Chubais twins shared a glance but didn't comment, returning their attention back to cleaning the weapons in their hands.

# XXV.

The body opponent bag fell back and bounced back up as, through the Tiger, Leila slashed with her hands curled like claws. This pattern of working out in the mornings helped, but she could feel the Phoenix biding its time, waiting in the shadows, and storing energy to explode once more. Now with the recognition of the Dragon, nothing could stop the inevitable. There was no way their two dark sides wouldn't clash again.

Surprisingly, though, her explosions hadn't disrupted the flow of the Spetsnaz's lives. Leila had been accepted easily, and she grew comfortable around the men. In an odd way, both she and the Phoenix slotted into the Spetsnaz like the hole was meant for them. Leila was inclined to think she belonged…

*Stop,* the Phoenix's order threw off her punch. Her fist barely skimmed the bag.

*Stop what?*

*This foolish hope that we fit.*

*I don't think it's hope; it's a possibility.*

*You know how to see through things. The heart has fooled you before.* The Phoenix conjured up the belief of feelings with David and Miguel.

In denial, Dragunov's laugh rumbled within her, warming her heart and bringing a smile to her lips. She had replayed that moment so many times it was stored in her soul. Neither David nor Miguel had ever made her feel grounded like Dragunov; he touched her in a different way.

The Phoenix scoffed. *You can't possibly believe that! Love-sick teenagers tell themselves that. You aren't naïve! The Dragon feels threatened by me, so it is softening you, then will break you. You must remain on guard. I won't hurt you; he will.*

Doubt that Dragunov didn't care for her chipped away at the lightness in her spirits since that day. Could he be that cruel—build up her feelings only to crush them? Being a heartless, cunning Spetsnaz leader wasn't such a farfetched thought. As a last rallying effort, the memory of Dragunov laughing appeared.

*That wasn't real.*

Her heart hit the floor.

*Quit acting like there is something to mourn. Straighten up!*

She shut out the Phoenix's attempts at digging further and let her feet take her out, not noticing things of the house or if anyone called her. Exiting onto the patio, she leaned against a supporting beam. The cold reflecting from the snow didn't affect her; she was already numb from her realization.

A soft twang from a guitar brought her out of her thoughts—Ruben sat to the far right, seated on a patio chair and strumming an acoustic guitar. A small table beside him held a pen and various papers which he persistently checked. The gentle tune halted as he made adjustments to his sheet music.

"Should I go?" she asked, ashamed of intruding on him.

"Not unless I distract you." He picked up where he left off, nodding in approval of the change.

She hesitated to leave, enjoying Ruben's music and needing to be out—not enclosed by walls. Her presence failed to bother him for he continued to play, stopping to make readjustments and then testing them, lost in his own world.

Finally catching him playing his guitar made Leila stay. She seated in one of the patio chairs near him, entranced by his fingers plucking at the strings. Her eyes drifted with the music to the serene Russian wilderness. Those troubling thoughts that brought her outside dissipated like Ruben's song as it echoed through the trees, gradually growing unintelligible.

"Ruben, can I ask you a question?"

The tune never faltered. "I am here."

"Have I become a monster?"

"Only if you hold that image of yourself. You have not been monstrous here. Remember, we live with the Dragon. Your monster is no different than his."

She looked at him. "But my dark side—the Phoenix—is monstrous. Since it is part of me, does it make me the same?"

The tune slowed as he thought. He finally looked up when he found an answer. "Perhaps *it* is a monster, but you decide how much *it* is truly a part of *you*."

Ruben resumed playing as Leila thought about his words. "What about Dragunov?"

His mouth opened to reply, then stopped, thinking of something else. "Do you see him as a monster?"

The second-in-command wasn't looking at her so he couldn't see her blush. "No." Hopefully, he didn't catch the quickness of her answer either.

"That is because he found a compromise. It took some time."

Sighing, Leila turned away. Hyun wouldn't boast that he had told-her-so, but he did. She looked back at him. "Do you know what he did?"

"Not entirely, but I know he did not give in; he fought back. And I'm sure he still fights every day."

"Why do you think that?"

"Something is missing in him; ever since I've known him. He's not balanced yet—his scale lacks weight on one side."

"You don't know what it is?"

Ruben chuckled. "He's as open with his personal life as you are." He considered her a moment. "You should ask him."

Leila scoffed. "Asking him to open up would force me to do the same. I don't think so. Besides, confronting him again... may bruise our hands. Why can't you do it?"

"As you implied, you may come to blows. You can go toe to toe with him; I can't."

She turned from his knowing eyes. He knew she could—the Phoenix would enjoy that challenge. "What makes you think he'd open up to me anyway?"

He didn't answer right away; the music had even stopped. Leila looked at him, meeting his dark eyes blocking his thoughts.

Ruben turned back to his guitar. "Because you would understand."

He didn't say any more. From his answer, he knew Dragunov had experienced some life-altering event, and since Ruben saw the tournament, he knew she could relate from going through David's death.

Nevertheless, it came down to what she feared: to know more about him, she had to let him know about her—all of her. That was not happening. She wasn't that comfortable around him.

Maybe that was the Phoenix trying to further distance her from Dragunov...

# XXVI.

A dim green lit the cold, clammy, and dark concrete hallway. It wasn't so dark where Leila couldn't see the walls, but it was black enough that she couldn't see the end. Like looking at a funhouse mirror, the hallway behind her curved away into darkness. The vertigo effect gave Leila an uneasy feeling in the pit of her stomach.

Staying still in the middle of the hallway made her nervous—she needed to move. Leila glanced between one way and the other. Which way?

Sensing something, she looked back ahead—a form stood in the darkness. She strained to make out the image of a man. Nothing else was visible.

Curious, Leila walked closer, hoping to discern who he was. He didn't move, shift weight, or seem to breathe. Ice crept up her neck at the recognition of his stance.

Leila stopped. "It can't be."

For the first time, she didn't feel rage toward him but shuddering fear. She backtracked, unable to take her eyes off him.

"How could you know where I was?"

A shadow moved beside her, heading toward the faceless man at the end. This black figure remained indiscernible, but brought a menacing, angry aura like the other was trespassing on his territory. His arrival warmed every inch of her, ceasing the trembling.

Another shadow caught her eye to the left. It was much slimmer and reminded her of—

She froze. "No."

At the sound of her voice, it turned as if in recognition. His eyes landed on her, soft and gentle.

"Please, not again. Get away!"

The form continued to look at her, and she couldn't move. The darkness lightening on his body began to uncover a face, but he still hid behind a black veil. It wasn't instantly identifiable—like a confusing blend of faces she knew. But the smile meant to reassure her that everything was alright.

"Run!"

His head snapped back from an invisible force. The body fell limply to the ground, a hole between his eyes.

"DAVID!" she screamed as she jerked up in bed. Her scream pulled her out of the nightmare, but not soon enough.

Leila trembled from the inside like her blood was now ice-water. Her hands had frozen. She wanted to cry, to scream, to wail, but she covered her face to keep it in—she couldn't silence her whimpers from holding in her emotions though.

*I'm here, I'm here,* the Phoenix said. *Let me—*

Her door flew open, interrupting her dark side; she jumped at the suddenness to find a worried Dragunov on the verge of running in. "Leila, are you alright?" His eyes took in a quick search of the room.

The Phoenix growled, irritated by his intrusion.

She ducked her head in embarrassment and to avoid the concern in his eyes. "I'm sorry; it was… just a dream. I didn't-didn't mean to wake you." Her wavering and frail voice betrayed how bad the nightmare had shaken her.

"I was already up."

The silence built between them.

"I was about to brew tea," he said suddenly. "Would you care for some?"

Leila looked at him; his eyes weren't pitying, and his face wasn't expectant. She felt that he hadn't been in the middle of that process but offered to be polite. "Sure."

Dragunov nodded and left without another glance.

Most would linger and probe, but the undertone in her voice indicated that she wanted time alone. Or he understood her need for isolation.

Probably both, but she was glad either way. Leila got out of bed and headed for the bathroom. Since she was up, she took care of her needs, then rubbed water on her face to knock off the nightmare's lingering chill. She also brushed her hair to tame the bed hair.

Even with the bad dream, she appreciated the timing, being the second day into the squad's routine break every three weeks. If they were there, Alek would've expected her to talk about it, and Silvestrov would insist on checking her vitals or something. At least she had only disturbed the Spetsnaz leader.

*Like that's any better,* the Phoenix mumbled.

Looking better, Leila headed down to join Dragunov. She found him in the kitchen, standing at the stove with his back to her. At her approach, he looked at her and nodded in greeting.

Seeing him in a plain white T-shirt and dark-red plaid lounging pants—not in his sharp commanding attire—was odd. It made the Spetsnaz leader more normal.

"I'm sorry about waking you up," she said.

"You don't need to apologize; I was already awake."

"I feel like I should though." She took a seat at the island separating them. "I haven't had a nightmare in months."

He turned the stove off and removed the kettle. "Was it a recurring dream?"

The Phoenix stared at his back as he poured their mugs. It tried to raise her defenses. *He's trying to probe.*

Leila felt okay to answer. "It had the same theme, but no, it wasn't the same." Her ease of ignoring it and opening to the Russian stunned the Phoenix.

Dragunov handed her a mug. "What was different?"

She wrapped her hands around the warm cup—it was peppermint tea, proven to relax. The minty smell eased her tension. "The setting, and I couldn't see everyone's faces. They just reminded me of people." She took a sip to avoid describing everything, especially since she thought of him when she felt safe.

Neither would she mention it felt more like a vision, so she changed the topic. "Why were you up?"

"Couldn't sleep." His quick answer hinted at more.

"Is something bothering you?"

Dragunov looked at her over his mug as he took a drink. "Possibly."

"You can tell me."

She could see the decision working over in his head whether to tell her. "The Chechen are gathering again."

Not what she wanted to hear. "Is it me?"

"You haven't been mentioned. Nothing has happened yet, but I don't know what they're planning."

"What are you going to do?"

He looked at her for a long time, his soul-searching eyes doing their thing. "I'm meeting a friend to discuss details the day after tomorrow. He is closer to the Chechen than I. Would you care to come?"

His offer almost made her choke on her tea. She fought to keep surprise from playing on her face. His expression revealed nothing—not like she expected it to—but he waited patiently for her answer.

"Umm, sure. Where are we going?"

If he was pleased with her answer, only his eyes showed any response—a slight light brightened them. "Noyavinsk; a day and a half's drive from here. It will be cold, so I'll ask if Svetlana can spare some clothes. She was about your size before her pregnancy."

DRAGUNOV CALLED ALEK IN THE morning. He joyfully arrived wearing a grin stretching from ear to ear. Leila changed into some of Svetlana's warmer clothes he brought, packed the rest of the loaned wares in her duffel bag, and Leila and the Spetsnaz leader left for Noyavinsk before the sun had even awoken.

Throughout the long drive, Leila considered Ruben's suggestion of asking Dragunov to talk about himself, but talking about personal matters wasn't a long-distance-driving discussion. Besides, they had avoided awkward silences with leisurely conversation—no point in ruining the peaceful atmosphere.

Two hours into their drive, the landscape changed in an instant. Dense forests remained the only sights, but the warmth of the weak winter sun vanished behind bleak clouds. Snow wiped away any color, and the temperature inside the SUV dropped, unable to resist the cold outside.

Leila rubbed her hands together. "Are we going to the North Pole?"

He adjusted the heat. "Not quite. It'll get much colder than this."

She held her hands to the vents. "I thought New York winters could be bad."

"This isn't winter yet."

She looked at him in disbelief. "So, this is still fall?"

He nodded.

"I'm going to turn into a popsicle."

Dragunov chuckled. "I'll keep an eye on you. You're not used to this weather; I have to remember that." He looked at her. "Put on that *ushanka*—it's warmer than you think."

Leila did as he suggested, retrieving Svetlana's black fur hat, and grabbing the gloves in a side pocket of her coat. Putting the Russian hat on made a world's difference, and combined with the gloves, she started to sweat. Dragunov regulated the temperature to where they were comfortable again.

They only made stops at gas stations to refill the SUV, for restroom breaks, and to grab food or coffee, then they were back on the road. Leila thought about their quick departures—Dragunov said she wouldn't be recognized under the *ushanka,* but he wasn't taking chances.

With the coming of night, the temperature outside the vehicle dropped for the third time. Leila had wrapped Svetlana's coat around her, and the gloves and *ushanka* kept her warm, so Dragunov didn't have to adjust the heat again. Since their steady conversation had diminished, the quiet combined with the SUV's gentle movement and the cozy cabin eased her into closing her eyes.

# XXVII.

Gray skies brightening from a warm rising sun stirred Leila awake. Sleeping against the car seat left a crick in her neck, and she rubbed feeling back into it as she looked at Dragunov.

"Morning," he said when he looked at her, then turned his attention back to the road.

"Morning. Did you stop last night to rest?"

"I'll sleep tonight in Noyavinsk."

"You shouldn't have let me sleep all night; I could've given you a break from driving."

"I'm fine. You needed it; you didn't sleep well the night before."

She looked out at the landscape moving past. No snow fell—at the moment—but white still dominated the view, and the trees weren't as dense.

"How far until we reach Noyavinsk?" she asked.

"We'll get there about 2; it's 9:30 now."

If not for his urgency to get there by driving all night, it would be a day and a half's journey—instead, it would be less than a day's.

They stopped at a gas station for their usual routine, and like Dragunov had said, they arrived at their destination a minute before 2. Noyavinsk wasn't large and busy like St. Petersburg but quaint and calm. Dragunov drove into the heart of the town and parked close to a marketplace. Few vendors managed stalls in the square while others were in the warmth of their stores. Some locals accounted for the attendance, but tourists made up the majority.

"Is there a festival or something?" she asked.

He didn't bother looking. "No, this is a small tourist attraction."

Leila opened her mouth to ask what for, but he had stepped out of the SUV. She hoped Dragunov would allow her to look at the vendors' wares after they met his contact—not that she had money—as she followed suit.

They met up in front of the vehicle. Dragunov laid out the plan. "We will wander the stalls, and Makari will find us. We'll gauge whether it is too crowded or not and if we need to move off to discuss." He looked at her. "I hope you don't mind that we use you as cover."

She smiled. "I was actually hoping you would let me look around. I am a woman."

He shared her smile, then gestured toward the marketplace. They walked in and mingled with the gatherings effortlessly. With the gas station stops, Leila had practice remaining unidentifiable by limiting eye contact, keeping her scarf and coat close to her, and wearing her *ushanka* low.

Dragunov stayed beside her as they visited the stalls, and when she asked merchants to explain the Russian trinket they sold, he would lean in to translate if she needed it. He appeared at ease with their aimless wanderings as Leila admired the merchandise, not once peering around for his friend.

The town enchanted her. Warm-colored fabric displayed in store windows shimmered in the sunlight; a vendor advertised charming homemade wooden carvings; another store captivated her with jeweled rings and sparkling silver jewelry. The timeless age that seemed to encompass the small town made Leila fall in love with Noyavinsk.

Leila tried to ignore her numb nose—Makari wouldn't be able to spot them in an enclosed building. Objects at one stall made her forget about the cold; she headed over to admire the strategically arranged Russian dolls. Two themes separated the nesting dolls: one painted with bright colors on traditional black shells, and the other with flesh tones painted with a realism the other cartoonish faces lacked.

One in the collection of less traditional dolls caught her eye: it reminded her of her, so she picked it up. It was entirely handmade, from the paint to the wooden carvings of the little maid. Instead of red hair partially hidden under the *Sarafan*, the doll had long black hair. She had always paired the country with the toy but hadn't seen one yet.

"*Матрёшка*," Dragunov said beside her. "Most are toys, but some are said to tell a person who they really are. The further one goes removing the outer shells, the more one sees of themselves."

Leila froze at his words. He asked the vendor something, and he motioned at the toy in her hands.

"You have picked such one."

The little doll's face wasn't so charming now. But if it could reveal her… A hand rose to pull the top shell off to see what lay beneath, but two things interrupted her: the merchant grabbing her hand and speaking in Russian and someone saying Dragunov's name.

Dragunov snatched the merchant's arm in protectiveness. Leila recognized the tightening of his jaw, and the sudden fear in the vendor's eyes to know the Dragon glared at him. "Hang on, Makari."

"B-buy first, see l-la-later," the salesman stuttered in Russian.

Leila put a hand on Dragunov's and looked at him. The Dragon retreated from his eyes as he removed his hand. After placing the doll back down, she shook her head to show the merchant she wasn't buying. She turned away from his displeasure to see Dragunov's consultant.

Makari was the epitome of a homely dad. He stood about 5'6" with dull brown hair and plain features. Inactivity gave him a slight pudge around his middle. Nothing stood out on this average man, which was probably his best asset on remaining undercover. Being seen with the tall and imposing Spetsnaz leader would draw curiosity by itself; Leila wondered how these two obviously different men met.

He looked at her after Dragunov's introduction. Cunningness twinkled in his plain gray eyes. His appearance portrayed obliviousness, giving him the opening to slip in undetected to strike. This was no ordinary man to be overlooked if the enemy valued his life.

"It is a pleasure meeting you," Makari greeted as he held out his hand.

She took his hand and replied likewise.

He winked at her. "We'll run into a store to grab some coffee soon" —he said under his breath before turning to Dragunov and spoke normally— "but what are you doing up here?"

The two Russians launched into their native tongue, first upholding the ruse of reuniting friends if a passerby eavesdropped. Makari spoke about the Chechen's dealings without stating the name to prevent recognition. Leila also helped by further perusing the stalls like she meant to give the friends space. But she had an ear toward them to catch snippets of the Chechen happenings. Her Russian lessons with Alek were paying off, for she could now keep up with the rapid language.

Deciphering Makari's cagey way of hints, the Chechen were gathering to renew their reigns of terror. Their primary focuses weren't Moscow and St. Petersburg but towns and cities she wasn't familiar with. What prompted them to start again, even

Makari didn't know. Fortunately, Leila never heard her name as being back on the Chechen's radar.

It didn't take long for Makari to fill in what Dragunov's intel lacked. Nor did it take much persuasion for Leila to stop window shopping and go with the men into a small café for coffee to get warm.

MAKARI STAYED UNTIL DINNER, SINCERELY catching up on what Dragunov had been doing, but not delving into the topic of Leila's presence. He had to have been updated previously since he didn't ask questions involving her situation. When he left to return to his family, Dragunov also thought it time to go.

He drove them away from town. Noyavinsk's ample lights from the street market and main crossroads faded as they headed north.

"Okay, where are we going?" she asked.

Dragunov smiled but refused to answer. Since they had left the café, the Russian seemed to be in an uplifted mood. At some marker he watched for, he slowed the SUV to a stop.

He looked at her. "Close your eyes."

She blinked at him. "What?"

"Close your eyes—there's something I want you to see."

Because of the slight playfulness in the air, Leila shut her eyes to play along. She felt Dragunov looking at her, probably testing to see if she could see. The pressure of his gaze lifted, and the vehicle spurred back into motion.

With her eyes closed, it felt like they drove for hours. The car turned and moved onto less-smooth terrain—they had gotten off the main road. She had to admit, all the mystery from Dragunov tempted her to peek.

Eventually, the SUV came to a gentle halt. "I'll help you out," Dragunov said, then his door opened and shut.

As she waited for him to walk around, she felt for her seat buckle. She pushed it open when the passenger door opened. Cold air blasted in and took away her comfort from being in the toasty vehicle. But Svetlana's clothes did their job as Dragunov helped her out and into calf-deep snow.

Her hands wrapped around the Spetsnaz leader's arm to maintain balance, and she kept her eyes shut. She enjoyed the suspense as she teetered on the verge of peeking. Dragunov moved, and the car door shut behind her.

His free hand held onto hers clutching his arm. "I have you. I won't let you fall."

He escorted her through the snow to their unknown destination. Trudging through the thick snow was slow. After some high stepping to some spot, he stopped her.

"Open your eyes."

Leila opened them quickly, eager to see the prize. Above her, a glow brought her eyes up, and she gasped.

Slowly swimming green auroras with slight hazes of purple lit the dark sky. The lights gently writhed in the sky, hypnotizing her—she couldn't think of anything else. Even the Phoenix seemed nonexistent. She had never seen something so beautiful and serene. Completely entranced, she would have had no problem staying out in the cold all night to watch the amazing light show. It seemed like the world stopped to watch the show too.

Remembering Dragunov beside her—and still holding her arm—she pulled out of the trance. She couldn't look away from the lights though. "Thank you, Dragunov. This is… breathtaking."

Leila felt his gaze landing on her. "You never have to thank me for anything, Leila."

She ignored her gut warning that it wasn't a good idea and tore her eyes away from the northern lights to him. Her heart stopped beating. The auroras above cast an ethereal glow on the

Spetsnaz leader's face. The play of light and shadows gave him a sinister look—even a chill ran down her spine. But because she knew the sharp angles, scars, and hard planes of his face, the light softened his features.

They highlighted his dark eyes the most—those two depthless orbs not only reflected the light but captured the illumination, giving him strangely colored irises. Instead of being disturbed by the otherworldly look, Leila was brought closer because that blankness seemed to be wiped away with the coloring of his eyes. The tenderness she had felt before hummed through her.

Her heart resumed beating but at a faster rate. Goosebumps rose and shivered on her arms as she leaned in for a closer look. She could've sworn he leaned down…

The Phoenix found its footing again to come up between them, pulling Leila back. No surprise or resignation crossed Dragunov's face; he remained as stoic as ever.

*See? He doesn't care; neither should you.*

*I think he could if you would let him.*

Unhappy with her reply, the Phoenix forced her to look away from him, severing the magnetic eye contact. The auroras still gently swirled in the sky, unchanged, but they had lost their attraction now.

"I feel like I should thank you for this," she said to avoid awkwardness.

"You're welcome." His reply sounded clipped. "The hotel's back in town."

She understood the meaning behind his words even before the snow crunched under his weight as he headed back to the SUV. With a last look at the auroras above her, Leila turned and followed Dragunov's lead.

# XXVIII.

Dragunov planned to investigate Makari's leads when they returned, but he wasn't worth an ounce of work. From the trip to the hotel two days ago to the entire ride back home, there was practically no conversation between him and Leila. Not at all close to the carefree talking on the way up to Noyavinsk.

He rubbed his temple. It was that damned Phoenix—her dark side somehow slipped in just as Leila enjoyed a break. When he recognized that hollowness in her eyes, he had lost her. She was probably like that laid-back attitude before it ever showed up in her life.

*If that thing could've stayed back a little while longer…*

No; he couldn't do what-ifs. Nothing was meant to happen between them right then. It wasn't the right time. Something would happen when it meant to, for both of their sakes. To push either of them—or their dark sides—before they were ready… He shook his head at the thought of them exploding again and not being subdued.

But he couldn't be the only one to feel something between them. The men knew it. Everyone—other than Alek—had restrained from giving him knowing looks, probably in fear of his condescension. Ever since he brought her home, Alek hadn't been discreet in his encouragement of them. The trip to Noyavinsk didn't improve things either. He beamed at their return until he noticed their obvious distance from each other. The only respite was that he hadn't asked nonstop about the trip.

Leila had to have felt some possibility between them. She even looked to be accepting of it when they almost kissed—and God, did he want to kiss her! The light of the auroras gave her an indescribable beauty; he had trouble breathing. If he hadn't known any better, he would've thought she wasn't real. How else could a perfect woman be by his side, and with a dark side matching his? It couldn't be possible, but it was.

Dragunov released a heavy breath, trying and failing to get his mind off her and back on track.

He could only settle with one answer: she fought the idea of loving him. The chance of her not caring about him existed… But he didn't want to consider it. He had waited so long—

Hesitant knocks on his door pulled him out of his thoughts. "What is it?"

The door opened to a worried Alek. "Dragon, I think it's Lei. She went to the weight room, and I haven't heard anything in a while now. I don't want to go in there in case… you know… the Phoenix. I can't take her like you can."

It probably *was* the Phoenix keeping her in there. He could surely understand. The Dragon used to keep him locked away and isolated from the men so he could safely release it.

He thought about leaving her alone—she obviously wanted space—but he got up anyway. She may need help getting out from under the Phoenix beating down her soul. He understood that too.

All the men were present: Ruben sat at the piano, softly playing while Silvestrov read on one of the couches, and the twins talked at the dining table. Alek walked with him to the start of the hallway leading to the weight room, then stopped. He was genuinely worried; Dragunov went to the door, alone, and knocked. With no answer, he let himself in.

Alek's worry infected him when he didn't immediately see her. His eyes swept the room to land on the obstructed view of her legs. Something didn't feel right. He moved farther in to see past the weight rack and found Leila slumped against the wall, crying.

Recovering from his shock of seeing her crushed, he hurried to her side. "Leila, what's wrong?"

She didn't answer, seeming to not even know he knelt by her. Tears rolled down her face, but her eyes remained glazed, blankly staring ahead.

"Dr. Moretti says I imagine him," she whispered, so quiet he wouldn't have known she had spoken if he hadn't seen her lips move. "It's getting harder to feel him... Was he right? Has David ever been with me?"

"You know he is."

"Then why... why is he fading away?"

Dragunov hated that hope rose in his chest—perhaps he started to take David's place.

She hung her head. "I can't do this alone anymore. I'm so tired." Her voice broke at the end, and fresh tears streamed down her face.

"Leila, please don't cry." His hand reached out to touch her face; it hesitated before making contact.

His touch turned her head toward him. "I just want to give in..."

Her water-lined eyes shook as they focused. When she realized it was him, a fierce and angry firmness seized the blank glazing. He recognized it when the Dragon took over—the Phoenix.

Leila shot to her feet, glaring down at him. "Don't think you have a chance because I faltered. I will never let you in." She swept past him, leaving him to fight against his own dark side wanting to reprimand this uncontrollable Phoenix.

Any time he reached out to Leila, and she drew close, the Phoenix emerged to snatch her back. He tired of this tug of war with her too. Nothing he did helped.

It was time both dark sides *truly* met.

The Dragon marched after her.

She had almost reached the end of the hall, blazing past Alek without a word. Instead of standing in the middle, he hugged the wall—from living with the equally moody Dragon, he had recognized the Phoenix, so he gave her room to avoid being scorched.

"Stop right there, Phoenix!" the Dragon bellowed.

She stopped, back rigid at the heat of his order. Leila slowly turned, and the Phoenix looked at him with mild curiosity.

"Who are you to order me so boldly?"

"I'm the only one who can from being you. I've thought like you." He stopped at arm's length so neither could lash out at the other.

The Phoenix gave a dry, humorless chuckle. "You are not me. Not even close."

"No? How am I not?"

She surged up to him. "I am fire; you are ice. I burn with a vengeance that all feel and do not deny. I am the Phoenix; you are the aloof, cold Dragon of Russia. I have earned my title; you were given it."

"You're not the only one to burn with revenge. Have you ever tasted it?"

"I imagine it sweet; delicious."

"It is bitter ash. Achieving it solves nothing."

The Phoenix smirked. "You try to dissuade me. Tell me: do you regret it?"

He couldn't answer honestly, and with her growing smile, she knew it. "Dark sides like you revel in it. Leila would be destroyed."

It didn't break eye contact as she stepped back. He saw it in her eyes like she had spoken out loud: the Phoenix planned on it.

"I am set on what I will do, and I will do it alone." She turned to head up the stairs.

That thing eliminating Leila's aura worried him. He followed. "Don't you run away from me."

"I run from nothing."

"Then face me."

She whipped around. "What do you have to say that you can't say to my back?"

He stopped on the step below her, eyes now level with hers. "I am not going to watch that power spiral out of control and consume you. You are destroying yourself."

"What do you know!"

The Dragon awoke in a roar. "I've been you! You may have found strength rising from ashes, but not once you burn everything!"

"And how are you going to stop me? You said you weren't going to save me again!"

"But neither will I sit back and do nothing!"

Her eyes narrowed. "Why do you care?"

Dragunov paused, choosing his words carefully. Telling her how he felt—with the Phoenix dominating her—wouldn't be taken well. "I won't let you lose who you are, Leila. I won't let it."

"This *is* who I am."

"I don't believe it. I saw someone different in Noyavinsk. Someone in control of herself: Leila; not you, Phoenix."

Murder blazed over her features. The Phoenix tried to strike him, but he dodged, and when she tapped into her fighting skills, he deflected the kick, caught her arms, and pinned her to the wall. A leg held hers back so she couldn't kick him. Completely immobilized under his firm grip, her eyes burned holes into him.

It was the Dragon's turn to smirk. "You can't intimidate me; my demon is the same as yours."

She struggled under his hold. After the failed attempts, the Phoenix observed her predicament and came to some conclusion. "I've encroached on your territory, and you feel the need to defend it. Can't handle two demons, can you? You're threatened by my being here."

He got closer to her face so she wouldn't mistake the absolute affirmation in his eyes. "Not. At. All."

Her mouth popped open to fire back when she froze. In an instant, the Phoenix disappeared in her eyes, and her taut body collapsed. Dragunov caught her as her knees buckled.

"Leila?" The Dragon vanished just as quickly, and concern took over.

She didn't look up at him and kept her face turned down. "I'm sorry. Let me go… please."

Her complete shutdown worried him, but because Leila was back at the helm, he set her on her feet. *Only this once.* He made sure she remained steady before letting go.

Leila apologized again before hurrying up the stairs and shutting her door.

Dragunov stared at her door. He could feel the men watching behind him. That kind of shutdown only happened when another voice of reason appeared. Could it have been David? She said he was fading away, so she had been hearing him.

Shame stung him from the jealousy beginning to burn. At least someone could be with her right now.

*Next time, I'll be there.*

# XXIX.

Leila wanted to retreat and hide in her room. She couldn't face Dragunov after what the Phoenix pulled yesterday. Letting the Phoenix seize control like that shamed her.

As she had been working out, her thoughts drifted to the auroras and Dragunov until he alone remained. No David, no Foster, and no Phoenix; just Dragunov. It belittled her for considering the Russian, even for a second, then it grew relentless in its attacks—shaming her for throwing David's memory away, criticizing her for believing she could abandon her quest against Foster, and repeating Dr. Moretti's words that everything she held onto existed only in her head. That finally broke her and gave the Phoenix an opening. Then Dragunov appeared and enraged the Phoenix even more.

Leila fought for control, but the Phoenix's hold was too strong. She became a helpless onlooker to the dark sides' clash. David finally got a word in under the Phoenix's momentary falter, and Leila was back.

Fortunately, when she had gone down for breakfast—trying her hardest to avoid eye contact—the men pretended like nothing had happened. They included her in the conversations and jokes like usual. To the side, she started to apologize to Alek, but he stopped her, saying it wasn't any different than when the Dragon was new and touchy.

Dragunov never joined them for meals or just to visit. Leila thought it was because of her until she heard his phone constantly ringing—it would go quiet for a moment, then start again. Days dragged on with that phone being the only sound.

Ruben and the twins were deployed first, followed by Alek and Silvestrov. She watched the news for updates to find the Chechen had gotten on the ball. Terrorism drove the northeastern part of the country to run for their lives. No one could go anywhere to be safe.

Leila wanted the men back. She had grown attached to them, and there was a strong possibility they weren't coming back. These terrorist attacks were far more dangerous than the ones she had dealt with back in New York. Most targeted someone in power, but these were aimed at the common people. No pattern existed, magnifying the terrifying uncertainty of the attacks.

Now she stood at his closed door, searching for the courage not to run to her room and lock the door. She hoped that he wouldn't immediately send her away because of what the Phoenix had said and done, and then she entered the Dragon's Den.

He stood at the island, looking down at the touchscreen, then referred to the tablet in his hand. The television, set on some news channel, reported the newest attack. He didn't look up at her entrance—either not aware she had come in or ignoring her.

Before she could speak, an update about an attack near Moscow on the television distracted her. She looked back at him when the report finished and took a breath. "Dragunov, is there anything I can do to help?"

He remained studying the touchscreen for a long time before looking at her. She jolted with guilt at the strain in his eyes. He hadn't slept in a while, and she hoped it didn't include her episode. But a fierce determination hid the tension. In that one look, she knew why he never showed emotion: he had to remain the solidarity others could depend on when the world crumbled.

She also saw in his eyes that he held no animosity toward her. "Perhaps there is." His eyes drifted back down to the touchscreen.

She took his hint and joined him at the island—on the opposite side not to push things.

Dragunov motioned toward the screen with a map covered in markings. "These markings indicate where the attacks have been and their severity." The markings ranged in color: yellow/minor; orange/average; red/severe. The attacks were only in the northeastern section; everywhere else remained free of attacks. Red lines branched from the attacks to different sections, but most ran together at one location.

"What are these for? And what's important there?"

"I've tracked active radio waves coming from this area. There's nothing but a small industrial town." He looked at her knowingly.

"Sounds too suspicious not to be something."

He nodded as he looked back to the screen. "My exact thinking. A friend keeps an eye on things for me there. He's never seen commotion, but there's an abandoned bar that's too convenient."

"What has your friend said about these attacks?"

His dark eyes pierced her again. "He hasn't responded."

Her thinking headed toward betrayal, but his thoughts seemed to drift toward another darker option. He looked concerned, and it made her uneasy.

"These radio waves aren't something to ignore. I've been through too much to believe in coincidences," he said.

"Neither do I."

Silence fell over them. He appeared to be considering the map, but his thoughts were somewhere else because his face hardened, and he blew out an angry breath. "I should never have delayed looking into Makari's concerns."

Those already dead or injured weighed on him and on her. She worried she had been the cause of his delay. "I'm—"

His head lifted to speak—all signs of his frustration gone. "I'm headed for Akrino now. Care to come?"

Leila took a moment to straighten up—she still hadn't adjusted to his sudden mood shifts. She nodded. "Anything to help."

Dragunov smirked. "I see why you fit in so well with the rest of us."

LEAVING A MESSAGE IN CASE one of the men came back early, Leila and Dragunov left for Akrino. Since they left in daylight, she caught her first glimpse of the plain, two-story house. Nobody would expect that it housed six Spetsnaz and an American fugitive.

Nor would they find it. Leila knew it lay deep in a dense forest, and she had felt the turns when they had left for Noyavinsk, but she couldn't see exactly how many. During daylight, she thought it would be easy, but the many twists and turns ran together and turned her around. She asked Dragunov how many times he had gotten lost.

He laughed, and her heart fluttered at its mere simplicity. "Some, but not as much as Alek. He turned himself around so much, he called me to come find him and ended up being at least a mile and a half away from the house. He claims he wandered for three hours." He ended with a smile, doubting it was true.

"What helps you remember the way?"

"You make six turns in all, but it's arranged in two number fives laid next to each other. The one nearest the house is upside down while the second one is flipped. But you make one wrong turn and it's nearly impossible to get back."

They finally came to the edge of the dense forest to look at a blacktop road. Their arrival back from Noyavinsk had been too late for her to see where they entered the nameless forest. She wasn't expecting a blacktop road or to be this close to civilization.

Dragunov read through the muddled silence hanging heavy around her. "You're confused." Amusement laced his voice.

"Of course I would be. I assumed we were in the middle of nowhere."

"No, we're right here—hidden in plain sight." He looked over at her. "The best place to hide is where your enemy won't look: his shadow."

"So, where do you enter the forest?"

"After the tree with a twisted trunk. I'll point it out when we return."

They had already discussed the whole hiding-tracks-in-the-forest issue on their way to Noyavinsk. Precautions ranged from driving on the same tracks to false ones cut for other paths, rain determining if they hold off entry, and a tarp pulled behind the vehicles when it snowed.

About fifteen minutes later, they reached Akrino. The sleepy town included one main road with no traffic light, a general store, and a few other struggling buildings huddled close together. Dilapidated paint and faded signs implied that focus had shifted to maintaining larger 'attraction' cities.

The SUV ambled through, and Dragunov parked behind some storage building.

He nodded to her left. "There's the bar."

She looked. The old four-story building seemed to only be standing because of the two semi-newer buildings on either side holding it up. The newer buildings looked like they held life within their walls, both appearing to be apartments, and one even had glass windows on the roof for a small greenhouse. But the bar looked sad from lack of use as it sagged between the buildings.

Dragunov caught her attention by handing her a holstered gun. "Just in case." He stepped out of the car.

She quickly clipped it to her waist and jumped out. She felt like the detective again, armed with the pistol.

They headed for the unused building, noticing the unnatural silence and emptiness of the town—it felt like a ghost town. Leila unclipped the safety holster.

Dragunov eased the splintered doors open, and they groaned in protest. Like every bar, it used to be boisterous, full of drunken laughter and gay spirits; now, dust and cobwebs covered everything. Glass shards and bottles littered the floor equally with broken chairs and tables. The air was musty and still alcoholic from the decades of spilled drinks. The actual bar stretched along the opposite wall alongside a staircase leading up to the second floor and vacant bedrooms.

Footprints in the dust showed life. A path had been walked quite frequently to and from the bar. Some strayed from the path but still went the same direction.

Leila pulled her gun out in sync with Dragunov. His eyes remained locked on the bar ahead of them. "I told Polkesin to meet us here," he whispered.

"Could he already be here?" Her voice was just as soft as his, only a wisp of air.

"I don't know. This looks staged…" He looked at her, and she could see his unease. "Stay close."

She did as he asked, sticking by his side as they crept to the bar, careful not to kick bottles, debris, or glass shards. The footprints wound around the bar to where a few branched off to a back room, but the main path disappeared under a trap door. A trickle headed toward the staircase.

Dragunov motioned for her to wait as he ducked a head in the room for a look. He pulled back quickly and shook his head. He pulled out a small flashlight, and with a finger, he positioned her on one side of the trap door, and he guarded opposite. She kept her sights on the door as Dragunov crouched down to grab it. He looked up to see if she was ready, then flung it open, gun and flashlight aimed downward.

The spotlight revealed nothing but steps leading farther down into the cellar. Dragunov walked around to angle the light better. Still nothing. He looked at her as if in seeing what she thought.

His relinquishing of authority in wanting to know her opinion stunned her for a moment. Hopefully, he didn't notice her surprise. "You look into the cellar; I'll check to see if the other footprints are a dead end."

He considered her plan, then nodded. Once again, tenderness and a sense of concern came into his eyes. "Don't go far."

The Phoenix puffed up indignantly. *Don't be fooled by his eyes! He doesn't want you to get the glory of the first find.*

*No; he wants me to stay close in case something goes wrong.* She agreed with him. "I'll stick to the first floor until you come back up."

The Phoenix turned her away from his eyes to follow the other trail. Leila felt his eyes stay on her for a moment longer before they disappeared. She looked back to find the Russian gone into the cellar.

Even though she knew Dragunov was still with her, Leila felt alone and unprotected. The Phoenix inflated again.

*Smooth your feathers. I'm used to him always being beside me.*

The Phoenix had some grumbling reply, but a revolting smell hit Leila's nostrils, and she couldn't concentrate on what it said. A hand sealed off her nose, but the potent odor lingered.

Something dead—either some creature had crawled in to die, or a homeless person had while trying to find shelter.

She tried her best to avert her focus back to the trail. The footsteps walked to the foot of the stairs to where they vanished under something wiping the dust. She looked up at the stairs. They looked terrible: steps were cracked, splintered, or missing entirely.

Something glistened halfway up the stairs. She started to head up to get a better look when she caught sight of another glistening object closer to her. Bending, she found it to be a small speck of blood. Leila observed the stairs a bit more: broken and splintered not only from age but a recent fight.

She had dismissed the smell of death too quickly. She backtracked and thought about calling out for Dragunov when she saw the faint smearing of blood curving around the stairs. Someone had tried to wipe away the evidence. The streaks matched the act of dragging a body.

Leila considered calling Dragunov again, but the Phoenix made her feet follow the trail. An overwhelming stench forced her to close her mouth because she couldn't breathe. The streaks led to a closed door under the stairs. She reached for the handle, but the muffled buzzing of flies stopped it. After preparing herself to see a body, her hand grabbed the doorknob and pulled.

Flies rushed out as black as a group of bats. Leila had seen murdered bodies before, but nothing as mangled and decomposed as the heap within. She just knew the rotting, maggot-covered remains were Polkesin.

Leila did her best to keep from retching. She staggered back but couldn't take her eyes off the decaying man. She didn't restrain the horror in her voice. "Dragunov!"

He came to her with unbelievable swiftness for such a big man. He glanced at the corpse for only a second before he jumped into action. "We have to go." He grabbed her frozen arm and tugged her toward the exit.

She got over her repulsion and ran with him, but when they neared the door, cylinders broke through the broken windows. Dragunov spun, grabbed Leila in midstride, and pushed her down under him as the tear gas exploded.

The Spetsnaz leader returned to his feet, hauled Leila to hers, and fired into the smoke. Leila followed his lead, hoping their bullets found the targets since they were firing blind. As they fired, Dragunov pushed her back toward the stairs.

Their attackers suddenly returned fire. Leila and Dragunov abandoned defense and ran for the stairs.

They flew up the stairs only to meet Chechen at the top. Dragunov dove straight at them, taking four down with him. Leila quickly disarmed the two still standing and tossed one back down the stairs. As she turned to take care of the other, he was knocked in the back by the body of a comrade. They soared down the stairs and rolled into the dispersing smoke.

Dragunov appeared again, and he waited as she hurried the rest of the way up. The men Dragunov disposed of littered the landing. She had to jump over one of the immobile men. He led her toward the back, searching for a fire exit.

Shouts and bullets thudding into the wood around them had them ducking and scrambling for shelter.

"Stairs!" Dragunov ordered as he shot back. He covered her as she scrambled for the next flight of stairs. He followed right behind her. She started to break off on the third floor, but the Russian kept her going up. They sprinted up to the fourth, an exact replica of the floor below them. Again, with no fire escape in sight.

"Where?" she asked just as the floor shook beneath her. It threw them off their feet, and the building tremored from another explosion. The men below had abandoned chasing them—they would collapse the building on them with grenades.

"Jump through the windows!" Dragunov yelled.

Leila didn't question it; she shot at a window to break it, then soared through the frame and glass. She tried to keep her legs under her, but she rotated. The world spun around her until it halted abruptly. All air had been knocked out, and she almost lost consciousness. She landed hard on her back on the two-story building next to them—right on the glass skylight. The glass crinkled under her weight but somehow held together.

Just as she opened her eyes, something shattered the glass, and she fell again.

The hard floor met her quicker this time. She remained in her stunned position as her nerve receptors throbbed in a chaotic orchestra. Her head spun, her shoulder burned from landing on it, and there wasn't one area that didn't ache from strain or sting from fresh cuts. A roaring sound filled the air. Smaller explosions went off until the noise shut off. Everything went still like stunned silence.

Leila forced her eyes open and allowed her disorientation a moment to straighten out. Once her head leveled out, she sat up against her protesting body. The shattered glass roof still dropped shards, and she had landed among potted plants. She quickly inspected herself for major injuries, but she only found bloody nicks with glass lodged in the cuts, soreness, and stiffness.

*Dragunov.*

She looked around for him.

"Dragunov?" her voice cracked. No reply. "Dragunov!" Still none.

Leila got up on shaky legs, which gave out as she tried to step over a pot. She crashed to the floor as the pottery shattered beneath her. Getting up to her hands and knees, she looked up and found him.

Dragunov lay on his back with his head turned away from her—immobile.

The pain vanished as fear and adrenaline took over her. She stumbled over to the fallen man. He had deep cuts everywhere and losing a lot of blood from a gash in his head, but he was breathing.

She tore off her light over-shirt and wrapped it around his head to stop the bleeding. After inspecting the rest of his body, she found nothing broken.

Leila tried waking the unconscious man, but he slept on. *Someone's bound to have heard all the noise.*

She looked and found two doors, both opposite the other. Limping to one, she eased it open, and stairs led down into the apartments, life stirring with startled occupants. She closed it and hurried to the other—it led to a fire escape. Down the street sat the parked SUV.

Leila hurried back and attempted to rouse the big man again but failed. She braced herself and draped the Russian over her with his arm over her entire back and her arm wrapped around his waist to have him leaning on her. He was extremely heavy, and her muscles screamed with all her wounds.

"Help me, Phoenix; I have to get him out of here," she whispered as she struggled to drag the man toward the exit. A rush of strength and adrenaline pulsed through her veins, joining with her exhausted body, but it was different, stronger. *Must be David too.*

With her body energized, and Leila holding on by sheer willpower, she dragged the unconscious Dragunov out of the ruined greenhouse and onto the roof. As she made her way across to the fire escape, a gaping hole glared at her where the old bar used to stand.

Leila slowly descended the fire escape along with the limp Russian onto the street below. She took a breather, then adjusted

Dragunov over her body and headed for the waiting black car. Being preoccupied with the fallen building, she hoped no one would see them leaving. She dragged the Russian to the car, rummaged in his pockets for the keys to unlock it, then sat him in the passenger's seat—his head rolled back against the headrest, but he slept on.

Leila hurried to the driver's seat, woke the sleeping engine, and proceeded to leave the now-awakened town of Akrino. Through the gathered crowd of concerned townspeople and the various emergency vehicles, Leila saw the remnants of the abandoned bar: nothing but smoke, fire, and smoldering rubble.

# XXX.

Leila faded fast. Adrenaline had left her like wringing out a wet towel; drained of any energy, she could feel the aches. The constant throbbing in her body at least kept her awake. She kept asking the Phoenix or David to keep her conscious. Either of them or both—she couldn't tell which right now—would supply just enough power to do so, but whenever she glanced at Dragunov—who still refused to wake—her energy level rose. She would think about it later, once they were safe again. If she got them there.

She drove the SUV down the forest-lined road. It remained free of traffic—she wouldn't accidentally swerve into the other lane and strike a car. But no one could help if she lost consciousness and crashed into a tree. Regardless, she continuously checked her rearview mirror for pursuit.

Between watching the road and checking for pursuit, her eyes stayed on the forest line, searching for the twisted tree. It took all her strength to keep her eyes open, hands on the wheel, and a foot pressing the gas. Panic crept in that she had driven past the hidden entrance. It should've been close…

The tree with a twisted trunk didn't stick out—it blended right among the other trees around it. A small victory lifted her spirits at finding the entrance. If she hadn't been looking for it, she would have driven past, never knowing anything different.

Neither would she have suspected the path she turned into be anything other than a hunters' path. She was careful to stay in the previous tire tracks as they led her deeper into the forest. When the woods sealed off her view of the blacktop behind her, a fork in the path forced her to stop: one path veered to the left, and the other curved right. Both ways appeared to have been traveled recently.

She glanced at the sleeping Dragunov, wishing he would wake and take control by directing them home. But he wasn't waking anytime soon.

*No one will save you,* the Phoenix said.

*You said that last time and look who showed up.*

*But not now. Look at him; you have to save him this time.*

The Phoenix caring for someone other than itself surprised her. Until she realized that in saving him, she would save herself. "Still selfish," Leila mumbled, but the Phoenix was right—it was up to her.

Refocused, she turned back ahead, replaying the instructions in her head: two number fives—the first normal, and the second flipped. It was plain convenient that he had told her when she so needed it now.

The sharp left beckoned for her to enter. *"You make one wrong turn and it's nearly impossible to get back."* Dragunov's words haunted her.

"Let's hope I'm not wrong," she said as she turned down the left fork.

Now on top of her pain, weariness, the paranoia of possible pursuit, and concern for the Russian, was the fraying of her nerves that she had taken the wrong path. The foliage around her now appeared no different than the trees and shrubs when she entered the maze—nothing stood out. The car crept down the pathway until it stopped at another fork in the road, but this time with three options: continue going straight, take a left gently curving, or take a right that looked to lead back the way she came.

Leila huffed, trying not to become too frustrated that she couldn't think.

*Concentrate,* the Phoenix ordered.

She closed her eyes to imagine a number five—the next part of it was the big curve. She opened her eyes and looked at the left pathway. It curved.

Ignoring her doubt, she turned left again. She could imagine tracing a large number five as the SUV followed the wide curve. When she came out of the curve onto a straight path, Leila sighed in relief. She increased the speed as she followed the 're-versed' number five—she just made every left turn a right.

The forest thinned on coming out of the last curve. The house gradually came into view, but the other SUVs weren't there. She hoped the men had returned and could help her. Leila didn't think she had enough strength left to get Dragunov out of the vehicle and into the house, but she didn't have another choice.

She parked the car, unlocked the door on the house first, then went to fetch the Russian. With a humongous strain, she draped the man over her again. Under his weight, her knees buckled, and she headed for the snow. Heat burst within, strengthening her muscles.

*I'm here to help as much as I can,* the Phoenix reminded.

Leila used the car door to return to her feet, tightened her grip around Dragunov, then she advanced to the house. With every step, she wanted to collapse on the ground and sleep. But the Phoenix and her concern for the Spetsnaz leader kept her going.

She made an awkward advancement into the house as dragging a limp form sideways across the threshold almost made Leila lose her balance. They had to go up to her room—she knew exactly where the medicine was in the cabinets in her bathroom. So, straining and pulling, she stumbled up the stairs. She went down a few times, but the Phoenix drove her back up. Leila ran on empty, and her dark side was supplying her reserve.

She dragged his lifeless form to her bed. Laying him upon it pulled her down on top of him. Leila was okay with passing out on his chest, but she had to tend to him first. So, she stumbled back to her feet, went to her bathroom to grab the First-Aid kit, and headed back.

Even though pale from the immense blood loss from his head and also knocking himself out, Dragunov breathed evenly, lost in the blank world of his subconscious. With no chair available, Leila sat beside him on the bed. Doing so sent a wave of dizziness through her so fast, she almost tumbled off. After closing her eyes for a moment to steady herself, she reopened them and removed her bloodied shirt from his head. She tossed her ruined shirt in the trash bin, rummaged through the First-Aid kit for antibiotics, and then cleaned the wound and wrapped it with gauze. She applied ointment to the cuts, but her hands shook so badly she couldn't do anything about the glass in his wounds.

Leila had trouble keeping her eyes focused throughout the entire procedure. Her own skin looked pale from exertion. She planned to treat her own wounds, but the drive to take care of Dragunov sapped all the energy she had left. After a final look at the resting man, she considered the space beside him and lay down.

LEILA JUMPED AWAKE AT THE light touch on her shoulder. She would've fallen off if not for the quick hand snatching her back. As she recovered from the jolt, she struggled to concentrate on the dark eyes looking back at her.

"Dragunov! Oh, thank God." She immediately relaxed seeing him conscious again. "How are you feeling?"

He tried to brush off her concern. "I'm fine. You—"

"No, *I'm* fine," she corrected briskly. She hadn't rested nearly as long as her body needed, and the Phoenix wasn't letting him be overbearingly masculine by pretending he wasn't hurt. He had more color to his face, but his pale complexion still bothered Leila. "You were the unconscious one. So, how are you feeling?"

The Dragon flashed in his eyes at her tone. But he blinked it away and didn't argue with her. Even though he clearly didn't like being reprimanded, he sighed in resignation. "I don't think there's one place that isn't bruised."

"It was your idea to jump out a window."

"Didn't expect the fall to knock me out though." He hadn't taken his eyes off her nor had he released her arm. From the furrowing of his brow, he didn't like what he saw on her face, and if he had let go of her arm, she would've fallen off the bed. "You're pale, Leila, and you have a lot of cuts."

His other hand almost touched the wounds on her face, but she looked down to discourage the tender act. "I'm just tired from getting you here and all."

How didn't he hear her heart thundering in her chest? The noise was deafening in her ears, pounding faster and faster the more her imagination ran wild. To Leila's shock, the Phoenix didn't rise up, offended; instead, it kept silent like it sat back, watching.

Leila kept her eyes down, preventing him from seeing her confusion.

"You're not—You're bleeding!" he said in a panic.

His fear overtook her; she looked down at her waist where he stared. She had more cuts on her arms—already starting to clot—and her tank top had tears, but multiple dark blots dominated the navy-blue shirt, none wet and painful to the touch.

"It's not—"

Dragunov started to rise. "You've got to lie down—" What color he had in his face drained away in an instant. His eyes rolled back, and he fell onto the bed.

Leila lunged to catch him before he crashed into the headboard. Moving so suddenly sent a wave of dizziness over her, and his dead weight pulled her down on top of him again. She had no strength to push up. He remained motionless as he focused on getting air.

He surely had to feel her heart pounding now since it lay above his. But she couldn't tell what caused his to increase: her being this close or his body fighting to find equilibrium.

"Are you okay?" she asked, breathless.

His answer came after some labored breaths. "No moving for a bit."

Embarrassingly, his scent was so intoxicating, she couldn't think of anything else. She yearned to stay on him, warm and comfortable, but the Phoenix returned. It cleared her foggy mind and gave her the strength to rise off his chest. "It's not my blood; it's yours."

He opened his eyes and met hers—she was almost nose to nose with him. She couldn't break the stare because everything in her froze, like she had grabbed an electric fence and couldn't let go. Those eyes were no longer dark and menacing but soft and strangely hesitant. Dragunov's confidence disappeared like it never existed, and Leila found it hard to breathe.

But once again, the Phoenix pulled her back—not jerking, angry, just as if to say it wasn't right. Since the entrapment he had put over her was broken, Leila had the freedom to straighten. Dragunov didn't restrain her from getting up, and she couldn't see how he took her distancing herself, for she kept her eyes away from being trapped in his again. He also didn't have her arm anymore, so she kept a hold on the bed to maintain balance.

An uncomfortable silence fell around them for a while. Dragunov broke it, "Where did you find the strength to get us back? I'm not light…"

She chuckled. "No, you're not, but I just did." With him bringing it up, Leila wondered where the strength *had* come from. It was stronger than the Phoenix and David—it came from her concern for Dragunov…

"But that strength is waning," he said, breaking her train of thought. "You're beginning to sway." His hand drifted over to grab the one holding onto the bed.

Leila didn't think too much about it; with her resolve wavering, she wasn't going to demand that he remove the hand giving her security. "I'll lie back down soon. Too much movement has made me dizzy."

She wanted to beat him before he could suggest that she lie back down beside him and felt it okay to bring up the topic. "I'm sorry about Polkesin."

"He lived a good life—he died protecting Mother Russia. That's how we should all go, protecting something we love."

She looked at him, seeing the understanding and pity in his eyes. David was a prime example of what he said, and Dragunov knew it. "It is."

Dragunov suddenly looked behind her, alerted. "Someone's here."

Leila cursed as she spun to her feet with gun in hand: she had left the door open and probably left a trail of blood leading straight to them.

A voice yelled from downstairs—a question is a language Leila didn't recognize.

Dragunov responded in the same language. Tension relaxed in his form; Leila assumed it was some code. "It's—"

She didn't hear him finish from collapsing into blackness.

# XXXI.

She ached. Her body refused to move; her muscles were stiff as if they had been stretched out and dried in the sun and hadn't returned to their normal length yet. Everything in her whined in protest at waking up, but Leila forced her eyes open. A slight glow behind curtains and the light beneath a closed door gave her enough to see in the dark room. The two beds, another closed door, and the double doors of a closet made this room foreign.

Her recollection of the ambush at Akrino returned as she grew more awake. She had gotten Dragunov back, treated him, then laid down beside him. When the memory of laying on his chest and being trapped by the possibility in his eyes came back to her, she thought it was her imagination.

No way. The Phoenix wouldn't have allowed such closeness. But it wasn't a dream, and Leila's cheeks warmed. He hadn't been discouraging at that moment, and Leila had to admit that she hadn't either. Neither would make the first move, uncertain on how the other would react, but they both hoped the other would take the step—

An opening door brought her attention to the right. Light grew as the door opened. Whoever was at the door tried not to wake her. She had to blink rapidly to discern Alek in the doorway.

He cringed with guilt at disturbing her. "Sorry, Lei; I was just checking on you."

"It's alright. I need to get up anyway." Leila forced her body up from under warm sheets and the bed conforming to her form.

Alek switched on a lamp as he hurried to intercept her sitting up. "I think you should stay down. You definitely deserve more rest."

He couldn't stop her from rising. "Perhaps."

Alek sat beside her on the bed, and after a brief hesitation, he hugged her. He gently held her but tightly, like he feared letting her go. "I'm so glad to see you awake again. You scared us passing out yesterday."

The act and his words stunned her. A hug wouldn't be a huge surprise from Alek, but he had been scared, and even his shaking voice demonstrated his concern. And he said he wasn't the only one.

Leila finally recovered from her shock and returned the hug. "I'm sorry. I hope I didn't worry any of you too much."

"Dragon checked on you about every thirty minutes." He pulled back. "Now, how are you feeling?"

Alek expected her to change topics so quickly like him and talk about herself. Dragunov's actions displayed his concern, but she was still shocked at hearing it. She longed to know about Dragunov's current condition, but Alek focused more on her condition right now. "I guess as good as one jumping out a window and landing on a roof can be."

"So, fantastic?"

Leila laughed with him. "I wouldn't go so far as that."

"No? You jumped through a window, fell two stories, fell through more glass, dragged Dragon back here, and treated his wounds, not yours." Alek shook his head. "Your exhaustion would keep anyone in bed, but you're sitting up—you're Wonder Woman."

"I'm not that either. I was just… driven."

"Like you are every day. You're really strong, Lei, you know."

If she didn't stop Alek, he would continue his praises. "Enough about me; how is Dragunov?"

Alek began to answer, but a different voice spoke for him, "Well."

She and Alek turned to find Dragunov in the doorway, back to an imposing presence commanding attention. A fresh bandage had been wrapped around his head—and done correctly since Leila had been so exhausted yesterday, she probably didn't wrap it right. He had improved so much from a day's rest: he stood steady on his feet, had color to his face, and didn't show signs of fatigue or pain.

But she knew better. His body had been taut yesterday in pain. He couldn't be back to normal like he was portraying. Like most men, he put up a front.

She wanted to run to him and check him out herself. And the tension she could see in him had her thinking he had the same desire. "From what I saw yesterday, you should still be in bed."

He smirked. "And so should you, but here we are. I suppose neither of us can be kept down long."

"No, but I wasn't the one with a head injury."

"You could've sustained one when you fell yesterday; we didn't know." The sternness in his eyes melted away and replaced with such compassion Leila's breath hitched in her throat. "But it's a relief seeing you conscious again."

He had been worried. It was now obvious that Dragunov wasn't just captivated with her—he cared for her. Hope made her heart pound faster. He kept her gaze, trying to tell her something before he turned away. "I'll send Silvestrov up to remove that glass in your arms."

Air came back to her when he removed his gaze. With his departure, the room seemed empty and cold. She finally realized what he had said and looked down to see clear glints in her cuts.

Alek chuckled as he lay back on Leila's bed. "You are starting to change us, Lei. The change we've needed for a long time."

She had forgotten he remained and tried to cover it up by joking back, "What change, Alek? You were happy and laughed all the time before I came along." She carefully stood, with Alek providing a helpful hand and eyeing her stability.

He laughed as she headed for the bathroom. "This might not be good: I think my sarcasm is rubbing off on you."

"I was sarcastic long before I met you, so don't worry, you're not contagious." Leila shut the door on him laughing again. Her muscles still weren't cooperating, making her stumble as she moved around tending to her needs. She felt like she weighed a million pounds, and she looked in the mirror to see how badly it showed.

Face pale, hair disheveled, eyes strained like she hadn't slept in days, and body drooping in exhaustion. If not for the numerous slices and dried blood on her face, arms, and shirt, she would've looked like she had just come off a busy shift. She had pushed herself too far this time.

*You weren't supposed to let me,* she thought as she turned the water on.

David chuckled. *"When have I ever been able to stop you?"*

Repeating the first morning she woke up here, she rubbed the cool water on her face to further wake up and scrubbed off what blood she could. Voices made her turn the faucet off to hear that Silvestrov had arrived. She opened the door and pulled him away from his discussion with Alek.

The medic headed over and went to work by grabbing her hands and looking them over. "Don't you or Dragon get in any more trouble. I don't know how much more my heart can take."

"What fun is there without some blood?"

Silvestrov looked at her as Alek snickered behind him. "It sounds like you've been hanging around Alek."

Leila laughed. "He thinks it's his fault, and it's bad for me."

He looked at his comrade. "I'm shocked; he's finally right about something."

Alek shrugged. "It happens."

"Not often." Silvestrov turned back to her and felt her pulse. "How are you feeling though? Dizzy? Hot? Cold? Numb anywhere? In any kind of pain?" He felt her forehead as he spoke.

"Nothing; just tired."

Silvestrov removed his hand. "I'm glad that's it." He then pulled her into a hug. "I'm so glad you're okay."

Leila warmed, stunned again, but she recovered to hug him back. Even as much of a headache the Phoenix had caused, she had somehow found a way into these Spetsnaz hearts. It felt nice finding somewhere she was cared for again.

The scarred man pulled back. "Tell me if anything changes, but let's focus on your treatment now." He gestured to the bathroom.

He sat her on the stool by the countertop, and Alek brought in another chair for Silvestrov to sit. Alek returned with a small tray carrying disinfectant ointments, gauze, glasses, tweezers, small scissors, and other surgical supplies. After setting it on the countertop, he propped against the doorframe.

Silvestrov put the glasses on and chose to begin with her left arm. After giving it a thorough look, he grabbed the tweezers. "Tell me if there's any pain," he said as he began removing the glass in her arm.

Leila did her best to stay still. She sat hypnotized by his experienced hands removing piece after piece of broken glass and dropping them in the metal tray, which answered with a soft clink. They moved like a butterfly—moving from tray to her arm, softly landing to extract glass, before flittering away to do the routine again. She didn't feel a thing.

"Alek" —Leila broke the trance the surgeon had cast on them— "what language did you and Dragunov speak yesterday?"

"It's not real; we use it for codes. It's a mixture of Russian, Romanian, and Latin. Ruben made it."

"And, who sacrificed their room to me last night?"

Alek lifted his hand. "Me. I wanted you and Dragon close so I could check on both of you easily."

"Then where did you sleep last night?"

His face fell as he tried to answer. "Uhhh…"

"In his room," Silvestrov answered as he disinfected Leila's arm, wrapped gauze around the deeper cuts, and moved on to her next limb.

"In the other bed," Alek hastily explained. "I wanted to keep an eye on you because we didn't know how extensive your wounds were…"

An eyebrow rose. "We?"

"Dragon and me."

"And me," Silvestrov butted in.

Alek continued on with his story, "Dragon didn't like the fact that you escaped easier than he. You really alarmed us when you passed out, and he worried that something was wrong. He practically yelled at Silvestrov for trying to reach him before checking you out completely."

"I *had* looked her over; I was trying to stop him getting out of bed before he collapsed too," Silvestrov corrected.

"Oh, I know. Everything went by so quickly: seeing the car parked wrong, seeing the door open, finding blood, then finding Lei unconscious and Dragon almost so nearly shot my nerves."

"That's why I'm the medic; you can't keep calm."

"Then what am I?"

"Useless."

Alek picked up their usual playful banter, but Leila couldn't hear the rest—caught up on what Alek and Silvestrov had said. Checking on her every thirty minutes proved Dragunov's concern, but him straining to get to her in disregard of passing out himself screamed that he was frantic. He cared more about her safety than his.

But so had she. Leila had shown it, and it was no secret. That equality or balancing of their concern for each other shot up her heart rate. She fought to control her rapid breathing so Silvestrov wouldn't notice and call her out on it.

Thinking back on their clashes, they balanced each other out, much better than she and David did or her and Miguel. Leila didn't feel empowered by clashing with Dragunov but uplifted.

The idea of finding love in Dragunov had her feeling light and energetic, wanting to jump up from the stool, run down to him, and leap into his arms. But a doubt brought down her heart and kept her sitting: what if he didn't feel the same? That would be her last shatter, one she couldn't piece back together.

*More time,* the Phoenix urged. *Wait a bit longer until you're sure.*

*You're okay with this? Letting someone into my heart and turning me away from your control?*

*He won't be kicking me out. He has one like me, so he'll teach us how to coexist. Just like him.*

*What has changed you? You were so adamant about refusing him.*

*I have… grown comfortable with him around. Our fights have me acknowledging his power and control. And I see how you seem to fit together.*

*So, you like him?*

It took a moment for the Phoenix to answer. *I think I do.*

Noise silenced. She read Silvestrov's lips to understand that he needed to check her back. Leila leaned forward to prop against the countertop, and, once again, she didn't feel his probing. Even if removing the glass out of her back caused pain, she was too numb from the Phoenix's confession.

And at the possibility of loving the hard Dragon of Russia.

LEILA FELT BETTER WITH THE embedded glass gone from her skin and in a fresh set of clothes, but she forced herself to restrain her good mood and keep casual as she walked into the Dragon's Den. Dragunov stood watching a news report about the sudden halt to the terrorist attacks. But he turned at her approach, and she nearly lost her control—his eyes still held that deep pool of compassion she had seen earlier.

*Don't move too early,* the Phoenix reminded her.

Having her resolve strengthened, Leila moved farther in, and she stopped close to the Spetsnaz leader.

"I know you're hurting more than you're showing, so how are you, really? Alek and Silvestrov are busy so they can't hear." She whispered to reassure him.

Dragunov held her eyes captive, allowing her to see what he tried to hide. He smirked. "The same as you."

Him admitting that he hurt—even though vague—meant a lot. But she did see something in his eyes that didn't comfort her: a suspicion.

"What's wrong?"

He knew exactly what she asked about. "Akrino. I said it felt staged, and the brand-new equipment I found in the cellar points to that. And now all attacks have stopped since the bar fell."

"So, an ambush for us?"

He kept his eyes on hers, telling her he leaned toward a different option. Her joyful mood now darkened as her gut twisted.

"For me."

"There's no point hoping I'm wrong when we both know better. You're not in the clear. Whoever it is is still after you."

"Dragon? What happened?"

Dragunov's attention lifted from her, and she turned to find Yurii, Yakov, and Ruben standing in the doorway. The twins both held looks of bewilderment, and Ruben just scrutinized them.

"Lei, you too?" Yurii asked.

"Alright, what the hell happened?" Yakov demanded.

"We may have missed the fight," Ruben suggested.

Leila smiled and dipped her head in embarrassment. It was the most logical conclusion to come to with their behavior toward each other in the past weeks.

Dragunov chuckled. "A fight, but not between us."

# XXXII.

Dragunov blew on the coffee before raising it to his lips. Five days had passed since Akrino—plenty enough for him and Leila to heal—but the elapse of time hadn't deflated their attitude toward each other. Something had changed in Leila; something she tried to hide, but he saw through her façade. By the look in her eyes, his hopes rose that she was falling for him as much as he for her—more with every passing day.

He froze in thought when he heard—and sensed—Leila coming down the stairs behind him. She headed for her usual morning routine in their small gym to work out and practice. He had secretly watched her quite a few times, and she was far more intimidating in-person than on television. She would be an interesting opponent, especially challenging when they would spar for Alek.

"I must warn you: Alek's been sneaking in and out of the room," Dragunov stated without turning around. He had seen him slinking around, looking like a sly fox sneaking into the chicken coop.

She stopped at the foot of the stairs. "He wouldn't try to pull something on me." Her statement wavered slightly in doubt.

Silvestrov chuckled as he turned, cleaning a mug in his hands. "I wouldn't count on it. The only one he hasn't been able to get is Dragon. I don't think you're an exception, Leila."

She probably considered the hallway before scoffing and heading for it. "He wouldn't dare."

Silvestrov watched her go, then turned back to the sink. "Do you think he *would* set a trap for her?"

"Has he ever excused someone from his initiations? Even Svetlana fell victim."

Dragunov wasn't able to get a third drink before Leila's scream—like the air had been snatched out of her—answered their wonderings. Silvestrov bent over the sink in a laugh and shook his head; Dragunov smiled into his mug as he took another sip of coffee, then he went to rescue her from whatever Alek had left to snare her.

As soon as he arrived and took in the scene before him—of the door flung open, a large and empty bucket lying against the door, a dark splotch in the entrance, and a drenched Leila doubled over trying to catch her breath—Dragunov knew what happened. Alek had balanced a bucket of ice-cold water on the semi-opened door.

"You tried to warn me, I know; you don't have to remind me," Leila said through gasps of air as she used the front end of her drenched shirt to wipe off her face.

Her lower torso revealed defined abs and smooth skin except for a circular scar, identical to the one he saw near her heart when he woke her for the phone call. He knew what a bullet wound looked like. Her injuries intrigued him even more, and he wanted to know about them, but most people were sensitive about such wounds that could be hidden. Questioning would be for later—if ever—so Dragunov averted his gaze from her exposed abdomen to grab a small towel so she wouldn't catch him staring. "Didn't think I needed to. Here, you're shivering." He tossed the towel to her.

She turned to catch it, and with a mumbled thanks, she returned to dabbing her skin with something dry. But even with her wet hair matted down on her head and slightly smudged mascara, Leila was just as beautiful as any other day, only looking small, defenseless, and charmingly miserable standing there in dripping clothes.

Dragunov found himself unnervingly protective of her; he cleared his throat as he turned his attention off her. "I am surprised Alek wasn't here to watch. He's always wanted to see his pranks… through." Just then, he caught sight of the open laptop and live webcam.

Leila followed his gaze to the computer, then marched over and snapped it shut. "So, am I initiated now?"

He bent and grabbed the bucket with a smirk. "Not quite. You have to return the favor."

Her lips twisted mischievously as she walked over and took the bucket from him. "I think I have an idea."

A WEEK LATER, THE SOFT footfalls above him brought Dragunov's attention away from the computer screen listing numerous rumors of Chechen locations to the ceiling. Leila's room sat above his, and from the direction of her silent steps, she headed for the stairs. With her determination not to disturb anybody, and from it being three in the morning, this was her getting Alek back.

He waited until her timed descent meant she reached the kitchen before getting up, slipping out of his room, and moving toward the blackened kitchen.

Familiar with the layout of his home, he worked his way in the darkness with relative ease. Dragunov propped against the island separating the kitchen and living room as his eyes focused on the dark form crouching down at the refrigerator.

The usual bright fridge light had been partially covered when Leila eased the door open. So, Silvestrov was in on this too. She opened it enough to grab a bucket—full of ice-cold water, he presumed.

Just as she placed it on the floor, she must've sensed his presence. She whipped around and clamped a hand over her mouth to prevent the yelp from escaping.

The same hand dropped from her mouth to press against her heart. "I thought you were Alek," she whispered as light as a breath of air.

"I'm glad I'm not," he whispered just as quiet.

"I am too." She turned back to shut the door, plunging them into total darkness, and took time for her eyes to readjust before she picked up the bucket as she stood.

"While he's sleeping? He'll be expecting it."

"And he won't."

Even with no light, he could see a glint of triumph in her eyes. Leila moved past him with sure-footed steps, and he followed her up the stairs to Alek's room. "I would like to watch," he explained to her turn of the head.

With a quietness few could match, they ascended the stairs, Leila careful not to spill a drop. She repositioned the bucket when they reached Alek's door to reach for the handle, but Dragunov stopped her hand.

"If I have trained him any…" He gently pushed her back, then crouched to crack open the door. He found the tripwire wound to the door, and if opened too far, it would pull a weight down onto an air horn hidden above the doorframe.

Alek had actually listened and paid attention to his instructions on outsmarting your opponent… even if he used the information for a prank. Dragunov whipped out a knife, cut the wire, and after another quick check for any more, he motioned it safe for Leila to proceed.

As quietly as before, Leila moved into Alek's room like a shadow. Her form halted abruptly, then changed direction to creep to the other side of Alek's bed—he guessed she saw another booby trap. He straightened in the doorway just as she stopped beside the edge of the bed Alek faced.

Leila reared back and then threw the three-gallon bucket full of freezing ice-cold water straight into Alek's face.

His breathless scream mirrored hers from before, just at a slightly higher pitch. Leila dropped the bucket as she doubled over in laughter as he continued to yell and squirm his way out of his drenched sheets. Dragunov laughed with her, enjoying the moment of Alek finally being pranked—no one else had been able to get him back.

Alek escaped his sheets and lunged at Leila. They crashed to the floor, them wrestling with Leila struggling to breathe from laughing, begging him to get off because he was getting her wet, protesting that it wasn't fair that he got to retaliate, and Alek denying her through chattering teeth.

The others soon gathered behind Dragunov to watch the spectacle. "She did what we couldn't," Silvestrov admired.

"So, she passes," Yurii said.

"I don't think it would've mattered if she did or not; she's already been accepted," Ruben said. Their silences spoke their agreement.

Dragunov couldn't take his eyes off Leila's laughing face. Ruben was right; it didn't matter what she would've done—or even if Alek hadn't sprung his initiation ritual on her—Leila had already been welcomed into the men's hearts. His especially.

# XXXIII.

Even with the success of getting even with Alek and being initiated into the Spetsnaz team, Leila's mood dropped a few days later. Consumed with the whirlwind of adjusting to the Spetsnaz, her growing affection for Dragunov, and the chaos of the terror attacks, she hadn't realized the coming of October. Tomorrow was the second: David's birthday and also the day of his death. A full year had passed without him, but it seemed like her entire life.

Luckily, her bipolar-like change coincided with the men's break. None were at the house to witness her decline except for Dragunov—who she managed to dodge since phone calls in the command room kept him tied up. Not more Chechen terrorism but something else.

She sat on her bed, looking out the window—not seeing the beauty of the Russian wilderness blanketed under seamlessly thick snow. She didn't know how she should act. Just the coming of the anniversary of his death replayed that horrific scene, woke the ghosts of those bullets, and struck her with the memory of her ranging emotions then. She had come so far in escaping those suffocating memories, only to have them surging back.

Gentle, almost hushed, music pulled her out of her stupor: someone worked the keys on the piano into a dark serenade. She assumed it was Ruben but got up to investigate.

Ruben sat at the piano producing the haunting, seductive tune. It didn't sound like any she had heard before: it was gloomy, mesmerizing, beautiful but sorrowful, and Leila ached at the sadness of it. Before she knew it, she stood at the bottom of the stairs having been ensnared by the luring melody.

The song came to an end, holding such weight on the last key as if the song was a burden. A familiarity encircled the song—something she had become used to, but Leila couldn't put her finger on it. The tenor drifted off into silence, leaving the room naked and deathly quiet.

"Didn't mean to disturb you," Ruben said, voice as low and mysterious as the song he just played.

He brought her back to Earth, but she still had to focus on what he said. "You didn't. I heard the music and wanted to hear it better." Once fully snapping out from under the music's spell, she walked toward the couch. "That song's beautiful, like a dark lullaby. Did you compose it?"

He nodded. "That was *Dragon's Serenade*."

"It was for Dragunov?" Replaying the song in her head, she now realized why the song had felt so familiar. Secrecy, darkness, anguish, and an alluring quality all circled the tune. It described the Spetsnaz leader perfectly.

"I create a song based on everyone I get to know."

"Everyone?" She wasn't sure if she liked the sound of that, but she sat down and got comfortable against the arm of the couch.

He turned back to the keys; vastly different from Dragunov's song, the tune sped up, holding liveliness and warmth. If the notes could've been seen, they would've been bouncing around with energy. The peppiness of the song brought her mood up and kept a smile on her face.

"Alek."

Ruben nodded. "*The Crane's Charisma*, since he's so charming." The fast, upbeat song slowed dramatically. The tune reflected the soft, precise keys he played. The melody took its time, and Leila envisioned Silvestrov gently removing the glass from her skin a week ago. His song held just as much coolness and tranquility that the medic did. "*Remedial.*"

The relaxing chords transitioned into a series of dueling notes, pairing the lighter end of the keyboard against the deeper end. Ruben's talented hands battled as he struck the louder end hard and played soft on the other end. Eventually, the two opposing sides mingled in the middle, and the varying notes made a singular tune.

Yurii and Yakov came to mind: Yurii relating to the softer, carefree side, and Yakov belonging to the harder, firmer side.

"*Dissimilarity Within Similarity*," Ruben announced as the song came to an end.

Leila blinked in realization. "You must have one for you."

He considered her for a moment, then began to play. His fingers remained caressing the deeper keys, occasionally adding in some tinkling to lighten up the tone. Overall, it was a deep and graceful song, possessing an intrigue to the keys. Just like the quiet man.

The song faded. "Yustina says it fits me, but it sounds better on guitar."

She took a moment to recall that Yustina was his girlfriend. "I can see why. Do you have a name for it?"

"She calls it *Enthrall.*" But through his voice, he didn't agree with the title.

Ruben remained quiet for a while, thinking something over. "This is *The Firebird's Lament.*" Without glancing at her, he launched into playing the song.

The introduction maintained a steady beat with keys struck in a repeating drone. The repetitiveness carried Leila into a trance as her routine life with David in the force went by in her mind. Some different pitches and keys snuck their way in—like the sparse moments that disrupted her routine—but the lower keys continued their dullness.

Then the monotony broke as a fast tone built, combining both high and low keys. As the tune grew faster, so did the scenes race by in Leila's head: David dying in the bank, various fights in the tournament, her internal struggle and turmoil. The song climaxed as she defeated the Changeling David by embracing the Phoenix. It halted for a second before only the high keys played, matching the slow monotonous rhythm from the beginning. The sets of notes eventually separated, filling the room with the sad, isolated taps. They grew slower and slower, decreasing in number, like the keys held on. But that persistent hovering stopped on the last key, and the note faded into silence.

Leila was stunned. Not only did his composed song stir up flashbacks, but it captured her every emotion. Simplicity at the beginning turned into a fast whirlwind of disbelief, pain, and being lost at David's death, changing into even more extreme emotions at the tournament—coping with them all while confronting the internal Phoenix. She experienced triumph for a second with the fall of the Changeling until she turned numb, isolating herself while the Phoenix faced the world.

Ruben had watched the tournament, but how could he have seen the internal dilemma plaguing her? She had never been on the receiving end of going under a magnifying glass; she felt so exposed and ashamed. He somehow knew she wasn't as strong and stable as she projected. That meant the others in the house knew too.

He had his eyes on her, waiting for a response, but she kept her face away, hoping Ruben couldn't see how shaken she was. He had sifted through her soul and laid it out for her to see through music. Not in a cruel way, but he saw her that way by living through those hardships.

She finally found her voice. "Why a Firebird?"

"The Firebird is like a Russian Phoenix. In Slavic folklore, these birds live a harsh life, and so when they are captured, they are both a blessing and a curse to its captor."

*A blessing and a curse?* Alek's comment on how she was changing them echoed in her head, but the curse… *I'll bring destruction to this home?* A dark apprehension chilled her to the bone; she tried her best to brush off the feeling, but it lingered.

"What do you mean by 'a curse'?"

Ruben didn't answer right away.

"Please, let me know," she begged. "I will leave now if I can protect you. I cannot bear the thought of bringing any more harm to any of you."

His eyes widened—her statement of leaving startled him. "No, you cannot leave. Doing so would cause more harm than good."

"But this curse—"

"Do not think too much of it; it is only folklore."

"Someone told me that mythology was a way of explaining reality." She locked eyes with him. "I wouldn't be named as the Phoenix or the Firebird without a reason."

"No, you wouldn't have. Those birds represent a surviving strength after complete destruction that brings about renewal. The 'curse' I referenced can mean pain; heartache; strain from being close to one, like you. And you can agree with me—all of those have been felt here."

Leila couldn't argue. The Phoenix had definitely stressed this house quite a few times, so maybe it meant that—living with a Firebird wasn't easy. But she couldn't get out from under a chilling premonition.

Not able to combat his logic, she stood to leave. She could delve into her worry about 'the curse' in the quietness of her room.

"I can't possibly see how your coming here is a curse," Ruben stated.

She considered the usually silent man at the piano. His features remained guarded like on first meeting him, but now his defenses seemed lowered; he was open and talkative to her, and more life shone in his eyes—not so dark and withdrawn.

Leila and the Phoenix hadn't been complete screw-ups to these men's lives; they had needed her.

"I hope you're right." She thanked him for the music, then headed up to her room, head already spinning with outcomes for 'the curse'. As she ascended the stairs, *The Firebird's Lament* flowed through the house again and shadowed her footsteps, taunting her that another inevitable event was coming.

# XXXIV.

Ruben's tormenting music kept Leila from falling asleep, and as it repeated in her head, the music became the background music to David's death scene. They would run into the bank, fight Foster, she'd watch David get shot, then blackout… then it rewound and played all over again.

Leila tried to divert her thoughts, but *The Firebird's Lament* wouldn't go away, so neither did that horrific memory. Even the Phoenix could do nothing except watch her writhe in discomfort. She had overcome her guilt at his death, but that didn't soothe her much for she had been there… and done nothing.

She flipped over in an attempt to get away from that horror movie playing that one scene on the bare wall, but she caught sight of the red digital numbers of the alarm clock: 4:30. The time she had woken on that day.

The anniversary of his death now truly began. Leila didn't hold back the tears as she flipped back over with a pillow pulled around her head so Dragunov wouldn't hear her crying.

YESTERDAY HAD BEEN RUBEN'S TURN to return to the house; now Leila and Dragunov were alone. All meals were silent as Dragunov's thoughts lay heavy on something, and Leila wasn't in the mood to pretend everything was fine.

Other than the meals, Leila remained in her room, reliving the tragic day and dealing with the accompanying emotions. As David died again and again in her mind, her heart remained on how everybody back home handled the anniversary. Even if she had still been at her worst with the Phoenix, she needed to be with them on this day. She desperately needed them, and their comfort, their understanding, their support—she hoped they thought the same about her.

As much as she hated the idea, she needed to talk to someone and let out her stored-up feelings. She needed Dr. Moretti.

Her eyes drifted to her semi-closed door. She forced the thought out of opening up to Dragunov. Yes, she had started developing a bond with him, but this was far too personal, and she couldn't share that much.

*Is it that you're afraid he won't understand?* the Phoenix asked.

*No; I can see that he's been through heartache too.*

*Then do you think he can't give you the comfort you need right now?*

*You think he can?*

*He has changed toward you…*

Leila picked up her previously discarded thought of going to Dragunov. She stood and headed for the door before her mind could change, but her determined steps slowed as her courage faltered. That option looked so inviting, but she had never been good at letting out emotions through words—it was much easier to internalize them instead of risking being overwhelmed by those emotions.

Her feet led her away from the door, and she paced, debating on going to him or going down to the weight room to release her emotions the usual way. The more she weighed her options, the more she warmed to the latter, remaining in her comfort zone.

She had turned for the door, decided on beating out her emotions, when her foot collided with the brown chest. She yelped as she hopped over to the bed on one foot. She sat to nurse her injured toes, but her mind returned to the box. The heavy thing had barely budged, but it wasn't empty—something had shifted within the chest's stomach.

Curiosity not only got the best of her, but it had also bitten the Phoenix. Even with her foot still throbbing, Leila limped back to the aged chest. She watched the doorway for a few moments to see if Dragunov had heard her exclamation and come up to check on her. With no sounds of him coming up the stairs, she hefted open the heavy lid.

Nothing but a dark brown box sat inside. The box was in poor condition with scrapes, dents, chips, and scorch marks. She pulled it out of the chest and wafted up a faint smell of smoke.

"Fire," she whispered.

Leila seated back on her bed as she continued to look at it. Made of dark wood, swirling designs had been chiseled into the wood. Some of the engravings retained faded jewels sprinkled throughout.

A finger traced one of the swirls to the back where it hit something cold. Leila turned it around to find a metal knob to wind— A music box.

It was pointless not to listen to the lullaby a music box created. She glanced at the empty doorway again and hoped Dragunov's work kept him from hearing. She twisted the knob, mechanisms clicking inside as she wound it up. When it grew too tight to twist anymore, Leila lifted the lid.

A mechanical tune flowed out. Even with the outward damage, the insides appeared to be in a good state. Apparently, it was homemade with its plain and fading velvet lining. Even though cracked and rusty, a small oval mirror was set into the lid. But unlike the music boxes Leila had when she was younger, no spinning figurine caught the eye as it danced to the song. Instead, the majority of the box, kept safe behind the glass, was the mechanics producing the lullaby. The tarnished gears and apparatuses slowly turned each other, hypnotizing Leila with their repetitive movements. A shallow space held keepsakes and trinkets.

The Russian lullaby continued with a steady and deep, yet sorrowful beat. It reminded her of *Dragon's Serenade*—both beautiful and mesmerizing but sad and carrying so much weight. And like Dragunov, a story of heartache and grief lay behind the notes.

That was why she couldn't dig through the belongings. The music box, the stored items, and the song were too personal; she would be trespassing on someone else's cherished memory. And cherished they were, even loved and cared for. Just holding it had Leila feeling guilty at snooping.

The lullaby began to fade, growing weaker as the mechanisms lost tautness. With strain, it emitted its last note, drifting off into the silence, and the music box stilled.

Leila couldn't hear herself breathing. The room was left deathly silent because of the song. Reason came to her about returning the music box to the chest; doing so might shake off the stillness seizing the room, but dread froze her. That presence she had come to recognize and enjoy was now there. Leila feared what she would find on his face as she looked up to Dragunov in the doorway.

He did not meet her eyes—fixated on the music box in her hands. His face remained placid, and his eyes were as dark as ever, but she could feel the emotions raging within him even at a distance.

Leila was more uncomfortable than ever before with Dragunov frozen in utter silence, no movement, no hint of reaction at all. She wanted—*needed*—him back, so she began to close the lid.

It snapped him out of his trance, and he moved toward her. "No, wait, don't close it yet."

She opened it back up as he sat beside her. The reflection on his eyes in the mirror showed an onslaught of memories bombarding him. Motionless as stone, Dragunov reminisced in a silent moment. So, without asking, she passed the box to him, and he accepted it without words either.

Dragunov had recognized the music box, but he didn't know how to respond to that flood of memories. He stored them away inside just as he did to the music box—Leila could understand. It was easier locking memories away than dealing with them. But they build up, and the reopening of the dam engulfs.

And Leila had done that.

She had to break the unbearable silence—there had never been this awkwardness between them. "Dragunov… I didn't mean to… I'm sorry."

"No, it's fine. I've put off facing this for far too long."

She looked at him—the harmless box possessed the past he must confront. Whatever memories it held for him were those he tried to avoid, like hers with David. Leila hoped she could help him through it painlessly. Unlike her.

"You knew who this music box belonged to?"

Perhaps a lover, a wife, or a daughter.

At first, Dragunov didn't react like she had spoken, but then a hand sifted through the trinkets and letters, and he pulled out a small square—a photograph.

He handed it to her. "Edith Vladimirnaya." It was a burned picture of a petite Russian girl—around six with a bob of black hair. She had a small button nose and wide eyes—looking like a little pixie. The picture had been shot from the waist up, and she wore an enormously wide, joyful smile on her small face lighting up her eyes.

"Who was she?"

"One of the children in Chergyn I'd been stationed at for my first solo assignment. I was seventeen and tasked to be on the lookout for Chechen."

He smiled at the picture. "On arrival, I had to check in with Edith's father, and when I did, my welcome was his handshake and her wrapping around my legs."

"How did you take that?"

"As any new Spetsnaz fresh out on their own: like an assault. I ripped her off and nearly sent her flying, but I stopped from flinging her when I realized it was a little girl, not an attacker." He chuckled at the memory. "I held her by the arms, five feet above the ground, trying my best not to show my bewilderment, and she just beamed at me. 'I know you'll protect us,' she said. 'I feel safe with you.'"

She could imagine his shock being used to seeing rookies right out of the academy overreacting in a minor incident.

"From that point on, we were nearly inseparable. On my daily patrols, Edith sat on my shoulders giving me directions." He pulled out another badly burnt picture and handed it to Leila: one of a seventeen-year-old Dragunov and Edith sitting on his shoulders, grinning from ear to ear. His hands held onto her skinny legs, and the smile Leila loved seeing shared Edith's mirth.

He handed her another picture; this one of Edith in his arms, both enjoying each other's smile. Physically, Dragunov had changed by becoming bigger, stouter, but his smile remained the same—spellbinding and wholehearted. And the complete adoration in his eyes nearly choked her up.

Dragunov remained lost in the past. "The only store in the village was resale, and I found that music box. It was in such bad shape; it didn't even play anymore. I bought it anyway, touched up the colors, added sequins thinking Edith would like them, laid new velvet inside and fixed the gears, and then I gave it to her.

"Whenever you saw her, she had the music box under her arm. She loved it so much I think she even slept with it. For a return gift, she had her father engrave two gold heart-shaped lockets: one with my name and hers in the other. She gave me hers to wear, and she wore mine."

Leila enjoyed the peaceful bliss in Dragunov's eyes at sharing the heart-warming memories. But however joyful the memories sounded, she noticed one thing: he spoke in the past tense. With the photographic evidence in her hands, Edith had perished in a fire.

She hated to disrupt his serenity, but he couldn't move on if he didn't talk about what happened. Ironic that she would take Dr. Moretti's advice when she hadn't done it entirely herself.

"What happened?"

His mood darkened in an instant, and the joy vanished from his eyes. "May 15, 1996, 3:04 a.m., the Chechen attacked. Mortar fire woke me, and I rushed outside, first set on killing any terrorists I could find. I did so, but then the Chechen began targeting the townspeople with their assault rifles. So, I focused on shepherding them out of their houses and to safety."

"You were the only one fighting?" she asked.

"Some men of the village tried to assist, but they lacked battle experience. Instead of helping, they were being slaughtered, so I made them remain with the women and children. But yes, I was on my own."

His eyes shut against seeing the memory, but Leila knew it replayed behind his eyelids—her memories did. "Edith and her family weren't among the townspeople seeking shelter. I headed for her house to find the front door blocked by debris from a neighboring house. A mortar landed near me and pelted me with shrapnel—that's where I got most of these." Dragunov showed her his hands crisscrossed with faded scars.

She had never seen his hands up close, but the sight of the scars triggered Deja-vu. She failed to remember from where before Dragunov continued.

"After gaining my bearings again, I refocused on getting to Edith's house. I braced myself to barge in through the front door. Something was thrown out the window, a mortar hit the house, and it flung me back in a blinding flash."

He paused for a moment to shake off that image. "I awoke the day after in a makeshift hospital set up in the resale store. I searched the wounded and the gathered dead for Edith, but I couldn't find her. I went out to see that there wasn't a village anymore. Other than the surviving store, every structure had been destroyed, and homes were burning skeletons.

"Edith's house had been reduced to smoldering rubble. Her music box lay a few feet from the rubble where she had thrown it out the window. Right where the window should've been lay a small skeleton wearing my golden locket. I put it in her music box, found those pictures, buried Edith and her dad, helped with what I could, then left. I've never gone back."

His story ended with a brick wall, but Dragunov's memories, unfortunately, kept going, pulling him farther down the road of reliving that nightmare. His adoration of her then and his continuing devotion by speaking so reverently now tore her heart in two. Her loss didn't seem so devastating in comparison to losing one so young that he had loved as a daughter. Leila wanted to comfort him, to say something, but she found her mouth dry. What could she say that wasn't hollow, and that she hadn't told herself? Words could easily be spoken without sympathy.

But she did understand, so she recognized his pain—she lost someone too. Perhaps sharing her own story—the whole of it—would give him the correlation he needed that he wasn't alone in his pain—or convince her that *she* wasn't so alone either.

A hand lifted from the music box and touched something at his neckline; she couldn't see what he touched, but she could imagine what it was—Edith's locket.

She looked down at the box to prevent her emotions from swelling and overflowing at the tenderness of caressing that trinket. She concentrated on the fact that Dragunov had just opened himself to her so she wouldn't back out from doing the same.

"You… you said you had seen a fight in the… in the tournament." In the corner of her eye, his head turned toward her, but she kept her eyes locked on the music box. If she would've returned his gaze and had seen the sorrow in his eyes, she would've lost her nerve.

He picked up on her unspoken question. "Your last fight."

She closed her eyes, hating that he saw that one in particular. But now knowing which fight he saw explained his acceptance of the Phoenix's outbursts. "Then you know about David."

His silence was enough.

"And why you didn't question Bryan Foster's name before."

Again, he didn't answer.

She tore her gaze away from Edith's music box to land on the blank wall before her. It became the surface the reel of that night began to play on.

"David and I weren't only partners; he was my boyfriend for five years. Foster killed him the night of his birthday… which happens to be today."

Leila carried on retelling the memory before he could respond. "We were the first to arrive at the bank and found Foster's first victims for that night—seven security guards. Hearing a noise coming from the stairs, I figured he had the missing security officer as a hostage and decided we should search instead of waiting for backup.

"On the third floor, we found the security guard dead, and Foster jumped us. We fought him; he threw me on a table—breaking my arm—then he… he somehow got an opening to pull out his gun. Even with my broken arm, I shot at him, hoping to avert his fire from David—he turned on me. I woke three days later in the hospital and learned that David had died—shooting Foster made him jerk his arm up, sending a bullet through David's head."

She turned her head further away from Dragunov so he couldn't see the tears welling in her eyes. That guilt had haunted her so much, and even though the Phoenix and David had reassured her that she wasn't at fault, she had been there.

Dragunov's hand gently grabbed hers, and she clamped onto his. The support and comfort gave her the courage to say the rest. "Back home, his mother had boxed up my things in his apartment and left them for me. Inside the box, I found that he had planned to propose five days after his birthday, which became the day of his funeral."

She forced out the image of the Phoenix's Eye on her ring finger, but she could feel its ghost from trying it on so many times. But having that hand secured under Dragunov's banished it.

"That night when I blacked out, I met David in this emptiness. I stood in the blackness and he in this golden light. He told me that he had died, I was in The Between, and he had never been meant for me—someone else was. And he's right, we weren't connected like I thought we were; we didn't balance one another.

"But he didn't completely leave me; he's able to talk to me. I couldn't have gotten through the tournament without him, and he's controlled the Phoenix many times when I couldn't."

"That's why you changed so suddenly during our last fight," Dragunov said.

Leila nodded. "As I worked out, my thoughts had… drifted, and the Phoenix belittled me for it." She left out the fact that her thoughts resting solely on him was the reason. "I gave the Phoenix an opening, and I couldn't stop it. By just saying my name, David returned the reins to me."

Neither said anything else nor moved to make a sound. Leila went back to the memories of David as she remembered him—playful, brimming with life, his crooked grin—and she figured Dragunov did the same with Edith.

Dragunov took in a breath in an audible show of breaking the silence. "You being so quiet and preoccupied had me thinking the Phoenix had retaken you. I came up here to check. Then I saw Edith's music box…"

"And I brought back the memories." She looked at him. "I'm so sorry." Her apology had a double meaning—sorry for bringing the box out when she should've left it alone, and sorry for Edith's death.

He understood what she meant but shook his head. "Not for unearthing those memories. I had shut Edith out—blocking out the good with the bad. I needed to face them again as if in apology for doing so. Thank you."

Dragunov turned to her, eyes not dark and distant in mournful memories but tender and open. "But you… I am sorry for what this day holds in your heart. A day meant for celebration is tied with sorrow. It pains me to think about what you've been through."

She turned away from him. "But I had to."

"To become who you're meant to be. I understand. I also understand the Phoenix's need for revenge."

She looked back at him to explain.

His eyes hardened again. "I tracked down those Chechen, and I killed every single one of them, slowly, making sure they suffered."

A chill ran up Leila's spine at his confession—like he still savored the act. Dragunov must've noticed her reaction for his thumb rubbed the back of her hand and the severity left his eyes. "I justified it as vengeance for Edith and all of Chergyn, but I only tried to justify my revenge. And it did nothing to help my soul. The butchering just drove me to withdraw, making me the perfect Spetsnaz for feeling nothing, and the Dragon took my place."

All hardness disappeared, and the open Dragunov returned. "So, I can understand, but I also know it's not worth it. You'll lose who you are, Leila, to the Phoenix, and I won't let you do that."

"Then what can I do? I have to do something."

"I don't know right now. But you know that if you go after him right now, however you justify it, you would be killing him in revenge."

Leila turned away from him, indignant that he could see through her so easily and frustrated that even *he* didn't have a solution for her. Why else had the Phoenix emerged if not to kill Foster? A question made her turn back to him. "How did you come back?"

Dragunov kept her gaze. His eyes weren't boring into her like he demanded an answer, nor were they intimidating and harsh like she's seen so many times. They were soft, gentle, and oh so tender. Her breath hitched in her throat. His eyes held the answer: the reflection of her.

"I didn't until now."

His admission seemed like a confession of feelings. She couldn't think, and her whole being had no reaction. She had gone numb. The Phoenix remained back, fully renouncing command to her, allowing her to make the choice.

She struggled to breathe. She couldn't take her eyes away from his. The longer they stared at each other, the deeper she fell into his heart and his soul which she had grown to love, more so now that he had let her in further.

"Dragon? Lei?"

They jolted apart. They hadn't heard the Chubais twins coming in. Leila wished the brothers hadn't come home at that moment; she longed to know what would've happened between them. Perhaps it still wasn't the right time.

"I've never opened up to anyone before," Dragunov said quietly.

"Me either, not entirely."

One of the twins called out again, now with a worried undertone.

"Our pasts aren't meant to be told to just anyone." He turned to her and kept her gaze as he lifted her hand and kissed it. "Don't let that past keep you awake."

"I don't think it will now," she said.

Dragunov smiled as he gave her hand a final squeeze, then he let go, tore his dark eyes away from hers, and headed out, closing the door behind him.

Leila now drew in a breath. Her heart pounded, sending warmth to every corner of her body, replacing the ache of the coldest wound.

The idea of loving Dragunov seemed easy. She definitely loved the sensations of feeling again that came with it. But the final act of giving over to him wasn't going to be easy. Or maybe it could…

She looked over at Edith's music box. She picked it up and wound the knob to play the lullaby. "What should I do, Edith?"

She didn't get an answer.

# XXXV.

A few days passed, and Dragunov remained entrenched in her thoughts. Not only was Leila struggling with what to do, but just having him in her mind kept her warm and comfortable; she wanted more but also feared to have it.

She turned the news off and headed for the stairs, deciding on grabbing a jacket and checking out the Russian winter.

"Lei!"

A flustered Alek flew down the stairs, skipping some steps in his hurry. He never slowed. "Say yes, but don't mention me!" With a smile, he passed her and disappeared around the corner.

Leila stood stunned on the stairs, replaying what had happened because he had gone by so quickly. She thought she had missed something. *And, say yes to what? Don't mention him to whom?*

"Leila."

She loved to hear him say her name. She turned to Dragunov at the top of the stairs.

His dark eyes searched behind her for a moment, then returned to hers. "What did Alek say?"

"Nothing; he just ran by." It was hard to fib with his eyes on her.

The smirk told her that her lie fell flat, but the sight of it had her heart fluttering. "I highly doubt that; he can never keep something to himself."

She fessed up, "He told me to say yes, to whatever that is."

He shook his head, but she saw a smile. "Of course he did." He looked back at her. "He wants you to say yes to my question."

Leila waited for him to ask it.

Dragunov's eyes never left hers. "Every year, our head Spetsnaz leader hosts the Winter's Ball, and I wondered if you wouldn't mind accompanying me."

The invitation took a moment to register, but once it did, Leila's heart stopped. *Of course!*

She hoped her voice didn't come out too excited. "I know what Alek wants me to say, but how do *you* want me to answer?"

That dazzling smile hypnotized her again. "*I*… hoped you would say yes as well."

*How could I say no to that?* Leila returned the smile, even though she wanted to run up and hug him in delight. "Then I say yes."

As impossible as it was, his smile grew. "I'm glad. I have a friend that makes dresses; she'll be coming soon."

Her excitement about the upcoming event waned as she realized something.

Dragunov noticed. "What's wrong?"

"I've never been to any kind of formal ball, so I don't know how to dance… formally."

"We can't be having that. Good thing I'm a dance instructor too."

She turned to a grinning Alek at the base of the stairs. "Along with being a language expert and a Spetsnaz?" she asked.

"I'm a jack of all trades, Lei."

"Thanks for giving her an answer, Alek," Dragunov sarcastically commented.

That made the blond Russian smile even wider. "You're welcome. Always like to prepare someone before a shock. But it's not like she needed it. I knew she would say yes."

ALEK TAUGHT LEILA HOW TO waltz accompanied by Ruben at the piano. She had less trouble learning the flowing steps than she did with the fast tempo of Miguel's Tango. After she had mastered the steps, Ruben changed up the lineup of slow ballroom songs to one of the traditional Russian songs. At the fast, uplifting tune, Alek dropped the professionalism and performed the Russian short kicks. Leila backed out, and he tried to get Silvestrov or the twins to join him. Yurii did, matching Alek in every kick and hand raise.

Now the house was quiet again, for the men had left for their monthly break. Back home, they were enjoying Thanksgiving. Even though she still longed to ease their worry over her missing, her homesickness lessened by the day. Now comfortable with the Spetsnaz, if she went home, her heart would be somewhere else.

She was folding her laundry when a new set of voices drifted up to her. Dragunov's call of her name didn't give her time to eavesdrop. She finished folding her shirt, then headed down.

Walking across the catwalk, she found Dragunov's visitors were an elderly couple. The man had receding white hair and many sunspots from working out in the sun, but that constant movement kept his skin taut. Much shorter than him, the woman's white hair glistened, pulled back in an elegant bun. Her put-together attire from her pearl studs to the black heels showed her class. Their nearly wrinkle-free appearances counteracted the much older age the hair portrayed.

At her entrance, they looked up, and their faces lit up in delight. They both already had sweet and open faces, eyes sparkling with the life behind them and the prospect of the days to come.

Dragunov was smiling before Leila made it down the stairs. His own eyes were lit in pleasure—he was happy to see the elderly couple.

"Leila, this is Eremey and Adeleïda Semyonov; they are good friends, and Adeleïda will make your dress."

Like a grandmother, Adeleïda hugged and kissed her on the cheek in greeting. Leila didn't stiffen for the hug fit her personality, but the suddenness surprised her. They had just met, and Adeleïda embraced her like she had known her forever.

"Oh, Leila, I'm so glad to meet you. Your beauty will outshine the dress we make."

"Oh, well… I-I don't think that'll happen," Leila stammered.

Eremey moved with the same energy as his wife but took her hand and kissed it. "Nonsense; you are beautiful, inside and out. Dragon chose the right one to rescue."

Leila glanced at Dragunov to see his reaction. His eyes now became deeper, more tender, just like that night when she found Edith's music box.

"I believe I did."

"Come! Come!" Adeleïda broke in, breaking her eye contact with Dragunov. "We have much to do." She accepted a few catalogs from her husband, grabbed Leila's hand, and headed for the stairs, tugging her along.

Leila caught Dragunov's eyes twinkling in humor before she was turned around so she wouldn't trip up the stairs.

Adeleïda headed straight for her room, placed the books on the bed, sat, and then turned to a new page in her notebook.

"Alright, Leila, do you have a favorite color, or do you already have a dress in mind?"

Leila closed the door and took the time to sit beside her to think. "Well, I like fiery colors, but I don't have anything in mind. I've never worn a ball gown before."

Adeleïda smiled as she wrote down color ideas. "Great! We get to start from scratch. Those are always the most fun and original to make. Here" —she handed Leila a homemade catalog— "scan through and tell me what you like or don't like."

She did as asked, flipping through the pages and stating what she liked about one dress and didn't like on another. No to ruffles, no to a lot of tulle, and yes to straight line and so forth.

Alongside Leila's preferences, Adeleïda sketched a dress, combining some of the options and discarding those choices as she sketched another dress. She kept repeating one though, trying out different necklines or types of dress.

"What is that?" Leila asked.

Adeleïda chuckled. "When I saw you, this dress popped into my mind. I can't get it out of my head, but neither can I get it just right."

"I like some of the ideas there. Is there one thing you're sure about?"

"The color: gold. I have this gold fabric; it's beautiful. It's not the dull gold but a glowing gold, and it shimmers on its own in movement and when it catches the light. I also see you wearing gold gloves to the elbow and all your hair pulled up." She looked at her. "What do you think so far?"

"I'm loving the picture in my head."

"Tell me what you see."

With Leila describing her version, the dress became 'A-line' and the 'sweetheart' neckline transitioned into a choker of sorts—it gathered at the neck in five strips but still had spaces in between to show slivers of skin. The back mirrored the front except it came down as three pieces.

"I like it. No more changes?"

Leila shook her head. "I'm ready to see it."

Adeleïda laughed. "You have to give me three weeks first." She put her sketchbook down, relocated her notepad, and unrolled a measuring tape. "Now to the part women love the most."

DRAGUNOV WATCHED LEILA GET PRACTICALLY dragged back to her room. Even at seventy-eight, Adeleïda had enough spunk in her to act like an excited child, especially when it came to designing dresses. He hadn't seen her so eager before; it had to be because of Leila.

When he had called her to ask for her dress-making skills, the line went quiet for a moment, then Adeleïda asked so many questions. He filled her in on Leila's predicament that brought her to his home but told her she would have to meet her to find out what she was like.

He had heard in Adeleïda's voice the exhilaration she fought to suppress. To hear that, for once, he wasn't going alone to the Winter's Ball thrilled her, but he knew it meant more than that—she was elated that he finally found someone. And the way she accepted Leila with open arms showed her approval.

And now he sat with Eremey, listening to his commentary on what had transpired since Dragunov last saw them a year ago. He spoke when he needed to but let the older man ramble about his life. He could feel the hesitant air around Eremey as he danced around the questions he wanted to ask—Dragunov was positive Adeleïda told her husband everything she had learned on the phone—but Dragunov let him beat around the bush until he was ready to quell his curiosity.

Eremey had exhausted the tale of his life and looked at him. "So… Leila…"

Dragunov looked at him. "What do you think?"

It took him a while to respond as he thought. "One word: lovely. She captures your attention when she walks in. Adeleïda loved her immediately."

"She seems to have that effect."

Silence fell over the two men. Dragunov knew his admission stunned Eremey.

"It took some time to admit it to myself," Dragunov said. "It was a possibility that I loved her almost as early as when we met, but I truly realized it when we clashed."

"Clashed?"

"We both struggle with a similar dark side—vocal and violent. That connection pulled me even closer to her. And now I know that our dark sides emerged because of relatable tragedies. I'm not as alone as I thought. Someone can understand me without forcing me to change."

"You even love that dark side?"

"I do. I don't want her to change. I love everything about her."

Eremey sat quietly for a little while. "What about her? Does she feel the same about you?"

"I can see that she's close to giving in too, but she's hesitant, and I'm not pushing her." He looked at Eremey to explain. "Her previous boyfriend nearly became her fiancé but was killed in front of her, on his birthday. Later, she learned he planned to propose and found the ring. The day he had chosen to propose became his funeral. She's also struggled with the guilt that her actions contributed to his death."

Eremey shook his head. "Poor girl. I can't imagine how hard it is to lose someone you loved, then to love someone else."

"And put a dark side on top of that."

"I understand her hesitancy."

The sound of Leila's door opening ended their conversation. Dragunov knew Eremey wouldn't rudely blurt out what he just learned in front of Leila but could count on him sharing with his wife. And as the two conversing women descended, he also knew Eremey looked at Leila with a new perspective.

They stood to meet them, and Dragunov retrieved the catalogs, sketchbook, and notebook from Adeleïda.

"Make a decision, ladies?" Eremey asked.

She answered. "We did, but" —she shared a knowing look with Leila— "it's our secret. No one will see the dress until Leila has it on." She turned to Dragunov. "And you are to wear your black dress coat, black cap, and white slacks."

Dragunov pictured the attire she specified, trying and failing to guess the color of Leila's dress. But he smirked to play with Adeleïda's head that perhaps he had guessed the color.

It didn't work. "I gave nothing away. Those color choices can go with anything."

"Even I can't see? I'll play a part in delivering it," Eremey said.

"Not even you. My shop will be closed off to you."

"But your workshop is *in* our house."

"That means you're not allowed in half of the house."

Adeleïda thought better of it and took her notebook and sketchbook out of Dragunov's arms. "So, you don't try to peek."

Eremey shook his head as he went to get the door. Adeleïda looped her free arm through Leila's before heading out, and Dragunov followed them out to their car.

He laid the pile of books in the back seat and straightened to find Leila's ear close to Adeleïda's mouth as she whispered, Leila's eyes sparkling in humor. The whole time she looked at him. He wondered what the older woman told her, but regardless, he loved seeing the playfulness in those hazel eyes.

Leila laughed at her whisper. "I will try my best."

Adeleïda looked at him. "Yes, try your best, but I know he's hard to resist."

Eremey came up to shake his hand in farewell. "Women; when they get together it usually means trouble. I see it too," he added quietly. With Leila's eyes on Dragunov, Eremey saw the possibility of her loving the Spetsnaz leader.

Adeleïda hugged him.

He kissed her cheek, and she beamed at him.

She embraced Leila again. "I'll see you again in three weeks. Take care." She looked at Dragunov holding open the car door. "Both of you."

Adeleïda got in the car, and they watched the elderly couple drive off into the forest.

"What was she telling you?" he asked.

"To deny your questions about my dress. She said you're not used to hearing the word 'no'." She looked at him. "I told her I have before."

He chuckled. "You've been the only one brave enough to do so."

"Usually 'foolish enough' follows that phrase."

"It didn't turn out to be a disaster."

"I'm going to be successful here too."

"I get what I want."

She scoffed as she turned for the house. "Not this time."

"We'll see."

He wasn't talking about her dress.

# XXXVI.

Outside the frosty window, the heavy fall of snow slowed. Being the first week of December, it both felt and looked like winter. The land had been completely bleached overnight. Gray colored the sky, and a flawless thick blanket of white covered the ground, unmarred since the men spent the season with family. Adeleïda would return in two weeks with her dress.

Two weeks until she'd go with Dragunov to the Winter's Ball. Leila both looked forward to it and dreaded it. Other than prom in high school, she had never gone to such a formal event. With the men gone, she expressed her nervousness, and Dragunov soothed her by describing what happened every year. He recapped everything, and it sounded routine—nothing to stress over.

Her hands began to sweat, thinking about it all. Luckily, Adeleïda had paired gloves with her dress, so Dragunov wouldn't feel her hands sweating. She rubbed her hands on her jeans to dry them—nothing had ever made her react this way.

But she would be out of her comfort zone in a ball gown, dolled-up, in heels, and on the arm of a handsome man with hundreds of eyes on her.

And she was expected to dance.

Nothing to worry about.

Leila closed her eyes, forcing herself to think about something else. Her thoughts went to Dragunov and their continued visits.

She smiled, her nervousness already forgotten. Their visits and late-night talks—which grew later every night—were simple, liberating, and refreshing to just *talk*. Topics ranged from Leila's detective career to the Spetsnaz, David, and Edith.

Even though she enjoyed the visits and talks immensely, they continued to raise her sensitivity, which, in turn, raised her nervousness. There was no doubt that they were attracted to each other, but that threw Leila's imagination wild on what could happen between them at the ball—and how the Phoenix would react if it doubted that even Dragunov wasn't meant for her, just like Miguel.

But she did look forward to that alone time with him every day with absolutely no chance that the men could walk in on them, disrupting them. They hadn't tested the waters again like that moment between them when she had found Edith's music box.

She glanced at the box beside her Morning Glory on the nightstand. A lack of movement drew her eye back to the window. The heavy fall of snow had disappeared to sparse drifts of white swirls.

For some reason, the snow called to her. Leila added a few more layers of clothes, slipped into her boots, and headed down. Dragunov's door was closed—probably for some call.

She eased open the sliding door, slowly exposing herself to the frigid air. The cold stealing the breath from her lungs tempted her to shut the door and forget about venturing outside to remain in the comfortable warmth. Determination made Leila slip onto the patio and close the door behind her.

The deep snow had iced in the negative temperature, so her boots didn't sink far—the snow and ice crunching underfoot had just fallen. No wind blew to drop the temperature further, but the extreme cold still stung her face and bit into her skin, muscles, and bones under the layers of clothing. Her hot breath seen in puffs of smoke instantly vanished into the bitter air.

The coldness and sharp pains in her body eventually faded into numbness; she knew when to gauge it dangerous, but right now, she didn't care—the Russian wilderness had been turned into a winter wonderland. A pure white covered everything, long icicles drooped on the branches, the sky appeared serene, and snowflakes drifted down lazily. There were no sounds, other than the occasional muffled thud in the forest from a falling glop of snow.

When it snowed in New York, Leila hated it; it was just cold and bothersome from the wrecks it caused, complaints and headaches of being snowed in, the increase of emergencies, and the obvious struggle of chasing a criminal. It had never mesmerized her as it did now. The snow in Russia seemed magical, transforming the landscape and completely negating all sound.

Leila lifted her face, watching the snowflakes fall from the gray-and-white sky. She closed her eyes and enjoyed the icy touch which quickly melted, turning into liquid.

*"I bet doing this in the snow is great too. The feeling of the cold snowflakes melting on your face."*

David's voice melted away just like the snowflakes on her face. The memory brought a small smile to her lips. She lay down in the snow, and even though the frozen snow made her even colder, the shallow depth didn't make her feel buried. Being surrounded would take away from her contentment. Even though David wasn't there to enjoy it with her physically, she decided to pretend he was.

*"I am here with you,"* David said, his voice warming her heart.

*I know you are, but just not beside me.*

*"I don't have to be."*

"Leila?"

Startled, Leila turned to Dragunov standing a foot from her; being so focused on David's voice, she hadn't heard him walking in the snow. She had to answer the question in his eyes for people didn't voluntarily venture out into the Russian winter.

"The snow looked so quiet; I wanted to feel it too."

"Loud mind?"

From himself dealing with the Dragon, he had guessed at her dark side acting up again. "I guess you can say so, but thoughts, not the Phoenix."

He considered the white landscape. "It is quiet—never really noticed it before."

"It's even quieter when you become part of it." She closed her eyes against the desire to keep looking at him. He didn't bother her, but his arrival had distracted her, increasing her heart rate, making her body awaken when it had grown sleepy, contented and numb; she had lost the serenity she had gained.

Dragunov didn't verbally respond but accepted her unspoken invitation to join her. The snow crunching underneath him as he lay down beside her created the only sound for a moment before it faded, and the quiet peace returned.

Not a single sound disrupted the still air; even their breathing had quieted. Her body eased back down from being awoken, but it didn't lock up again because of the coldness; heat radiated off the body next to her, keeping her warm too. With Dragunov's comforting presence, she regained her serenity even quicker than before. Him beside her made it better.

"Tell me if you get too cold," he whispered, not shattering the peace but adding to it with his concern for her.

She felt a smile tug at her lips. "I don't feel the cold as much now."

"Numb?" The worry in his quick question warmed her further.

"No. Not anymore."

He didn't respond for a while.

"What gave you the idea to come out like this?"

She opened her eyes to watch the snowflakes drifting down—her turn not to respond quickly. A snowflake landed onto her eyelash, and she wiped it off before it could melt and turn to a tear. Her silence had the snow crunching as Dragunov turned his head to look at her.

"It was David's idea."

"He seemed very thoughtful. He had a lot of heart, didn't he?"

Leila smiled. "Yes; he wasn't afraid to show how much he cared about something. He had a lot of love—not just for me, but for everything and everyone around him. He was gentle." She had no problem opening up about David; she actually felt liberated.

"You were lucky to have known him. There are not many people like that anymore."

She looked over at him. "Everyone has the potential to be a gentle or a hard soul. Life makes you who you become, but it strengthens what type of soul you already have."

"What kind of soul do you think you have?" he asked.

Leila began to answer, but then she huffed out a puff of smoke as she turned back to the sky. "I really don't know anymore. I used to think that I had qualities like David: gentle, caring, loving. But when he died, I withdrew from everyone. I became hardened; I isolated myself; it seemed that I didn't care for anything, and I didn't… feel anymore. It felt like I became a completely different person."

Silence fell between them until Dragunov finished her statement left hanging. "You became the Phoenix."

"Unintentionally."

"But out of necessity."

Snow crunched again as she turned for his explanation.

"You had to become the Phoenix so you could carry on. You experienced something that robbed you of your caring, gentle, and loving soul. The Phoenix is your way of protecting yourself from ever being hurt again and from having to rely on someone for strength.

"When you first got here, you weren't you; the Phoenix was you. You were… unapproachable. But not so much anymore; now I think I see the Leila you've always been."

*The Phoenix's fire is starting to die down,* she thought.

"What kind of soul do you think you have?" Leila asked. "And don't say 'cold' or 'hard' either because that's not true. You have a heart and a caring soul, it's just… hard to get under your scales."

Dragunov chuckled, making her heart flip. "Before, I would have said that, but now… I'm not so sure either. I've never been one to get attached. Edith had slipped in without me realizing, and because of her, I don't let things in. Even the men; I never extended our relationships beyond comrades. With our line of work, you don't establish deep comraderies, and I have lived by that standard.

"But the men all care for each other, and their bonds and efficiency are stronger because of it. I've failed to realize that before—to see that it is better to be warm and accepted than to be cold and alone." His eyes locked onto hers. "I want to spend time with everyone, all because of you, Leila. I used to be like this with Edith, and now you've woken me again."

Leila smiled. "The Dragon's not angry that he's been disturbed?"

He smiled back, and Leila felt his warm hand find hers in the snow. "No, he's not. He sees that he needed to be awoken a long time ago."

They grew quiet again, and Leila turned back to stare into the sky before she closed her eyes. She was back in Central Park, but instead of David's hand laced with hers and feeling the warmth of his body, it was Dragunov's.

# XXXVII.

Even though Dragunov dressed up once a year for the Winter's Ball, he had never felt so jittery before. Not going alone to the ball this year wasn't the reason but *who* he was bringing with him.

*The best one I could ever bring,* he thought with a smile.

The crunch of snow under a car wheel outside announced the Semyonovs had arrived. Dragunov finished buttoning his black shirt as he walked to the front door. He opened it to admit Adeleïda with a box of shoes and another labeled jewelry, a dress-bag-encumbered Eremey, and the cold winter air.

Adeleïda beamed up at him as she stepped in. From that twinkle in her eyes, Dragunov knew Eremey had told his wife about him being in love with Leila. She rose up on her tiptoes to kiss his cheeks in greeting. "I see you still have a way to go. How is your beauty faring?"

"I'm sure she is coming along fine." He nodded to Eremey in greeting since the older man couldn't shake hands.

"I haven't been able to see it," Eremey said in regret.

"Of course not!"

He leaned closer to whisper, "She popped me quite a few times."

"I warned you what would happen if you tried to peek." Adeleïda began to head up the stairs.

"I could train you to become a better sneak, Eremey," Dragunov said.

Adeleïda pointed a warning finger at him as Eremey laughed. "I might take you up on that."

She frowned at her husband, then turned and continued up, mumbling all the way in Russian.

"I'm sure they'll kick me out, so I'll be back down soon." Chuckling at whatever Adeleïda had said under her breath, her husband followed.

Dragunov returned to his room to finish getting ready as well. Probably just as meticulous as the women, he had every piece of his attire laid out in order of how he should adorn them. Each individual medal—arranged in a specific order—lay next to his red sash, then next in line was his black cap, and finally, his white gloves.

His appearance had to reflect leadership, sharp and in command—no loose clothing, no dullness, and absolutely nothing out of order. Freshly washed and pressed, his shirt conformed to his torso, and the slacks were as straight as ever. He had polished the medals and black dress shoes the night before, so they shined on their own. The black cap rested evenly on his head without roughing up his hair, and there wasn't a space in the white gloves. Not a single hair was out of place on him.

Once again, he tried to imagine the color of Leila's dress based on what he wore. His color scheme was predominantly black with a gold stripe running down the sides of his white slacks. The ribbons of the medals ranged from purple to green, red to blue, yellow to white, and in between. He had every color present on him. Regardless, Dragunov had complete trust that Adeleïda would make him and Leila coincide perfectly.

"Only got to the door before Adeleïda kicked me out," Eremey said as he came into Dragunov's room.

He straightened the red sash running down his right breast. "How is Leila faring?"

"Didn't see her, but she sounded fine."

Eremey propped against the doorframe. "And how are we doing? Anything I need to get?"

He finished molding the gloves to his hands. "I'm good."

The men fell quiet as Dragunov added the finishing touches by making sure everything lay perfect. "How disappointed the ladies will be tonight, seeing you are taken," Eremey said.

Dragunov chuckled. "Indeed, they will."

"I think it best if you stay close to Leila to make sure they don't try to steal you."

Dragunov's reflection smiled back at him. "I don't think I have to worry; Leila can take them."

Eremey chuckled. "Then you might have to watch the men for they might try to take Leila from you."

"I'd like to see them try."

He stopped fidgeting and looked in the mirror. At first glance, his pristine attire would showcase his leadership if the numerous medals didn't. But he knew the medals would lessen in importance when he had Leila by his side.

His heart swelled in pride as he pictured escorting her down the stairs when their names were called. All would turn and be starstruck. He probably wouldn't even be able to take his eyes off her to notice. He couldn't wait to see her.

"So, any progress?" Eremey asked as he walked out, hinting at him and Leila.

"We have grown closer since we're able to talk more freely now." For the final time, he readjusted the cap until he was satisfied that it sat symmetrically with everything else, then followed the older man.

He sat at one of the couches. "Any expectations for tonight?"

Dragunov stared at the short hallway and closed door that kept Leila hidden. He released a heavy breath; he knew what he wanted to happen, but he also knew it wouldn't happen if he forced her. "I have to let the night decide for us."

Eremey shook his head. "You have a lot of patience—more than what others have."

He turned and sat on the long couch carefully, determined to make it through the night without a crease in his pants. "That's what this requires, and Leila deserves it. She doesn't need to be pressured anymore."

"Ah, you're talking about her dark side."

Dragunov nodded. "Just like mine, the Phoenix is pushing her toward revenge. She's holding out longer than I did."

"She has had too much put on her. How does she do it?" Eremey asked.

"She has a strong heart."

"No one should have that much put on their shoulders though—no matter how strong they are."

"No, I wish she didn't have to prove it either. But because it is her burden to carry, I hope she'll let me help her carry it."

Eremey chuckled. "She's changed you so much already."

Dragunov looked at him to explain.

"You've never expressed thoughtfulness before; you're not one to think about others—not that you're selfish—but you've always been… blank toward others. And now you look like you're more aware of the world around you—you're not so closed off. You have a different look about you."

"A good one?"

"A *great* one," Eremey corrected.

Because of his perception of him, Dragunov reflected on his changes through the months since Leila joined them. He knew his views had changed, but he hadn't realized it had been so noticeable. All the men had probably known that he loved her—probably before even he realized it. He shook his head in disbelief. "I'll never be the same without her."

Eremey nodded understandingly. "A woman will do that to you. But it also seems that we do it to them in return."

Something above Dragunov caught Eremey's attention. "*Там нет слов…*" He exhaled as he slowly rose, transfixed. *There are no words here.*

Dragunov could now hear the gentle swoosh of fabric. Heart pounding, he took a deep breath and released it in hopes of steadying him as he stood and turned.

Adeleïda stood out of the way as the overwhelming beauty made her way past. Her gold dress had a slight fullness to give it shape, it gathered at her neck, and the fabric itself shimmered in the light, giving the impression of an angel descending from Heaven. Her long black hair was sophisticatedly pulled up, and dangling earrings caught the light at every movement. Gold gloves covered her slender forearms, and a dainty bracelet sparkled on her wrist.

But the woman! The neutral colors of her makeup enhanced her natural beauty. Her dazzling smile never waned. Leila took his breath away—she spurred his recollection of goddesses from old stories.

He moved around the couches to wait at the bottom of the stairs but couldn't take his eyes off her. She seemed to float down the stairs; a gold glove on the railing kept her balanced for her eyes remained locked on his, entrapping him in those sultry, hazel eyes. Dragunov could do nothing except be further drawn into the deity's eyes, speechless at her beauty.

Leila stopped on the last step, so they were eye level. They gazed into each other's soul, Dragunov falling deeper and deeper in love.

He swallowed. "You are… absolutely beautiful."

Leila's smile grew even bigger. "You clean up nicely as well."

He smiled in return, then composed his face and bowed while kissing her hand, without breaking eye contact. Leila's eyes alighted with the memory of his last brushing kiss on her hand. His thoughts went there too, also landing on the intimacy between them, and he hoped it happened again. Perhaps even more.

"May I cut in now?" Eremey asked, shattering their concentration on each other.

Dragunov stepped out of the way as the older man took Leila's hand. "Oh, my dear, you are gorgeous! Let's have a look." He helped her down the last step, then held her hand as she twirled for him, laughing the whole way. "Stunning, just stunning."

Movement to his left brought Dragunov's eyes up to Adeleïda descending. He held out a hand to help her down. "*Ты не разочаровываешь*, Adeleïda." *You don't disappoint*, Adeleïda.

"Oh, you don't know what you're talking about." She stopped beside him and admired Leila smiling at something her husband said. "A dress is just fabric sewn together—it cannot be astounding without the wearer. Now, stand next to each other."

Their eyes met again as Dragunov stepped up next to her. Leila could very well stand out on her own, but next to him, they were undeniably together.

Adeleïda clapped her hands together in delight. "You are perfect! Exactly how I pictured it! But you two can stare later; you have a ball to get to!"

Eremey snapped back to the present and headed toward the door. Dragunov waited as Adeleïda placed a fur coat over Leila's shoulders to keep her warm in the winter air. When she turned to him, he held his arm out for her to take. With a smile, Leila placed a hand on his arm, and he led her out to the black SUV.

At seeing them exit, Eremey opened the car door to the already running and warm SUV.

"You two have a great time," Adeleïda told them.

"I'm sure we will," Leila said as she hugged her. "Thanks again."

She hugged Eremey before Dragunov helped her into the passenger side. He tucked her dress under her before shutting the door. He turned to say farewell to the elderly couple.

Adeleïda cupped his face. "Dragon, I'm so happy. You're meant for each other."

He smiled and kissed her on the cheek. "I know; I just have to tell her so."

She hugged him tightly, then let go at Eremey's urging. He shook his hand with a nod for encouragement.

Dragunov broke away from the couple to join Leila in the car. With a smile shared between them, Dragunov drove the car toward the Winter's Ball, looking forward to the outcome of the night.

# XXXVIII.

"You remember my warning?" Dragunov asked Leila as another valet opened the glass doors for them to enter, staring in mute bewilderment at the woman.

Leila's eyes lingered on the stunned valet. "I've been steadily reminded so far."

He chuckled. "Making sure."

Leila and Dragunov stepped into the lobby of the expansive ball house. Two enormous chandeliers hung from the high ceiling painted with a beautiful fresco of heaven and angels, gold leaf adorned the columns, and portraits of tsars that ruled Russia dotted the walls. Tsar Nicholas II, Tsar Peter the Great, even some of Catherine the Great and other empresses. Painted against dark backgrounds, the lifelike subjects in colorful regalia jumped from their frames. A steady flow of people ascended the wide marble staircase leading to the second floor.

"The lobby is unbelievable in itself," Leila whispered.

He helped her remove the heavy fur coat. "Wait until you see the rest."

Dragunov handed her coat to a servant, then offered her his arm again.

With a hesitant twitch of her rose-tinted lips, Leila placed her hand in the crook of his elbow. His free hand patted it.

"You will be fine."

"YOU MUST SIT, SVETLANA," ALEK continued to beg. "The doctor only allowed you to come because you promised to rest. He says you're close, and you could advance things. I don't want to deliver our child here; do you?" Her purple dress draped in a Roman style masked the length of her pregnancy. Even her tied-up red hair matched.

She continued to arch over him to see the staircase. "Oh, to hell with his orders! I know my body better than him! I cannot see Dragon and Leila sitting down."

He tried to herd his pregnant wife back to their designated table. "He's had far more experience than us. I think he knows what he's talking about."

Svetlana glared at him. "Are you treating me like a fat cow, herding me like this?"

Alek looked around her at the table where the medic sat with his family. "Silvestrov, please?"

Seated beside his wife, Nataliya, he had Klara on his lap. He looked too amused to help. "Welcome to fatherhood."

Nataliya turned on him. "Silvestrov…"

"*Папа*," his daughter pouted. *Daddy*.

With both women ganging up on him, he relented. "You know I'm poking fun at Alek," he told her. "How about this: after we say hello to Dragon and Lei, we go dance together. Deal?"

Klara couldn't resist. "*Сделка!*" *Deal!*

He looked at the husband and wife. "Svetlana, you should sit down. That boy of yours is bound to arrive earlier if you don't, and no one wants to see this ballroom become a delivery room."

Nataliya joined in to help. "Once we hear their names, we'll all get up to see better. Come sit."

Svetlana sighed in defeat and let Alek help her back to the table. She sat with a heavy sigh and ran a hand over her swollen belly. "Andriyan is so heavy, I want him out, but I don't want to ruin this night for Leila, so I'll stay down… for now."

Nataliya laughed. "I can understand. Nine months is a long time, but the last month is the worst." She looked over at her daughter, hand locked with her father's, attempting to pin the other's thumb down in a game of thumb war.

"Ruin it for Lei? What about me?" Alek asked.

Svetlana looked at him. "You've had how many years here? Seven? I think her first time trumps your seventh."

"I think we can also consider this as Dragon's first ball," Ruben said as he approached with Yustina at his side. The deep wine color of her dress accentuated her green eyes and made her pale skin glow.

"I thought Alek exaggerated when he told me what has gone on. Has he really changed that much?" Svetlana asked.

The twins walked up, each with their girlfriends on an arm. "Knowing Alek, he probably added embellishments," Yurii said.

"You'll see soon enough," Yakov said. "If his change is noticeable for men to see, you ladies will definitely key up on it."

"Spetsnaz leader, 'The Dragon', Dragunov, and Detective Leila Wells, from New York City, New York, the United States of America," the announcer called out.

A stunned silence overtook the ballroom for a brief second before every head turned for the stairs. Alek and Nataliya helped Svetlana to her feet, and Silvestrov held his daughter up.

"Oh… my…" Svetlana breathed. Leila embodied a goddess on Dragunov's arm. Her golden dress shimmered and shone like the sun as they descended. She bet the detective became even far more beautiful up close.

But the smile on Dragunov's face stunned her the most. In the seven years she had known him, Dragunov had never beamed like now. He was proud of the woman on his arm, and if what she heard from Alekseev proved true, love created that smile and glow around him.

"You'll see when they get closer," Alek whispered in her ear. He couldn't take his eyes off the entrancing woman, just like everyone else in the ballroom.

"I see it now. But I can't wait to see them close. I've never seen him so happy."

"None of us have," Silvestrov said.

"I like it," she said.

Alek chuckled. "We do too."

EVEN WHEN THEY REACHED THE base of the stairs and a new couple was being announced behind them, no eyes moved off her. Leila kept a smile on at all the faces staring at her and tried not to pay attention to those whispering to their neighbor about her. Dragunov being beside her kept her steady, but inside, she shook like a leaf.

Dragunov led her away from the stairs and to the right, through the sea of guests. The crowds parted for them, but not without further ogling and whispers she could now understand.

"Dragunov," she whispered.

His free hand covered hers on his arm. "I know." He looked at her. "I'm here."

His hand on hers already started to ease her tension. "Don't leave me alone."

She walked right beside him, but his eyes drew her in even closer. "Never."

A woman—possibly in her fifties but the wrinkles made her look even older—stepped in front of them. Many jewels and diamonds reflected all light, and she dressed just as exclusively in a fringed red dress. She had a white ermine draped around her neck. A cloud of strong perfume thickened the air around her.

"Dragunov," she purred and held out her hand with a ring on every finger.

"Ms. Lebedva." He took her hand and kissed it. "You become lovelier every year."

The caked-on makeup made it hard to tell if she blushed, but the dimpled-smile and fluttering of her eyes said she had been a victim of his charm. She turned her attention to Leila.

"And wherever did you unearth this jewel?"

"I did not." Dragunov looked at her. "She came to me already polished."

"Hard-cut, I think is what you mean," Leila corrected.

Dragunov smiled. "No, you had already gone through the flames. I was on the receiving end."

"Even so, I don't think I'm polished."

"There are some edges, but you're still the right cut."

"Sounds like you match this one perfectly," Ms. Lebedva said, breaking their focus on each other, reminding them of her presence. "Now, I must go and find a dancing partner; he will be a poor replacement." She grabbed Leila's hand and squeezed it. "You are gorgeous, darling; one that will be greatly envied tonight—not only for your beauty either." Her eyes flickered to Dragunov. "Farewell." She walked off without a backward glance.

"Well," Leila began as they watched her disappear, "are all of your past dates like that?"

Dragunov chuckled. "Most."

He continued to lead her through the crowd with a few acknowledging him in passing. When the masses grew lighter, they had reached the tables and his team at their reserved table. The men were dressed similarly to Dragunov but in all-black, not mixed like him. Their medals also varied in color and numbered less. Everyone stood when they approached except for Alek and the woman who Leila assumed to be his wife, Svetlana.

Alek explained why they remained sitting down. "I'm having to restrain her; the doctor said she shouldn't be on her feet a lot."

They greeted them with smiles and hugs on the parts of the women. Yurii's girlfriend, Sacha, brown-headed with a single streak of blonde and dressed in a bright blue dress, extended her hug into questions about the States. Elizaveta was also brown-haired and wore a light pink dress, but so petite, she stood a good three heads shorter than Yakov—she stayed nearby to hear Leila's answers. Yustina had greeted her but then retreated to stay by Ruben; she appeared to be just as quiet and mysterious. Nataliya and Klara were both blonde and wore matching shimmering navy-blue dresses. Svetlana's purple dress brightened her fiery red hair.

The tuning of wind instruments from the orchestra at the end of the ballroom announced the beginning of the ball, ending their Q&A session. After some more adjustments, the orchestra began a slightly upbeat song.

Klara bounced up to her father. "*Папа, ты же обещал! Первый танец!*" *Daddy, you promised! First dance!*

Silvestrov nodded. "*Да, я сделал.*" *Yes, I did.* "Excuse us, Leila." His daughter pulled him toward the dance floor, skipping.

Leila watched the father and daughter go out to the dance floor, then turned to find Yurii, Yakov, and Ruben had disappeared with their dates as well. Nataliya had joined Svetlana and Alek at the table. Dragunov walked up to Leila.

"I haven't spoken with Svetlana yet," she said. Even though it sounded like a poor excuse for being nervous, she truly hadn't yet.

He nodded and gestured at the table. "Whenever you want to go but know we don't have to dance if you're not comfortable."

"And waste Alek's lessons? I don't think he'll be pleased."

Dragunov chuckled as he walked her around the table to an opening by Svetlana. He helped Leila sit by pulling out her chair, but then a man approached them. He and Dragunov conversed in Russian, but Dragunov kept a hand on her back, providing reassurance that he was still there.

"So, Leila, is Russia what you thought she would be?" Svetlana began.

Leila chuckled. "No, not at all."

"What did you expect when you first learned you were coming?" Nataliya asked.

"Honestly: nothing. I saw this as another job in a different place. I had just finished an assignment in Michigan, so I figured it would be like that but colder."

The women laughed. Dragunov finished speaking with the man and sat beside her.

"Mother Russia's been good to you so far though, hasn't she?" Svetlana asked, eyes straining not to glance at the Spetsnaz leader beside her.

Leila understood what she hinted at. After taking a moment to think, she smiled; she appreciated everything that had happened, even the bad. It had all been a test for her, to reveal her relationship with the Phoenix—now an accepted part of her—and brought her to Dragunov—an equal, and the love she felt she deserved and needed. "I think so."

She looked at Dragunov to find his dark eyes warm and twinkling, understanding what she agreed to.

Klara and Silvestrov returning to the table caught their attention.

"You seem a bit out of breath there, Silvestrov. Getting old, are we?" Alek began smugly as the father sat beside his wife and lifted Klara onto his lap.

"I'd like to see you get out there, Alek. I thought young people have more energy."

Alek grinned. "Can't. My pregnant wife is ready to pop; I don't have a dance partner."

"You do too. You have Leila; I recall you teaching her how to waltz."

His smile disappeared—caught. "She's Dragon's date. I can't steal her. He won't have anyone to dance with then."

"If you want so desperately to dance, ask Leila," Dragunov said.

Alek looked questioningly at Leila. She nodded. "Of course, I'll dance with you, Alek. I have to show my teacher what I learned."

"On how to step on your partner's toes?" Svetlana asked with a smile, turning to him.

Her husband scowled. "No, and that was one time."

"Or did you show her how to look ridiculous?" She laughed.

Alek looked at Leila. "See, Lei? Even my wife picks on me."

Svetlana placed a hand on his cheek and turned him back to her. "Because we wouldn't be as much fun if we didn't laugh at each other." Alek smiled—he couldn't resist her.

The notes in the air changed as the band shifted into a slow-paced song. Feeling more comfortable, Leila looked at Dragunov in question. He stood, offered a hand to her, and helped her stand. "Sorry, Alek, but I'm dancing with her first."

"By all means," Alek said with a smile as he waved them on.

They headed to the dance floor and joined the other dancers in the waltz. At first, Leila knew she remained stiff from a number of things: being focused on executing each step Alek had taught her, not wanting to embarrass Dragunov from messing up the graceful dance, and from feeling all eyes in the room on them. But the gentle encouragement from Dragunov on getting out of her head to enjoy it and him saying he had her, eased her into doing just that, letting him take control.

Once she did, they fit in perfectly with the other swirling dancers as they flowed with the music. Just as she got the hang of it, the waltz came to an end. However, it transitioned into another song, so Leila and Dragunov stayed dancing. This next round was less formal, so Leila relaxed even more. The constant smile on Dragunov's face and his arms around her made her not want to leave.

But the song came to an end, and a faster-paced Folksong came up—one with more intricate steps. They left the dance floor before they could be swept up into the dance. As they headed back to their table, a man approached them.

"Finally, I catch you," he said with a smile as he firmly clasped Dragunov's hand. "I thought Lebedva wouldn't let you go."

"Me either, but I'm glad she did. I can breathe this year," Dragunov said.

A deep laugh rumbled his large frame. He was as tall as Dragunov but on the wider, less lean side. A long brown beard and blue eyes as hard as steel finished his solid appearance. Even in this relaxed atmosphere, he emitted a dangerous and lethal aura. Leila had first imagined all Spetsnaz to look like him.

"Leila, this is Vyacheslav. He expunged your name of all accusations," Dragunov introduced.

He turned to her. Those sharp-looking eyes softened as he took her hand and kissed it without breaking eye contact. She felt that his eyes penetrated to her soul. "It is a mighty pleasure to finally meet you, Leila Wells."

"It's my pleasure to meet you as well and thank you for what you did."

He straightened. "Oh, no need to thank me. I enjoy a good challenge." Vyacheslav looked at Dragunov. "And it's not every day Dragon comes to me for help. But now I see why.

"I'll let you be now." With a final handshake and a meaningful look at Dragunov, he bowed to Leila and disappeared back into the crowd of people.

LEILA APPEARED TO BE ENJOYING herself. He surely was. The women had included her immediately, and since the first dance, she seemed to have shrugged off the stares still directed at her. Dragunov saw them, and at his attention, those stares quickly vanished, but now that they didn't bother her anymore, he felt that they could look all they want.

Laughter from Leila and the other women sounded as beautiful as his date looked, making it hard to keep his eyes off her. Her soul enchanted him more, though. Even after everything she had been through, she never lost her determination to survive. He truly hoped she could see herself as he saw her. Strong. Magnetic. Independent. Lovely.

It surprised him that she didn't question him about Vyacheslav's comments. Even though the Phoenix seemed to have slackened its temperament on what would set it off, Dragunov remained careful on letting her know how much he cared for her. He would have to get onto Vyacheslav later.

Another slow song came up; Alek looked to his wife, then to Leila who looked at Dragunov. He simply nodded. Alek kissed his wife, then whisked Leila off to the dance floor. Silvestrov and Nataliya had also slipped off to dance while Yakov's magic tricks entertained Klara. He would pour Elizaveta's drink into his hands and make it vanish or make a fork disappear and reappear behind Klara's ear.

"I'm so glad to finally see it in you, Dragon," Svetlana began. The others were too preoccupied with Klara giggling and asking for more tricks to pay attention to them.

He lowered his champagne and lifted an eyebrow. "See what?"

She smiled warmly. "Love."

Dragunov held her gaze for a moment, then looked to the dance floor. He knew exactly where Leila and Alek were after just taking his eyes off her to respond to Svetlana. Leila laughed with Alek as they danced; Dragunov shared her merriment, smiling. He absolutely loved seeing her being carefree. "Is it that noticeable?"

Svetlana laughed. "Not unless someone knows you, which I do. Leila has opened your eyes again and holds your heart. You can't seem to do anything right without her, can you?"

He chuckled. "No, I can't. It's frustrating."

"Oh, I know how that feels." Svetlana leaned back in her chair with a hand drifting over her swollen belly. "Alekseev frustrated me so much when he stumbled into my life. I couldn't get him off my mind, and I didn't seem to be living if he wasn't with me. So, I married the fool." She glanced at the dance floor. "I found out he had my heart that very first day we met." She looked back at him. "And I had his."

Dragunov watched Leila and Alek walk back to them and found Leila's eyes locked on his as well. At first sight, he had been besotted back at the Seaport, but it took a while for him to realize that it was love. Could it be the same for her?

He stood to hold out her chair. *I'll find out soon enough.*

AFTER AN UNEASY START, LEILA'S confidence grew to where she and Dragunov nearly stayed out on the dance floor. She didn't want to lose one chance of dancing with Dragunov. Even though Leila felt herself tiring from dancing and the late hour ticking away, she wished the night wouldn't end. As she moved closer to him, Dragunov never pulled back. Their magnetism—their attraction—wasn't a flimsy imagination.

Something in Dragunov had changed after she and Alek returned from dancing. A new sense of determination in his eyes meant he was set on something. And the way he wouldn't remove his eyes off her had her stomach flipping.

For three songs in a row, the orchestra played slower songs that didn't require much footwork. The third song happened to be an instrumental version of a familiar love song, but the name slipped past her. But the name—and the music—didn't matter as Dragunov held her in his arms; she couldn't think on much else. The room swirled around them, but Dragunov remained the only thing firm.

The song softened to an end, slowing the swirling dancers to a stop. But the room continued spinning as Leila faced Dragunov. He had pulled her in tighter to him where they breathed each other's air—their faces inches apart. Her heart pounded so much it hurt, and it wasn't from the dance. Feeling his heartbeat against hers lessened the pain.

"Leila, I—"

A familiar set of chords striking at a sad pace froze them. The recognition of the tune blew away the intimacy building between them with an icy vengeance. Never would she have thought Edith's lullaby was a Russian song the orchestra would play.

The lightness in his eyes hardened into a deep hollowness as he replayed the night Edith died in his head—that same void came into her eyes when she thought of David's death. "Dragunov…"

An organ joined in to emphasize the deep timbres in the mournful lullaby. "For Edith."

His face remained blank but stern as he experienced that dreadful night over again; like he had forgotten Leila's presence, and nothing else existed. As they danced, David's death played in her mind as well, stirred up by Edith's lullaby since she had shared her wounds with Dragunov that night too.

But she forced those pains tied to David's death away. Dragunov meant more now. Leila noticed nothing but him, concerned that he wouldn't come out of his memories in ample time—when she fell back into reminiscence, it always took time for her to return to the present, or the Phoenix emerging would snap her back.

Each couple first danced individually, but when the violins, cellos, percussion, and drums joined in the mournful song, Leila and Dragunov merged with the rest in spinning around the dance floor.

The composition slowed into solo thumps of drums, seeming to finalize the deaths they both had shared. After the sets were repeated twice, the singular chords from the beginning replaced the steady thuds. Those isolated taps sadly drifted off into the ending.

An eerie silence swept across the ballroom. Leila didn't even notice if the orchestra had begun a new song or if the dancers swirled around them, wondering why they were frozen in the middle of the dance floor. She could only think about Dragunov. His set, firm stare hadn't changed during their dance.

Edith's locket popped into her head, and after taking a deep breath—hoping the action could bring him back to her—she placed a hand against where it hung. She felt the shape of the heart locket under his shirt.

It worked. Dragunov blinked the blankness out of his eyes and looked down at her hand on his collarbone. He enveloped her hand in his and looked at her. Those dark eyes, once light, were now strained with the sorrow he had experienced at the expense of Edith's lullaby.

Leila could understand his withdrawal, and she knew he recognized the silent apology in her eyes. The Phoenix and the Dragon found solace in the understanding of each other's pain.

# XXXIX.

Leila woke the next day with sore feet. She wasn't as tired as before in the tournament, but the dancing had drained her. She forced herself to get out of the warm bed and headed to the bathroom on tender feet.

Silvestrov and Nataliya had been the first to leave, with Klara asleep on her father's shoulder. It was past one when the rest did the same. Poor Svetlana entered the lobby in a stumbling exhaustion to where she concerned quite a few people waiting. Alek had her sit as they waited for the valets to pull up their vehicles, and she almost passed out against him.

The closeness of Leila and Dragunov went unnoticed as all attention stayed on the pregnant woman—even by them. By the fatigue on her face, Leila could see her going into labor soon or at least in a few hours.

When Alek's car pulled up, Dragunov helped Alek pull her to her feet and walked her to the car. Yurii, Yakov, and Ruben went with them, holding open doors; their dates stayed with Leila in the warm lobby.

They came back in to retrieve them. Dragunov looked at her as she slipped her arm through his. "We will be seeing Andriyan soon."

Leila was surprised she wasn't awoken by Dragunov getting the call. On the ride back, she had made him promise to wake her if he did. She knew Russian women were strong, but Svetlana couldn't fight it for long.

Her mind was still replaying the night when she stepped out of the shower and began to dress. She would never forget it—without a doubt the most fun she'd had in a long time. All because Dragunov enjoyed it as well. He seemed more laid-back, and he nearly never stopped smiling.

Then the dance before Edith's lullaby… He had kept her close to his chest, even when she meant to twirl out—he didn't want to let her go. And neither did she want to let go of him. Their lips had been so close.

She looked up at her reflection, still blurry because of the fog.

"Do I love him?"

*"Why do you ask that?"* David asked.

"I'm still in love with you, but at the same time, I'm falling for Dragunov."

*"Lei, you are in love with a memory—my ghost. I can never come back. I will only remain in your past. Dragunov is here, hurting in the pain of emptiness that you are filling. You just need to completely let go, lay me to rest, and latch onto him."*

"Leila?" Dragunov's voice jolted her heart to speed faster in response. She opened her bathroom door and stepped out to find him easing open her bedroom door.

He held up the phone in his hand. "Svetlana's gone into labor."

She threw her damp hair up into a ponytail and rushed back into the bathroom. "She lasted longer than I thought!"

LEILA AND DRAGUNOV WALKED DOWN the hospital hallway in the maternity section, headed for room 102. Dragunov tapped on the door.

"Come on in," Alek answered.

Dragunov pushed open the door for Leila to enter first. Pale and with strained eyes, Svetlana gave a courageous smile at their approach, holding a small bundle. Alek sat on the other side of the hospital bed with an arm draped around the back of his wife for support, looking worn out as well but glowing in pride.

Ruben and the Chubais twins were already present, propped in various places in the small hospital room.

"Glad to see you two," Alek greeted.

"Thank you for coming," Svetlana added weakly.

"Wouldn't have missed it." Dragunov gave her a peck on the cheek.

Leila gave her a hug. "I expected us to be here earlier."

Alek chuckled. "So did I."

"Andriyan wasn't ready," Svetlana said.

Leila looked into the small bundle: Andriyan already had a head full of blond hair under the blue stocking cap. He slept with a tiny hand closed by his face.

"Do you want to hold him, Leila?" Svetlana asked.

"Sure."

"He's heavy," she warned as she handed him into Leila's arms. She sat as she continued to look him over. Her heart warmed at the new life.

A scarred hand suddenly appeared by Andriyan's smooth face as Dragunov leaned down, an arm gripping the seat behind her to look. The baby boy's little hand clasped around his large finger.

Dragunov chuckled. "He's got more strength in one hand than your entire body, Alek."

"Ha ha," he mocked.

A soft knock brought Yurii to get the door. He opened it to Silvestrov and his family. Klara beamed with excitement, pulling her father along.

"How are you faring, dear?" Silvestrov asked of Svetlana.

She smiled. "As good as a mother coming out of childbirth can be."

Nataliya chuckled. "I can understand that."

"What? No concern for me? I suffered through quite a bit myself," Alek complained.

"You'll manage."

Klara led him over to where Leila sat with the baby. Klara stared at Andriyan until a hand stretched out and stroked his cheek. She giggled. "*Он такой мягкий.*" *He's so soft.*

Silvestrov leaned down to admire the baby. "Well good, he looks like Svetlana; he'll be handsome."

THE NEW FAMILY WENT HOME after a few days. Leila and Dragunov visited often to help them adjust and provide a break since they were the closest.

Leila sat talking with Svetlana on the couch as she held Andriyan. Dragunov and Alek stood in the kitchen. He suddenly brought his phone to his ear. His eyes shot to her before he turned away.

"*Что случилось?*" he asked. *What is wrong?*

Alek watched his leader listening to whatever the caller had to say. Since he stood beside Dragunov, he could overhear the dialogue. Quickly, Alek glanced at Leila, then turned back, attentive to the conversation.

Leila was worried now. The caller had to have mentioned her name since Alek had looked at her. Svetlana watched the men, and even Andriyan had stopped cooing like he knew he needed to be quiet. The entire house stilled in apprehension.

Dragunov ended the call with his back to her.

"What's happened?" she asked.

"Evgeniya." Dragunov turned to face her—the tightening of his eyes told her it wasn't good. "She knows you're with a Spetsnaz team, but she hasn't narrowed it down to us, yet."

Fear froze her. She wasn't afraid of the woman, but the unknown behind her bothered Leila. And Dragunov implied that they would discover her location.

Andriyan started crying as though he felt the anxiety in the room. His wailing snapped everyone back to the present. Svetlana began cooing, rocking her son back and forth, telling him everything was going to be fine.

Dragunov whispered something so low to Alek that Leila couldn't hear it. His gaze went back to her as he walked toward the couch she sat on. Leila stood, reading the urgency to get home in his eyes.

"We'll handle this, Svetlana," Dragunov began. "Don't think you're in any kind of danger."

"I know you'll manage it; you always do." She stood to hug them goodbye. "Be careful, both of you."

Alek hugged her, then they immediately went to the SUV and headed home.

# XL.

Evgeniya's emergence meant that whoever used her as a front man searched for Leila again, and the concern in Dragunov's eyes meant that they were closing in. She had nearly forgotten about Petrishchev's wife, but Dragunov had kept tabs on her because her involvement left him uncertain.

Dragunov gave her a backpack to fill with a few days' supply of clothes. "Just as a precaution."

But Leila could see the uneasiness in his eyes—he didn't like being so lost in the dark with the only light being Leila.

NIGHTS LATER, LEILA HAD EDITH'S music box in her lap, trying to focus on the mournful lullaby, but failing every time she heard Dragunov's phone ring. It rang for the tenth time in two hours.

Her backpack full of clothes had been sitting near the door for a week now. One week and nothing new. It made Dragunov more uneasy by the day. The rest of the team voluntarily returned from the seasonal holiday to shadow Evgeniya in St. Petersburg.

The others came in for a breather—and Alek to check on his son—but Ruben stayed. His reputation for stealth and infiltration made him invaluable. He knew how to become a shadow and stay invisible.

She didn't like it. It felt too much like a ploy, spooking them into immediate action, and once they began to settle—thinking it nothing—then the trap would spring. If she could think that then with them being Spetsnaz, they could see through the deception and not fall into it—especially since Dragunov hadn't discarded Evgeniya. But with Leila being endangered, she worried they would overlook the signs because of their concern for her.

*They're too experienced to make mistakes,* the Phoenix said.

*Look who trusts someone else. Usually, I would be telling you to have faith.*

*We have both changed. I have always made you bold, but now is not the time for that.*

*But you don't like this hiding either.*

*Of course, not; I would prefer to face this head-on while keeping them back, so they don't get hurt. But that's what they're doing, and I agree with it; your safety is all I care about right now.*

*What if this unknown figure is Foster?* Leila asked.

*It doesn't matter if it is or isn't. They can't do anything to hurt us; we are too strong. Just stay calm.*

The music box stopped playing and she rewound it. *Calm,* she repeated as she lay back with the music box on her stomach and closed her eyes, trying her best not to let her imagination run wild with possible scenarios.

"YOU KNOW WHO I AM."

The little girl did look familiar smiling in front of her. She looked so sweet with her bob of black hair, a cute button nose, and wide innocent eyes making her look like… a pixie.

Leila gasped as she recognized the six-year-old Russian girl.

"Edith?"

The same beaming smile captured in Dragunov's pictures appeared, happy that she had finally named her—like Leila had just won a game show.

"And I know who you are: you're Leila."

"How do you know me?"

Edith giggled. "Because Dragon loves you! He thinks about you all the time instead of me now! I'm so happy! He's finally letting me go!"

Leila stared at the little girl. "He… loves me?"

She clasped her hands and jumped up and down. "Yes! But he's so nervous to say so! I think it's so sweet!" Her brown eyes turned on her. "You want to love him, but you're scared too!"

"Wait!" Leila's hands came up as if they could physically stop her. "How do you know what I feel?"

"Because we've been watching you two." David Neal, Jr. appeared to stand beside Edith. The little girl looked up at him in adoration.

Leila stared at her dead boyfriend. "David? Are we in The Between again?" She looked around. An inky blackness surrounded them but not close to being as cold. Warmth caressed her bones.

"No. We're paying you a visit as you sleep."

Edith held up a finger. "A very important visit!"

"How so?" Leila asked.

David's molten chocolate eyes locked on hers. "We're here to urge you to let me go—like Dragunov is letting go of Edith."

Edith smiled. "I know why you are scared to, Leila. You think that loving someone else would be betraying David. But you won't. Dragon has been so lonely since I died, but you're filling that hole. He feared loving you too because he didn't want to replace me."

That wide smile appeared again. "But he's not, and he's seeing that. I still have a place in his memories, but you have his heart! Dragon's realized that he has enough room for both of us!"

David took over, "Dragunov has realized that Edith will only be a memory, and he can't change that by holding onto her. I will only be in your past too."

Both he and Edith looked over at something, and Leila followed their eyes to see a picture of Dragunov standing outside in the snow, gazing up at the bright moon.

"He loves you, Leila, with all of his heart," David said.

Another picture came up, of her dream in Woodlawn Cemetery before she left for Russia. And that portal with those dark, intense eyes and the scarred hand of a man reaching out for her. The hand and eyes belonged to Dragunov.

There—she had recognized his eyes and hands from the portal. She had loved him from the very first day. Her subconscious knew she found the one destined for her, but she fought it, not wanting to believe it. Leila looked over at David and Edith with tears in her eyes.

"I knew from the beginning… Why did I fight this for so long?"

David chuckled. "You *are* stubborn."

She laughed with him.

"You've been his all along. He is your future. Go to him."

"I couldn't have gotten this far without you, David."

He smiled that crooked grin. "Love you too, Lei."

Edith ran to her and threw her arms around her waist. "You're perfect for him!"

Leila moved to hug her back, and she woke. She still lay on her back with Edith's music box playing on her stomach—like nothing had happened.

She sat up and looked down at the music box in her lap. The churning mechanisms caught her attention first, but she tore her gaze away to the stored trinkets. She pulled out the picture of Edith sitting atop Dragunov's shoulders. His hands holding Edith's legs drew her eyes. They weren't scarred, but she knew they were now.

Her heart pounded in her chest as she sat Edith's music box aside and ran out of her room. She loved him, and he loved her.

He was meant for her. He had gently brought down the walls she had built around herself, just like how David said he would.

Leila flew down the stairs and found him just as she had seen: outside the patio in the snow, his dark silhouette gazing up at the moon. She pulled open the door and went out into the freezing Russian night without a jacket.

He turned at the opening of the door. "Leila, where's your jacket?" He began to take off his.

"I don't need one right now," she said as she trudged out to him. She spoke the truth—the negative temperature may have iced her body, but she didn't feel it.

He placed his jacket around her, but her cupping his face halted his reply. "I love you, Dragunov."

She didn't wait to see his reaction; she lifted to kiss him, but he met her at the same time. Her heart exploded in warmth like a river bursting through a dam after being held at bay for too long. Her wounds and painful memories were swept away in that loving flood like debris clinging to stay afloat. The warm river continued to rush through her limbs, making them awaken as they wound around him, pulling him closer.

Their kisses were long and deep, showing their need for each other. Her body fit perfectly against his, warmed by his enveloping heat, and needing to feel his heartbeat against hers. Dragunov's hand slid up her back, firm and solid, keeping her pressed to him as their desire deepened.

They finally broke away, panting for air, but stayed locked together, forehead against forehead. No cool air could be felt between them.

"I love you too, Leila," Dragunov whispered.

Tears streamed down her face. She didn't realize how much she craved to hear those words from him. "Say it again."

He softly wiped them away. "I love you, Leila Wells."

She kissed him. "How did we last this long apart?"

"I don't know, but I never thought I would need something as much as you."

"Me either."

Dragunov caressed her face. "You're the one I've been waiting for."

Her breath hitched at his words. Even though she clung to him for support, her knees gave out underneath her, but his arms around her kept her standing. All pressure had been lifted off her soul, crushing her ever since David died. Now she could breathe.

"David told me to look for the one to say that," she said.

He kissed her head. "You found me."

Leila ducked into his chest, and he held her to him. The stinging winter air didn't touch them.

# XLI.

An ugly storm rolled in the next morning and hung around for days. The heavy rain pounded the roof, lightning cracked viciously across the darkened sky, and the wind howled like a furious beast.

Dragunov called all the men, except Ruben, in from St. Petersburg. He explained to Leila that perhaps the reason Evgeniya refrained from doing anything could be that she—or whoever was behind her—had felt their presence. Making it appear like they abandoned surveillance on her might make her—or whoever—comfortable enough again to move, where Ruben could catch them.

"This has worked before; it will again," he said.

"But will it have the outcome we want?" she asked. She had barely left his side since they had finally professed their love for one another. The blissful relief of giving in that night had almost faded. Combined with the storm holding a dark premonition, fear loomed over her, making her need the security and confidence Dragunov provided. She had never felt this anxious before.

He wrapped her up in his arms and kissed the top of her head. "Whatever happens, we will adjust. Don't worry."

BY THE MIDDLE OF THE second week, the sky calmed, and the storm slowed to a steady drizzle. The previously fallen snow had turned into a nasty mess because of the downpour.

Leila stood at the glass doors watching the weather improve. Maybe the change was a good omen. But even as she tried to convince herself of that, the dark premonition hadn't been dissipated with the clouds. The Phoenix stayed on high alert—unconvinced of closure.

The front door burst open, whipping everyone around with guns aimed at Ruben.

"Evgeniya's dead."

"Move," Dragunov ordered.

The Spetsnaz team did so, separating to retrieve their own emergency packs of clothes or to the arsenal hidden somewhere.

Leila did the same, hurrying up to her room, slinging on her backpack, and running back down. Dragunov followed her out to an SUV, shut the door behind her in the passenger seat, then got behind the wheel. Alek and Silvestrov sat in the back. Ruben, with the Chubais twins, pulled out first, and they trailed. The swiftly deserted house disappeared behind them.

The forest looked innocent as the SUVs wound through it, but Leila nervously watched the tree lines for any kind of sudden or foreign movement. She had never been forced to run for her safety. Or she had been put in situations where she should've, but being in control, Leila hadn't felt the need to. Now she didn't know what to expect. She shivered from unease.

It took a while for Leila to steady her voice. "Where are we going?"

"Ivankeynar," Dragunov answered, his eyes shifting from one side of the woods to the other.

"It's our closest and easiest to access safe house," Alek said.

"Fewer people around to see us too," Silvestrov added.

The cabin fell quiet—its occupants too preoccupied and tense to carry on a conversation. But Leila needed something to distract her from overthinking what could possibly happen. The Phoenix diverted her focus to watching for abnormalities.

Dragunov reached over and enveloped her cold hand in his. She clutched his. His silent show of encouragement calmed her. They neared the big curve of the reversed five.

Ruben suddenly swerved in front of them, banking hard left to avoid something. Dragunov's hand shot out to hold Leila back as he slammed on the brakes; he fought to maintain control as the slick tires sent them fishtailing. Ruben corrected the swerving vehicle to miss something else. But as he straightened the car, the rear tire ran over a hidden land mine. It exploded, catapulting the SUV in a high arc before crashing upside down.

The unharmed SUV stopped at a distance before the burning vehicle. Shock kept everyone frozen for a second before panic smothered caution in Leila. She started to fling open her door, but Dragunov held her back.

"No." She turned to question him, but his eyes searched the surrounding forest. "Perimeter search."

Alek and Silvestrov jumped out with guns to scan the woods.

"Stay close to the car," Dragunov said before he got out; Leila right behind him.

After a quick but thorough perimeter search, Silvestrov ventured out to the burning vehicle with eyes glued to the ground. He stopped. "11 o'clock."

Leila froze. The Russian medic made a mark where the land mine sat, then moved on with his sure-footed walk, continuing to call out and marking the locations of other mines.

He reached the overturned vehicle, and after a quick sweep for mines, hurried to help them.

Alek stepped in Silvestrov's footprints in a zigzagged path. Leila shot Dragunov a look, ready to argue if he demanded she stay back.

"Follow his path precisely," Dragunov said.

She copied Alek through the treacherous path. When she reached the overturned SUV, she hurried to Alek's side and looked under the car. A bloody Yakov had already unbuckled himself, clawing his way to the middle seat.

"I'm fine! Yurii's hurt!" he yelled as he tried to reach his brother.

Leila moved around Alek to the squished frame of the middle window. She could see Yurii still belted to his seat, face bloody and twisted in pain as he fumbled to get himself free.

"Hold on, Yurii!" She slipped off her backpack and crawled through the broken window. The broken glass cut into her arms, but she helped unbuckle Yurii, and with both of their strengths, she eased him to the ground.

Yurii clutched at his bloody and torn pants leg where a large piece of the vehicle had been blown into his leg from the explosion. Blood gushed out of his thigh—a nicked artery.

Dragunov appeared at the space where she crawled through. Leila helped the twin force himself through as Dragunov pulled him out. He looked at Leila.

"Help him first!"

He disappeared to be replaced by Alek, and he helped her out. Dragunov and Silvestrov held the injured Yurii between them as they went back to the second SUV. She grabbed her backpack and hurried to join them. Silvestrov quickly applied a tight tourniquet on Yurii's leg while his twin watched from the passenger seat.

The rain had begun to wash the blood from Ruben's pale face and arms, but he leaned against the car, supporting himself. Dragunov turned to him, bent his head close, and whispered something only Ruben could hear.

Nodding, Ruben headed for the driver's seat. Dragunov herded Leila and Alek back from the reversing SUV. It turned around and sped back the way they came. It disappeared before long to head down another pathway.

Dragunov grabbed her hand as he looked at her. "They'll be fine."

The three of them ran off into the forest. They were deep within and far away when they heard the abandoned car exploding.

NOBODY VENTURED OUT INTO THE rainy night in Krasvina. The freezing rain combined with wet snow made it not worth venturing out into.

The three pairs of eyes watching the slumbering village didn't have a choice. Whoever planted those land mines knew they would go to Ivankeynar to keep Leila safe, so Ruben drove the wounded men to Krasvina, and the others ran.

Leila shivered uncontrollably as she stood in the cover of the woods. Drenched and chilled to the bone, they had run a long way to the village. The rain had picked up drastically from when they began running. Warm with the thought of dry clothes in the safe house helped her push through the pain and exhaustion.

Dragunov had been standing beside a tree at the edge of the forest for about ten minutes now, not moving. He had explained on their run over.

"We have a routine when one is at a safe house and one is trying to get in. Every hour, one of us will place a white fabric in a window for a total of ten seconds and then take it back. If the fabric is red, it isn't safe. If no fabric, they aren't there."

*God, I hope we won't be waiting out here for an hour.*

She found Alek in the darkness, and the few streetlights of Krasvina highlighted his worried face. She knew his thoughts lay heavy on Svetlana and Andriyan—as hers were now—wondering if they were in danger. He sensed her watching him, turned, and smiled.

The silent Dragunov finally moved. "It's safe." He draped an arm over Leila's shoulders, and they ran out from under the cover of trees into the steady downpour of rain; Alek ran behind them, looking like people trying to get out of the rain.

They stuck to the cover of the building as Dragunov worked on the chained door. He unlocked it with a key of his own and ushered the other two inside.

As Dragunov chained the door again, Leila looked around as she shook the water from her clothes. Dust covered the broken furniture, and cobwebs hung from every corner, spun between the legs of chairs at the table and from an old lamp on an end table. The walls had holes—exposing sheetrock and rusted pipes—a chandelier lay shattered on the floor, the pieces among debris and garbage.

Dragunov passed to lead them again. They skirted around the broken chandelier and went down a hallway. Leila glanced through open doorways to see more destroyed furniture—one room contained an intact rocking horse for a child. All the remains were skeletons of the lives that used to dwell there. Leila had a fleeting thought that she would prefer outside than this unfriendly, gloomy home inhabited by ghosts.

In the kitchen, they had to sidestep discarded pots and pans to pass through a doorway leading down to a wine cellar and storage. Dusty bottles of wine still filled holes in the wine rack, but many were missing. Barrels and boxes sat stacked in the corners and along a wall. A fat rat scurried on top of one of the wine racks and ducked into a hole at the sight of the intruders.

Dragunov approached one of the wine racks and reached into a vacant slot. A heavy click echoed out of the hole. He pulled his arm out as the false wine rack slid behind the real side.

It stopped with a deep thud to reveal steps leading down to a hallway.

And coming down the hallway to greet them was a better-looking Ruben Severnov. Blood didn't dirty his face, only cuts, and he had more color.

They descended the stairs as the hidden pathway closed behind them by the false wine rack.

"Yurii?" Dragunov asked.

Ruben walked with them. "Well and resting. Silvestrov removed the piece of metal and stopped the bleeding."

They rounded a corner and came upon an even longer hallway, dimly lit with a soft green light, completely made of concrete with a few doors lining the walls and large crates placed throughout. The end of the hallway faded into a black abyss. A knot twisted Leila's gut—it looked so familiar. It resembled the many WWII tunnels and bunkers she had seen in documentaries, but her feeling came from more than a simple resemblance. She had seen that exact hallway before somewhere…

Ruben went into one room with the door already open. They found Yurii stretched out on a cot asleep and Yakov sitting beside him in a chair. On the other side of the room, thin screens showed different camera shots of the abandoned house—one even watching the hallway they were on.

"Glad to see you three again," he said quietly to not disturb his twin.

The cuts on his face had been treated, and his upper arm was wrapped in gauze. Yurii rested his injured leg on a few pillows, securely wrapped.

"Silvestrov?" Alek asked.

"Gone to shower," Yakov answered.

"Worried about me, Alek?" Silvestrov asked from the doorway as he finished drying his hair with a towel. "That's sweet."

Alek turned to him. "No. I just wondered when you were done using all the hot water."

Silvestrov threw the small towel into Alek's face. "Glad to see you made it in one piece, Alek."

He turned to Leila. "You good, Leila?"

Her mind had been pulled from trying to place how she recognized the hallway at him mentioning a warm shower. She nodded. "A shower sounds heavenly right now though."

"I'll show you to your room," Dragunov said behind her.

When they left the others, the emergence back into the hallway distracted her again.

Dragunov noticed. "What is it?"

"I… don't know yet. What is this place?"

"A WWII bunker we recommissioned as a safe house."

She had guessed right. "Could it have been filmed for a documentary?"

"There's a chance it could've before we got it." He looked it over. "Is that it? You recognize it from one?"

"Maybe." Her voice lacked confidence.

They went down to the next door on the right side of the hallway. "Here's yours. It's not great, but—"

"It's dry," Leila finished as she walked into the room—simple with a cot and another door leading to the bathroom.

He chuckled. "It's dry and has its own bathroom. We'll go down the hall to get ours."

She eased her damp backpack down near the cot, gently since it held her Morning Glory and Edith's music box. "Alek will be pleased."

"It has more than one shower head. He won't have to fight anyone for shower privileges."

Leila could tell he tried to lighten the fact that he wasn't happy being in this safe house. And her obvious unease at recognizing the place didn't help either. She turned and clung to his broad chest, absorbing the heat from his body.

"You don't like it here."

He held her to him, just as needy. "No, I don't. But it's safer than being home right now."

Dragunov kissed the top of her head. "You're safe here. That's all that matters."

It was barely there, but she heard it in his voice: uncertainty.

# XLII.

With the Morning Glory twirling in her hand, Leila paced, trying to remember where she recognized the hallway from. She had fought for recollection the whole day since they arrived last night. A movie? A picture? It stayed out of reach, on the tip of her tongue: the green lighting, the wooden crates dotting the corridor, looking identical at both ends. Even with the picture perfectly in her head, it still missed something…

She stopped. A dark figure standing at one end, awfully resembling…

Her dream. Deja-vu. The Morning Glory fell out of her hand.

The door to her room behind her opened.

She whipped around to interrupt Dragunov, "We have to leave."

Alarm wiped off the calm on his face. "What?"

"We have to go right now!"

"Why? What's wrong?"

"I remember where I recognized the hallway from: my dream, the one I told you about before we left for Noyavinsk. Foster stood at the end, shooting—"

He grabbed her face. "David's not here. You won't see him shot again; it was just a dream."

She shook her head. "It wasn't David. They just reminded me of him." She began to shake as the dream replayed. "Can we please go?" Emotion hitched her voice at the end.

He pulled her into him. "Alright. Okay; we'll go. Yurii's well enough to move—"

Gunfire cut him off, quick and singular at first, then joined by automatic fire. Dragunov already had his gun out of its holster when he propped against the doorframe. He looked around the corner, then retreated when the intruders spotted him and fired.

"*Десять противников*!" he yelled over the gunfire for his men to hear. *Ten hostiles.*

Fear had paralyzed Leila, forcing her to stare at her doorway, lighting up with each pull of the trigger. "Oh God. Oh God, please no."

Dragunov looked at her; the Dragon had awoken at the impending threat. "This isn't your dream. Don't think about it like it is. You don't know the ending."

More gunfire answered in retaliation from the Spetsnaz end of the hallway. Caught in the crossfire, Leila and Dragunov stood pinned down in the middle room.

*How did they get in?* Leila thought. *The cameras…*

*Had to have been altered,* the Phoenix said.

Dragunov left his post and moved to her, cupping her face. "Look, stay here. You can't get hurt in here."

The Phoenix finally snapped her out of her frozen state. "No, I can do this. I have to fight. I don't hide."

A second passed as he scrutinized her. "Get to the crate after twenty seconds. Stay down and run if I tell you to. Stay safe, please." He kissed her, then tore himself away and ran out into the fray, crouching.

Leila took his place at the doorway. Howls of agony blended in with the gunfire—fortunately only coming from the enemy side.

*Help me stay calm,* she asked the Phoenix.

*And deadly,* it said back, energized at the threat of danger.

She counted down the nerve-racking seconds as her heart raced. The gunfire grew closer to her, but from the side of the Spetsnaz. Movement in her peripherals made Leila turn—Ruben's head appeared around a crate before he pulled back, threatened with bullets.

*18… 19… 20.*

She crouched down and slipped into the hallway. Bullets flew over her head, thudding into the wooden crates or glancing off the concrete walls. She reached the crate nearest her door and took a moment before peeking around to see what they were up against. A few heads poked around the crates, equally using them for cover. Dragunov crouched behind a crate ahead of her. New gunfire forced her to duck back down.

Leila leaned around her shelter to fire at those she saw, then hid again. She continued doing so at alternate angles so the enemy couldn't predict where she would show. Howls or the thudding drop of bodies continued to confirm their hits and slackened the fire rate—they didn't bring enough reinforcements.

"*Граната!*" an enemy shouted. Men yelled in alarm, and the fire altogether stopped. Leila lifted her head to see figures scrambling before the detonation of a grenade consumed them. She dropped back down. The explosion intensified in the confined area, the hallway acting like a launch tube, sending a shockwave of energy, heat, smoke, debris, and possibly dismembered body parts all around her. Taking the brunt of the blast, the crate protected her.

The hallway fell deathly silent, but her ears still rang. Leila peered around her heavily damaged crate to find Dragunov, unharmed and searching for her. Once he saw her uninjured, he turned back around to check out the destruction. Looking behind her, the others emerged from behind their covers. She rose to see the damage for herself.

That end of the hallway was completely dark. The grenade had taken out the light, and lingering smoke made visibility even more impossible. As the smoke dissipated, she saw that nearly everything had been obliterated. All crates were gone, splinters showing where they used to exist. Some of the concrete walls had chips blown out of them, but they were black from the gunpowder residue. Two burnt bodies were discernable as human; everything else lay in pieces—a finger here, a whole hand there.

Alek came up next to her. "You alright?"

"I'm fine. Would we have thrown a grenade?"

"No. We're not stupid enough to take such a risk in a tight area."

Dragunov began to venture closer. Deja-vu dawned on her at his movement. She wasn't entirely certain if her imagination formed the dark figure materializing out of the darkness or not. But the scene was set.

"No!" Again, time slowed. She turned to Alek, moving to shove the oblivious man out of the way.

The single gunshot rang out, just as she remembered. Alek's head snapped back. He limply fell to his back; eyes frozen in front of him, a single line of blood trickling from the hole between his eyes—the same as David. Alek was dead.

Leila stared in disbelief. Alek's face blended into David's and back again, sharing the same bullet hole. She stood there, locked in Alek's dead stare.

Alek was dead, and she had been left alive.

Again.

Wind brushed her as two forms ran past her, toward the other end. A gray head knelt down as someone approached and put a hand on her arm, blocking her view of Alek's body.

She snapped. Leila hit the hand off her, tried to shove the immovable chest away, and fended off the reattempts to contain her. She screamed in frustration. The strong arms secured her flailing arms and hauled her away from the dead man.

Leila fought the man dragging her back. She needed to be dead with David and Alek. She couldn't do this again. She couldn't go on knowing someone else died for her. This couldn't be happening.

The man called out to her, but she couldn't understand him. This was all a bad dream. Alek still lived; he would go home to Svetlana and Andriyan.

"LEILA!"

She looked up at Dragunov—moisture threatened to overflow the disbelief in his eyes.

"Alek's dead! He's not coming back!"

"No, he can't be!" She couldn't—*wouldn't*—believe it.

"I'm sorry," he said as a tear rolled down his cheek.

Leila continued to fight him. He trapped her arms against his chest by pulling her into him. He placed his cheek against her head and continued to try to soothe her by apologizing. She cried into his chest. It was happening all over again.

# XLIII.

The ride back remained quiet. No one said anything as all five Spetsnaz and a woman piled into the one SUV. Alek would've cracked constant jokes or would've made some sort of snide remark to one of the twins just to get them going and pull everyone's mood up with a smile.

But he wasn't squeezed in like the others. Dragunov still had trouble believing it. He had never lost a man before. Even when the mortician had arrived, it didn't seem like Alek was the one in the body bag. He knew it would be finalized when he told Svetlana—something he dreaded doing.

Not only was he lost in disbelief, tainted with sorrow, but there was guilt. No matter how much he felt though, Leila held so much more. She had had the dream predicting Alek's death. She had tried to save him only to have his blood splattered on her. She was the one who relived David's death at the same time.

Leila hadn't said a single word since Alek died yesterday. It wasn't her fault—no one blamed her—but he knew he wouldn't be able to say anything that would convince her otherwise.

She still wouldn't speak now, face turned to the window, not moving an inch—delving deeper and deeper into those thoughts that beat a person down, and probably struggling with the Phoenix too. He could rely on the Dragon arriving later with anger, insulted that someone had trespassed into his family's life to inflict a lasting wound, and eager to return the pain. It did so when Edith had died. But right now, it was only disbelief and mourning.

When they arrived back at the house via another pathway, since Ruben's burnt SUV still blocked the main one, everyone except for Dragunov and Leila got out to inspect the house. It didn't appear to have been visited by any intruders.

"Leila, don't for a second believe it was your fault," he began.

She didn't respond, verbally or physically.

He reached over to grab her hand. "Please don't withdraw from me and let the Phoenix take your place. I need you to stay with me—especially now."

She inhaled uneasily from emotion. "I'm not going anywhere." After a moment, she turned to him. "It hurts, but it hurts less when you have someone to share it with."

A thought suddenly broke her composure. "Unlike Svetlana."

Dragunov pulled the crying woman into him, wishing he could somehow eliminate her sorrow and grief.

"She has us."

DARKNESS SURROUNDED DRAGUNOV WHEN HE stood at the front door of Svetlana's home. He fidgeted, uncomfortable, but Svetlana needed him to tell her—she would need his strength.

His hand seemed to be controlled by someone else as it rose and knocked three times against the door. The knocks echoed dully into the surrounding darkness.

Sounds of shuffling moved toward the door. Dragunov took a quick steadying breath before the door opened, and light temporarily blinded him.

Svetlana's eyes widened at finding him on the doorstep instead of her husband.

"Dragon? What—" Understanding quickly dawned on her from his somber silence.

"No," she breathed.

"Svet—"

"Dragon, he can't! Alekseev can't be dead!"

He hated he couldn't bring better news. "I'm sorry, Svetlana."

She fell into Dragunov, sobbing.

"I know. I know."

Dragunov held the weeping woman against him, stroking her hair for comfort. Not far into the living room sat one of Andriyan's cribs; asleep within, he would become a spitting image of Alek.

# XLIV.

Alek's funeral was nothing near the size of David's, consisting of Leila, the Spetsnaz team, Svetlana and Andriyan, Vyacheslav, and the attending priest in the snow at a small graveyard behind its church. But the same emotions and strain not to show those overwhelming emotions were very much present.

The priest performed the Russian burial ritual, no additional words were asked to be shared from the attendants, Alek was buried, and it was over. Svetlana remained stoic for her son throughout the short funeral, but her eyes held devastation.

Leila tried to remain in the back—as if not to have her presence felt—but being beside Dragunov and in line with the Spetsnaz team prevented that.

She stared at Alek's coffin as it lowered, vowing to never attend another funeral where she lived from the dead ensuring it.

AFTER RETURNING FROM THE FUNERAL, they all gathered in the command room to watch the surveillance videos from the safe house. Different hallways and angles inside and around the abandoned house flipped on the three screens. They needed to see how the Chechen gained entry, and if they had all been killed.

Leila sat beside Dragunov at the controls, Silvestrov on his left, and the Chubais twins and Ruben propped against the table behind them. All focused on the screens flipping through the different vantage points, trying to catch sight of where they entered.

The first 'South Entrance' camera showed the Chechen breaking into the house. Every inch of the exterior was wired, so any tampering from an intruder should've raised an alarm. But the Chechen had somehow gotten past the alarm system under the guidance of the one clearly in charge. How he knew to get past the safeguards eluded them and angered the Dragon even more.

The man led them through the East Wing, down the hallway of another angle, to the other secret entrance through a fireplace in the servant's quarters. He pressed the exact order of false bricks to reveal a stairwell leading down into the bunker. But he oddly held back in the corridor that turned into the main hallway when the Chechen opened fire.

Leila kept her eye on him the entire time—his movements seemed familiar. At every angle, he had his back to the camera, and wearing all black made it impossible to recognize him. He seemed to know where the cameras were located, and the fact that he knew about everything else meant that he had unsettling access to study the blueprints.

The man peeked around the corner to check on progress. Her eyes switched over to the center screen with the footage of the main hallway and found it to be when they had greatly reduced the Chechen's numbers. Right before the grenade exploded.

He pulled back around, grabbed something from his waist, hesitated a second or two, then rolled something into the hallway and retreated. The center screen lit up with the explosion.

"He killed his own men," Leila said in disbelief.

"I know," Dragunov said. "I've been watching him too."

The man walked back on screen. "Why would he have thrown the grenade?"

They watched him advance to the corner, then slowly poke his head around to check out the damage he caused.

"Can you zoom in on him?"

Dragunov did the best he could with that angle.

Even with the zoom, the man's face stayed in shadow since the light had been taken out by the blast. They found the murderer, though, for he stepped boldly into the hallway and shot one bullet. With the deed done, he retreated, but not without coming into the dim light under the camera. Ruben and Yakov appeared seconds later, chasing after him.

Ice flowed down her neck, and her heart raced when he entered the light. He lifted his face and smiled directly into the camera, like he knew she would be watching. She couldn't breathe. Those sharp, cruel, green eyes shot through her soul like a lightning bolt. Even the Phoenix was floored at the recognition.

"Leila?" Dragunov asked beside her.

Numbly, she backed from the screen, but couldn't remove her eyes from where he had run off camera. Smiling. Gloating at the death, knowing how it would affect her.

"Leila?" Dragunov stood up, concern lacing his voice.

She bolted. She ran out of the room, flung open the glass door, and flew out through the patio and into the snow, ignoring the calls behind her. The thick snow hindered her run, but she didn't stop. The bitter and dry air made her gasp for breath in between the sobs. Maybe if she never stopped running, she could escape and keep everyone safe behind her.

But her run slowed as a thought dawned on her: no matter how hard she ran, she could never escape. No matter where she went, she would always bring destruction.

How did he know to find her here? Why couldn't he have chosen her to kill? Why keep her alive just to twist the knife deeper in her soul? As she continued to race through the questions in her head, the Phoenix heated.

*Like I first guessed, he was the one behind Evgeniya. He used the relationship between the captain and Petrishchev to pull us to him. He let us come to these Spetsnaz. He planned the ambush at Akrino, wanting it to fail. He allowed* everything *to happen. Why?*

It combed through Alek's death, frantically searching for the answer. *Dragunov was the easier kill being closer. He chose to kill Alek. He aimed for him.*

Leila stopped at its revelation.

*He… aimed… for him.* Its fury shook its very thoughts, making it strain the words. It couldn't believe the realization itself.

The Phoenix exploded in rage. Leila screamed as she dropped to the snow, a combination of a furious, primal scream and a roar of frustration. Her violent yell scared the birds in the trees into a frantic flutter of wings, echoing endlessly through the vast forest.

How could he do that? Why would he do that! He had to know killing Alek would rekindle her vengeance—he just threw gasoline on the fire.

Enough. He wanted her to come after him. Leila's body clenched at the takeover of the Phoenix. Its anger literally radiated off her, melting the snow around her. Her vision turned red.

He would get it.

"I will kill him. I will annihilate Bryan Foster; there won't be a piece of him left."

Dragunov stood behind her, watching and listening to her rave through her anger. Now he dropped down beside her and lightly touched her arm.

"Leila, I feel just as angry as you. He will pay for this, but don't let anger control what you're going to do. I've been through this exact situation, so I know to calm down, step back, and look. Don't let your fire consume what you don't want to burn."

The Phoenix still vehemently rampaged in her head, engulfing Dragunov's words.

She understood his warning. *STOP! Listen to what he just said!*

*He's trying to stop our revenge! it fired back.*

*No, he's not stopping us; he's trying to warn us. You will engulf everything in your path for revenge. What if in the trail of ashes you leave is something I loved? What will it do to us?*

The Phoenix stopped raging long enough to reflect on his words. Grasping the reality of the danger cooled it down, and Leila took back control. Her temple stopped throbbing and left her thoughts blank.

The sudden silence, though, allowed the gravity of Alek's death and Bryan Foster being the culprit back in to overwhelm her. Leila stared blindly into the woods, not seeing a single thing.

"Alek didn't deserve this just for knowing me."

"No one deserves punishment for knowing you. It's not your fault," Dragunov said.

"But he wouldn't be dead if I wasn't here."

"Leila." Dragunov grabbed her arms so she would face him. "Alek brought laughter to our lives, but you being here brought us all back to life. Alek's death is a price we wish we didn't have to pay, but there will never be anything that can make us regret the day you came. You mean the world to me. Alek would've always chosen him to keep you safe. Do you understand? All of us think that way."

He cupped her face. "The thought of losing you…"

She could see the complete loss and disorientation in his eyes at thinking about it. Leila choked up with emotion, close to losing her control over his love for her. It hurt her just the same in thinking about losing him—her soul, her reason to breathe, would be gone.

"I don't know what I would do. You are my air now, and without you, I couldn't breathe. I would *want* to stop breathing."

His statement broke her restraint. Leila sobbed, crying uncontrollably because of the guilt of Alek's death now paired with David's death, the persistent pressure of Bryan Foster, and the profoundness of Dragunov's love for her.

He pulled her to him for comfort, his head against hers. "We will do what we have to do, together. You're not alone in this."

# XLV.

A week had passed since Alek died. Life resumed like it always did, but his absence echoed dully in their hearts—the house seemed stuck in a never-ending chill without the sun. Leila recalled him predicting that he 'provided the fun' and 'they would miss him if he was gone'. They did; they sorely missed him.

They all met almost daily to discuss retribution against Foster but couldn't decide on what to do. The first problem was that they didn't have a clue on where he could be. Through Vyacheslav, Dragunov notified all Spetsnaz across the country about Foster and to contact him if spotted.

Knowing his MO, Leila figured he would have already left Russia. He knew every Spetsnaz would hunt him down once he was identified—especially with how he looked up at the camera after killing Alek.

All a part of his plan in involving her. She just hoped they wouldn't fall into his plan… whatever it was.

"LEILA."

She looked up from Edith's music box to Silvestrov in her doorway. His soft yet harsh, craggy face was tense. Hard. Even his stance seemed tight. In the eight months she had been with them, she had never seen anger in his gray eyes.

She jumped up. "What's wrong?" Her mind flew through hundreds of scenarios before jumping to the next one. All of them rotated around Dragunov, the Spetsnaz, and Foster.

He opened his mouth to answer, but nothing came out—hesitation was out of character for him. "We need you." He turned and left.

Now her mind went into overdrive. Dread kept her legs locked in place until the Phoenix woke her body and nudged her to move. Leila put down the music box before heading out on the catwalk to see Silvestrov entering the command room.

She headed down the stairs but lingered at the door out of fear from what she saw: everyone present but tense and glaring at the screens to her right and out of sight. Jaws were set and eyes flashed murderously. Heat radiating from the room raised cold goosebumps on her arms. But at her arrival, they turned to her with concern and uncertainty.

Leila was terrified now of what she would find on the screens. News of more killings by Foster? Sightings? She cautiously stepped into the room. Her eyes went straight to Dragunov when he came into sight, but he didn't return her look—the enraged Dragon focused on the only bright screen.

Once fully in, she turned to see what had him so set and furious. She froze.

The bland face with piercing green eyes grinned like a wolf. A new voice greeted her, patronizing, and at the same time, mocking—detached and derisive.

"There you are, Lei," Bryan Foster said.

If you loved this book, please leave a review on Amazon and Goodreads—it helps me and potential readers!

Thanks again!

# TURN THE NEXT PAGE FOR A SNEAK PEEK

at the finale to The Phoenix Trilogy!

# I.

"There you are, Lei."

Leila Wells could only stare at Bryan Foster grinning on the screen—too stunned to even blink. The green-eyed devil with a square face and buzzed hair was there. The one who had destroyed countless families, tortured Detective Uehl and caused Detective Washington's suicide, and killed David Neal, Jr. and Alek. No one moved in the room of five Spetsnaz or even seemed to breathe.

Not even a second ticked by before the Phoenix exploded at the sight of his face. Scorching rage swept through her veins like a blazing tornado. Her dark side itched to be unleashed. It took every ounce of her to restrain the Phoenix from lunging at the screen and ripping it from the wall.

"I hate seeing that hollowness in your eyes again, Lei," he said, but with absolutely no remorse. "You looked like you were controlling the Phoenix and began to heal. You smiled all the time." He chuckled. "It affected me."

The Phoenix broke through. "WHAT DO YOU WANT?"

He grimaced at her shriek. "Tone the Phoenix down some, Lei. We're not going to be able to talk with you screaming at me."

She shook under the Phoenix's kept-in fury. So furious, she struggled with what to do next.

"Then I'll ask. What… do you… want?" Dragunov asked slowly as he held back his own fury. Hearing the strain of containing the Dragon sent chills racing down her spine. Leila thought the Phoenix had pulled the Dragon out before, but only in part. Anger tightened the dark-haired Russian's jaw, and his eyes had sharpened like knives. That little taste of the fully infuriated Dragon was terrifying—she hoped she would never see his dark side in its entirety.

Foster turned his eyes on him. "This is between your woman and me."

"Not when you killed one of my men and invaded my home by surveilling us. How did you?"

"By hacking—how else? Besides, that still doesn't give you the right to be included."

Dragunov ground his teeth. "Anything that involves Leila involves me."

A smile grew wickedly on his face. "Sounds like we have a commonality. I thought we would get along just fine."

"It involves all of us," Silvestrov said. The gentle, soothing, gray-haired Spetsnaz medic and chef seemed like he wanted to slice open Foster's neck with a butcher knife.

"Leila is family," Yurii Chubais began.

His identical twin—with darker brown hair—Yakov Chubais, finished, "And we protect our own."

"I stand like a wall for my relatives," Ruben Severnov said in Russian, then translated. His dark eyes usually hid emotions, but the burning fury couldn't be disguised.

These dangerous Spetsnaz were pissed.

Foster's eyes scanned each face, meeting fierce gazes. "What loyalty you've found here, Lei—each willing to jump in harm's way to protect you. And it's already been proven once."

"Alek didn't jump in the way; I tried to push him down. You aimed for him," she spat.

His gaze landed back on her. "He still would've jumped in front of you if the roles had been reversed."

"Why did you shoot him? Why not me?"

"We're not here to—" He stopped. "You? Never! You're too important!"

"WHY? WHY ME?"

He lifted his hands like that could pacify her. "You'll find out in due course. Which brings me to why I'm talking to you: I will be at Panordom next year. Xander is a good friend, and as such a fan of the last Rulers of the Realms, he's allowing me to come for free to watch in person. I only got to see one fight last time." He shut his eyes as he scowled. "I wasn't too happy about that."

He opened them and put on false peppiness. "But never mind about the past. It'll be better this year—I'm sure of it. So, I hope you decide to come, Lei; we can meet up. Have a nice little reunion—it'll be fun. Oh, and bring your Russian. Until then, take care of yourself." Foster waved, and the screen blinked black.

No one made a sound or moved after the screen grew dark. Leila couldn't believe how easily Foster had shredded her spirit. She thought she had grown tougher. But she had already let Foster under her skin—just like the captain said—so he bided his time, extending his roots until they became long enough for him to strike something vital. Something that would cripple her but leave her alive: Alek.

The Phoenix wanted to rage—*needed* to destroy something. With just words, Foster tore apart that drive of resolve. His offhand manner was worse than if he had been impassive and malicious. She had absolutely no anger, no energy to spend on punching bags. Foster had broken and beaten Leila down. Again.

Feeling Spetsnaz eyes watching, weighing her stability on how she would react—especially since she ran off when she first realized Foster had killed Alek—she turned and left for her room. Her thoughts ran unbelievably fast; she strained not to run with them. The Phoenix kept tugging her toward the weight room, but the conference left her numb, drained. She reached her room and closed the door behind her.

Order *Dueling with Snakes*!

# WANT MORE?

Need a fun, light-hearted story after that emotional rollercoaster in Russia? Read about Alek's mischief in the companion short story, *The Crane's Dance.*

*Available only as an ebook!

# ACKNOWLEDGMENTS

I've heard that writing a sequel is usually hard—keeping the story rolling, interesting, and true to its predecessor—but for me, this was my favorite part of Leila's story to tell. (Mainly because I came up with *The Dragon of Russia* before *Ascension of the Phoenix*... Oh well. I'm different.)

There are quite a few people to thank for helping me with the publication of this book. As always, God deserves my praise and thanks first. Second, Mark Gardner for his formatting skills, marketing advice, and allowing me to vent about this self-publishing venture. (There are many ups and downs.) Fay Lane made this phenomenal cover—I love the dragon! Major thanks to Paul Martin with Dominion Editorial for being a fantastic editor. Once again, thanks to fellow authors, Simon Hillman and Michael Holiday for being beta readers. My proofreaders, Savanah Allen and Pamela Wilson. Hassan/Roach on Discord for correcting my Russian and John St. Clair on Twitter for further help on my Russian names.

My family, Mom, Dad, Dadoo (John), and Jacob, for never telling me I couldn't chase my dreams and making me laugh—even when I didn't want to. My grandparents—Mawmaw Mae and Pawpaw John—thank y'all for being with me, too.

To my church family at Mangham Baptist Church for encouraging me on my writing journey.

The #WritingCommunity on Twitter deserves some recognition for helping me expand my little reach and so many authors on there having my back and giving me support. Thanks, everybody!

And finally, to you the reader. I wrote this story mainly for you to enjoy. Without readers, authors wouldn't exist. If you enjoyed my writing, keep an eye out for more books!

# ABOUT THE AUTHOR

**Jessica Piro** is the author of The Phoenix Trilogy, which has won multiple accolades, writes in multiple genres, and is in a wheelchair with Type 1 Diabetes. Her work caters to young adults, new adults, and adults.

She graduated from the University of Louisiana at Monroe in 2015 with a Bachelor of Arts in English and a minor in History. She lives in Northeast Louisiana with her parents and two brothers.

You can find her on X (formerly Twitter) @AuthorPiro or Instagram @authorpiro. For updates on upcoming books, or even access to FREE works, visit jessicapiro.com.